I0692776

The Billion Dollar Heist

Ben Lovejoy

Published by Airbook Publishing

AIRBOOK PUBLISHING

www.airbookpublishing.com

First published in Great Britain 2015
by Airbook Publishing.

Second edition.

A catalogue record for this book
is available from the British Library.

ISBN 978-0-9931922-1-0

Acknowledgements

I would like to offer my grateful thanks to those who read an early draft of the novel and took the time and trouble to offer detailed feedback on the technical aspects.

Simon Bradley, for assistance with matters military.

Katrina Lowe, Adam Golding, JW Hubbers, Stephen Armitage and Martin Stoll for proof-reading and early feedback – with a special mention for Henry Cooke Smith, who also demonstrated the reason I'm a writer rather than a mathematician...

My fellow members of the Write Together group who made the writing process a rather less solitary one than is generally the case.

**A closed night-club in Brooklyn, New York.
10am Friday.**

Jessica Sullivan reached into the attaché case next to her and pulled out a block of $50 bills. She dropped it onto the table in front of her. None of the seven others gathered in the backroom of the closed nightclub reacted in any way.

"You've all seen your share of those in your time. One hundred bills. A strap. In this case, it's fifty dollar bills, so that's $5000 there."

Sullivan looked round at the bored expressions. This wasn't news to any of them, she knew, but she was enjoying the build-up: she wanted to see at what point the energy in the room shifted.

She reached back into the box and pulled out nine more blocks, forming them into a neat row, end-to-end.

"Ten straps, that's a bundle. $50,000."

Nobody looked impressed: they'd all seen much more money in one place.

"I'll dispense with the visual aids now, I'm sure your imaginations can fill in the gaps. Package four of those bundles together, you've got a brick. $200,000."

Shrugs. There were eight of them in the room. $25k each was ok, but they were used to bigger things.

"Package four bricks together, and you've got a cash-pack. $800,000."

Sullivan could see a couple of them visualising that. She was starting to get their attention.

"Package 40 cash-packs together and you've got a pallet, or a skid. Thirty-two million dollars in a space just over one cubic metre."

Nobody was looking bored now.

"Three pallets per load. $96 million."

Every eye in the room was on her.

"Twelve loads. One billion, one hundred and fifty-two million dollars. But let's keep it simple and call it a billion in round numbers."

"And just where might this billion dollars be found?" The tone of voice was casual, the facial expression blank.

Sullivan smiled: "It's the amount of currency printed three times a week at the Bureau of Engraving and Printing at Fort Worth, Texas, in the weeks leading up to the introduction of a new bill design. A new design like, say, the new $50 bill being introduced two months from today. Which was what gave me the idea."

A thin Hispanic man in his 40s spoke up: "And you think we're going to steal some of this cash from the BEP?"

Sullivan shook her head. "No. No, that's not the plan at all."

"So what is this plan of yours?"

"We're going to steal all of it. We're going to steal a billion dollars."

Three seconds of silence. Longer than she'd expected; not much fazed this team.

"And your plan for this is ... ?" asked the same man.

"I haven't the faintest idea," smiled Sullivan.

"Ok, just so we have this straight, you want us to steal a billion dollars. You want us to steal it from probably the most secure facility in the world after Fort Knox. And you have no clue as to how we might do it?"

"Fun, isn't it?"

"You don't think we're perhaps over-stretching ourselves just a little this time?"

"I seem to recall a similar sentiment was suggested last time."

Perez tilted his head in amused agreement.

"So," said Sullivan, "we have some research to do. Are we all in for the fieldwork stage? Maybe a few weeks' work and say $50k for initial expenses."

They'd worked together on other operations. The previous one had been on a sufficient scale that $50k between them was a pretty small investment, so she was confident no further discussion would be needed. "Let's do the roll-call."

* * *

Sullivan turned to the man on her left. Sam Young was of indeterminate age. A con-man with a long and impressive history of successful frauds, his various disguises could have him look as convincing as a 30-year-old as he did as a 70-year-old. Despite having known him for many years, Sullivan was never entirely sure whether the face he showed to her and the rest of the team was his own or merely another disguise. Certainly he varied his appearance regularly; right now he looked like a 50-year-old accountant who enjoyed his food rather more than his gym.

Young had as many names as ages, and not even Sullivan knew his real one. She did, however, trust him implicitly: he was a confidence trickster, and would lie to a mark without a second thought, but he was completely loyal to those few people he considered friends.

It was Young who had introduced Sullivan to her current life. Formerly Head of Security for a major bank, she'd uncovered a highly sophisticated fraud. Her problem had been proving it. While she'd worked out how it had been done and by whom, she'd been far from confident that either the bank or the police could prove it. Without proof, it was doubtful whether the culprit could be convicted or the funds recovered.

The sum of money involved was significant, and frankly the bank cared more about recovery and discretion than it did about convictions. She'd managed to persuade Young – though that wasn't the alias he'd used then – that quietly returning the money would be best for all concerned. She'd expected a battle, but Young had been remarkably sanguine about it. She was sure this wasn't his first major fraud and that it wouldn't be his last, so perhaps he could afford a casual attitude to such things.

Unravelling the maze had been such a challenge, such fun. She'd felt more alive than she had in years. She hadn't wanted to admit it to herself at the time. Hadn't wanted to name the feeling. But finally she'd had to. Every time she'd solved a new part of the puzzle, figured out one more element of the intricately-planned fraud, she'd felt admiration at the sheer ingenuity of what the fraudster – the man she would later identify as Young – had pulled off.

It was when she found herself grinning at the sheer cleverness and gall of one particular aspect of the fraud that she'd realized that, much as she wanted to catch him, her motivation was no longer to exact justice, it was to win this enthralling game. And to meet the man who'd pulled it off. She wanted, she'd finally acknowledged, to congratulate him.

Crossing sides – joining forces with Young – had been a long and gradual process. And yet, looking back on it now, it had begun less than halfway through that investigation, before she'd even met the man responsible for it.

When Young finally issued the invitation, she'd been expecting it. She'd been ready to lay down the law. Her law. Nobody got hurt. No individuals lost out – not by more than pennies, anyway. But Young had beaten her to it. He'd said that if she chose to join him, she had to agree to the principles on which he operated. They were almost word-for-word what she'd been about to say.

She brought herself back to the present. Young winked at her. He too loved the hunt.

* * *

"Chung?"

Mike Chung had been the third person to join the team. Most operations of any scale these days required IT expertise, and in the early days it had been just the three of them. While Sullivan liked and respected each member of the team, she still thought of the three of them as the core team. Sullivan, Young, Chung.

Chung didn't generally take much persuasion. A slightly-built 35-year-old Hong Kong-born Chinese man who could pass for ten years younger, he was a freelance security consultant. While his website described him as a former hacker, the past tense was pure fiction.

Sullivan was convinced the money they'd made was almost an irrelevance to Chung. Each of them maintained legitimate businesses to provide an explanation for their evident income, but most of them did very little work in those. Chung was an exception, with a substantial client-base for whom he worked hard. He operated a very personal brand of ethics: while he happily used access to his client systems to add to his knowledge of different systems, he would never compromise any client network. On a previous project when one of his client systems would have provided the perfect solution to a difficulty they faced, he instead spent several days breaking into a competitor system to achieve what would have taken him 30 seconds on the system to which he already had legitimate access.

Chung generally said little – until you got him onto the topic of computer systems, then he could talk for hours.

Chung simply nodded.

* * *

"Lewis?"

Katrina Lewis was the only other woman in the team, though she couldn't have been a greater contrast to Jessica Sullivan. While Sullivan was feminine and elegant in her dress, Lewis was secretly contemptuous of women who played that game. Not that she didn't respect Sullivan - she had to, Sullivan had more than proven her intelligence and determination - she just didn't see why women dressed up in costumes and paint just because men expected it of them, and was particularly disappointed when someone of Sullivan's intellect chose to do so. Lewis expected to be accepted for who she was, not her ability to match some male fantasy. Her short-cropped hair, absence of make-up and habitual uniform of baggy jeans and t-shirt was her way of making the point.

Part of it, she admitted, was a response to working in a traditionally male world. An electronics engineer who'd previously worked for the largest chip manufacturer in the world, she'd found it easier to fit in if she'd been seen as just one of the boys.

Lewis too loved her work. She boasted that there wasn't a circuit she couldn't design and build in her home electronics lab, and so far she'd lived up to that promise. She'd designed and built a sophisticated home automation system that managed everything from heat and light to running a bath.

Perhaps that was why they worked together so well as a team, mused Sullivan: they were all in it for the love as much as the money, and they all relished a challenge, no matter how much feigned grumbling they did at the outset.

"I'm in," said Lewis.

* * *

"Jackson?"

Scott Jackson was an ex-USAF pilot who'd flown everything from Apache helicopters to B52 bombers. He wasn't a soldier by instinct, but he had dreamed of flying since he was a five-year-old boy staring in wonderment at the turboprop aircraft that had over-flown his home when heading to or from a nearby airfield. It was not an unusual childhood fantasy, of course, but while other friends had moved on to dreams of being a firefighter or racing driver, he had never wavered from his vision of himself at the controls of one of those beautiful machines. One of four children in a not particularly well-to-do family, the military had offered the only route to fulfilling his dream, and he'd accepted the drudgery, discipline and disruption of military life as the price of the time he lived for: time spent in the air.

His flying career had been brought to a premature end in 1992 by the BRAC Commission. The Base Realignment and Closure Commission had been set up by the government to examine the USA's changing military requirements at the end of the Cold War. Jackson had for five years been a B-52 pilot. A key element of the nuclear deterrent strategy, they saw nuclear-armed service both as high-altitude bombers and as low-level infiltration bombers designed to fly beneath Russian radar. But with the fall of the Soviet Union, and the B-52 an elderly aircraft which had remained in production far longer than anyone had ever envisaged, Jackson found himself surplus to requirements. With just three years to retirement, he was one of hundreds of pilots retired to desk jobs. He'd deeply resented it, and when offered the opportunity for early retirement, he'd taken it without looking back.

Anything which provided an excuse to fly was fine with Jackson, and if there wasn't an obvious need for it now, he was sure he could find one.

"I'm in too."

* * *

"Perez?"

Raul Perez was the Hispanic man who'd expressed his scepticism. Ex-army OD (Ordnance Disposal), more colloquially known as bomb disposal, his service in Afghanistan had been the turning-point. It was, in his view, a clusterfuck. They called it a war while hampering them with rules of engagement more suited to a scout picnic than an armed conflict. They were allowed to shoot to kill only when in direct and immediate danger. The way that was defined meant that even if they were certain they could see insurgents placing a roadside improvised explosive device, they weren't allowed to shoot, they had to sit back and watch them complete it before moving in to disable it. The insurgents were well aware of this and frequently waited until the EOD team moved in before remotely detonating the device. There was only so much that could be done by robots, and Perez had watched too many of his friends die needlessly.

He was far from a coward. Cowards don't choose ordinance disposal as a career. He'd simply reached the point of not being able to sit back and watch more colleagues die without any meaning or purpose in a conflict which appeared to have no clear goal or exit strategy. He'd intended to wait the 18 months until his Service of Enlistment was up, but the death of a close friend attempting to defuse a car-bomb in a civilian area while they were as near-certain as they could be that the insurgents were just waiting for their approach to detonate it had been the final straw. A strenuous argument with the base commander had ended with a single blow to the commander's chin, a six-month stretch in Leavenworth and a Dishonourable Discharge.

There aren't many civilian careers open to you when all you know is bomb disposal, even fewer when you have a DD on your army papers. But to disarm explosive devices, you first have to be an expert in their design and construction. It had been fairly inevitable that he would find some unofficial means to put those skills to use.

He'd been friends with Jackson; it was not long before he was on the team.

He remained sceptical, but what else was he going to do? Besides, he couldn't really argue with Sullivan's point: all her ideas had sounded crazy when she first presented them.

* * *

"Pugh?"

Ryan Pugh, a rotund man in his late 60s with a beard which looked like he'd been growing it for most of those sixty years with scarcely a trim in sight, was a retired printer. Old-school, his career had been mostly spent in the days when type was set by hand and when it was not unusual to hand-cut print stencils for intricate work. He'd adapted well to first desktop publishing and then a graphic design world geared more toward the web than printed products, but missed the hands-on nature of his earlier work.

His retirement had not been entirely voluntary. When his wife had fallen ill with cancer, and their medical coverage reached its financial limits midway through her treatment, he'd needed a way to make a sizeable amount of money quickly. He'd received various approaches over the years for less-than-official document creation, and had always declined; Suzanne's illness changed that overnight. He'd got in touch with one of the men who'd contacted him six months earlier about some passports. Yes, he was told, there was always a demand for forged passports and driving licences, and if he could meet the exacting quality requirements of a forgery good enough to pass muster at banks, then he could be advanced the money he needed and work it off over a year or so.

His work had been good – extremely good – and he couldn't keep up with demand while also working in his day-job. He'd quietly started turning down his regular business, pleading pressure of work, and moved into his unofficial print business full-time.

Young had been his introduction to the team. A letter of credit had been required, good enough to remain undetected as a forgery for a week or two, and Pugh had been recommended as someone able to deliver the goods. His capabilities had been

13

considerably extended by a partnership with Katrina Lewis for documents requiring an embedded RFID chip. Between the two of them, there wasn't much they couldn't create. He nodded too.

* * *

"Evans?"

Aaron Evans was an unlikely member of the team. A magician specialising in large-scale illusions, he'd had a successful career first on stage and later on TV, and had not been hurting financially. For someone in his position to take the risk of engaging in criminal activities would have seemed inexplicable to anyone who didn't know him. But to those who knew him well, it would have been far less surprising: Evans was enormously ambitious, and harboured the dream of being considered the greatest magician of all time. To have a series of big-time crimes pulled off thanks to his genius offered perhaps the most promising route to this, albeit one which could not be known until after his death. But that was ok with Evans: the knowledge of his future legacy was enough.

A billion dollars? To come up with an illusion to make that possible would surely guarantee his place in the history books!

"Definitely," he said.

Eight yesses, including her own.

Sullivan nodded: "Then we have some research to do. I've done a little googling, and the good news is that the vault opens at least three times a week. Bank notes wear out, and need to be replaced, so three times a week new bills leave the vault and are transported to the twelve Federal Reserve Banks scattered around the USA. All of the commercial banks get their cash from the Federal Reserve. The exact amounts presumably vary with the denominations involved, but the BEP website says that the total amount transported averages over $700 million a day, alternating between the BEP facilities in Washington DC and Fort Worth. But in the weeks leading up to a new bill design, the daily amount hits over a billion."

"How is the cash transported?" asked Evans. "I assume they don't just stick it in a few Brinks Mat armoured trucks and schlep it halfway across the USA?"

"No," replied Sullivan. "Army convoy to Carswell Air Force Base, then it's transferred to Galaxies and flown to air force bases local to the Federal Reserves. From there, another army convoy. I flew out there for a few days for a little recce work, observing the convoys as they leave."

"And what did you learn?" asked Perez.

"They would not make an easy target."

Perez gave Sullivan a quizzical look. "That's it? That's what you learned? I think we could have guessed that much!"

Sullivan grinned. "There are three separate convoys, each with twelve semis and a whole bunch of army vehicles, all of which look decidedly unfriendly. Six helicopter gunships overhead, following at low-level: they don't look terribly friendly either. The three convoys take separate routes, which appear to vary every day, with no obvious pattern. Whether the money is split between them, or there are two real convoys and one dummy, or one real convoy and two dummies, I don't know."

"Seems there's quite a lot we don't know," observed Jackson.

"That's what fieldwork is for," replied Sullivan, calmly. "I've only been able to witness the convoy departures. I was in a building high enough to get an overview, but it was too far away to see any great detail. What we need now are some more detailed observations at ground level. The convoys are Mondays, Wednesdays and Fridays. We need to get ourselves out there, and we have a few preparations to make, so I suggest we view the one on Wednesday."

"What time does it leave?" asked Young.

"Also random, as far as I can see. Sam, you and I will try to get a good view of the trucks exiting the BEP, hopefully with a view into the loading bay when the doors open. The problem is that the BEP complex is set into its own grounds, with no close buildings overlooking it, and the loading bay is around the back. But Sam and I will figure something out."

"I'm sure we will," said Young.

"So my plan is to hang around a short distance away until we see the army vehicles arrive, which gives us a few minutes' notice of the convoy departure, at which point we'll move in for a closer view. Mike, Katrina, Ryan, you three can ride motorcycles, so you'll be the mobile observation team, shadowing one of the three convoys as closely as possible."

"How do we know which one to follow? And how do we follow any of them, given we don't know the route any of them are going to take?" asked Katrina Lewis.

"Young and I will watch all three leave, but unless we get any clue to distinguish them, you guys will just follow the first one," said Sullivan. "We don't know the route, but we know where they're headed, so the idea is for the three of you to position yourselves at different locations, but all south-east of the BEP, as that's the direction they need to head in. We'll all be in contact by radio, of course. The helicopters overhead will provide a clue, and the local police close off junctions as they approach. When you see a closure go in, you can get up close to the cordon to watch it go past. As it passes a junction, radio in the street it has taken and then the next one of you can head in the right direction to meet it. The most direct route is 16 miles, so allowing for the fact they take indirect routes, you ought to get multiple opportunities for a close look in that time."

"What about me and Raul?" asked Jackson.

"You guys are going to be our air observation team," said Sullivan. "Rent a light aircraft, get as close to the base as you can to observe the arrival of the convoys."

Jackson frowned. "It's an airbase, it'll have the standard 3-mile 3000-feet Prohibited Area." Jackson was referring to the air exclusion zone around all military airbases: no civilian aircraft was allowed within three miles of the base unless it was above 3000 feet.

"A fuck-off big zoom lens would still allow us to see something, weather permitting," observed Perez. "A lot of the air surveillance we did in Afghanistan had to be at that kind of distance to avoid scaring off the bad guys. With aircraft vibration you have to shoot a lot of frames to get a few usable ones, of course, but with a digital SLR and a few big cards, you can just stick it on motor-drive mode and keep firing."

Jackson shrugged. "Worth a go."

"What about the vault?" asked Lewis. "How do we get a look at that?"

"I'm hoping Sam might have some thoughts there. There are BEP tours, and those include an elevated walkway above the print-room, but don't go anywhere near the vault. To see the vault, we need to get someone inside the BEP. Any initial thoughts, Sam?"

Lewis looked at Young. "Well," he said, "there are various ways to get entry to a building. The simplest is relying on good old-fashioned politeness: walk close behind someone, especially carrying a heavy-looking load, and they'll invariably hold the door open for you. Get chatting to them as you walk and a security guard will often assume you're together. But that only works at low-security buildings, so is no use here."

Lewis looked impatient. There was little Young didn't know about the art of deception, but he was prone to rather pedantic explanations at times. What was the point, she thought, of telling us something he knows won't work? She said nothing.

"Next level up," continued Young, "is a forged employee or contractor pass. It's easy enough to create a physical pass, of course, when we have someone of Ryan's talents available." He gave a respectful nod in the direction of Ryan Pugh, who looked embarrassed. "But at a facility like the BEP, we can be confident the passes will be smartcards, with embedded electronics of some kind. A chip or an RFID tag. And to get near the vault? There has to be some kind of biometrics involved. No," he said, "the only way to do that is to get a legitimate pass, and that means getting access to the employee database and creating a new employee. Mike?"

Unlike Young, Chung was not noted for his verbosity. "The BEP systems will be one hell of a tough target," he said, "but I'll see what can be done."

"Thanks," said Sullivan. "Ok, we'll fly out on Monday and get ourselves organised. I'll look into the travel arrangements and email through the details. As always, you'll each make your flight and hotel reservations so there's nothing to connect us. Meantime, I'll see what else I can learn about the vault from some more googling. Chances are they will boast about it somewhere online, and provide at least some idea of what we're up against. Vault security is obviously going to be ... impressive."

Despite the deliberate understatement, Sullivan had no idea just how inadequate a description that would prove to be.

* * *

As the team left, a figure inside the store-room breathed a sigh of relief. He'd expected the club to be deserted at that time of the morning, the perfect time for a spot of opportunistic burglary. He wasn't a greedy man, a few cases of spirits would do him. He knew a couple of local store-owners who'd be glad of a cash-sale, no questions asked. So long as he was careful not to take too much at any one time, he could keep hitting the same clubs every month or two.

Efficient, he called it. You worked out your way in, leaving no damage, and you got to know your way around inside, how to pick the storeroom lock. You judged the stock levels, figuring out how much you could take without the owners realising they'd been burgled. They'd know drinks went missing, of course, but that always happened in clubs. Staff members came and went, and not all of them were honest. A few punters would manage to grab a bottle or two when the club was open, usually drunken dares. Breakages. Stock-keeping errors. A few cases every now and then wouldn't cause any panic.

He'd just entered the storeroom and turned on the light when he heard the front door opening. He'd slipped the stockroom door shut, but not had time to lock it. There was no other door in the room: if they walked in, he'd be trapped. He glanced at the back of the room, spotted some folded tables and tried to memorise a clear route to them. He'd snapped off the light and moved quickly but carefully to the back of the room and crouched down behind the tables.

When it had become clear they weren't headed for the storeroom, he'd grown curious and crept slowly out to the door. He'd tried looking through the keyhole, but the angle hadn't allowed him to see anyone. They were too far away to hear everything they said, but he'd heard enough to know that this was big. Very big.

He didn't like snitching, it went against the grain, but times were tough and a man had to make a living where he could. He'd never do the dirty on anyone he was friendly with, but strangers on the turf were fair game, and he had an arrangement with a local precinct dick to pass on anything he happened across that might be worth half a yard or even a C-note on a good day. But this? This was major league stuff! It had to be worth a few Cs, at least.

He didn't think the visitors were coming back, but wasn't going to hang around to find out when he could make more from one phone call than he'd expected to get from the booze.

"Foster."

"It's Joe Rossie."

"Yeah?" asked Detective Rick Foster.

"I've got some info for you," said Rossie.

"I didn't think you were calling to invite me to your wedding, Rossie – what info?"

"This is big-time stuff. Maybe I shouldn't talk about it on the phone?"

"Nothing you know about is big-time, Rossie, and this ain't the movies," said Foster. "Now say what you got to say or say goodnight."

"You know about the Bureau of Engraving and Print in Fort Worth?"

"I went to school, Rossie, now quit wasting my time."

"There's this gang. They're going to hit it."

"Are you high, Rossie?"

"I swear, Detective Foster, that's what they said!"

"Who said?"

"I don't know who they are."

"And how is it this 'gang'-" the sarcasm was clear in his tone "chose to take you, a low-life nobody, into their confidence on this hit on the government?"

"I overheard it at Danny's twenty minutes ago."

"It's 11am, Rossie, Danny's is closed."

"I know, but they met there."

"And what were you doing in a closed club?" asked Foster.

"I didn't take a thing, honest."

"That doesn't answer my question."

"Look, ok, maybe I was there to conduct a little freelance removals work, but I didn't do it, ok? When

I heard what I heard, I was straight out of there and straight on the phone to you."

Foster sighed, picked up a pen and pulled a notepad towards him. "Descriptions?"

"I didn't actually see them, Detective, I just heard them talking. I didn't want to risk opening the door."

Foster put the pen down on the notepad and pushed it away. "This is bullshit, Rossie. Call me when you have something that you didn't find at the bottom of a bottle, ok?"

"It's true, I swear it."

"Let's pretend, Rossie, let's pretend I'm not a busy man with five hundred better things to do with my time than listen to your crap. How exactly is this little gang of yours planning to break into one of the most secure facilities in the world?"

"I don't know, I couldn't hear all of it. But they talked about the vault and following the convoy and getting a man inside the place, as an employee."

Rossie had heard one other thing – the phrase 'a billion dollars' – but he sure as hell wasn't going to mention that. Foster didn't believe him as it was, he'd think he was on crack if he mentioned that.

"And when is this crime of the century supposed to be happening?" asked Foster.

"I don't know. I heard something about Monday and Wednesday and Friday."

"Any other days of the week you want to throw in there, Rossie? Tuesday, Thursday, Saturday and Sunday, maybe?"

"I can only tell you what I heard, Detective."

"You heard crap, Rossie."

"This is big-time, Detective Foster. This has to be worth something."

"It ain't worth a dime. It's horsecrap, that's what it is. You come back to me with something decent and we'll talk."

"But–"

"Goodbye, Rossie."

Rick Foster shook his head as he replaced the handset. He didn't have time for this, he had real crimes to solve.

* * *

BEP, Fort Worth. 9am Monday.

"Luke Pritchard, Secret Service," said the tall man in his early 40s with prematurely silver hair, showing his gold badge, "and this is my colleague Tim Daniels." The unremarkable-looking balding man in his 50s displayed his badge too.

"Kate Lorrimar, Head of BEP Security." The petite woman in her 30s with a bob haircut, grey eyes and dressed in a conservative dress suit held out her hand. She had a firm grip. "Apologies for the security checks on the way in, I'm afraid not even a Secret Service badge gets you past those!"

"I'm glad to hear it," smiled Pritchard.

"Coffee?"

"Black without, please."

Lorrimar turned to Daniels with a questioning look.

"I'm fine, thanks."

Lorrimar walked to the coffee machine on one wall of her corner office at the Bureau of Engraving and Printing in the Blue Mound neighbourhood on the northern side of Fort Worth. She poured two cups of coffee, handed one to Pritchard and gestured for them to take a seat on the sofa.

"I hope you don't think we're here to tell you how to do your job," began Pritchard. "These five-yearly security reviews must seem a bit presumptuous, especially as it's always a brand new Secret Service team who start out knowing nothing about your procedures."

"Not at all," said Lorrimar, "I understand the 'fresh pair of eyes' concept, though I must confess to a certain degree of confidence in our systems and processes: we've averaged over $700 million a day here for twenty-three years without losing a single dollar, and the BEP as a whole has been printing bank notes since 1869, so we like to imagine we have some idea of what we're doing."

Pritchard smiled. "Believe me, I understand. I was part of the Presidential Detail at the White House for five years, and we have more contingency plans than you'd ever believe. Every possible attack scenario, and not a few impossible ones, has been considered, evaluated and a counter-terrorism plan put in place. We held exercises every single day. We practiced ceaselessly for things we didn't ever expect to have to do in real-life. We liked to imagine we had every base covered. But you know what? We had guys coming in every week to take another look at procedures, trying to find weakness. We had Special Forces teams briefed to find holes in the security. We had IT geeks trying to defeat the electronic measures. 99.99% of the time, they failed miserably. But every now and then, someone would find something new, something we'd never considered. That's why we did it, and that's why we do the same thing here. We figure once every five years isn't too great a hardship."

Lorrimar smiled. In truth, she appreciated the principle, but really didn't expect an outsider to come up with anything they hadn't already thought of. However, she'd spent her entire career in public service, and knew better than to try to buck the system.

"So," said Pritchard, "I've obviously read all the briefing documents, and I'll be going through the Operations Manual page by page-"

"Not exactly light bedside reading," interjected Lorrimar.

Pritchard grinned. "No, I imagine not. As I say, we'll review all of the paperwork along the way, but it would be a great help if you could start by providing an outline of what you see as the key security elements – the things you believe make a theft impossible. In my experience, if there is a blind spot, it's most likely to be in the things everyone takes for granted."

"Ok," said Lorrimar, pleasantly. "Let's begin at the beginning: with the paper and ink. The paper is manufactured at an undisclosed location. Most paper, as you know, is made from wood-pulp. The paper used for US bank notes isn't: it's a blend of 75% cotton, 25% linen. That gives it its special feel. The watermark and security thread are embedded into the paper at the point of production. There are three watermarks in the paper: one portrait, two numeric. The security thread glows under ultra-violet light. The sheets of paper are treated as if they are already bank notes: every single sheet made has to be tracked at every step of the way. Even the tiniest piece of waste paper has to be accounted for."

Pritchard nodded; Daniels looked on impassively. Both men had begun their Secret Service careers in anti-counterfeiting – the original remit of the Service – so were familiar with this, but it had been a while, so a brief refresher did no harm.

"The ink is likewise manufactured in secrecy. It's a special multi-hue ink which appears to change colour as you change the angle at which you hold the note. The ink is also ultra-low-spread, enabling micro-printing techniques impossible with standard inks. $20 and $50 notes use metallic ink which not only has a different appearance to standard inks but can be electronically detected. $100 notes use two different 3D techniques, raised printing and a holographic ribbon. The inks, like the paper, are subjected to comprehensive audit trails: if even a few millilitres went missing, we'd know about it."

"A few millilitres?" asked Pritchard. "Really?" Even with his anti-counterfeiting experience, that part was news to him.

"Really," nodded Lorrimar. "You can read chapter and verse in the manuals."

"Ok," said Daniels, speaking for the first time since declining coffee, "what next?"

"After the paper and ink are securely transported to the facility, they are loaded into the printing press. Loading is handled by robots, as is every aspect of the printing process. There are two printing presses at each BEP location, each capable of printing 10,000 sheets per hour. Each sheet contains 32 bills. Not a single human being enters the printing press room while printing is in operation. If there is a fault which requires the attention of an engineer, the entire press is shut down, the ink supplies and paper rolls are retracted into secure bays and single-step maintenance procedures apply."

"Single-step procedures?" asked Daniels.

"The engineer has to ask for permission to carry out every single step he takes. He wants to undo a bolt? He requests permission from the control room. The control room ensures that at least two cameras have a good view of the bolt in question and he undoes it. Next bolt - same process. He wants to pull off a panel once all the bolts are out, again, specific permission is required before he does it."

"Repairs must take a while," observed Pritchard.

"Fortunately the machines are extremely reliable, and because we alternate printing between DC and Fort Worth facilities, every other day is available for any routine maintenance required: it's not a problem if a procedure takes the entire day. It's mostly a precaution against alterations which would create flaws in a batch of notes – those, as you know, can turn an ordinary $1 bill into something worth thousands of dollars to a collector – but also ensures an engineer couldn't get up to anything of a nefarious nature. Again, you can read up on repair and maintenance procedures in the manuals."

Pritchard nodded.

"What happens next?" asked Daniels. He seemed to be taking more of a lead on the specifics.

"Robots pack the bills into straps, bundles, bricks, cash-packs and pallets," said Lorrimar.

Both men nodded at that: they were familiar with the different units of currency packaging.

"Once a pallet is loaded, the robots shrink-wrap it in extremely strong saran-wrap - much like the suitcase-wrapping services you see at airports. SARVs transport the-"

"SARVs?" asked Daniels.

"Sorry: Storage And Retrieval Vehicles," explained Lorrimar. "They're rather like computer-controlled forklift trucks that follow magnetic tracks embedded in the floor and are equipped with imaging systems that allow them to 'see' what they are doing. They transport the pallets from the printing press to the vault. There are no human beings on the route. BEP personnel are needed to unlock the vault – we'll show you that process later today – but it doesn't physically open until they have all cleared the area. The same process applies when the notes are transported: the SARVs transport the pallets to the loading bay and load the trucks. The only people in the loading bay are the truck drivers who must remain in their cabs at all times. The SARVs load and seal the trucks."

"I understand the time-lock on the vault is randomised, so no-one knows what time it will open?" asked Daniels.

"That's correct," confirmed Lorrimar. "We'll get to the unlocking procedure shortly, but it begins with the activation of a time-lock whose activation time changes randomly each day. Nothing else can happen until the time-lock has kicked in. Once it has, the ten personnel involved in the unlocking get 30 minutes notice. If you're one of the ten, you don't leave the building until that day's vault opening has happened. We all quickly learn to bring in a brown-bag lunch in case the opening isn't until the afternoon. Six of those people, and only those six people, are present in the vault ante-room for the unlocking process. Mr Pritchard-"

"Luke, please," said Pritchard.

"Luke, you have been added to the list of authorised personnel to enter the vault ante-room for today's opening only so that you can witness it first-hand. You don't want to know how many hoops we have to jump through to achieve that. That happens once every five years and only once every five years: you don't want to be absent when the call comes – you won't get a second opportunity."

"What about me?" asked Daniels.

"Sorry," said Lorrimar without further comment.

"So the vault opens every single day?" asked Pritchard.

"Six days a week," said Lorrimar: "three days a week for notes to go in, three days a week for them to come out."

"It seems incredible that we get through $700 million a day in notes – where do they all go?" asked Daniels.

"We're a country of 320 million people. The average person has $74 on them in notes at any given moment. The life of a banknote can range from a few weeks to a couple of years, depending on how soiled they get in that time. An increasing number of people insist on brand new banknotes when withdrawing cash from a bank, so production has had to ramp up to meet that demand. When the new $50 bill is introduced, daily production and distribution exceeds a billion a day."

"Ok," said Daniels, "let's talk about the vault."

"The two BEP vaults are the most secure vaults in the world – even more secure than that at Fort Knox, but please don't tell anyone I said that."

"Why more secure?" asked Daniels.

"Fort Knox is a repository. Most of the time, the gold just sits there. It's rare that the vault door needs to be opened, so the procedures are simpler. Our vaults need to be opened almost every day, so we take additional precautions."

"Ok," said Daniels, "talk us through those."

"To reach the vault, you'd have to pass through five separate security perimeters, staffed by a total of 105 heavily-armed BEP Police officers and a further 40 armed security guards. To reach my office, you've had to pass through two of those layers: there are three more between us and the vault. Progressively fewer people are cleared for each perimeter. Only the six named individuals are allowed past the inner perimeter – plus Luke today."

Daniels nodded.

"If you somehow reached the vault, it wouldn't help. The outer walls are three feet of solid granite. Inside that is a further six feet of steel-reinforced concrete. Inside that is an inner-lining of two six-inch thick steel plates sandwiching a one-inch copper plate to dissipate the heat of a thermal lance. The blast-proof vault door is ten feet thick, weighs 22 tons and it takes the combined actions of ten members of staff to open it, as Luke will see shortly. I'm afraid, Mr Daniels, that you will have to rely on your partner's description of the process."

Daniels said nothing; he did not, noted Lorrimar, follow his boss's lead in inviting her to address him by first name.

"Once the unlock team are gathered in the ante-room, the control room supervisor does a countdown on the PA. What follows is a complex unlocking procedure comprising ten separate steps, with each individual responsible for one of those steps. Six of those individuals will be in the ante-room today, two in the control room, two at our sister facility in DC. Each person has exactly 30 seconds to complete their step. Once they have done so, the control room supervisor gives a five-second countdown for the next person to do their bit. If any one of the ten people attempts their part too early, the whole sequence is aborted. If anyone of the ten takes longer than 30 seconds to complete their step, the whole sequence is aborted. If anyone makes an error, the whole sequence is aborted. An abort means an alarm is sounded, the entire team has two minutes to leave the room – just long enough for each person to clear the airlock – before the entire ante-room is flooded with fast-acting anaesthetic gas. At the same time, the whole building goes into total lock-down: nobody in or out, all internal doors electronically locked. Police and military response teams are automatically alerted."

Pritchard had to admit it sounded thorough. Even Daniels looked somewhat impressed.

"Once the entire unlocking sequence is complete," continued Lorrimar, "all six personnel in the ante-room have to clear it before the vault door actually unlocks. This only happens when both the automated security systems and the control room chief confirms there are no personnel left in the ante-room. I've already described the restrictions on entry to the printing-press; the rule for the vault is even simpler: no human being ever enters the vault under any circumstances. Not even the President of the United States himself. To ensure no human being enters the vault, the doorway is fitted with heat sensors, laser beams, pressure-sensitive flooring and additional measures that even I don't know about. If someone defeated those, a powerful anaesthetic gas would render them unconscious within seconds. While the SARVs are in operation outside of the vault, nobody has access to the areas in which they are operating."

"What if one of the SARVs breaks down inside the vault?" asked Daniels.

"The SARVs are capable of towing each other out. There's nothing else mechanical inside the vault, so no reason for anyone else to enter."

"What if one of the SARVs drops a pallet, and it splits, spilling bills on the floor?" persisted Daniels.

"It can't happen," replied Lorrimar. "All the SARV movements are pre-programmed: they just repeat precisely the same movements each time."

"But if it did?"

"If it ever did, we can manually control the SARVs remotely from the control-room, so we'd figure out a way to sort it out using those. Nobody enters the vault, ever, under any circumstances."

Both men recognised the steel in her voice.

Lorrimar walked over to her desk, opened a drawer and pulled out a pager. She handed it to Pritchard: "My assistant will show you to a conference room you can use to begin your documentation review. When the pager signals, she will come and bring you to my office, and you'll accompany me to the vault ante-room. Don't go AWOL."

* * *

The two men had been sat in the windowless conference room for almost two hours. Pritchard and Daniels each held A4-sized ebook readers containing: 1,163 pages of The BEP Security Operations Manual (Fort Worth). The ebook readers themselves were special ones originally made for use on US naval submarines. They had no wifi or mobile data capabilities, no card slot, no USB port. There was no way for anyone to get materials on or off them outside of the secure facility responsible for them.

They'd had to sign for the readers, and had been informed that the devices would be automatically wiped if they attempted to take them out beyond the level 3 checkpoint.

Daniels, who had a near photographic memory, was on page 232. Pritchard was on page 149. The difference in pace was partly explained by the fact that Pritchard was taking occasional notes, but he couldn't deny to himself that another factor was the distraction of that silent pager sitting on the table by his right elbow. He had read 149 pages and had probably glanced at the pager at least half as many times.

It was crazy, he thought. He'd worked in the White House. He'd been with POTUS – the Service abbreviation for President Of The United States –

almost every day for five years. After that, nothing should impress him. A door? A hunk of metal? What was that in comparison, however sophisticated it might be? Yet the more he read, the more The Vault – he wanted to capitalise it – seemed to take on almost mythical status in his mind. It was just what you're used to, he supposed: the president is just a man when you spend every day with him; see him when he's tired, frustrated, short-tempered. The Vault – he felt himself mentally doing it again – was something new and unfamiliar. To the BEP personnel involved in the unlocking, he was sure it soon became a mundane rout–

BZZZT!

He'd been waiting for that sound for two hours now, yet still he jumped when the pager sounded. Daniels looked at him, smirked and said nothing.

Pritchard glanced at his watch: 11:09. It seemed an age before Lorrimar's assistant opened the door.

"Mr Pritchard, follow me, please."

She led him back along the short walk to Lorrimar's office, knocked once and opened the door without waiting for a response.

Kate Lorrimar smiled and stood up as they entered. "Productive morning?" she asked.

"Glad to be able to take a break from the theory," he smiled.

"We have plenty of time yet, but as I explained earlier, there is no leeway at all in the timings, so we like to ensure you're on hand. Normally I only head down there around ten minutes before, but it will take extra time with you, so we'll head down about ten minutes from now so we'll have 20 minutes to clear the two final security checkpoints."

"Ok," replied Pritchard.

"So, time for a coffee beforehand."

In the conference room, Daniels continued ploughing through the ops manual. He approved of what he read, but then it shouldn't be too difficult in an environment over which you had total control. This wasn't like the White House, where you had any number of visitors arriving at different times, and especially a presidential walkabout where your control was extremely limited. Those were the days Secret Service agents dreaded. Give them total say, and they'd have wide-area perimeters, pat-down searches and body-scanners for anyone to get within a block of POTUS. As it was, any nut with a gun and a grievance could walk right up to the rope-line. You couldn't relax for a second. Presidential protection detail was the most coveted role in the Service, but there wasn't a single agent who didn't breathe a heartfelt sigh of relief when it was over.

He turned his attention back to page 239.

"It's time," said Lorrimar. "You'll need to leave your jacket here, I'm afraid." She gestured to the door of her office: "You'll find a couple of hangers over there."

Pritchard already felt naked without his SIG SAUER P229, which he'd had to leave with Security at the entrance. No visitor weapons were allowed in the building no matter who you were. He slipped off his jacket and hung it on the back of the door. He was familiar with the no-jacket rule used in some secure areas: it made it easier to ensure someone wasn't concealing anything on the way in, or slipping anything into a pocket whilst there.

Lorrimar handed him a credit-card-sized badge. It was a featureless grey colour bearing nothing but the letters QQZ and today's date.

"Please ensure this remains visible at all times. It makes people nervous if you're within the inner perimeters without it."

Pritchard clipped the badge to his shirt pocket.

"Do I take my Secret Service pass with me?" he asked, gesturing to his jacket.

"No, that badge is the only pass that counts from this point on," replied Lorrimar.

No gun, no badge: this was no ordinary day, thought Pritchard.

Lorrimar continued: "Once you clear the final search at the entrance to the vault ante-room, you need to keep your hands in your trouser pockets at all times."

He nodded. Again, the precaution was a familiar one: it ensured a visitor couldn't touch any controls or papers.

They walked to a small unmarked elevator. There were no buttons, only a cardslot. Lorrimar inserted her pass into the slot and the doors opened immediately. The elevator had only two main buttons, Pritchard noticed, labelled Upper and Lower. Lorrimar pressed the Lower button and the elevator swiftly descended. A few moments later, the door opened. They were in a small lobby area: a desk containing nothing but a laptop and a featureless black box, one BEP cop sat behind it, and a second BEP cop stood next to a door with a keypad next to it.

"Mr Pritchard. Secret Service," announced Lorrimar. The cop behind the desk studied Pritchard's face then a photograph displayed on the screen in front of him. Several seconds passed before he was apparently satisfied that the features matched.

"Your pass, please, Mr Pritchard."

Pritchard unclipped it and handed it over. The cop took a pair of odd-looking glasses from his pocket, put them on and studied the card carefully, angling it in different directions. He then removed the glasses and waved the badge over the top of the featureless black box while looking at the laptop screen. He nodded and handed back the badge. Pritchard clipped it back onto his pocket.

The cop by the door approached Pritchard. "Legs apart and arms to your side, please."

Pritchard complied. Pat-downs varied in thoroughness, from the casual to the presidential. The one he received would have passed muster in the White House. While this was happening, the cop at the desk repeated the pass routine with Lorrimar's pass.

Lorrimar put her pass back around her neck and was also subjected to a thorough-looking pat-down check by the second cop. He nodded and Lorrimar stepped up to the door. The cop took a couple of steps forward, facing away from the door.

Lorrimar stood close to the keypad so neither Pritchard nor the cops could see what she was doing. A few seconds later, a green light came on. The cop by the door glanced at the cop at the desk, who was looking at the laptop. He nodded again: a man of few words, it seemed.

Lorrimar opened the door and held it open for Pritchard. "You have to walk ahead of me. It reassures the cops watching on CCTV that you don't have me at gunpoint. Straight to the end of the corridor," she said.

Pritchard smiled. It felt faintly theatrical, but he was here to ensure that there was no security precaution they had missed, and so far he couldn't fault anything.

Pritchard tried to spot the CCTV cameras but failed: the corridor appeared featureless.

"I'm guessing the cameras are not the only electronics hidden in the corridor," he commented over his shoulder.

"Indeed," replied Lorrimar. "Again, full details in the ops manual."

The corridor ended with a sliding metal door. It opened while Pritchard was still about 20 feet away. Another BEP cop stepped through and the door slid closed behind him.

"Another search, I'm afraid, Sir."

Pritchard assumed the position. The pat-down was as thorough as the last one. He approved: civilians often questioned the sense of repetitive checks. It wasn't like anyone could have acquired a weapon between one end of the corridor and the other, but professionals appreciated that the weakest point of any security system was the people. You couldn't rely on the fact that the last guy did his job properly. Multiple layers of redundancy was one of the watchwords of good security.

"Thank you, Sir."

The door slid open without visible signal from the cop, and at a gesture from the cop Pritchard stepped through. He was in a small featureless room with black walls and a matching sliding door at the far end. That door was closed.

"Full-body scanner," explained the cop. "You know the drill, stand as still as you can, legs apart, arms slightly away from your side, and remain still until the door at the far end opens, then step out."

Pritchard stepped in and stood as instructed. Nothing visible or audible happened. About ten seconds passed, and Pritchard was beginning to wonder whether something had gone wrong – the check should only take a few seconds – when the door at the far end opened. He stepped out into a small wood-panelled room. At the far side was a clear glass air-lock, with two BEP cops stood directly in front of it, each of them carrying a Heckler & Koch semi-automatic.

One of them gestured to the side: "If you would just wait here for a moment, Sir." He stood next to the left-hand wall, featureless except for a telephone handset.

He looked through the glass air-lock. It was a circular-shaped chamber just large enough for one person to stand in it. He looked through the air-lock, and there it was, visible on the far side: a brightly-lit room with metal-skinned walls and in the centre of one side the Vault Door. He found himself mentally capitalising it. Criss-crossing the door area was a mesh of red laser beams. Clearly Bad Things would happen were any of the beams to be broken.

He was staring at the door so intently he didn't notice Lorrimar step out of the body-scanner to stand beside him.

"Quite a sight, isn't it?" she asked.

"Yes," he said, simply. It was gun-metal grey in colour, round and approximately ten feet in diameter. It looked nothing like a standard vault door: there was no hand wheel or visible levers. There were, however, two outsize-looking keyholes in the door itself, and various black panels either side of it. Reflections from the spotlights glaring through the two layers of glass in the airlock made it difficult to see much more detail.

"You'll get a better look in a moment," she told him.

She picked up the phone handset.

"Lorrimar," she said. A pause, then: "Yes." Then a series of pauses and single syllable responses: "Yes. No. Yes. Yes. No." Another pause. "Golf Bravo Zulu Juliet Juliet Alpha Whisky Niner Two Seven Fife One." Another pause. "Confirmed."

She handed the handset to Pritchard. Surprised, he took it.

"Good morning, Mr Pritchard. I trust the traffic was not too bad on your way in?"

He recognised the coded question, used to establish whether an agent was being coerced in any way. It was a code specific to the Service, so he suspected he had now been connected to a Secret Service office. He gave the response indicating that all was well: "Rather light, actually, considering the time of day."

"Thank you." The line went dead. He replaced the handset in its holder.

Nothing visible happened. Pritchard could see no sign that anything had been communicated to the two cops, but they stepped aside, leaving the entrance to the airlock clear. The airlock door on their side slid open.

"You first," said Lorrimar. "Hands in your pockets now, please. Once in, obviously keep clear of the laser beams: you don't want to be responsible for an abort, not unless you want to spend the rest of your career guarding an obscure public monument somewhere in Nebraska."

"I'll be careful," he said.

He glanced at the cops, who were staring into space, and stepped into the airlock. The entrance door slid closed behind him. Nothing happened for several seconds. Then the door ahead of him slid open. Just that. No green light, no bleep, just the door opening. Efficient.

And there he was standing in the vault ante-room, alone. He stared at the door. He had at least managed to stop mentally capitalising it, he thought. Now that he had a clearer view without the glare through the air-lock, he looked at the black panels either side of the door. Two of them were clearly touch-style keypads, but neither pad had any numbers or symbols of any kind on it: all of the keys were blank. He recognised another panel as a palm-print reader, similar to the one used to access certain areas within the White House. He also recognised an iris reader. There were other panels he couldn't identify.

He looked around him and saw on the opposite wall a row of four metal shutters, each around 1.5 metres square.

The airlock door slid open and Lorrimar stepped out. "So now we know you don't have any explosives or ammunition on you," she smiled.

"Ah, explosives-sniffers in the air-lock," he responded.

"Conventional, plastic and nuclear," she replied, "there's a radiation meter in there too."

Lorrimar looked at her watch. "The others will arrive shortly," she said. "I'll talk you through each element of the unlocking process as it takes place, but I'll brief you now on my part in it as I won't have time while I'm doing it."

She pointed to the left-hand keypad. "An 8x8 pad. 64 touch-sensitive panels. There are no numbers or letters, we have to memorise the pattern. The number of combinations is greater than it appears:

the keypads measure not just the order in which the keys are pressed, but also the duration of each touch – like you might have a secret knock of three short, two long. I can't tell you how many keys have to be pressed, but if we used all of them the total number of permutations would be a shade under 4 billion. The sensors also have fingerprint readers built in, ensuring that it is the correct person operating them. The wrong person with the right combination would generate an abort."

"Quite sophisticated as combination locks go," said Pritchard.

"The one on the right is operated by my deputy. I have no idea what his combination is, of course, or whether it is the same length as mine. I will do mine first. I have 30 seconds to complete my combination. There is no feedback to indicate a successful code-entry, so that an intruder wouldn't even know it if they were somehow able to enter the correct code. An unsuccessful code entry, on the other hand, would be quite ... loud. Suffice it to say if we are asked to clear the room, we do so immediately."

"You said before that we have two minutes to clear the room," observed Pritchard, "which was just enough time for everyone to clear the airlock. That's normally six people, today it's seven – does the system make allowances for that?"

"Do you know," she replied, "you've managed to ask a question to which I don't know the answer. Congratulations! I'm afraid, though, that as it's first-in, last-out, you would be the guinea-pig for that particular experiment!"

"Let's hope no-one messes up! Erm ... have they ever?"

"Never in my time here, but apparently there were two occasions before my time. Rest assured it isn't a common occurrence."

"Glad to hear it."

"So, you'll hear the countdown over the PA. Ten seconds before the end of the countdown, the laser beams will be automatically switched off and both my deputy and I can step forward to our respective keypads. I will enter my code on the left-hand keypad, then step back. He will get a 5-second countdown then enter his. The rest, I'll talk you through as it happens, ok?"

"Sure," said Pritchard.

The airlock door opened and a man in his late fifties or early sixties entered the ante-room. He looked somewhat out-of-place in a crisp white shirt and tie but no jacket. He was carrying an enormous key, about two feet long. It looked like something out of a novelty store. Pritchard raised an eyebrow. Lorrimar laughed. "It looks like a joke, I know, but I assure you it's very serious."

A second man, younger, entered, carrying an identical key. Lorrimar didn't introduce either of them.

"There are two reasons for the keys being that size," said Lorrimar. "First, there is no way to secrete a key that size about your person."

Pritchard smiled: "I would imagine not."

"Second, the size allows an extremely intricate pattern, much more complex than a conventional-size key. And the lock isn't purely mechanical: some parts of the keys are electrically conductive, other parts are insulators, and the pattern of opened and closed circuits within the lock confirms that the keys are genuine."

A portly gentleman with an untidy shock of salt-and-pepper hair and matching beard was next, also looking half-undressed in suit trousers, shirt sleeves and bow-tie. "The Director," observed Lorrimar.

He was followed by a stylishly-dressed woman in her late 30s. "His deputy."

Over the next couple of minutes, the others joined. The room was now about half-filled with people.

"I assume each of them went through a similar security regime to get here," said Pritchard.

Lorrimar nodded. "Visual identification by the cops. Physical and electronic verifications of their passes. Keypad entry for the first door. Voice verification with coded responses before admission to the air-lock. These cops see the same people entering every day but nothing is taken for granted, nothing is assumed, everything is checked."

"Two minutes," announced a voice over the PA system.

Pritchard waited.

"90 seconds."

He looked around. The group didn't appear to be arranged in any particular order, and no-one seemed tense: they all looked perfectly relaxed. He noted, though, that there was no small-talk.

"One minute." There was total silence in the room.

"Where is the control room?" asked Pritchard, almost whispering. There was something intimidating about the surroundings and the near-silence.

"Above us," replied Lorrimar, gesturing. "One-way glass and the spotlights mean we can't see them, but they can see us, both directly and via the cameras."

"30 seconds."

It felt like waiting for a Space Shuttle launch. Back in the day when we had a Space Shuttle, he thought, sadly.

"20 seconds."

"10 seconds."

The laser beam grid vanished. Lorrimar stepped forward, as did a younger-looking man Pritchard assumed was her deputy. Each stood in front of the keypads.

"Keypad 1 in 5, 4, 3, 2, 1. Go."

There was nothing to see. Pritchard could only see the backs of the two people stood at the keypads. Lorrimar seemed to be taking a very long time – surely she had exceeded the 30-second window by now?

After a few more seconds, Lorrimar stepped back.

"Keypad 2 in 5, 4, 3, 2, 1. Go."

Again, there was nothing to see.

After what again felt like an age, the security deputy stepped back. The two men with the comedy keys stepped forward, positioned either side of the vault door.

"Keys 1 and 2 in 5, 4, 3, 2, 1. Go."

Both men inserted their keys into slots in the walls alongside the door, then looked at each other. The man on the right nodded and both turned the keys simultaneously.

"The key turning has to begin simultaneously to within two seconds," commented Lorrimar. "It would be physically impossible for one person to simultaneously turn both keys, or to get from one to the other fast enough."

Pritchard nodded.

The two men withdrew the keys and stepped back.

The Director stepped forward, standing in front of the two pieces of equipment Pritchard had recognised earlier.

"Integrated Personnel Identification System," confirmed Lorrimar. "Iris, palm and voice. His hand must be on the palm-print reader at the same time he looks into the iris-recognition visor, and he must remain in place as he speaks."

"Director recognition in 5, 4, 3, 2, 1. Go."

The Director positioned his right hand and looked into the visor. "Voice recognition, Duncan Ross, Director, BEP Fort Worth." He then stepped back and his deputy took his place.

There was no visible or audible confirmation within the ante-room of the successful completion of any element of the unlock sequence, noted Pritchard, approvingly.

"Deputy director recognition in 5, 4, 3, 2, 1. Go."

The deputy repeated the actions of the director, stating her own name and title, then stepped back

"Those are six of the ten steps," said Lorrimar, "which are the only ones visible from here. The next two steps take place up there." Lorrimar gestured upward at the unseen control room. The control room chief satisfies himself that he has six green lights, and that no-one has been coerced into playing their part. His deputy double-checks this. Both must then simultaneously enter different passwords into two different terminals on opposite sides of the control room. Both must be typing simultaneously for the passwords to be accepted. Again, there is no feedback of any kind that the passwords were entered correctly until the end of the 30-second window. At that point, green lights seven and eight come on."

"And steps nine and ten?" asked Lorrimar.

"Those happen remotely at the sister BEP facility in DC. The Director and Deputy Director there use the same IPIS unit to confirm their identities, and once that is done lights nine and ten come on."

"So they are in the vault ante-room in DC?" asked Pritchard, surprised.

"Correct. You sound surprised?"

"I am – I would have thought you don't want anyone in the ante-room unless necessary. Why not have additional IPIS units in their offices?"

"The offices are less secure locations. To reach the vault, they have to pass two additional security perimeters. I assure you it is not done as an economy measure."

Pritchard grinned. "So how will we know when the remaining four steps are complete?"

"The PA system," replied Lorrimar.

They waited. Still no-one else talking, he noted. He wondered whether Lorrimar and he had broken some unspoken code, their breach of etiquette the topic of canteen gossip for days to come.

"Thank you, ladies and gentlemen," said the voice over the PA system.

"That's it?" asked Pritchard. "The door is unlocked?" It seemed a massive anti-climax after all that build-up to have the unlocking of the door signalled by nothing more than a simple 'thank you' message. He'd expected ... well, he wasn't sure, but if not a siren, then surely a flashing green light or at least the whirring sound of bolts being withdrawn.

"Not quite yet: there is one final automated step," replied Lorrimar.

The team started exiting one at a time through the air-lock.

"Namely?"

"The computer system will verify that all six of us – seven today – have left the ante-room before the vault door actually unlocks."

"How does it do that?" asked Pritchard.

"It counts us all out through the air-lock, then uses feeds from both infra-red detectors and CCTV cameras to verify that the room is empty."

"Does the computer know that there are seven of us in here today rather than six?"

"Oh yes. You wouldn't have gotten in in the first place otherwise."

"Can I watch the SARVs work through the air-lock?" asked Pritchard.

"Afraid not," she said, "but there's a monitoring station upstairs – you're welcome to watch from there."

It was Lorrimar's turn in the air-lock. Pritchard turned around for one last look at the vault door.

He entered the air-lock. There was the briefest of pauses between the rear door closing and the exit opening: no security needed on the way out, he assumed.

As the two of them walked back to Lorrimar's office, Pritchard asked: "What is the actual locking mechanism?"

"There are two elements to it. The first is a set of twenty-four Inconel 625 bolts."

"Inconel 625?"

"The strongest metal in the world."

"I thought that was tungsten?" questioned Pritchard.

"Everyone does," she replied. "Tungsten has a tensile strength of up to 170,000 psi. It's used a lot in the aerospace industry because it retains that strength at high temperatures. Inconel 625 doesn't have the same temperature range, but that isn't needed in this application. It's tensile strength is 220,000 psi - a third stronger than Tungsten."

"Ok," said Pritchard, and the second element?"

"Powerful electromagnets. They are capable of holding the door closed against much greater pressure than even fifty people could exert." They reached her office. "Ok," she said, "let's watch some TV! Most people are fascinated by watching the SARVs at work."

* * *

Daniels flicked onto page 290. He'd taken out his notebook to jot down queries just four times so far – something he considered a considerable compliment to those responsible for the security procedures. The door opened and Pritchard poked his head round it.

"How was the show-and-tell?" asked Daniels.

"I'll tell you about it afterwards. Want to come and watch the SARVs remove $700 million from the vault?"

"When you put it like that ..." replied Daniels. "What happened to your jacket?"

"No jackets in the ante-room," said Pritchard.

Together they walked back to the desk of Lorrimar's PA, Deborah, where she stood up and led the way to an unmarked door. She knocked but again didn't wait for a response before opening the door.

Inside was a fairly typical security monitoring station: a horse-shoe shaped desk with two chairs in front of it occupied by uniformed security guards. In front of them was a huge bank of monitors. The two guards both nodded but neither spoke, and both quickly turned their heads back to face the monitors. Pritchard and Daniels stood a few feet behind them, while the PA excused herself.

Pritchard and Daniels surveyed the screens in front of them. There were eight large screens – around 40 inches – set into a curved facade. Above, below and to either side of them were a massive bank of smaller screens – they appeared to be around 20 inches. The screens curved about halfway round the room. Some of the smaller screens showed obvious locations: the outside of the building, the lobby area, each of the security checkpoints, corridors and so forth. But two rows of screens showed a series of completely featureless corridors with closed metal shutters at each end, four in total. Pritchard recalled the four metal shutters in the vault ante-room: the corridors were presumably what lay behind them.

But both men focused their attention on the eight large screens. The two on the left showed different views of the vault ante-room. The vault door was still closed. The two screens on the right showed the loading bay where 12 trucks were backed-up against a loading dock with four metal-shuttered doors in the wall behind them, and a further 24 trucks were parked on the opposite side. It was the four screens in the centre that really grabbed their attention: these showed the inside of the vault from each of the four interior walls. Like the ante-room, it was brightly illuminated to almost painful levels by floodlights set into the ceiling.

The vault was enormous – around 50 feet square and about 20 feet high. The floor was metal, the small sections of visible wall were the same. The ceiling presumably too, though it just appeared black against the glare of the floodlights set into it.

The inside of the vault door was, like the outside, completely featureless.

Most of the wall surfaces could not be seen as every available inch was covered in warehouse-style shelving. It looked oddly low-tech in this environment: it didn't look any different to the metal shelving you might see in any DIY store. The difference, of course, was the contents of the shelves: pallet upon pallet of shrink-wrapped currency.

The bills themselves weren't really visible through the multiple layers of saran-wrap. The pallets could have held almost anything: copier paper, flyers, tax returns, you name it. But it wasn't any of those things. They were, they knew, looking at seven hundred million dollars.

In the centre of the vault were eight SARVs. He was surprised to see them already in there as the vault door was still closed, but realised that the empty centre area in the vault was a perfectly sensible place for them to be stored when not in use, totally safe from tampering. Lorrimar had described the SARVs as robotic fork-lift trucks, but they looked more like straight-sided blue-coloured skips with one wall missing and two robot arms bolted onto the sides of the missing wall. Thick black cables ran in a curved path from the arms to a black box attached to the front of the unit. The small wheels were the only part of them that resembled a conventional fork-lift truck. None of the eight were moving.

The door behind them opened and Lorrimar walked in. "Usually the SARVs would begin work immediately, but I've arranged for a short delay so that you wouldn't miss anything. I'll briefly talk you through the process as the transfer to the trucks begins, then you can stay to watch as much of the process as you like."

"Is the vault unlocked yet?" asked Pritchard.

"Yes," said Lorrimar. "Usually the door would have opened as soon as we cleared the ante-room, but the whole process is on a short hold." Lorrimar lent forward and said something to one of the guards who spoke into a desk microphone in front of him. "Hold release requested."

Nothing happened for a few seconds, then they watched in fascination as the huge metal door swung very slowly outward. As the door began to open, Pritchard could see it was shaped like a slice through a cone, the inside smaller than the outside, leaving room for it to open out in an arc. It was interesting, he thought, how much of life is symbolic. In other circumstances, the opening of a door, even one as impressive as this one, wouldn't be deserving of more than a moment's attention. But here, now, he couldn't take his eyes off the screens, alternating between the interior and exterior views.

The conical shape of the door meant that the floor of the vault was at a slightly higher level than the floor of the ante-room. He knew from Lorrimar's briefing that the door weighed 22 tons, yet there was no visible means of locomotion: no telescopic arms pulling it or pushing it open.

"How is it moved?" he asked.

"Motors in the hinges," answered Lorrimar.

"Must be quite some motors," he remarked.

"They are. Very highly geared, hence the slow opening. Quadruple redundancy too."

The door swung all the way around to lay flat against the exterior wall of the vault. As the motion ceased, all eight SARVs moved simultaneously, two each moving toward each of the four walls. Pritchard knew that their movements were programmed to within a millimetre, and had somehow expected the precision to be reflected in slow, careful movement. But of course he was judging by human, not machine, standards: the SARVs in fact moved rapidly, looking almost as if it were a fast-forward replay of a recorded video. All eight SARVs moved in perfect synchronisation: it was like watching some bizarre robot ballet.

Pritchard turned his attention to one of the SARVs. It had rapidly positioned itself in front of one of the sections of shelf. The blue box unit was now raising rapidly in height, lifted by a scissor mechanism similar to that seen on the service carts used at airports to restock food supplies. The box extended until it was level with the highest of the three levels of shelving. The robot arms extended and slotted into the base of the pallet. The pallet lifted slightly, then rapidly retracted until it was inside the blue box. The scissor mechanism retracted until the box was once again at floor level. All around it, the other SARVs had matched the one on which he had concentrated, move by move.

"You'll now see the first four exit the vault, one at a time," said Lorrimar.

Even before she had finished speaking, the first SARV had done a 180-degree turn on the spot and 'driven' toward the wall containing the vault doorway. It did a sharp right-hand 90-degree turn, heading parallel to the wall in the direction of the doorway. It stopped in front of the open doorway and made a sharp left-hand 90-degree turn. After the barest of hesitations, it passed through the vault doorway, coping easily with the small downward slope of the doorway itself.

Pritchard switched his attention to one of the two screens showing the vault ante-room. He watched as the SARV drove forwards ten feet or so – sufficient distance to clear the vault door – then made another right-hand 90-degree turn. A short forward motion, another 90-degree left and more forward motion saw it heading for one of one of the four metal shutters. There was no halting this time: the metal shutter lifted as it approached and the SARV entered the tunnel beyond. As it did so, Pritchard could see that the second SARV had already exited the vault and was on its way to a second shutter.

Lorrimar leaned over to point to one of the smaller screens where the SARV could be seen passing through the corridors Pritchard had noted earlier. "There are various forms of detectors in the tunnels," said Lorrimar, "to ensure nobody is in them. Body-heat sensors, laser beams and so forth. The SARV doesn't enter unless the tunnel is clear. In the first section of tunnel is a highly sensitive weighbridge, which knows the precise weight of the loaded SARV; any additional weight, indicating something on the pallet that shouldn't be there, and the SARV reverses out."

The first SARV had already reached the far end, where the metal shutter had slid up as it approached so there was no delay. Lorrimar pointed to one of the large screens with the loading bay view where the SARV could be seen emerging. It did its now-familiar 90-degree turns-on-the-spot to position itself at the rear doors of the first of the twelve trucks. The right-hand robot arm extended and appeared to attach itself to some kind of plate on the back of the truck.

"The electronic lock for the truck door," explained Lorrimar. "You can't really see it well on the screen, but something rather like the wiring plugs used on a trailer unit has plugged into a matching socket on the truck. Computer systems on truck and SARV communicate with each other, each querying the other. The truck satisfies itself that the device connected to it is a BEP SARV, and the SARV satisfies itself that the truck is a BEP convoy one. If the SARV fails the truck's authentication query, the door won't unlock; if the truck fails the SARV's authentication query, it won't load the pallet onto the truck."

As Lorrimar explained this, the SARV disconnected and backed away.

"Problem?" asked Pritchard.

"No," replied Lorrimar, "it's backing up so that the truck door can open." As she said this, a large, thick section of truck door, looking much like a bank vault door itself, slid outward and upwards. The opening was slightly larger than the SARV. The skip moved forward on the robot arms until it was fully inside the truck. The arms withdrew and the SARV immediately turned and headed toward the metal shutter. It stopped just short of it. The shutter slid open and another of the SARVs emerged. The first

SARV, positioned to the left of the shutter, waited. The second SARV turned sharp right and headed toward another of the trucks. As soon as it was clear of the tunnel entrance, the first SARV moved forward, turned 90 degrees and entered the tunnel.

"There are computer-controlled motorised roller systems inside the trucks that position the pallets inside," said Lorrimar. "They will load all twelve trucks backed up against the loading dock. The twenty-four trucks parked on the opposite side are the decoys for the dummy convoys."

Pritchard and Daniels' eyes darted between the various screens as they watched the synchronised dance of the SARVs heading back and forth, each waiting like gentlemen to allow an oncoming SARV through a tunnel entrance or the vault doorway.

"I'll leave you to watch as much as you like," said Lorrimar. "Just come to my office when you're done."

Pritchard had to admit there was no logical reason to watch the entire loading process. Complex as the movement patterns were, they were all fixed in nature and the ops manual would doubtless contain detailed diagrams of the steps should it become relevant, but the orchestrated efficiency of it was mesmerising to watch. In a strange way, it was actually quite beautiful. Both men remained in the observation room until the loading of the trucks was complete.

On the screens showing the exterior of the building, they could see the convoy escorts waiting – but that could wait: they would be accompanying the money on both the convoy and one of the flights on Wednesday. For now, it was back to the manual.

* * *

12:20pm, Hertz car-parking area of Dallas Fort Worth airport

Sullivan secretly loved this stage. Right at the beginning of a project, when nothing was known, everything was new. You didn't even yet know the problems, let alone have any of the solutions. Others had their adrenaline rushes at the tense moments in the middle of the job, when seconds mattered and everything rested on their ability to play their part right then, right there. But she was the leader. Her job was to plan and support and encourage. By the time the job was underway, her job was done: she could only rely on each member of her team. This was her adrenaline rush, right at the outset.

Secretly, because she knew most of the others hated it. They liked solutions, answers, data. They each wanted to figure out their part, and only when they were confident they had a solution would they begin to enjoy themselves. But Sullivan, she lived for this.

Even the boring admin she'd done was enjoyable to her, because it represented the beginning of the adventure. Booking two Hertz rental pickups to get from the airport and to provide a flexible form of transport that could be adapted to any needs that might arise while they were there; three Harley Davidson motorcycles from a dealer in the centre of the city for pickup the following day; and a one-day self-fly rental of a Cessna 172 booked for pickup first thing Wednesday morning.

There was also the financial investment, of course. Thanks to their earlier projects, the combined $50k investment they'd agreed for the research stage wasn't a massive one, but it represented a commitment all the same. Like putting your initial table stake down in a poker game, it got you focused.

She climbed into the back of one of the two Ford F-150s she'd rented, sitting next to Chung. She'd been intrigued by his description of the BEP hack they'd need to get someone inside the building. One hell of a tough target, he'd said. Chung was noted for his laconical approach. If anything, he was usually too casual, too confident. If he sounded dubious ...

They obviously couldn't discuss anything on the plane, so she'd decided to sit next to him on the short ride from the airport so she could learn more. This was just curiosity on her part: if Mike said it was good, it was good, but she liked to learn, and she knew Mike enjoyed explaining things to her.

"So, Mike, this BEP hack: how would it work?"

"If it works, you mean."

There it was again. This wasn't like him.

"I start with the webserver," he said, "the one running the public website."

"Why the public site?"

"That's the only server whose identity is known, so it gives us a machine to target."

"Ok," said Jessica.

"I ping it–"

"Ping it?"

"Send it a little hello message. One of the things I get in response is the IP address. That's like the phone number."

Sullivan nodded; in her former role, she'd needed a reasonable overview of computer security, but mostly it was at the conceptual level: she'd relied on techs for the detail, then as now.

"Next up, I use a scanning tool to query the server for open ports. That basically tells us what services are running on the machine and what types of incoming connections are accepted from machines outside their network. Might be a number of those: FTP, SSH, etc, but a likely one is email."

"Ok, so the server accepts incoming emails?" asked Sullivan.

"Basically, yes. If the email port is open, it means the machine will allow a mailserver on another machine outside the network to talk to it. I can then telnet in and–"

"Telnet?"

"A piece of software that acts like a computer terminal in days of old. By sending the right commands, I can pretend to be a mailserver."

"And what does that achieve?" asked Sullivan.

"It tells me which email software it's running, and which version," explained Chung. "If we're very, very lucky, they will be running an old version with a known exploit. I can then use a buffer overflow exploit to get in."

"Ok, you just lost me."

"It's a special packet of data that causes the software to crash and drops you to a command-line. You're now inside the network. First thing you do is restart the mailserver so no outage is detected, then you have a poke around inside the network seeing what you can see. If you're fortunate enough to have root access, you may be able to hop from machine to machine inside the network. If I have sufficient access, I can add a superuser, then I'll be able to login as and when I like, and do pretty much anything. Including find the employee database and add a new employee to it."

"You make it sound easy."

"That's because you didn't hear all the ifs," replied Chung. "If there's an open port. If there's outdated software installed. If I have root access. If the employee database is on a server reachable from the webserver. Frankly, I'm not optimistic: if all of those ifs were true, their sysadmin should be fired. Personally, I'd fire them if any one were true."

"Ok," said Sullivan, "you just went from making it sound easy to making it sound impossible."

Chung nodded. "It probably is, but you just never know with these things. People are careless. The guy running the public webserver doesn't see it as a high-security environment because it's not: it's all just publicly-accessible documents. But what he may not realise is that anyone who can get access to that server may well be able to then connect to others."

"Right," said Sullivan. "Keep me informed."

1.30pm, BEP, Fort Worth

Pritchard finished talking Daniels through the procedure in the vault. He was a trained expert witness: his description was forensic in its detail and accuracy. Daniels, who had read through the procedures in the ops manual, nodded.

"So," said Daniels.

"Hmm," replied Pritchard.

"See any weaknesses at all in what you observed?" asked Daniels.

"Not a thing. And in your reading?"

"Not even the shadow of one."

"I hate to admit this," said Pritchard, "but it honestly looks to me like there'd be more chance of a bad guy getting into the Oval Office than into that vault."

Daniels nodded. Both men were silent for a few seconds.

"You know," said Daniels, "we ought to be happy about this."

"Ought to be, yes. But can you imagine how smug Lorrimar is going to be if we have to admit that all that stuff she said this morning is right on the money?"

"And we're not exactly going to look like conquering heroes back at the ranch if we go back to the office and report that we didn't think of a single thing to improve."

"Perhaps we're over-thinking this," said Pritchard. "You know the old thing: you guard against all the sophisticated stuff but in the end it's the guy who drives a truck through the crowd or gets off a lucky shot from the back of the rope line."

"So what's our equivalent here?" asked Daniels.

"Let's suppose one of our six guys goes rogue. Maybe willingly – they are all well-vetted, but there are seven hundred million reasons for any one of them to be tempted – or maybe someone takes their kids hostage. Let's ignore the weapons screening; it's good here, no doubt about that, but we both know it's never foolproof. A plastic gun taped to the inside of a thigh, rounds with non-conventional propellant, whatever. Let's say one of them gets a pistol past the metal-detectors, past the pat-downs and through the air-lock."

"It's a stretch," said Daniels, "but ok, let's say that."

"So, he pulls a pistol on Lorrimar, for example. Everyone does their bit or he blows her head off."

"I don't see Lorrimar entering her code even with a gun to her head, do you?"

"No," admitted Pritchard, "but we're playing Let's Suppose here."

"Fair enough," said Daniels. "So the bad guy and the five other people in the room do their stuff. Are we also supposing that both the control room personnel and the BEP Director and Deputy in DC play nice and keep Ms Lorrimar's head attached to her shoulders? Because I'm not sure they are that nice."

"Nor me," agreed Pritchard, "but we have five suppositions already, four more can't hurt."

"Ok, so, let's review. Rogue guy somehow gets a gun into the ante-room. Waves it at Ms Lorrimar, everyone quietly does as they are told. Now what? The vault door is still locked, and nobody – not anyone in the room, not anyone outside it – can over-ride the computer. And until the computer sees all six of them leave, the vault stays locked. Rogue guy is standing in the ante-room wondering 'now what?'."

"Right," said Pritchard, "so our bad guys need access to the computer too. A little reprogramming."

"How many things are we supposing now?" asked Daniels. "I lost count."

"Yeah, I know, but again ..."

"Yeah." Both men had known supposedly foolproof computer systems be defeated.

"Ok, so they pull the gun, get the locks unlocked. They hack the computer, and the door opens. Now our man is still outside the open doorway, presumably still with a hostage. So far, so good. His next problem is all the systems designed to ensure that no human being ever sets foot in the vault."

"Did you get that far in the ops manual?" asked Pritchard.

"Oh yes," said Daniels.

"Go on."

"Basically, anyone attempts to enter the vault, quick-acting knock-out gas is released. One breath, maybe two, and you're out."

"Triggered by?"

"You name it, they've got it. Let's start with pressure-sensitive flooring. The SARVs take very precise paths through the vault doorway. Any pressure that differs from the wheel paths and weights, bam."

"Ok, so our bad guy hops onto one of the empty SARVs as it enters the vault," suggested Pritchard.

"Uh-uh," said Daniels. "The empty ones are already inside, remember? The first one that comes out has $32 million on its back. Closely followed by its friends."

"Right. So our guy has to watch one batch of cash leave. Then he hops on an empty one on the return journey."

"Which now won't weigh the same as either an empty or a full one, so triggers the gas."

"Alright," said Pritchard, "but that must be a look-up on the computer system, and we've already assumed a compromise there."

"Are you going to play this card with every one of the security systems?" asked Daniels. "Because we might as well skip them if you are."

"Maybe," said Pritchard, "but that one has to involve the computer because it isn't just a simple mechanical thing – it has to compare weights with two different values to determine whether all is well – the rest might be simple self-contained triggers."

Daniels made a note in his notebook: Weight sensors computer or self-contained microprocessors?

"Ok," he said. "Next up is heat sensors. No communication with a computer needed there, just your bog-standard passive infra-red detectors. Anything of body-heat temperature, bam, goodnight."

"Foil suits," said Pritchard.

"Our man got those through the security perimeters, did he? One each for him and his hostage, as I assume he has to take the hostage into the vault with him." He held up a hand as he could see Pritchard was about to speak. "I know, I know: Let's Suppose."

Pritchard grinned.

"Ok, rogue and hostage don foil suits and hop on a returning SARV. Depending on the PIR sensitivity, those will work for what, 30 seconds? A minute? But ok, let's assume low-sensitivity PIR and top-notch foil suits. Let's say they get in, hop off the returning SARV, immediately hop onto a loaded one and back out into the ante-room. They now stay on the loaded SARV as it heads through the tunnels. That's their next problem," said Daniels.

"The tunnel detectors," nodded Pritchard.

"Right. Starting with the weighbridge. And while we'll check, my guess is you can't pull your computer hack stunt on this one: it's an entry-only weighing, so it simply has to detect the single weight of a loaded SARV."

"Let's run the list and see what we're up against."

Daniels had the annoying habit of rarely needing to refer back to anything he'd read. "Laser beams. Transceivers on the SARVs switch them off just as the front end arrives and on again as the back passes them. Now, bear in mind the tunnels are made-to-measure for the SARVs, there's no room for your bad guy – and his hostage, remember –" they both grinned at the vision of the bad guy having to defeat all these detectors with a hostage in tow at all times, "on top of the SARV or either side of it, so they are hanging off the rear of it. Laser beam gets switched back on, bam."

"What does 'bam' mean in the tunnels?" asked Pritchard. "In the vault doorway or ante-room, it's anaesthetic gas – same in the tunnels?"

"You got it," confirmed Daniels, "plus the shutters come down and stay down. Oh, and lots of men with guns come running."

"Ok, ok, what else?"

"Heat sensors, of course. Those foil suits are going to be well into overtime by now."

"True, but humour me," said Pritchard.

"We can discount the CCTV, given the hostage. Ok, so that's it. We'll grant the foil suits a 5-star eBay 'A++ would steal again' review and assume they're still doing their job. I'm even going to allow you a pass on the lasers for the moment – we can come back to those if needed. Your man and his hostage step off the back of the SARV which talks to a truck, opens the door and passes in the cash to the rollers. Is your guy going to hop into the truck with the cash, or stop the SARV doing the loading? I'm just curious, as there's an army convoy out there either way, and so far our guy has temporary possession of exactly one pallet. A sizeable haul, I'll grant you, but for this much effort he probably wants more."

Pritchard sighed. "I need coffee. Let's work this through one step at a time."

5.11pm

"I give up," said Pritchard. "You're right: it's impossible. It doesn't matter how implausible we get, how many ridiculous assumptions we make, how much luck we grant them, it can't be done. The vault cannot be breached."

"Agreed," said Daniels. "So tomorrow we rack our brains to come up with any tiny improvement we can think of to vault security–" Pritchard shot him a look– "I know, I know, but we'll think of something. Anything. Maybe. And then on Wednesday, we go play follow the money."

* * *

3pm Tuesday

'Damn it,' thought Detective Foster, as he thought back to the call for the fifth time in as many days. Rossie might be way out of his league on this one, but if something did happen and it got out that he'd been tipped-off about it and done nothing ... What was the first rule you taught the rookies when they were fresh out of police academy? CYA, baby: Cover Your Ass.

He logged onto the PC on his desk and looked up the Out Of State Police Department Directory. He tapped in Fort Worth to get the inter-force liaison contact name and number. Hmm, that's interesting, he thought: directly underneath it was a notation saying 'See also BEP Police, Fort Worth'. The note was a link, so he clicked on it. So, the BEP had its own police force; he hadn't been aware of that.

For a moment, he hesitated. These guys were solely responsible for the BEP, and weren't likely to welcome some guy from another city telling them how to do their job. Maybe he should just forget the whole thing. What did he have? A half-assed claim by some low-life snitch who'd be doing well if he learned of an ATM snatch, let alone anything as major league as this.

CYA, Foster, CYA. Better to be laughed at on the phone and let it be their problem if there turned out to be something in it. He read the number on the screen and punched the digits on his phone keypad.

"Lieutenant Mather, BEP."

"Lieutenant, this is Detective Rick Foster from NYPD."

"Afternoon, Detective, to what do I owe the pleasure?"

Foster took a deep breath. "I have an informant who claims there's a gang in NY planning a hit on your facility."

"Which gang?" asked Mather, grabbing a notepad and pen.

"Unknown," said Foster, cringing at how he knew this sounded. "The informant doesn't know them."

"He's supposed to know the local bad guys, yet these guys are completely unknown to him and they plan to hit the most secure vault in the world. Is your informant on drugs?"

"He's been known to deal, but he doesn't use, no. He's given some reliable tips in the past, but I'll be the first to admit that this one is way, way out of his league. Still, I thought I'd better pass on the report. Cover my ass, you know how it goes."

"Yeah, I do," said Mathers, softening. "Does he at least have good descriptions?"

More cringing. "He didn't see them, just overheard part of a conversation from a closed door."

"Do we have a date for this hit?"

"He doesn't know that either, but he thinks this week," said Foster, omitting mention of the fact that yesterday had been one of the days named.

"Does he know how they plan to do it?"

"He just heard something about the vault."

"So basically he knows nothing," said Mather.

"That's about the size of it."

"Ok, well, thanks, I guess."

"No problem."

Mather put down the phone. The idea was crazier than a box of frogs. He'd be laughed out of the room if he took this to Lorrimar. He put down the pen and headed out for a smoke.

* * *

Hicks Airfield. Wednesday 8am.

Jackson and Perez had driven out in one of the rented F-150 pickup trucks to a local flying school, where Sullivan had booked them a Cessna 172 for the day. With the convoy departure time unknown, and the convoys taking less than half an hour to make the short journey from the BEP to Carswell Air Force Base, they needed to be ready to take off the moment the call came through from Sullivan. They'd arranged to pick up the aircraft at 8am.

"Morning," said the cheerful Chief Flying Instructor who ran the school, "Jon Taylor, CFI."

"Charlie Shaw," said Jackson, shaking Taylor's hand, "and this is my buddy Richard Matthews." Pugh had run up the fake IDs, complete with pilots licence and logbook for Jackson showing the necessary qualifications and hours. The logbook was effectively a copy of Jackson's real one with enough details changed to make it untraceable.

"So, I understand you've got her booked for the full day, but you'll probably only be flying for an hour or two, is that right?"

"Yeah," said Jackson. "It's just a pleasure flight for my buddy here, but a couple more friends may be joining us if their boss will give them the time off, so we thought it best to book it for the day. If they get the time off, we'll wait for them, if not we'll set off as soon as we know."

"No problem," said Taylor. "It's just $300 for the day, plus $175/hour flying time from wheels up to wheels down. If you fly four hours or more, you pay only the hourly rate. We put a hold on the card for the $5000 deductible, refundable when the aircraft is returned undamaged."

"That's all fine," said Jackson.

"I just need to see your licence and your logbook."

Jackson slid them across the counter.

"Ah, ex-USAF. Always good to know the aircraft is in safe hands," he smiled.

Taylor turned to the last entry in the logbook. "Ok, no problem there, obviously. The aircraft has been upgraded to a glass cockpit, but I'm guessing you don't need a briefing on it, given your experience."

"No," said Jackson, "I think I'll manage."

"I do have to take you through the NOTAMs, though," said Taylor, "there are rather a lot of them. All to do with Carswell." NOTAMs was the aviation abbreviation for NOTices to Air Men, documents issued by the Federal Aviation Authority explaining any temporary restrictions on flight paths. These could be issued in response to anything from a local skydiving display to a visit by Air Force One.

"Oh?" said Jackson, though he had in fact already studied them online.

Taylor pointed to a flight chart mounted under the glass top of the counter. "We're here, and this is Carswell AFB." He pointed out the base. The normal Prohibited Area around Carswell is the standard 3-miles, 3000 feet." Jackson nodded; he was naturally familiar with the air exclusion zones around military bases.

"But we have an additional twelve exclusion corridors for some kind of special flights. The NOTAMs don't go into details, and the times are advised to ATC only half an hour in advance, but you can't really miss a set of a dozen big-ass Galaxies pulling out of there every other day."

"No, I'd imagine not. Any idea what that's all about?" Jackson, of course, knew exactly what they were.

Taylor shook his head: "The NOTAMs don't say anything about what they're up to, we just make sure we stay well clear. The time of day varies, but these same corridors are closed each time."

Jackson nodded.

Taylor pulled out a sheaf of A4 papers with details and simplified charts on them. "In a 172, the exclusion corridors only concern you for a short distance as they climb above 10,000 feet within a few miles." Ten thousand feet was the maximum altitude at which the non-pressurised 4-seater could fly. Taylor took Jackson through each of the corridors to make sure he was clear where he could and couldn't fly once the restrictions were announced by ATC.

"We've pre-flighted the aircraft up to engine start-up," continued Taylor, "but of course I won't be offended if you want to repeat the checks." Taylor was referring to the pre-flight checks that had to be carried out before every take-off. These ranged from simple visual checks – are both wings still attached? – through to checking that the fuel had no water in it by draining a small amount. There were eight sets of checks to be carried out before take-off, six of them before the engine was started.

"I'll do an abbreviated pre-flight," said Jackson. "I trust you, but old habits ..."

"Of course," said Taylor. "Anyway, the aircraft is yours: here are the keys."

"Thanks," replied Jackson, accepting them. "You know," he added, "I nearly got transferred to Galaxies, back in the day. I wouldn't mind seeing them in the air again – from a distance, of course," he added quickly. "Any chance you could let us know when you get the 30-minutes notice?"

"Sure," said Taylor.

Jackson turned to Perez. "Mind if we delay our little jaunt until they're due for take-off, so we can get a bit of a view of them?"

Perez picked up the cue perfectly. "Not at all, sounds like an interesting sight."

Jackson turned back to Taylor. "Is there somewhere we can get breakfast around here?"

"Sure, there's a canteen out back," said Taylor, indicating with his thumb.

"Thanks."

The two men walked across the apron towards the canteen.

"The PA around the base isn't going to make your life easy," said Jackson. "All I've got to do is fly the plane and stay out of the exclusion zones, you've got the hard job."

Perez shrugged. "The Bigma is the right tool for the job." It was the affectionate name for the huge Sigma 50-500mm lens he had attached to his camera. "I'll shoot plenty of frames, maybe one in 20 will be sharp given the distance and the aircraft vibration, but we only need a handful to see what's going on."

Jackson nodded. He took out his phone and hit the speed-dial for Sullivan.

"Morning Jessica," he said.

"Everything ok with the aircraft?" she asked.

"No problem," said Jackson, "keys in my hand. Raul and I are just off for breakfast."

"Enjoy," said Sullivan.

"Right," said Jackson, turning to Perez, "let's get ourselves a fry-up!"

* * *

Lorrimar's office, BEP. 9am Weds.

"You've finished reading the security operations manual?" asked Lorrimar.

Both men nodded.

"It's a lot to take in, I know, so I thought a brief summary might be helpful."

"Thank you," said Pritchard, "that would be helpful." In fact both men had read it thoroughly, but it was often helpful to have a verbal summary:

people sometimes covered things that weren't mentioned in the manual.

"First line of defence," said Lorrimar, "is the two dummy convoys. Each is identical to the real one in every respect. The computer randomly determines the order in which the trucks emerge, real versus dummy, and the control centre informs the drivers and the Captain in charge of each convoy. Nobody else knows which is the real convoy and which are the dummy ones."

"Not even the rest of the Marines guarding them?" asked Daniels?

"Correct."

"So the bad guys could get themselves killed attacking the wrong convoy."

Lorrimar nodded. "If they launch an attack, the intent is there regardless of whether they got it right, and the US Government has no qualms about them meeting the fate you can reasonably expect if you choose to take on two platoons of Marines."

Daniels smiled. "Two platoons of Marines and rather a lot of firepower."

"Enough to start a small war," said Lorrimar. "You've seen the convoy configuration diagram: an M2 Bradley heading the convoy and a second one at the rear; an M1114 Armoured Humvee alongside each truck; and IAV Strykers positioned after every third truck. So the first thing any would-be attackers are going to see is the business end of a Bradley.

"I imagine seeing a tank rolling toward you would have a fair bit of deterrent value," commented Pritchard.

"The Army refers to it as a 'tracked infantry fighting vehicle' – the Pentagon never uses one single-syllable word when four longer ones will do. But yeah, a 50,000-pound 600-horsepower vehicle that you or I would call a tank. Crew of three, and carries six fully-equipped Marines. Primary armament is a 25mm cannon capable of firing 180 rounds a minute. The cannon is capable of downing a helicopter or light aircraft at a range of 10,000 feet. Secondary armament is an M240C machine-gun capable of firing 800 rounds per minute, but its primary role here is air defence."

"I must say that impressed me when I read it in the manual," said Daniels. "The idea of the bad guys attacking via helicopter struck me as one of those really tiny probability things that might have been overlooked. I've seen Bradleys in action, and at close range a helicopter stands no chance at all."

"We try to cover all the bases," said Lorrimar. "Next up in order of capabilities are three Stryker armoured vehicles. Eight-wheeled and a lot more manoeuvrable than their size would suggest. Two crew and eleven deployable Marines. Equipped with the Protector M151 Remote Weapon Station – a fancy name for an unmanned machine-gun controlled from within the vehicle – fitted with a .50-cal M2 machine-gun. 635 rounds per minute, and will cut through most vehicles. This is the primary means of defence against a serious armed assault as the gun operator remains within the armoured vehicle at all times, meaning it can continue to lay down serious amounts of fire against any civilian opposition."

"The M2 can also cut through light armour," observed Daniels.

"Right, with the Bradleys available should the convoy come up against any heavily-armoured opposition. Finally, there are the twelve Hummers. M1114 Armoured Humvees, one per truck. They drive alongside their assigned truck, and are the immediate response vehicles to anyone attempting to stop or board the trucks. Each Hummer has a driver, radio operator and gunner. Hardened steel passenger compartment, bullet-resistant glass, kevlar-wrapped gun turret. Armament is the M134 Minigun, but don't be fooled by the name: it's a six-barrelled 7.62mm machine-gun capable of 2000 rounds per minute. It makes for a pretty formidable vehicle in its own right, but here it's just the baby of the team."

"And finally the helicopters," said Pritchard.

Lorrimar nodded. "Air cover is provided by two AH-64 Apache attack helicopters per convoy, with a combined firepower of 96 Hellfire air-to-air missiles, 456 Hydra air-to-ground rockets and a Hughes chain gun: a 30mm cannon with a total capacity of 7,200 rounds. One flies directly overhead the convoy at low altitude, at the rear so it has a view of the whole thing, the other provides wide-area cover from a higher altitude so it can look out for trouble further ahead but still be back with the convoy within 30 seconds tops."

"And then there are the randomised routes," said Daniels. "Both real and dummy convoys travel along one of 24 different routes, each of which is randomly assigned 30 minutes prior to departure, at which point Fort Worth PD is informed so that they can put the necessary road closures in place.

"I can see you've done your homework, Mr Daniels."

Daniels shrugged. "That's why we're here."

"Did you memorise the 24 different convoy routes too?" she asked.

"I could probably take a reasonable stab at them," said Daniels.

"He's being modest," said Pritchard: "he could draw you a detailed map of each."

"The Police are well-practiced with the road-closures, as you might imagine, using a rolling road-block system to close each road just a few minutes before the convoy reaches it."

"And all three convoys proceed all the way into Carswell," commented Pritchard, "and only once inside the base do the dummy convoys peel off to park while the real convoy proceeds to the aircraft."

"That's right," confirmed Lorrimar. "From here to Carswell Air Force Base is between 10 and 13 miles away, depending on the route, taking a little under half an hour. Once the convoy is safely inside the base, the pallets are loaded onto twelve C-5 Galaxy aircraft, each of which has a squad of 13 US Marines on board as escorts. Once the aircraft are loaded, F-16 fighter jets take over escort duties: two per Galaxy. Each Galaxy with its pair of F-16s flies to their respective regional USAF bases. The security arrangements at the far end are scaled back a little given they have only one truck to protect at each location, but you still wouldn't want to mess with them."

"How will we travel with the convoy?" asked Pritchard.

"You're in a very privileged position," said Lorrimar. "You will both travel in the cab of the lead truck of the real convoy, so will be two of the very few people to know which is the real one. Today's load is $50 bills, so each truck will have two pallets totalling $64 million. Total convoy load, $768M."

Lorrimar walked around her desk to open the desk drawer to pull out and hand over a pager.

"Again, don't go anywhere. When the signal comes, you'll need to go directly to the loading bay: nobody is allowed to enter once the vault is open, so by that time you have to be safely locked in the truck cab. Deborah will collect you and take you there."

"How do we collect our service weapons?" asked Daniels.

"You don't," said Lorrimar. "No weapons in the cabs, and no phones either – you'll need to leave those with Deborah."

The two men looked at each other. No weapons inside the BEP building was one thing, but being unarmed outside it? That was not something either felt comfortable with.

"Ms Lorrimar, Secret Service agents aren't in the habit of wandering around naked. The nature of our work is unpredictable, we need to be ready for all eventualities."

"As do we, Mr Daniels. We can't have two armed men inside the cab of a truck containing, today, $64 million, whoever they are. You needn't worry, there is a whole platoon of Marines surrounding you, and believe me, they are not short of fire-power. Any shooting that needs to be done, you can rely on them to take care of it."

Daniels was about to argue when Pritchard held up a hand. "It's ok, Kate, we understand."

Daniels shrugged; Pritchard always was better at recognising arguments they weren't going to win.

Sullivan was nervous. From her earlier solo observations, she knew that the army vehicles only pulled up outside the BEP 10-15 minutes before the convoys departed, which as far as she could determine could be any time during office hours. Her earlier surveillance had been from further away; today they would be much closer. The risk of an alert security guard or cop noticing them was higher than she would have liked, but there wasn't any way around that.

The BEP complex was not an easy target for surveillance. It was a white-coloured, low-level building set in its own grounds and surrounded by two layers of chain-link fencing. It looked like some kind of cross between an army camp and a retirement complex. There were no high-level buildings close to it, and the loading bay was at the rear of the building, meaning no view from the only road to run directly past the facility. When Sullivan talked about on-the-ground observations, she meant it literally.

There were only two possible observation points with any kind of view of the loading bay area: a residential road to the rear which ended in a turning-point about 300 metres from the loading area, and three roads which looked like they were earmarked for residential development but were currently open plots. These were a little further away, maybe 400 metres.

The plan was for Sullivan to be a jogger on the roads, while Young would be in coveralls and a rented white van temporarily decked out with cable

TV logos – magnetic vinyl signs created by Pugh – apparently working on a junction box at the end of the residential road. Given that a lone female jogger was unlikely to be seen as a threat, and a cable guy shouldn't stand out as unusual, they were hopeful that they could make their observations without drawing attention to themselves. Pugh had created false IDs for both of them that would pass muster in a casual check so that if they were questioned there would be no record against their names later.

Chung, Lewis and Pugh had parked up their Harleys at a diner a few miles south-east of the BEP facility. When the time came, Chung would remain where he was while Pugh and Lewis would head out east and west respectively so that they should be ready to intercept any likely route the convoy might take.

"This is fun," said Lewis, "I feel like we're a proper biker gang."

Chung smiled. "It's ok for you two, you kind of look the part. I look like a yuppie guy who's lost his Beemer."

"Plenty of yuppies on Harleys," observed Lewis.

Chung was the least comfortable with this type of fieldwork: he was happiest sat in front of a computer. Well, he thought, they could all relax for now.

BZZZT!

"They're singing our song," said Daniels as Pritchard reached for the pager to silence it.

Both men stood and made their way to Lorrimar's desk.

"Your cellphones, please." The PA held out her hand. Daniels passed his to Pritchard, and Pritchard handed them both to the PA. She put them in the top drawer of her desk and locked it, removing the key. "Follow me, please."

They entered the standard elevator, not the one Pritchard had used with Lorrimar on Monday. The PA swiped her pass through a card slot and then pressed the LG button. The elevator descended.

At the bottom, they emerged into a large room with white-washed brick walls, lockers along one wall and a kitchenette area on the opposite wall. In the centre was a table and chairs, sofas, easy chairs and on one of the end walls a large LCD TV.

"This is the rest area for the drivers," explained the PA. The sole occupant of the room got up from one of the easy chairs and held out his hand. He was a tall, muscular-looking man. He looked a lot fitter than the average truck driver.

"Karl Dawson," he said.

Pritchard and Daniels shook hands with him in turn, introducing themselves.

"Karl is the driver of truck 1," said the PA, "so you'll be keeping him company for the ride out to Carswell. I'll leave you in his capable hands."

With that, she disappeared back into the lift.

"We need to go straight to the truck," said Dawson, "but we'll have time to talk once we're all aboard."

On the wall opposite the TV was a metal door with a cardslot and keypad. Dawson inserted his card and tapped in a code. The door unlocked, he stepped through and held it open for them.

"No BEP Police guarding the door?" asked Pritchard.

"You need a pass to take the elevator down here and another pass for the door, and of course we're being monitored all the way," replied Dawson as they walked down a short corridor at a second door. "Any issue and the vault opening would be aborted." He again inserted his card and entered a code to open the door.

They were now standing in the large loading-bay area. In terms of layout, it didn't look very different to a factory or warehouse loading bay, thought Daniels. But there the similarity ended. First, it looked completely sterile: not a single pallet, box or even a piece of litter in sight. Second, it was completely devoid of people: all the other drivers were in their trucks. They were on the upper level of the loading dock, with the 12 trucks backed up against the dock ahead of them, and the 24 other trucks on the far side of the bay.

Dawson led the way down a set of steps to ground level. Looking across at the trucks opposite, Pritchard noted that the there were no passenger doors on the trucks, and Dawson led them to the drivers' side of the nearest truck. "You'll have to get in first," he said, "but first we need to get the truck lock released."

Dawson pulled a radio out of his pocket.

"Truck 1, control."

A brief pause then: "Control, Truck 1, go ahead."

"Request door open. Secret Service team present."

"We have a visual. Door unlocked."

Dawson gestured to the steps leading up to the door. "You'll need to get in first. The door handle will open the door now."

Pritchard climbed up first and tugged on the door handle. Nothing happened.

"It's heavy," called up Dawson, "you have to pull hard."

Pritchard yanked on the door. Wow, he thought, as he heaved the door open: Dawson wasn't kidding about it being heavy. The reason became clear as it opened: it was about a foot thick!

He clambered in and scooted over to the the passenger side. Daniels joined him, followed by Dawson who yanked the door shut. "It re-locks automatically," he commented.

The inside of the cabin looked more like a TV studio than a truck. There were TV monitors set into the dash showing the exterior of the truck from all angles, as well as two views of the interior. There was also a large bank of illuminated push-button switches, some with obvious icons or lettering, others with mysterious-looking ones. A few of them had clear flaps covering them.

"We have about 20 minutes before loading begins. You won't really be able to see much directly during loading, it all happens behind us, but you can watch it on TV." He gestured to the screens.

"I was about to ask about those," said Pritchard. "Both the screens and the buttons."

"Thought you might take an interest," grinned Dawson. "Let me talk you through it. The screens are obvious. We have micro-cameras set into the truck." Dawson gestured to each set of screens as he listed them: "We have forward views ... rear views ... this is looking down the rear of the truck ... this is the blind-spot directly in front of us ... the roof, forward and back ... the area between cab and trailer, from each side ... and the underside of the truck. The surface of the truck has a capacitive outer layer: anyone tried to climb onto the truck, an alarm sounds and the surround of the relevant screens flashes."

"And this is a GPS, I presume," said Pritchard, pointing to a large screen displaying a map of the BEP facility.

"Differential GPS, accurate to about 1 metre, with intra-convoy datacoms," replied Dawson.

Pritchard nodded: they were familiar with those from Presidential convoys. Differential GPS used military transmitters on the ground as well as satellite signals to give a more precise fix, while datacomms capabilities meant the convoy vehicles all communicated their positions to all the other GPS units in the trucks, so it displayed the positions of the other convoy vehicles.

"And the buttons?" asked Daniels.

"Mostly we rely on the Marines for protection, but the trucks are not totally defenceless." Again, he indicated the various buttons as he took the two men through the functions. "There are simple high-pressure water-jets. They should be automatically activated in the event that the capacitive sensors are triggered, but they can also be manually controlled from here. It's a non-lethal first-line of defence designed to simply knock an attacker off the truck."

Pritchard nodded.

"Then we have the rather more robust levels. There are flamethrower sheets set into the sides of the truck around both the rear doors and the drivers' door. Should an attacker prove persistent, I can activate them using these buttons – the ones protected by the clear flaps."

"Anything else?" asked Daniels.

Dawson nodded. "Three other things. These buttons here release CS gas from jets on the underside of the truck, around the entire perimeter. That's more for dealing with any civilians who fail to move away from the truck when requested, like a civil unrest situation. It just clears us some space."

"And the other two?" asked Daniels.

"Two last resorts. These buttons here, press and hold all three together and it activates automatic assault rifle mechanisms set into the top of the truck above both rear and driver doors, pointing straight down. Hollow-point rounds. They shouldn't be a danger to anyone who isn't standing right against the truck."

The expression on Daniels' face suggested he approved of those.

"How do you top that for the final layer?" asked Pritchard.

Dawson smiled. "The final resort is purely defensive, but very effective. Embedded in both rear and driver doors are thin channels containing a mix of aluminium, copper and magnesium powders. Operate these buttons here and small explosive strips release the powders and ignite them."

"You'll have to forgive my ignorance," said Daniels, "it's been a while since I did any chemistry."

"It creates a strong exothermic reaction," explained Dawson, "instantly welding the doors shut. It is an extremely strong weld. You don't ever want to trigger it by accident: if you do, you're going to be trapped in the cab for a very, very long time while specialist teams cut through the doors. I'm told it takes around 12 hours."

"Impressive," said Pritchard.

"So how do you end up in a job like this?" asked Daniels.

"Ex-Army," said Dawson. "All the drivers are ex-military. We have the clearances, and we're not going to panic in a firefight."

"Ever had any trouble?" asked Daniels.

Dawson shook his head. "You'd have to be pretty brave or pretty dumb to take on a platoon of Marines. The most drama we've ever experienced was a car that somehow made it through the police rolling block and headed towards the convoy. It turned out to be a perfectly innocent mistake by a very confused tourist, but neither Police nor Marines take kindly to visitors: two police cruisers rammed him and the next thing the driver knew he was staring down the wrong end of half a dozen assault rifles being wielded by six serious-looking men in khaki."

"I imagine he didn't give the place a very favourable write-up on TripAdvisor," said Pritchard.

"I'd imagine that too," smiled Dawson.

* * *

Carswell Air Force Base, also 9am

"Company ... company, ten-hut!"

The company of Marines standing in the parade ground came to a smart attention. One hundred and fifty-six right boots all hitting the ground in perfect unison. The company commander, Major Jack Timpkins, expected nothing less as he looked out at the twelve platoons assembled in front of him. Each platoon comprised twelve soldiers and a sergeant.

One platoon would be responsible for each aircraft. They were responsible for their security of the aircraft from the moment the call came through from the BEP to place them on standby – 30 minutes before the vault opening – throughout the flight and right the way through to the moment the convoy departed the airbase at the destination city.

Timpkins nodded. "Company ... stand at ... ease!"

"Stand easy, gentlemen," said Timpkins.

The men relaxed.

"Please ensure that you all have your Rules of Engagement cards and are familiar with their contents. They remain as usual. If anyone approaches without authority, you challenge and order them to halt. if they fail to do so, you are authorised to use reasonable force to halt and detain them. If they are armed, they get one warning to drop their weapons. If they fail to do so, you can use reasonable force, up to and including lethal force, to disarm them. If fired on, you return fire immediately, and in that eventuality you shoot to kill. Questions?"

The Marines were familiar with the wording, but it was a legal requirement that the ROE be issued both verbally and in written form any time lethal force was authorised. There were no questions.

"This morning, flight BEP 1 to La Guardia will be joined by two members of the US Secret Service who are reviewing shipment security. They have clearance to board and fly aboard BEP 1. They will be unarmed. I will be accompanying them, mostly to ensure that they don't get in your way, and to answer any questions they have. However, should they have questions for any one of you, you each have full authority to provide detailed answers; for the purposes of today's flight, they are to be considered part of the team."

There were some surprised looks at this: Secret Service or not, this was Marines business, and secrecy was second nature.

"Any questions regarding BEP 1?"

"Sir!" said one of the Marines.

"Yes, Williams," said Timpkins, who prided himself on knowing all of his Company by name.

"Major, what happens if one of them gets into our line of sight?"

"You instruct them to move, politely or not as the urgency demands. They are here as observers only, and their ability to see something is less important than your ability to do your job. Clear, Marine?"

"Yes, Major. Thank you, Major."

"Any other questions?"

There were none.

"Very well. You may now stand-down until the standby call is received. At that time, you will commence your final search of your aircraft and secure the area ready for the arrival of the convoy. You may dismiss the company, Sergeant."

"Company ... Dis-miss!" 156 men turned as one, and 156 right boots hit the ground in unison. The men dispersed, able to relax until the call came through. If there was one thing the military taught you, it was not to miss any opportunity to sleep or relax.

* * *

It was an experience common to military personnel the world over: hurry up and wait. For almost two hours now, most of the Marines had been able to relax while just a handful were left as perimeter guards for the Galaxies. When the PA announcement was made, it was once more back into hurry mode.

"Marines, standby call. Final aircraft checks."

"You heard it," yelled the sergeant, "let's go, let's go! Now, Nibbs, not next Thursday!"

Team 1 picked up their backpacks and weapons and double-timed to their aircraft: from the moment their final search was complete to the moment they boarded the aircraft for the flight to La Guardia, none of them would leave the vicinity of the aircraft, so they had to take everything with them.

The 13 men comprised three 'fire teams' – each of four men – and a sergeant. Each had their assigned search roles, and needed no instruction. Fire team A was responsible for the exterior of the aircraft, including the landing gear bays. Team B was responsible for the cargo bay, team C the flight-deck and common areas like the restrooms.

The men moved quickly but methodically, each starting their sweep from the front of their area and working backwards. Two members of team C were on the flight-deck. Everything that moved or was large enough to hide a small pistol was checked, from the rear of the rudder pedals to the seat-pockets containing the checklists. Team B was working through the cargo bay, looking behind every cargo strap, checking the seal on every fire-extinguisher, looking behind the insulation panels. Team A had a scissor platform under the front landing gear and was using powerful torches to look inside it. There had been cases of stowaways hiding in landing-gear bays of civilian aircraft, and while there was no route into the aircraft from there, and most of them froze to death or died from oxygen starvation during the flight, nothing was left to chance. By the time the search was complete, they would be confident that no-one and nothing had been snuck onto the aircraft.

* * *

Daniels looked at his watch: "How long now before loading?" Dawson pointed to a countdown timer on the dash. It read 00:03.

"On Monday, loading took 20 minutes – same every day?" asked Pritchard.

"Between 18 minutes 35 seconds and 19 minutes 10 seconds," said Dawson.

"Precise times, yet a variation from day to day?" queried Daniels.

"They're robots carrying out pre-programmed routines. Nothing varies once they leave the vaults, but depending on which shelves they load the pallets from, there are slight variances in the timing. For example, lifting a pallet from an upper shelf requires more time than pulling one out from a ground-level shelf."

Daniels nodded. "Ok, that makes sense. Which is how the convoy outside is able to time its arrival so precisely." He knew from the ops manual that the convoy only arrived at the facility a few minutes before departure, so as to give minimum notice to any unwelcome observers.

Chung, Lewis and Pugh walked back out to their motorcycles.

"No heroics, boys," said Lewis. "We get as close as we can without alarming anyone. The last thing we want to do is draw attention to ourselves."

"Don't worry," said Chung, "I'm a coward."

"And I'm too old for heroics," added Pugh.

"Glad to hear it," said Lewis. "Remember, the team radio will come through your earpiece, but keep the handlebar-mounted police scanner on the bars turned up high enough to hear it while parked but not so high that any nearby cops can hear it too. It's unlikely we'll learn much from it – I'm expecting the convoy to use its own military encrypted bands – but any info is better than none."

The two others nodded.

"Ok," said Lewis, "time for me and Pugh to fan out, you sit tight, Chung, and hit the radio the moment you sight the convoy."

Pritchard and Daniels both had their eyes fixed on the screens. Watching the SARVs at work on the screens in the observation room had been fascinating, but it had felt like they were spectators watching a performance. Sat here in the cab of the truck, watching the SARV approach and open the rear door of the truck, then turning their attention to the inside cameras to see the motorised rollers pull the pallets inside and automatically apply locking bars had quite a different feel. Before, they were observers; today, they felt like participants.

To think that just behind them, separated only by the admittedly thick cab and trailer walls was $64 million was a thrilling thought even to men accustomed to wandering the corridors of the West Wing.

Sullivan, now dressed in jogging sweats, trainers and an iPod, squeezed forward between the seats of the van and into the passenger seat.

"Very fashionable," said Young, glancing across from the driver's seat.

"Yeah, yeah, and you look like a catalogue model, I suppose," she replied, looking pointedly at his cable technician's uniform and baseball cap.

"The ultimate urban camouflage," said Young, putting the van into Drive ready for the short five-minute drive to the residential road behind the BEP. "No-one will notice either of us."

The last of the SARVs withdrew into its tunnel, and the metal shutter dropped down.

"Control, Truck 12 loaded and ready," came the voice over the cab radio.

"Truck 12, control: confirmed. Standby."

There was a short delay. "Control, Trucks 1 to 12, you are first out. I say again, trucks 1 to 12 are first out. Five minutes. Standby."

"We're out first," explained Dawson. "The sequence is random, and all the trucks are identical, so there's no way for the bad guys to know which is carrying the cash and which the newspapers." The two men knew from their reading that the dummy trucks were loaded up with old newspapers, so that they weighed exactly the same as the real trucks.

There would be no clue for even the most observant to tell them apart.

Young was crouched down by the junction box watching the loading bay when he heard the unmistakeable sound of helicopters approaching. He discreetly pressed the transmit button on the radio in his jacket, speaking into the headset.

"All personnel, standby."

Receiving the transmission through what looked like iPod earphones, Sullivan glanced across and came to a halt. She bent over, acting like she was out of breath. She was further round the complex than Young, and could see the side of the buildings as well as the rear. Nothing ye– Wait! There they were: the army vehicles! What looked like the iPod controller was a microphone switch; she used it now.

"All personnel, stage 1 confirmed. Stage 1 confirmed."

The first helicopter came into view, swooping low over the building and pulling up to stop faster than she would have imagined possible, to hover a couple of hundred feet above the loading bay area. From a distance, it had simply looked rather oddly-shaped, like some kind of gigantic insect. From this distance, it looked terrifying! She could see whole clusters of missiles slung from pods mounted on struts sticking out to either side of the helicopter. The cockpit body looked really narrow. There was something round above the blades, and all kinds of protrusions that she couldn't identify and which just added to the menacing appearance.

A second helicopter approached from her left – from the front of the BEP facility. It too was only a couple of hundred feet up. It hovered off to her left. Scanning around, she spotted four further helicopters, maybe two miles away.

While Sullivan had seen the convoy before, albeit from a distance, Young was seeing it for the first time. In the lead was a dirty great tank! Make that two tanks, he thought, as he caught sight of the one at the rear. Both looked like something that belonged in Iraq or Afghanistan, not on the streets of Texas. The incredibly noisy helicopter perched overhead facing away from him nose-on to the metal shutters of the loading bay added to the surrealism of the scene.

He was surprised at the speed of the tanks: he'd always thought of tanks as lumbering great things, but these were zipping along nicely at what looked like a good 40mph. In the middle were a whole bunch of Hummers – he counted twelve – and three odd-looking vehicles that looked something like a kind of mini-tank with huge wheels instead of tracks.

He thought about turning back to the junction box so as not to make it obvious that he was studying the convoy, but he knew that half the time when people tried not to look conspicuous, they did so in such an obvious way they stood out. Any innocent member of the public seeing a sight like this would stop to gawk.

Christ, even the Hummers looked like harbingers of death, and they were the smallest of the vehicles. The armour was obvious, as was the bulletproof glass. And a gunner on top with what looked like an extremely lethal machine-gun.

We might as well abandon the convoy surveillance right here and now, he thought: there was no way in the world a small group of them could take on that lot. Their only hope would be that the soldiers were laughing so hard at the attempt that they'd forget to operate their weapons.

The convoy came to a halt on the far side of the wide apron in front of the four loading bay shutters. For a couple of minutes, nothing happened, then Young saw the shutter doors opening simultaneously. He hit the transmit button on his radio.

"All personnel, stage 2, stage 2."

The exit procedure was clearly carefully choreographed and well-practiced, he thought: the lead tank pulled forward and the first truck emerged to stop directly behind it. At the same time, one of the Hummers pulled in behind it. A second truck was already on its way, and a second Hummer pulled in behind that. The same with the third truck and Hummer, then one of the weird-looking eight-wheeled tank type things lined-up behind. It was smooth and precise: these guys were no amateurs.

He looked casually around before taking the calculated risk he'd decided would be acceptable only for a few seconds. Pulling the baseball cap further down his face, he quickly slipped a small pair of binoculars from his pocket and raised them to his eyes. He swiftly tracked to one of the open shutter doors.

Out of his field of view, the closest Apache helicopter began rotating slowly to the right.

Young could see nothing at all inside: the contrast between the brightly-sunlit exterior and the artificially-lit interior meant that the doorways just looked black. He hurriedly put the binoculars away and looked back to the bay.

Fuck! He'd been seen using the binoculars! The Apache had turned 180 degrees and was now facing directly towards him! The 16 missiles slung beneath the attack chopper were pointing straight at him.

He froze, unsure of what to do. As he stood there, the Apache rotated slowly right. What was it doing now, he wondered? It continued rotating right until it was again facing the loading bay doors. Young almost collapsed to the ground with relief: it hadn't seen him at all, it was simply doing a 360-degree survey of the surroundings.

Trying to persuade his heart-rate to return to normal, Young watched a replay of the routine with the next three trucks, Hummers and eight-wheeler. The routine was repeated again with the three after that. The only difference with the final three was that the second proper tank took up the rear in place of an eight-wheeler.

Young heard distant sirens from the direction of the road, but could see nothing from where he was. The convoy moved off almost immediately, and he again hit transmit on his radio.

"All personnel, stage 3, stage 3."

As they had no way to know which of the convoys was the real one or ones, they'd opted to track the first one to leave.

As soon as she'd made her radio report, Sullivan had resumed her jog in the direction of the main road so that she could report which direction the convoy turned. As she approached the main road, she could see a police motorcycle parked across the junction, blue and red lights flashing. As she got closer, the motorcycle cop held up a hand in an unmistakeable 'Wait' signal.

Perfect. She wanted an excuse to stop and watch the convoy drive past, and now she didn't need one. She could see there was another motorcycle cop blocking the far side of the junction. She was to the left of the BEP facility, so that seemed a pretty sure sign the convoy was turning left but she'd wait until she was sure.

She didn't have to wait long. About a minute later, four more police motorcycles came past, sirens wailing and lights ablaze. They were closely followed by the tank. Although she'd seen the convoys before, that had been from high up and a fair distance away. Up close like this, the tank looked far scarier. For a moment, she was too fascinated by the sight to remember the radio call. She thumbed the transmit button.

"All personnel, status Lima, status Lima."

Lewis got back on her motorcycle: a left turn out of the facility meant that it was heading towards Pugh. Her job now was to ride on an intercept course to get ahead of Pugh in the same direction. She headed towards 287 and Bailey. Chung would head toward Meacham.

Sullivan watched as three trucks came past, each with a Hummer to the offside. They were immediately followed by what looked like an eight-wheeled armoured personnel carrier. Three more trucks with Hummer escorts, another eight-wheeler, three more trucks and Hummers, another eight-wheeler, the last three trucks and Hummers, another tank and two police cars with lights but no sirens.

As the first convoy departed, she spotted the second approaching, about a quarter of a mile away. The three successive convoys would depart a few minutes apart.

The motorcycle cop waved thanks to her, and pulled out. As she watched the convoy disappear, the two motorcycles overtook the convoy ready for the leapfrog pattern she'd seen from afar on her previous trip.

Their part of the observation was done, and she wasn't sure what, if anything, they'd accomplished. Perhaps Young had seen something useful?

Young had packed up his kit and returned to the van shortly after the convoy departed. He slowly drove towards the main road, where he would pick up Sullivan. He knew that sometimes a surveillance operation could appear useless at the time, but you'd later realise you'd seen something of significance. He wasn't all all confident that would prove to be the case this time. The convoy had looked even more intimidating than he had expected.

The only small glimmer of hope he'd seen was the shutter doors to the loading bay. He'd imagined something far more like bank vault doors, but these ones had seemed pretty standard to him. Could that be a weakness, he wondered? It was frustrating that he'd seen nothing at all of the interior of the loading bay.

He drove slowly back toward the main road, and pulled in as he saw Sullivan jogging slowly towards him.

"Strobe lights," read Perez from the laminated checklist in front of him in the Cessna cockpit as they taxied out toward the runway.

Jackson checked the switch, though he had switched it on just a few minutes ago. "Check."

"Radios slash avionics."

Jackson had again switched them on earlier. "Set."

"Auto-pilot."

Jackson glanced at it. "Off."

"Flaps set for take-off."

On this aircraft, flaps were only used for short-field take-offs; here, there was no need for it. Jackson checked it was in the zero position.

"Set."

"Parking brake."

An experienced pilot, Jackson was completing the checklist during taxying, so the brake was already off, but he gave the expected response. "Released."

"Windows."

"Closed," replied Jackson, checking both sides. The runway threshold line was 300 feet ahead – perfect timing.

"Pre-takeoff checklist complete," said Perez. He wasn't a pilot himself, and didn't know what all the checklist items meant, but reading out a checklist and checking that the responses were the ones printed on the card was simple enough.

Jackson pushed the transmit button on his radio: "Hicks Tower, November Niner Seven Eight Charlie Papa."

"Niner Seven Eight Charlie Papa, Hicks Tower," came the response from the air traffic controller.

"Hicks Tower, Charlie Papa, VFR, two on board, requesting permission for take-off," said Jackson.

"Charlie Papa, winds 290 at 12, altimeter 29.91, runway 32, cleared for takeoff."

"Charlie Papa rolling."

Jackson taxied onto the runway and lined-up with the centre-line. He placed both feet on the brakes, pushed the throttle forward to the take-off position, waited for the engine to reach take-off revs and released the brakes. The aircraft lurched forward and picked up speed. As the airspeed indicator reached 60 knots, Jackson pulled gently back on the yoke. The nose wheel lifted and a moment later the Cessna was back in her natural environment: the air.

Jackson pushed the yoke forward slightly, adjusting to the best climb speed of 72 knots.

"Ok," he said, "let's see what we can see!"

* * *

"Left onto Old Decatur," came the voice from the cab radio in the truck.

Pritchard looked through the windscreen at the junction ahead, and saw the police motorcycle escort which was blocking traffic for them. He saw the Bradley ahead of them turn left, and looked at the monitor screen showing the offside view of the cab to check the Hummer was still alongside them. It was. He shifted his view to the GPS screen, and saw colour-coded dots representing the positions of the other trucks, their Hummers, the Strykers and the two Bradleys. All of the vehicles were where they were supposed to be.

Pritchard was taken back to the days of Presidential convoys. Now, as then, there was the knowledge that there were people out there who would not even blink at the thought of killing you if it allowed them to reach their target. And the odd mix of security and vulnerability. This truck, like the President's Limo, was one of the most secure vehicles in the world. A huge amount of thought and care had gone into protecting it against almost all eventualities. It had as impressive an escort as you could ask for. Yet at the same time, there was no such thing as total safety, and there were any number of people out there actively trying to figure out a way to defeat all the precautions that had been taken.

As the truck turned into Old Decatur Street, Pritchard looked ahead as far as he could see. The next pair of police motorcycles had already blocked the next junction. He could see no sign of any vehicles that looked out of place. That was a skill that really got honed on Presidential Detail, he thought. Half the time, you couldn't even put your finger on what it was that had set your senses tingling, you just knew that something didn't look right about a person or a vehicle.

He smiled at himself. He wasn't even part of this protective detail, he thought: just an observer. In theory, he had no responsibility for any of this, he was only here to see whether he could spot any weaknesses. If there were bad guys up ahead, it wasn't his job to deal with them, and he couldn't exactly do much without his SIG SAUER P229. It still felt very odd to be out and about with an empty holster.

But whatever the official position, Pritchard knew that he and Daniels wouldn't be spectators. If there was anything they could do to help protect the truck, they would. With their bare hands if it came to it. Sitting back and doing nothing at a time of crisis just wasn't in their nature.

Pugh was parked up in a lay-by roughly midway between two junctions. Given the direction in which the convoy was moving, he expected to see it arrive at one or the other. He had a good view of the junction ahead of him, and a reasonable view of the junction behind him in his mirror. He had his radio in his hand, his thumb over the transmit button. His engine was off, as he expected the first sign of the convoy to be the sound of the approaching choppers.

He was correct, but it didn't help much as he found it hard to tell the direction from which the sound was coming. He slipped his helmet back on and started the engine.

There! A police motorcycle appeared from the left at the junction directly ahead of him. He quickly thumbed the transmit button of the radio:

"Mobile Echo, Mobile Echo," indicating that the convoy was on the East side of the potential routes. Slipping the radio back into his pocket, he snicked the Harley into gear, did a shoulder-check and eased out onto the road. As he approached the junction, the motorcycle cop held out a hand. Pugh waved and came to a halt about 30 feet back: he wanted to be close enough to get a good view of the convoy without being close enough for the cop to get a good look at his face.

He could see the arrangements for blocking a 4-way intersection. Three police motorcycles were used. One positioned itself across each side road while the third did the same with the oncoming lane. He glanced casually down at his watch. It estimated it had been around 20 seconds since the first motorcycle cop arrived. He didn't have long to wait: it was about a further 30 seconds before the huge Bradley tank rolled through the junction without pause, closely followed by the first of the trucks with a very serious-looking Humvee alongside the rear of it.

He slipped his iPhone from his pocket and acted as if typing a text message while activating the camcorder. He zoomed in to get the closest view possible.

Almost as quickly as it had appeared, the final tank disappeared and the police motorcycles were rolling within a second or two. Pugh crossed the junction: his work now was done – they didn't want the cops seeing the same person twice.

"What do you think?" asked Sullivan, having changed back into street clothes in the back of the van before slipping back into the passenger seat.

Young frowned. "Wish I could be more optimistic, but frankly that looked as scary as hell. Those guys looked like they were on their way to take over a small country."

"The convoy did look rather ... purposeful, didn't it? Could you see into the bay?"

Young shook his head. "Not a thing. I just scared myself half to death when the Apache chose the moment I pulled out the binoculars to have a little look around, but I couldn't see into the interior at all. The only encouraging thing I saw was that the shutters don't, from a distance, look anything special. But without knowing what's on the other side of them, that's not much help."

"Well, hopefully Chung can provide the opportunity to find out."

Chung was, at that moment, engaged in rather lower-tech work. He'd managed to spot the low-flying Apaches from an overpass and could see that that the convoy was going to pass beneath him within a couple of minutes. He'd put on his hazard lights and pulled into the emergency lane. Feigning frustration for the benefit of any traffic cameras, he got off and kicked the bike. He was ready with a story of it over-heating and having to wait a few minutes for it to cool in case a highway cop appeared.

He bent down as if inspecting the engine, turned up the police scanner mounted on the handlebars and slipped the team radio from his pocket:

"Mobile Sierra, Mobile Sierra," indicating the convoy was on the South diagonal. He slipped the radio away and wandered casually to the railings and leant over them, both arms resting on the wall, looking out at the landscape below him. The convoy was only around 30 seconds away now.

He reached into his pocket for a camera and again rested both arms on the wall, the camera just peeking out from between the top of the wall and his arm. His index finger was on the shutter button so he could fire off a whole bunch of shots. The police motorcycles passed beneath the overpass and he began snapping away.

The motorcycle cop had been doing the job for 14 years and didn't miss much. The biker on the overpass looked casual enough, but it was a bit of a coincidence that it was parked directly overhead. He hit the transmit button on his handlebars.

"Dispatch, 23."

"Go ahead, 23."

"I have a 10-37 at J12A on the B20. Harley, black jacket, silver helmet, blue jeans. May be nothing, but parked on the overpass directly over the convoy. Request a unit be sent out to check it out."

"10-4, 23."

Wow, thought Chung, listening to the exchange on the police scanner – these guys didn't miss much. He made a show of checking the temperature of the engine, thumbed the starter and nodded. He climbed back on the bike and pulled back onto the highway.

"Two more junctions and we'll be there," said Dawson.

Pritchard nodded, looking down at the GPS screen to see the base on the map. For the first time, he saw another moving dot, this one some distance away, next to the base entrance.

"What's the hollow yellow dot?" he asked.

"There are two of them," replied Dawson. "They indicate the positions of the other convoys. Since we don't need to know the detail, it just displays the position of the lead Bradley – the front of the convoy."

"So one of the convoys has already reached the base."

"Right. They took a more direct route than us. They'll drive onto the base then park out of the way, while we go straight through to the aircraft."

Almost there. Far from relaxing, Pritchard felt his tension level increase: the Service trained you to expect an attack on every journey, and if it hasn't happened yet, then it's going to. The closer you got to your destination, the greater the chance that an attack would take place within the next few seconds. He scanned the screens showing each of the camera views.

Daniels was doing the same. He reached out a finger and tapped the screen showing the view of the Humvee alongside them. "What about the Hummer crews?" he asked. "If I were planning an attack, that's where I'd want to be, inside that. You're inside the perimeter, you're in an armoured vehicle, you have heavy firepower and you have the advantage of both surprise and confusion."

"A rogue Marine?" asked Pritchard. "Or rather, two of them, since I can't see either the driver or the gunner being in a position to launch an assault without the active assistance of their partner. If they're not Marines, then they had to have somehow taken out two Marines and commandeered their vehicle without any of their colleagues noticing. Either prospect seems like rather a long-shot."

"I agree," said Daniels, "but do you see any shorter odds here?"

Pritchard considered the matter for a moment. "No, I don't."

"So let's look into whether the Marines have any additional vetting, and examine the security arrangements for the convoy before it leaves the base."

"Dispatch, 67."

"Go ahead, 67."

"I'm 10-23 at J12A on the B20. No sign of anyone here now."

"10-4, 67, return to patrol."

Lewis was left with the trickiest role of the three bikers: trying to observe the convoy's arrival at the base. Even allowing for the fact that the convoy was likely to stay off residential roads, there were four main roads it could take that would bring it in on a pretty direct approach from its last-known position, and yet more if it took a more roundabout route. Lewis couldn't cover all of them without getting close to the base gates, something she was keen to avoid.

However, it seemed pretty likely that it would end up on Carswell Access Road, and she'd found a grocery store by the side of it. She parked her bike outside and wandered in to buy a coffee, figuring out that she wouldn't look out of place sipping that while gazing out of the window, and the sound of the helicopters would give her enough time to discard the coffee and wander outside as the convoy passed.

She didn't have long to wait. She'd only drunk about a third of the cup when she heard the unmistakeable sound of a chopper. Trying to look casual about it, she tossed the cup in the trashcan, put her helmet back on and wandered out to her bike. She could hear sirens now and rode her bike toward the car-park exit, timing it so that she would arrive there just as the motorcycle cops came past.

She was within 20 feet of the convoy as it passed on the opposite side of the road. This close, the Bradley leading the convoy looked incredibly menacing. She'd never realised just how large they were. Viewed on the TV, usually in the desert with nothing close by to lend a sense of scale, they looked little larger than an SUV. Close-up, they were enormous.

The first of the trucks passed her. Despite the lack of visible weaponry, it too managed to look threatening, and that was before the Humvee passed with its gunner poking through the roof.

This was utterly insane, she thought.

"Dispatch, 67, priority."

"Go ahead, 67."

"That 10-37 is back, this time at Carswell and Gillam. Same bike, same helmet, maybe a different jacket. Can we get a patrol there on silent approach?"

"67, that's a Harley, black jacket, silver helmet, blue jeans?" queried the dispatcher, reading from the earlier CAD entry.

"Dispatch, maybe a blue jacket now, but rest confirmed."

"67, standby. Units in the vicinity Carswell and Gillam, a 10-37, Harley Davidson motorcycle, dark jacket, silver helmet, blue jeans. Possible convoy surveillance. Silent approach."

"Dispatch, 14 responding, I'm half a mile away. Silent approach."

"14, 10-4."

Hearing the message on his scanner, Chung decided he'd heard enough. He climbed aboard, thumbed the starter and headed for one of the residential roads. He'd pull up as soon as he was out of sight of the main road, swap jackets for the red one in the left pannier and swap the silver helmet for a blue one. Within a minute or two, he'd no longer match the description of the bike the police were looking for.

A siren wailed for ten seconds, followed by a PA announcement:

"BEP teams, convoy arrival. All non-involved personnel, clear the area."

The standing rule was that anyone not part of the BEP team had to remain indoors or completely clear of all access roads used by the convoy, as well as the apron on which the Galaxies were parked. The latter instruction wasn't really necessary: the perimeter of Marines surrounding the C-5s, all with weapons drawn, made the point with sufficient clarity.

The gate barrier was raised as the first of the three convoys entered the base. The lead Bradley pulled off to the right and stopped. The trucks, Humvees and Strykers all passed by. The rear Bradley pulled off to the left. Both Bradleys then did a neat 180 on the spot to face out of the gates. The two Apache helicopters overhead broke off and began climbing.

The dummy convoy turned off down a wide side-road and parked. The real convoy was just one minute away.

* * *

Dawson hit transmit on the radio.

"Carswell, BEP 1."

"Go ahead, BEP 1."

"BEP 1 on approach."

"Acknowledged."

Ahead of them, the base gates swung open as the lead Bradley approached.

"Once we park up," said Dawson, "you'll be met by Major Timpkins who will take care of you from that point, but please don't attempt to exit the cab until we have clearance, otherwise things could get messy."

The Bradley lead them through the gates, along the approach road and onto the apron where the twelve C-5 Galaxies were waiting. They were enormous aircraft, and twelve of them made for an impressive sight. The Bradley pulled off to one side and a Marine with paddles usually used for directing aircraft beckoned them towards the left-most Galaxy. He guided them to a position about 100 feet to the left of the cargo ramp underneath the huge raised nose of the aircraft, then directed them hard right. Dawson swung the semi round in a 180 with practiced ease. A second Marine indicated for them to creep forward then halt. Standing next to him was an officer.

"That's Timpkins," said Dawson. He picked up the radio mic: "BEP 1 on station, request unlock for guests."

"BEP 1, standby." A short pause, then: "BEP 1, unlock confirmed."

"I'm not allowed out of the cab," said Dawson, "so you'll have to clamber past me." He swung his feet round to the side and pushed a button on the door. There was a sharp sound then he released the handle and pushed the door open with both hands. Daniels climbed past and looked down from the doorway. There were two Marines waiting for him. He climbed down the steps, Pritchard close behind him.

The officer stepped forward: "Major Timpkins," he said, holding out his hand.

"Luke Pritchard and Tim Daniels," said Pritchard, each of them shaking hands in turn.

"Apologies for hurrying you, but we operate to a tight schedule," said Timpkins. "Follow me, please."

He led them along the side of the truck to the left side of the loading ramp of the Galaxy. As they walked back, the two men could see that a group of Marines had surrounded the area between the rear of the cab and the cargo ramp of the Galaxy, each facing outwards, on one knee, assault rifle resting on their other leg.

There were two more Marines guarding the ramp, one positioned about ten feet to either side of it, weapons pointing toward the ground. Pritchard looked inside the gaping cargo hold. Despite having read up on the aircraft, he couldn't believe just how much space there was inside.

Timpkins gestured for them to stand between the Marine on the left and the ramp.

"You'll want to observe the transfer of the currency to the C-5s, but we need to keep you out of the way. In particular, we want to keep you out of the line of fire in the unlikely event of an enemy engagement."

Once more, Pritchard felt naked without his service weapon.

"Please stand here and don't move from this position unless asked to do so by one of the marines," continued Timpkins. "I'll talk you through what's happening, but we won't have time for detail – there'll be plenty of time for that once we're airborne."

"One quick question now," said Daniels. "Has there ever been an attack on the base?"

Timpkins shook his head. "Never, but that doesn't mean we relax for a moment. Our job is to expect bulldozers to plough through the perimeter fencing and helicopters to swoop in at any moment, and if that happens, we're ready for them."

Looking around at the Marines, neither man doubted it for a moment.

"During loading," continued Timpkins, "the convoy Marines provide perimeter security, while the Marines assigned to the aircraft monitor the loading and provide close security. The Apache helicopters have now climbed to 1000 feet and provide air-protection. We load one aircraft at a time, to minimise the exposure. This is Flight BEP 1, so this gets loaded first."

They watched as two fork-lift trucks drove down the cargo ramp. The sergeant at the top of the ramp said something into a headset.

"The forklifts belong to the C-5, and are equipped with the same encrypted datacomms systems as the BEP SARVs," said Timpkins. "They are driven by Marines, and the same forklifts are used for unloading on arrival. We like to have complete control. Only one is used – we move the pallets one at a time – the other is simply a backup."

The driver of one forklift positioned it off to the side, while the other arrived at the rear of the truck. A telescopic arm reached out and connected to the datacomms socket on the rear of the truck. After a few seconds, the forklift backed away. As before, a large section of the truck door opened outward and upward. The forklift manoeuvred forwards until its arms were inside the doorway.

"The truck has sensors that tell it when the forklift is correctly positioned, then the computer system activates the rollers and places the pallet in position. Once the pallet is ready to lift, a radio signal is sent to the forklift and the driver sees a green light. He is then free to lift the arms and reverse out."

They watched this happen. Pritchard looked at the pallet. Somewhere inside all that shrink-wrap, he thought, was $32 million and he was standing about 30 feet away from it.

The forklift did a neat 180 on-the-spot turn and headed toward the ramp. The $32 million was getting closer. 20 feet. 10 feet. And then it was on the ramp, passing them. Both men turned to watch as the forklift climbed the ramp and disappeared inside.

"Marines on board the aircraft will secure it manually once it has been positioned by the forklift," said Timpkins.

Daniels leaned over the ramp for a better view, placing his hand on it. The Marine standing next to them snapped his rifle across his chest: "Sir! Do not touch the ramp, Sir! Step back, Sir!"

Daniels complied.

"Sorry about that," said Timpkins. "It's not that we don't trust you, simply that this is a very carefully-controlled process, and the Marines are trained to be professionally nervous."

"Understood," said Daniels.

"How's that?" asked Jackson, trying to hold the aircraft as steady as possible as they flew directly south at 1000 feet three-and-a-half miles west of Carswell AFB.

"It's pretty tricky," said Perez. "The auto-focus was hunting all over the place, so I've now switched to manual and set it on infinity, but the haze makes it difficult to see much from this angle."

"I can go higher and closer," said Jackson, "but I'm a bit concerned about cloud cover." The PA rules allowed them the choice of coming down relatively low but remaining more than three miles from the base, or staying above 3000 feet and coming closer. Jackson was trying the former first as there were scattered clouds at around 2000 feet. Nothing major, but even very isolated clouds had an awkward habit of getting in the way at just the wrong moment on observation flights.

"Ok, let's complete this run. If it's no good, we can try the higher and closer approach."

"You got it," said Jackson.

Perez was bracing his arm against the window and resting the camera on his forearm as a way of dampening the vibrations, but zoomed in to 500mm a movement of even a few mm translated to a shift of tens of feet in the view captured by the lens. Couple that to the haze rising from the hot ground beneath them and it was next to impossible to get a clear view of anything on the base.

Jackson was flying the light aircraft around 5 knots above stall-speed to keep the ground-speed as low as possible, to maximise the time Perez had to work, but nothing was helping. As they passed to the south of the base, Jackson began a sweeping right turn.

"It's no good," said Perez, "this is hopeless. We'll have to try high-and-close."

"No problem. This thing takes a while to climb, so I'll head out east for a while then do a 180 and head somewhat to the left of the base, and bank gently right to give you the best possible view." The high-wing aircraft design coupled to a right-hand bank meant that Perez would be able to see almost directly down.

While the Marines at the front of the Galaxy continued to load the pallets, the flight crew were running through their checklists.

"Startup checklist, please," asked Captain Dave Turner.

His co-pilot, Neil Gill, pulled out a spiral-bound booklet of laminated cards and flipped over the page. "Startup checklist. Throttles."

The pilot put his hand on each and confirmed they were in the idle position. "Idle."

"Engine 1, fuel-flow," said Gill.

Turner switched on the fuel for the outer engine on the left wing. "Engine 1, fuel-flow on."

"Engine 1, start."

Turner pressed and held the start button for engine 1.

"Check N2 greater than 20% flow."

Turner checked the dial. "Check."

"N1 increasing N2."

"Check."

Jackson had climbed to 3200 feet and was around half a mile to the east of Carswell. He put the aircraft into a gentle right-hand bank.

"This will bring us nice and close," said Jackson. "You'll be looking down at about 30 degrees."

Perez was already looking through the lens. "This is much better," he said. "Once we get overhead, I'll start shooting."

The air traffic controllers in the control tower at Carswell were able to relax somewhat during loading of the BEP flights. All other flights into and out of Carswell were suspended from the moment the convoy arrived until the final Galaxy was off the ground. All they had to do until then was monitor the civilian traffic in the area around the base.

The controller responsible for the sector to the east of Carswell was, however, feeling a little less relaxed. He'd been monitoring a light aircraft heading almost directly towards the base. It was now less than half a mile away, and only just above the 3000 feet PA. Military controllers didn't generally speak directly to civilian traffic except in emergency, but rather directed enquiries to the civilian tower. Any incursion into the Prohibited Area counted as an emergency, but that wasn't quite the case yet.

"Sir!" he said, signalling to his supervisor.

"What is it?"

"This aircraft here." He pointed to it. "He's at 3200 feet, but he's cutting it rather fine."

The supervisor studied the scope.

"What were his movements earlier?" he asked.

"He started out southbound over here, then turned and climbed to the south of us, then continued climbing as he turned back towards us."

"Ok," said the supervisor. "Keep a close eye on it and I'll check out the tail number."

"We don't hang around once we're loaded," said Timpkins, "so let's get you strapped-in ready for take-off."

"Sure thing," said Pritchard.

Timpkins led them up the ramp and into the cargo bay. The first of the two pallets were already strapped down in the centre while there were bench seats on either side. Timpkins gestured to the bench seats on the left.

"I'm afraid we can't offer much in the way of creature comforts."

Daniels smiled. "It's not my first time in one of these. Last time they threw us out halfway there, so staying on board for the landing is a luxury."

Daniels strapped himself in while Timpkins showed Pritchard how to fasten the harness: a waist-strap with twist-release buckle and inertia-reel shoulder straps that snapped into the top of it.

"Once we're in the cruise, I'll take you up to the flight-deck and you can talk to the flight-crew," said Timpkins.

"Thanks," replied Pritchard, watching as the forklift came up the ramp with the second pallet.

"Marines! Board!" yelled the sergeant. The Marines paired-up, one continuing to face outward with rifle drawn while his partner used the webbing straps on his back to guide him backwards. When they reached the ramp, the same procedure was used to reverse up the ramp. Pritchard saw no sign of a signal, but the moment the Marines were on-board the ramp began to raise.

Perez finished his photography of the loading of the first aircraft. It was tantalizing. Around $700 million dollars sat there in the open. And in a few weeks' time, it would be a billion. But on a secure airbase and surrounded by more Marines that you would ever want to meet unless they were very firmly on your side.

"Ok," said Perez to Jackson, "we're done."

Jackson nodded. "I'll pull well clear of the PA corridors, and we can watch the Galaxies take off from a safe distance."

Jackson headed north, back in the direction of the airfield.

* * *

The ramp continued to lift and the giant nose cone descended. It was quite an awe-inspiring sight, thought Pritchard, and that was before you got to grips with the idea that you were now sat in a cargo hold with $64 million for company.

Four marines remained stationed at the rear of the ramp, assault rifles raised, one monitoring the left, one the right and the other two the rear. The remaining marines guarded each of the doors, with one assigned to the door to the flight-deck.

Perez and Jackson watched as two F-16 fighter jets leapt up off the runway and went straight into a vertical climb. Jackson smiled: it was always a pleasure to see the raw power of an F-16, like some kind of rocket-aircraft hybrid.

The F-16s climbed to 3000 feet and peeled apart. Perez watched in alarm as one of the fighters headed straight for them! It was closing on them at a terrifying speed. Jackson too was growing increasingly worried as the distance between them closed. Just as Jackson began to fear a collision, the F-16 pulled up and over into a half-roll to over-fly the base again.

"What the fuck was that about?" asked Perez. "I thought the pilot was going to end up sitting on my lap!"

"I think he was hinting that he would like us to remain well clear," said Jackson, his pulse now returning to normal. "Those guys practice close-formation flying all the time, so they probably considered that a fairly laid-back friendly word."

"I sure as hell wouldn't like to meet them when they're being unfriendly."

"That wouldn't be good," replied Jackson.

The supervisor returned to the controller. "It's a C-172 belonging to the local flying school," he said. "What's it doing now?"

"Headed north away from the base. One of the F-16s did a little flypast just now. Looks like he's taken the hint and is headed back to the airfield."

"Ok, guess he's just doing extended circuits. Those guys know the drill, so I shouldn't imagine they'll infringe on the C-5 corridors, but keep an eye on it just in case."

"Will do."

A Marine passed ear-defenders to the three men. "You'll want these for take-off," said Timpkins.

"Will we be flying at pressurised altitudes?" asked Daniels.

Timpkins nodded. "Yes. And yes, the assault rifles have frangible rounds," he said, anticipating Daniels' question. The Secret Service men were familiar with these: aluminum or plastic bullets designed to break up quickly on impact with solid objects, effectively turning into dust. In soft material – like a person – they did the job they were designed to do, but they wouldn't pass beyond. The Secret Service used them to prevent injury to innocent bystanders; the Marines on the Galaxies used them to ensure rounds didn't pass through the aircraft fuselage, depressurising it.

The nose cone continued to descend.

"The two F-16s assigned to us took off first, providing air-cover from the moment we begin our take-off roll. They'll accompany us all the way to La Guardia and remain overhead until the Apaches take over air cover for the journey to the Federal Reserve. En-route, we're additionally protected by air-exclusion corridors. Any aircraft breaching those is considered hostile."

Pritchard nodded.

The moment the nose section locked into place, the four jet engines spooled up to power the aircraft forward, the revs dropping once the Galaxy was moving and headed along the taxiway towards the runway.

On the flight-deck, the crew were completing the pre-takeoff checklist.

"Flaps 80%," said Gill, pointing to the lever. Procedure called for both pilots to check every item on the list. The pilot-not-flying pointed to the appropriate control or dial to indicate that they were checking it, and the pilot-flying responded verbally.

Captain Turner set the flaps to the extreme setting used for take-off on the massive aircraft. "Set."

"Spoilers."

Gill checked the level. "Retracted."

"Instruments."

Both men scanned them. "Check," said Turner.

"Take-off data."

"V1, VR, V2, check."

"Crew alert."

Turner activated the horn button three times to warn the Marines in the hold that they were about to take-off.

"I check you, Sir," said Gill. "Take-off checklist complete."

Perez watched the Galaxy lumber down the runway at what seemed a hopelessly slow speed. It didn't seem possible the thing could actually fly. For an incredibly long time it didn't appear to be gaining speed at all, but finally it lifted itself reluctantly from the runway and began to climb.

"Ok," said Perez, "I can't see anything to be gained from watching the others go through the same routine, and I don't fancy any more F-16s taking such a close interest in us – let's head back."

The Galaxy took 11 minutes to climb to its cruise altitude, the engine revs were reduced and two short bursts of the horn indicated to the crew that they were free to unstrap.

With the engines reduced to the cruise setting, the aircraft was considerably quieter than it had been for the take-off and climb. The C-5 was exempt from noise-reduction measures which required airliners to reduce their power settings soon after take-off to climb at a reduced power setting: the C-5 maintained maximum power all the way to the cruise.

Timpkins removed his ear-defenders and twisted the buckle on his harness to retract the shoulder straps and release the lap strap. Pritchard and

Daniels followed his example. Despite the reduced revs, the men still had to yell to be heard.

"I'll take you up to the flight-deck now," yelled Timpkins.

Pritchard nodded.

Timpkins gave a thumbs-up signal to the Marine by the staircase to the flight-deck, and the Marine returned the signal. Timpkins led the way up the stairs.

Another Marine was stationed outside the flight-deck door. Timpkins nodded to him and the Marine nodded back and knocked on the flight-deck door. There was a short delay before the door opened. A crew member nodded and exited the flight-deck, walking past the three men.

"There isn't much room to spare in there, so I'll wait outside," said Timpkins.

"Ok," said Pritchard, surprised. The Galaxy was a massive aircraft, so he'd expected the flight-deck to be relatively spacious. As he walked through the door, he immediately saw what Timpkins meant: the flight-deck was pretty cramped. Up front were the two pilots, the entire space between them occupied by the centre console. Immediately behind the console was an empty chair, presumably vacated by the man who just left the flight-deck. Behind that and off to one side was a flight engineer facing a complex-looking panel of dials and switches.

"Welcome aboard!" said the man in the left-hand seat. "I'm Dave Turner, this is my first officer, Neil Gill, and one of our two flight engineers, Charlie Keen. Sorry we only have one seat to offer you."

"Luke Pritchard and Tim Daniels," said Pritchard, shaking hands with each in turn. "And that's ok, thanks, we can stand. I hope you can spare your other flight engineer?"

Turner laughed. "Yes, we joke that he's a part-timer: most of his work is monitoring things during take-off and landing, he doesn't have much work in the cruise."

"Like us, really," smiled Scott, indicating the auto-pilot.

"It's certainly the time everyone can relax," said Turner. "It's a little different to a combat mission."

"In what way?" asked Pritchard.

"In combat, we have to assume hostiles are trying to shoot us down. We have to be alert for ground-to-air missiles and enemy fighters. On this mission, we don't have to worry about that?"

"Because of the F-16s?" asked Pritchard. "Where are they, by the way?" he asked, peering out through the windscreen.

"Just behind us and either side," replied Turner. He flicked a switch on the radio panel to the right of him and hit the transmit button on his radio. "Escorts 1 Alpha and 1 Bravo, BEP 1."

"BEP 1, Escort 1 Alpha."

"Would you mind coming up-front to give our guests a little look-see?"

"Wilco."

Pritchard and Daniels crouched down to see the two F-16s converge in front of them in perfect synchronisation. The left one lifted, the right one dropped and they neatly swapped sides within the space of about three seconds, all while remaining no more than about 30 feet in front of the nose of the Galaxy.

"Impressive," said Pritchard.

Turner thumbed his radio. "Thank you, gentlemen."

The two F-16s slipped outwards and backwards, out of sight.

"I can see why you can relax a little," said Daniels.

"It's not just that," replied Turner, "it's the fact that any hostile here won't want to shoot us down: all that would get them is a fireball on the ground. They want the cash, and they can't get that by firing things at us."

"How could they get it?" asked Daniels.

"Pretty much only by forcing us down somewhere, and the F-16s might have something to say about that. Additionally, this aircraft is fitted with all the usual defences against air-to-air and ground-to-air missiles – chaff, flares and so forth – but those are really there for its wartime role."

"Armaments?", asked Daniels.

"None," replied Turner, "but the F-16s are there to do any fighting required."

Daniels nodded. "What about GPS jamming or something to divert you off-course?"

Turner pointed to the moving map in front of him. "This is in GPS mode," he said, pointing to a 'GPS' label on the top-right of the screen. "There are three independent GPS receivers, operating on a voting system: all three are comparing their readings, and if one of them gives a different reading to the others it is automatically 'voted' out. The GPS position is also constantly being compared against our INS position." He again pointed to the GPS lettering and flicked a switch. The label changed to INS.

"INS?" asked Pritchard.

"Inertial Navigation System. Basically some highly-sensitive accelerometers, much like the one your smartphone uses to know which way up you are holding it. We tell it our initial position on the ground, and it logs every single movement we make. It knows how far and how fast we have moved and in what direction. From those two things, it can calculate our current position. Again, there are three INS systems, with the same voting approach."

"That doesn't sound like it would be too accurate?" asked Daniels.

"You'd be surprised. In the days before GPS, airliners navigated primarily by INS, and at the end of a 5,000-mile flight, it could tell them which gate they were parked at."

Daniels raised an eyebrow, and nodded.

Turner flicked the switch again. The label changed to ECT. "Now we're receiving our position from the lead F-16 behind us. Which also, of course, has both GPS and INS, and also has three of each. Additionally, our position is being tracked by air traffic control radar: if we deviated from our planned course, they would be on the horn to query it. Believe me, diverting us off-course without our knowledge isn't an option."

"Ok," said Daniels, "what about sabotage? Doing something to the aircraft while its on the ground to force you down somewhere?"

"At 6am, the maintenance engineers go through the aircraft with a fine toothcomb. Every hatch, every panel, is opened. These guys know the aircraft intimately – anything that shouldn't be there will be spotted. Prior to loading, the Marines back there make their own search. The aircraft is sterile and remains under guard until take-off. No-one but those authorised to fly on it get on board."

"But supposed they managed it somehow?" persisted Daniels.

Turner pointed to a green button on the centre console with a glowing green light next to it. "This system here is our deadman switch. Every 15 minutes, there is an audible bong, and the light turns red. We have to press the button to reset it. If we don't, it automatically squawks 7500."

"Sorry ... ?" said Pritchard, looking puzzled.

"My apologies," replied Turner. "Jargon is an occupational hazard. Every aircraft in-flight within a given air traffic control sector broadcasts a 4-digit transponder code, known as a squawk code. That code shows up on ATC screens so they can see which aircraft is which. A squawk code of 7500 is the international signal for a hijacked aircraft. When that code is set, it automatically alerts controllers. At that point, additional F-16s will be scrambled. Post 9/11, you can imagine that hijacked aircraft get a rapid response no matter who or what they are, so add on our special status and anyone trying to hijack us would face rather a robust response."

"Ok," said Daniels, "what about a hijacker on-board? Let's suppose a couple of the Marines go rogue."

"When the hijack system is activated, it does two further things. First, it switches on an internal GPS jammer so any GPS devices the hijackers may be using are rendered inoperable. Second, the primary navigation system is switched into a simulation mode. We can use buttons on the yoke to tell the navigation screen what we want it to display – left, right, up down – while we follow a discreet indicator on the secondary display to head to the nearest USAF base."

Daniels looked at Pritchard. "Can you think of anything else to ask?"

Pritchard shook his head.

"Me neither," said Daniels.

"Well, feel free to come back up if you think of anything else," said Turner. "Just make sure you get the ok from the Marines before climbing the stairs. Even though you've been up here once, they are trained to assume nothing."

Pritchard nodded approvingly. "Well, thank you for your hospitality, we appreciate it."

"Anytime," said Turner.

* * *

Perez was flicking through the shots on the LCD screen on the back of the camera as they taxied back in.

"How do they look?" asked Jackson.

"A lot of blurred shots as expected," replied Perez, "but we have enough sharp ones to see what's going on."

"See anything that helps us?"

"Not a thing."

"Well," said Jackson, "maybe we will when we review them properly."

"Maybe."

* * *

Lieutenant Mather's mind kept wandering back to the call from Detective Foster in NY.

The idea was totally nuts, he thought, but the precinct cop had the right idea: CYA was rule 1 in the force these days. He didn't have to claim to give the idea any credence, all he had to do was report the conversation. He got up from his chair and walked towards Lorrimar's office.

* * *

Chung had headed off to a local coffee-shop and pulled a laptop bag from one of the motorcycle panniers. He grabbed a coffee, then opened up his Alienware M18x-R2 laptop. It was as far as you could get from the slim and sleek ultrabooks in fashion at the moment: a massively thick base, an 18-inch screen and acres of plastic, it looked like someone's 1980s idea of what a laptop might look like in 20 years' time. It was a laptop built for one thing and one thing alone: raw power. The laptop of choice for gaming enthusiasts, it delivered high-end desktop computing in a (somewhat) portable form.

He pressed the power button, blue LED lighting came on around the keyboard, trackpad and front ducts. Garish as it looked, the machine proved its serious nature when it booted up its 512Gb SSD into FreeBSD in nine seconds flat. The solid-state drive did all the heavy lifting, containing both operating system and applications, while the 1Tb hard drive in the second drive bay stored most of the data.

His browser automatically connected to a rotating list of anonymous proxy servers. This session it selected a proxy server in Hamburg, so anyone looking at the logs of any connection he made would see an apparent visit from Germany. Any attempt to trace the connection beyond that would lead nowhere.

He connected to www.moneyfactory.gov – the website of the Bureau of Engraving and Printing. He opened up a terminal window and typed:

 # ping moneyfactory.gov

Almost immediately he saw the message:

Pinging moneyfactory.gov [206.188.192.208] with 32 bytes of data

This told him the IP address of the webserver. Next, he needed to see what ports were open on the server – what type of incoming connections the machine would accept. He typed:

 # nmap -v -sT 206.188.192.208

The response came back showing that ports 23, 80, 143, 443 and 465 were open. The bad news was there was no SSH access: the usual method for using a server remotely as if you were physically connected to it. But port 465 was very encouraging, thought Chung. This was the port used for secure email connections, meaning the server was likely located within the BEP network rather than with an external hosting company.

Next, he needed to pretend to be a piece of email software attempting to login to the mailserver. Without a username and password, he wouldn't be able to complete the login, but he didn't need to: he simply wanted to know which mailserver software was running, and which version. If he was lucky, it would be running an out-dated version with a known exploit. If this turned out to be the case, he could send a packet of data that would crash the mailserver and drop him into a command-line. At that point, he would be able to explore the server to see what else it was running. He typed:

 # telnet 206.188.192.208 465

This told the machine to connect to the mailserver running on port 465. The machine responded:

Trying 206.188.192.208 ...

This was simply his PC telling him it was attempting the connection. A couple of seconds passed, then:

Connected to int-smtp-in.1.moneyfactory.gov

Sendmail v8.14.5

Escape character is '^]'.

220 mx.moneyfactory.com ESMTP n5si12368360paw.254

Damn! That was the latest version of Sendmail, and there were no known exploits for that version. It also suggested that the sysadmin was good at keeping the server software updated. He would try the other ports, but he wasn't optimistic.

* * *

Jackson and Perez had also headed to a coffee shop to review the photos on a rather less sophisticated laptop. They'd grabbed a corner booth so nobody could look over their shoulder, and far enough away from the other customers that they couldn't be overheard.

"I don't think you should plan a new career as a photographer," said Jackson as the fourth blurry photo in a row came up.

"If you could fly a plane in a straight line without bouncing around like a monkey on crack ..." responded Perez.

Perez had known that most of the photos would be blurred by the vibration and movement of the plane, so had set the camera to high-speed 'motor drive' mode, firing off five or six frames at a time, and shooting five or six batches of each. That gave him 25-35 versions of every photo he wanted, and in those kind of conditions he expected only one or two of them to be sharp.

"There," he said, pointing to the latest photo to appear on the screen. It showed a forklift truck midway between the truck and the Galaxy. Even with a 500mm lens, it was still quite a distant view, but with 36 megapixels to play with, he could zoom in a lot and still get a sharp image. He pressed the + key several times to zoom. There it was. The pallet clearly visible on the forklift. "$32 million dollars, right there in the open air."

Jackson whistled.

Perez nodded: "Quite a sight, isn't it?"

"It certainly is. Not so keen on those guys, though." He pointed to the Marines. The assault rifles couldn't quite be clearly seen, but the stance of the Marines could, and that was enough to convey the message that visitors were not welcome.

They continued flicking through the photos, deleting the hopelessly blurred ones until they were left with a decent set showing every stage of the operation from the arrival of the convoy to the departure of the first Galaxy. Perez flicked back to the start of the photos that were left.

"That's some serious firepower in the convoy," said Jackson. "Are those Bradleys?"

"Looks like it, yes. Then the armoured personnel carriers – they look like Strykers. And those are Hummers."

"All armed to the teeth, no doubt," said Jackson.

"Count on it."

"And then there are the Apaches. Both of them. Those will be bristling with missiles. And, of course, the F-16s. Those only took off shortly before the departure of the Galaxies, but they can be in the air within 2-3 mins if needed earlier."

Perez nodded, frowning. "I think Sullivan finally got too ambitious."

"Well," said Jackson, "perhaps the ground teams have spotted an opportunity."

The two looked at each other.

"No," continued Jackson, "I don't think so either."

* * *

Chung had worked his way through each of the ports in turn; no luck with any of them.

He closed down the laptop. It was time for another approach, but he would try that back at the hotel.

* * *

The team met back in the mini-suite Sullivan had booked as their temporary base. There was little chatter, and the facial expressions told their own story.

"I'm guessing from the lack of excitement in the room that nobody has yet spotted any weaknesses," said Sullivan.

"Not a one," replied Perez. She looked around the room.

"Nope."

"Nothing."

"Zilch."

"Well," said Sullivan, "if it were obvious, someone would have done it by now, right?" Shrugs. "Anyone think we need to observe more convoys, or do we have enough data?"

"More than enough," said Lewis in a low voice.

Sullivan turned to Chung. "Any luck in getting into the system, so we can get someone inside that building?"

Chung shook his head. "Not yet, but I'm not out of ideas yet."

"Ok," said Sullivan, "Mike, you work on that when we get back to New York. In the meantime, let's share our observations, photos and video and then we can start giving some thought to possible approaches."

Lewis smiled to herself. Her view right now was that this was a non-starter, but you had to give Sullivan that much: she wasn't easily deterred. She'd proven herself right in the past, so Lewis was willing to let things roll for now.

* * *

"Enjoy the trip?" asked Lorrimar with a smile as she Pritchard and Daniels met back in her office on their return from New York.

"I'm not sure that enjoy is quite the right word," replied Pritchard, "but it was certainly a memorable experience."

"I'd imagine that with your backgrounds, it takes rather a lot for something to qualify for that description."

"True."

"Well, I know you have a lot to think about and to review, so I don't want to keep you from your work, I just wanted to check in with you."

"We appreciate it," said Daniels, rising from his chair.

"Oh," said Lorrimar with a grin, "I should probably let you know you have some opposition."

"Oh?" asked Daniels.

"We had a call from a NY precinct cop. Apparently one of his low-level snitches claimed some gang no-one has ever heard of plans a hit on us."

"Are they taking it seriously?" asked Pritchard.

"No!" she laughed. "The snitch is apparently some nobody who couldn't tell the cops who they were supposed to be or any kind of credible story about what it was they planned to do."

"Ok, thanks."

The two men walked back to the conference room they had made their temporary base at the BEP.

"What do you make of that?" asked Pritchard.

"The snitch? Hard to say, but without any details, I can't see any way the story impacts us. The steps to protect against a non-specific threat are the steps we'd want to take anyway."

Pritchard nodded. "On the subject of which, we need to come up with some. The Service is going to wonder why they're paying our salaries if we can't find something to comment on!"

"This is true," said Daniels. "Let's take it from the top, review everything from the loading bay onwards and see what we can think of."

* * *

"So what's the next tactic in breaking into the BEP computer system?" asked Sullivan as the cab dropped them back in Brooklyn.

"Come up to my apartment and watch if you like," said Chung.

Techies liked an audience, Sullivan had found. Both Chung and Lewis enjoyed showing-off their skills, and she indulged them partly because she knew it motivated them and partly because it was fascinating watching them at work.

"Sure," she said, "I'd like that."

It took only a few minutes for them to walk up to Chung's apartment. There were two types of bachelor's apartment, she thought: incredibly messy or incredibly tidy. Chung was most decidedly in the former camp. There was a dining-room table with six chairs. The table surface was covered in papers, and every one of the chairs had something on it: papers, clothes, bags.

"Sorry," said Chung, picking up a pile of papers from one of the chairs and looking round in a vain attempt to find a clear space to put them down. He settled for dumping them on top of yet more papers on the black leather sofa.

"Don't worry," said Sullivan, smiling.

Chung reached into his bag to extract his laptop. He didn't attempt to clear any of the papers on the table, merely placing it on top of them. He opened it up and hit the power switch.

Sullivan was amused by the blue glow. Very Star Trek.

"So what's the plan?" she asked, sitting in the one empty chair.

Chung picked up a bag from the chair next to her and dumped it on the floor so that he too could sit. "The first thing I tried was quite crude," he replied. "I basically tried an attack which relies on the system having outdated software on it. That wasn't terribly likely in a secure environment, it's just the first thing to try. What we'll be trying today is a little more sophisticated."

"Ok," said Sullivan.

Chung opened his browser, which automatically connected to a new random anonymous web proxy, and selected the BEP website from his bookmarks. He clicked through into the jobs section.

"I'm going to do a search for jobs. That means it will be querying the HR database, and that's the one we need to access." He clicked into the search-bar.

"So how does a search let you break into the database?" she asked, puzzled.

"What happens when you enter text into the search-box is that the webserver takes the search-term and effectively pastes it into the database software. The database software then processes the search text and passes the results back to the webserver." Sullivan nodded. That much made sense to her. "What we are going to attempt is something called an SQL injection attack. Basically we enter a search-term that contains a small piece of code. If we're in luck, the database will see that code as a command. If it works, we can then access the HR database exactly as if we were logged-in locally."

"Wouldn't you need a login to do that?" asked Sullivan.

Chung nodded. "Yes, but we can query the system to see which database software it is running. There are default admin logins for each, just like your home wifi router has a default login. Those continue to work unless the sysadmin has actively disabled them. They should, but many don't because it's easier to have a quick way in that works no matter which box you are talking to."

"So you can literally just type a piece of computer code into the search box of a website to gain access to the database behind it?" asked Sullivan. "That sounds scarily simple."

Chung smiled. "Well, that depends. First, we don't know what database software they are running, and we can't find out unless we get in. Different software has different codes to allow us access, and we just have to use trial-and-error to see which, if any, works. Microsoft SQL Server is the most common database software used as the back-end to website searches, so we'll try that first. Second, a sysadmin can configure the webserver to trap commands and discard them rather than pass them to the database software. Effectively you tell the webserver these are a bunch of search terms you should reject. If they have done that, then the commands won't work even if we use the right one for the database software because they won't get that far."

"So we just try it and see."

"Yep." Chung typed into the search box:

; Select * from sys.tables

"The semi-colon is a statement terminator that tells the SQL query processor that the next bit of text is a new statement." Chung always did this, thought Sullivan: started simple then wandered off into jargon once he got into his stride. She took the smile-and-nod approach at these times to forestall lengthy explanations. She smiled and nodded.

Chung continued: "The remaining text will, if we're lucky, be processed as a database query command. That particular command tells the database software to give us a list of all the tables – individual databases, effectively – that it has in the system. There are similar commands that do the same for mysql and Oracle, the two other main database systems they may be using."

"And if we're unlucky?"

"Depends how unlucky. If we're moderately unlucky, it will generate an error message that gives us a clue as to whether we've guessed the database type correctly. If we're more unlucky, then we have ourselves a sysadmin who knows their stuff and has configured the webserver to trap database commands. In that case, nothing at all will happen other than a null result for our search."

Chung pressed enter to send the query to the website.

No results found

Chung tried the equivalent command for mysql.

No results found

He moved onto Oracle.

No results found

Two minutes later, Chung had tried the commands for increasingly obscure systems; all had failed.

"Sorry," said Chung.

"Nothing else we can try?"

"Not without physical access to the network. If Young can get me access as a visitor, then maybe, but I'm not optimistic."

* * *

Janice Reid had been sysadmin at the BEP for three years, and took pride in running a tight ship. Not all admins did, she knew, but for her there was no satisfaction in sloppy work. In the webserver, for example, she'd trapped SQL commands and configured it to automatically email her the log entries any time an SQL attack was attempted. She was looking at one of these logs now.

The search was in the jobs section of the site, which suggested an attempt to hack into the HR database. The command had been trapped, and had thus failed as it should, but she wanted to see if she could learn more. She looked at the IP address. The attack had not originated from within the BEP network, she saw, which was good news: an internal hacker potentially had access to more systems than an external one. She next did a lookup on the IP address.

Xi'an, China. That was less good news. The US government had been concerned for some time about attacks on its computer systems originating from China. The strong suspicion was that much of it was State-sponsored, but that was difficult to prove and diplomatically awkward to raise as a suggestion.

Well, she thought, the attack had been thwarted, but given the apparent origin, she'd drop an email to Security just so they were aware.

* * *

Lorrimar looked at the email. Janice Reid was someone who very much erred on the side of caution, so receiving an email about an attempted hack was not terribly unusual, but the timing was interesting, coming so soon after a tip-off about a planned hit. It was, though, hard to see a connection between the Chinese government and some unknown gang in New York.

Unless, she thought, this wasn't a government-sponsored attack at all. A Triad? An attempt to access the HR database could be in order to get home addresses of the personnel responsible for unlocking the vault. Kidnap a spouse or child and hold them hostage?

It wasn't much to go on, but she didn't like coincidences. She picked up her phone and dialled the number for Lieutenant Mather.

"Lieutenant, could you join me in conference room 3? I have something I want to run past you and the Secret Service team."

"Sure, I'll be right up."

Lorrimar pushed back her chair and walked the short distance to the conference room where Pritchard and Daniels were reviewing the ops manual in the light of their experience of the convoy and flight. She knocked on the door and poked her head round the corner.

"Got a moment," she asked.

"Sure," said Pritchard, gesturing to an empty chair.

"I've asked Lieutenant Mather to join us, he'll be up momentarily."

Mather arrived and Lorrimar quickly and succinctly filled them all in.

"It was a scenario we discussed," said Daniels. "A rogue employee, either willingly or coerced, but after running through the game-play we couldn't see any way for it to succeed. With nine other people required for the unlock process, they'd need to get a weapon into the ante-room, which is a stretch, and all the electronic counter-measures mean that they don't get very far even if they manage to take possession of one of the loaded SARVs."

"What if the target is the convoy?" mused Pritchard. "Again use a hostage – one of the truck drivers – to try to force the convoy to divert?"

"Wouldn't work," said Lorrimar. "You know State policy on these things: we don't give in to terrorists or criminals as that just encourages further attacks."

"We know the theory," said Daniels, "but Pritchard and I have both been in the room where these situations have been discussed. Even at presidential level, there's still a strong desire to resolve things without bloodshed. If it can be done quietly, and without conceding too much, sometimes these things do happen."

"Yeah, but a semi driver versus the $64 million or thereabouts in the back of his rig?" queried Pritchard. "I hate to be a cynic, but ..."

"Yeah."

"The hard fact of the matter," confirmed Lorrimar, "is that all of the personnel involved in the transfer of the cash know that we'll do our very best to protect them, but both policy and reality is no-one gets the cash."

"So," said Daniels, "what now?"

"This snitch," said Pritchard to Mather, "is he in a position to learn more?"

"I don't know, but I can ask the question."

"Let's do that. Let's put him on the payroll for a few weeks, see if he can hang out in the same place and learn anything more. Let's also talk to NYPD about Triad activity there and see whether they have any intelligence which might suggest they have anything planned."

"Ok," said Mather, "I'll see what we can arrange."

* * *

Sam Young picked both his payphone and his timing carefully. The payphone was at the back of a convenience store, and at 10.30am it was pretty empty. He waited until there was nobody nearby and then dialled the number of the BEP switchboard.

"Good morning, BEP, how may I direct your call?"

"Ah, good morning," said Young. "I'm calling from Siemens in New York. Sorry, my opposite number in Fort Worth is off sick today and I'm not sure who I need to speak to."

"How can I help, Sir?"

"We're upgrading your conference call system, and we have a new engineer on the team. I'm not sure whether he needs anything other than his normal employee pass as ID?"

"Yes, Sir, all visitors need security clearance. You need to fill out the online form at least 48 hours before access is required. Would you like the web address for the form, Sir?"

"Yes, please."

The telephonist gave him the website URL.

"Thanks very much," said Young, "I appreciate it."

"You're welcome, Sir."

Young wandered a few doors down to a Starbucks. He pulled out his iPad and connected to the web address he'd been given. He scanned through the form. Social security number. Full employment history. References. This wasn't good, he thought. There are various different levels of security clearance, but asking for this much information suggested it would be more than a basic one. They weren't going to go as far as positive vetting for a visitor, but with these kinds of checks, you can't just invent an identity: it has to be a real person, and their details had to check out.

He put the iPad away, walked out of the Starbucks and down the street. He pulled his cellphone out and called Chung. Maybe he could help.

"Nothing is impossible," said Chung, when Young had outlined what they needed, "but it would be a major undertaking – and a risky one. I don't know your view, but it doesn't strike me as a worthwhile bet on the unlikely off-chance that I could, as a visitor, get access to the network."

"I agree," said Young. "If we're going to be able to do this at all, we have to do it without having anyone on the inside."

* * *

Sullivan and Young had compared notes on security when they first started working together. With their respective experience as both cat and mouse, they had been able to bring both perspectives to the table.

They'd jokingly termed the executive summary of their conclusions 'Don't be dumb'. Most of those who operated on the wrong side of the law were. They got caught because they were stupid people who did stupid things. And getting caught was the dumbest thing of all, because once you'd been caught for one thing, the authorities knew who you were and would come knocking on your door next time. The team had never been caught.

Most of the precautions they took were commonsense ones. Don't be seen together, for example. They had a rule that no more than three of them would visit any of their homes. No meetings on fixed days or at fixed times. Never meeting in the same place twice running.

Much of it too was about balancing competing risks. Meeting in a different place every time was safest from a surveillance viewpoint, but borrowing more places potentially meant exposure to more people. So you compromise. They had a couple of places they used, and alternating between them and meeting on different days at different times gave a sensible balance.

By day, the tyre-fitting shop was full of cars, fitters, customers and the buzz of wheel-nut guns. By night, it was empty and silent. The team had gathered in the customer waiting area, the harsh fluorescent lighting somehow managing to be at once painfully bright on the eyes while leaving the room feeling murky.

"Ok," said Sullivan, "let's review where we're up to, from the top."

"Faking an employee or contractor is a non-starter," said Chung. "The system is too well-secured from outside the network, and getting a visitor in is non-trivial."

"Too much risk for next to no chance of success," added Young. "Most organisations, there are ways to get someone in as a visitor while creating opportunities to plug into a network without being observed, but at the BEP we don't see it happening."

"And no visitor is going to get anywhere near the vault," added Sullivan, "so direct observation isn't on the cards. Which means we know no more about the vault than we did at the outset."

"Tunnelling in is a non-starter," said Young. "Unless we can get someone inside, we don't know where the vault is located in the complex, and there are no buildings anywhere remotely close to give a starting-point."

"From the googling I've done," said Perez, "even if we could tunnel right up to the external wall, trying to blast our way in would be a hopeless task."

"So I think we have to eliminate the vault as a feasible target," said Sullivan. There was no argument with that one.

"Any further thoughts on the convoy?" she asked.

"One," said Perez, "but it gets us one truckload at best, and it's a non-starter in reality."

"Let's hear it anyway," said Sullivan, "it might trigger some other ideas, or we may be able to solve the problems."

"If we could find out the route, I could lay small explosive charge strips on the road. Blow the tyres of one of the trucks, forcing it to stop. When one of those tyres blows, you stop pretty quickly; when several blow, you stop pretty much instantly, so we could conceivably get one stopped right where we want it."

"Which is?"

"Over a manhole cover. Come up from under the truck, cut through the floor, grab the cash, disappear down into the water system, emerge a safe distance away."

"And the problems?"

"Working backwards, we begin with the problem of getting the cash down the manhole cover. The only way to do that is to break it down into bricks at most, maybe even bundles. That takes time. A lot of time. And we only get to start that after we've cut through the bottom of the truck. A conventional armoured truck, cutting through the armour takes 15-20 minutes. Those trucks look like a considerably tougher target."

"Not to mention their tougher company," said Lewis.

"Right, which is the next problem. One tyre blowing could be chance, but several clearly isn't, so the Marines are going to be instantly on the alert. It isn't going to take them long before they look beneath the truck."

"Certainly a hell of a lot less time than 15-20 minutes," said Pugh.

"But the biggest problem of all, of course, is that we can do nothing without knowing the route in advance – and without knowing which of the three convoys is the real one," said Perez.

"It would be irritating to do all that work only to cut through into an empty truck," said Pugh.

"Which brings us neatly back to the inside info it appears we have no way to get," said Lewis.

"Any other thoughts?" asked Sullivan.

The room was silent.

Sullivan looked at Young, a hint of a smile playing on her lips. Only he knew what she was about to say. She'd been prepared to run with any other idea raised in the meeting, but in the absence of same …

"We're going to attack the shipment at its weakest point," said Sullivan.

"Which is?" asked Lewis.

"While the cash is in the air."

"Excuse me?" said Jackson. "The cash is in big-ass Galaxies flying at 23,000 feet in twelve different directions, each with a squad of Marines on board, each escorted by two of the most advanced fighter-jets on the planet – and that's the weakest point?"

"Precisely," replied Sullivan. "It's the one part of the journey they won't be expecting an attack."

"It occur to you there might be a reason for that?" persisted Jackson.

Sullivan ignored him, continuing her briefing like a college professor explaining a particularly obvious point to a rather dim-witted student.

"We have," said Sullivan, "six problems to solve."

"Only six?" asked Lewis sardonically. Sullivan ignored her.

"First, how we divert the aircraft."

"That'll be the Galaxies with the F-16 escorts," chimed in Perez.

"Those ones, yes. We need a method of getting them to land in a place of our choosing."

"Perhaps if we ask nicely," suggested Jackson.

"Perhaps so," responded Sullivan, lightly. "In any case, that's the key to the whole game, so you, Sam and Katrina will work on that." Sullivan had no idea how they might pull it off, but a military pilot, a con-man and an electronics whizz seemed like a reasonable team.

Young smiled, Jackson looked sceptical, Lewis shrugged.

"Second," continued Sullivan, "we need a suitable landing strip. Galaxies are heavy aircraft, 'big-ass' as you so eloquently put it, but they were built for dirt-field landings. We need a lot of space, but not necessarily an actual runway."

"That's a lot of space with a capital L and a capital S," said Jackson. "I've never flown a Galaxy so I'll need to bone-up, but they're going to need three or four thousand feet to land, probably double that to take-off, assuming we plan for them to take-off again afterwards."

"We do," said Sullivan, "if for no other reason than to get rid of the twelve squads of Marines they carry between them. I don't fancy trying to make our getaway with those guys in the vicinity. Which brings us to problem three: how we deal with the Marines. If you were choosing people to mess with, US Marines would not be high on your list."

"That's basically the short-form job description of a Marine: 'be someone you don't want to mess with'," confirmed Perez.

"Which is why they got this job," continued Sullivan.

"Eight civilians versus twelve squads of them," mused Perez. "That's eight of us and 156 Marines."

"Like I say," replied Sullivan, "they wouldn't be my preferred opponents, but since we don't have a choice in the matter, we have to figure out how we mess with them anyway."

"We don't have a choice?" queried Perez.

"Not if we want the billion dollars."

"There is that."

"Problem four. How we stop the fighter-jets attacking once we have taken possession of the cash. The F-16s will be circling overhead with the capability to reduce any vehicle and its occupant to their component pieces at the touch of a button, so if we want to leave the scene of the crime, we have to have a plan to prevent them doing the same to us."

"Wouldn't a missile attack also destroy the cash?" challenged Lewis.

"Sure, but this is the government: the cash is just so much paper to them. If it gets destroyed, no harm is done, they just print some more."

Lewis tilted her head in acceptance of the point.

"Problem five. Assuming we divert the aircraft, create an improvised landing strip, deal with 156 US Marines and render ineffective 24 F-16 fighter jets, we have to make good our escape. The police will have roadblocks on every road within a 50-mile radius, and they'll have helicopters watching our every move. We have to somehow evade them."

"That would seem to be my territory," observed Aaron Evans calmly. "The key to any illusion is misdirection. We simply have to ensure the police are looking in the wrong direction."

"Um, can't we be rather confident they will be looking in our direction?" The question came from Chung.

Evans smiled. "That's what every audience thinks."

"You sound like you have an idea already?"

Evans shook his head: "Not the faintest inkling of one. But that's what makes this fun."

"And the final problem?" asked Jackson. "Problem six?"

"Once we have made our getaway," replied Sullivan, "we have one point one billion dollars in fifty dollar bills. Laundering that much cash would be challenging at the best of times, but these are brand-new bills. Brand-new sequentially-numbered bills. The theft is going to be highly embarrassing to the government, so if it's possible to play down what occurred, my guess is they will. We'll probably be able to spend the cash at our local Walmart without any trouble, but the serial numbers will be circulated to every bank in the country within hours. None of the usual outlets will be able to handle anything close to this quantity of cash. Laundering the money will therefore be ... non-trivial." Both Sullivan and Young had been racking their brains on that one; neither had come up with any ideas yet.

"Do we get to assess your craziness now?" asked Perez.

"Go for it," invited Sullivan.

"You've come up with some whacky ideas in the past, but those were do-able. We demonstrated that. But this one?"

"None of the past ideas were do-able until we figured out how."

"Right, but on a scale of 1 to 10, the impossibility of this one has to be a good 15-20."

"I think we've done an 11 or 12 before," said Sullivan. "So do we write it off now, or put some thought into how we might approach it?"

"We've come this far," said Evans, "and some thought can't do any harm."

"There's not a chance in hell we can pull this off," said Lewis, "but it'll be fun to see how many problems we can solve, so sure, why not pretend we're going to do it."

"I don't like giving up too easily," said Chung, "and yeah, it's fun to think about."

"Sure," said Jackson. "I agree with Lewis that there's no chance, but it's fun to think about."

"I'm not sure what I can contribute," said Pugh, "but why the hell not?"

"Nuts," said Perez. "I'll play make-believe with the rest of you boys and girls."

"Then let's see what we can come up with," said Sullivan.

* * *

"Detective Foster."

"Detective, it's Lieutenant Mather, BEP."

"How are you doing?"

"Good, thanks. No news from your snitch, I assume?"

"Nope. He says he's been in there every morning, from 9am through to early afternoon, and they haven't been back since. You want us to pull him off? I'm conscious we're burning through money here, and I'm very dubious about the whole thing."

"No," said Mather, "let's hang in there for a bit longer. Were any of the faces he saw Chinese, as a matter of interest?"

"Hang on," said Foster, flicking back through his notebook. "Yes, one of them was, why? You have a lead?"

"Not a lead, more of a thought at the moment. Do you have mugshot books for known Triad members?"

"Sure."

"Could you bring your snitch in for a look through them? It's just a wild idea at the moment, but can't hurt to check it out."

"No problem," said Foster, "I'll get him in this afternoon."

* * *

"So how the hell do we get a dozen of the world's largest military aircraft to do as we tell them?" asked Young.

"What about generating false GPS signals?" asked Lewis. "They are extremely low-power so it's easy to override them with more powerful ones. I know US forces did that in Iraq to confuse Iraqi forces."

Jackson shook his head. "That was aimed at missiles and ground-forces, it wouldn't work on aircraft." He explained about INS. "Besides which, military pilots are old-school, we still use paper charts as backup. With compass readings, speed and time, you know pretty much where you are even if all the electronics fails."

"Fake weather radar signals?" suggested Chung. "Make it look like a major storm system, to force them to divert?"

Jackson again shook his head. "They'd have the latest weather reports just before departure, and anything that came out of nowhere would be interpreted as a likely technical glitch. They'd be on the radio to ATC who would report clear weather."

"Combine it with radio jamming to fake ATC exchanges?" asked Lewis.

"ATC transmissions are very powerful," said Jackson. "Hard to block those unless we could get very close, and with a dozen aircraft all flying in different directions, we can't be close to all of them at the same time."

The three sat silently for a minute, before Lewis spoke again: "If they were civilian flights, it would be trivial. But up against Marines, I'm stumped."

"Why trivial if they were civil flights?" asked Jackson.

"Put bombs on board and threaten to blow them out of the sky unless they land where we want them to. Civilian aircraft, they're not going to take any chances. But I'm guessing Marines aren't going to run scared."

"No," replied Jackson, thoughtfully, "but we don't have to scare them for the threat to work."

"What do you mean?" asked Lewis.

"You have to understand the military mindset," said Jackson. "Marines are the meanest, toughest sons of bitches out there. Every last one of them are willing to die to achieve a mission, and the generals are ruthless in dispatching them to their deaths when a military objective needs to be achieved and putting soldiers in harm's way is the only way to get it done. But nobody will let them die senselessly. If we can get bombs aboard the aircraft, and they are faced with the choice of landing or being killed for no gain, they're going to land."

"And risk all that money?"

"They're not likely to see it as a big risk. Ok, we can get the planes down on the ground, but you then have twelve squads of Marines on the ground ready to defend the cash. That is 156 Marines equipped with assault rifles defending against ... us. A small group of, as far as they know, civilians. They're going to be 100% confident of their ability to prevail, and frankly I can't see any reason to question that confidence. But for getting the planes on the ground, bombs would do the trick."

Lewis shook her head. "You know Rule One. No violence. No-one gets hurt." It was the first thing Sullivan and Young had agreed on when they started working together. They were gentlemen thieves, not thugs.

"We don't need to actually blow the aircraft out of the sky, just have enough explosive capacity on board to be able to persuade them that we have the capability. We'll destroy something non-critical that will make our point."

"Leaving the small matter of getting the bombs on board the Galaxies, of course," observed Lewis, laconically. "These are military aircraft that spend their lives on military airbases. We're hardly going to be able to just wander in and plant the bombs."

"True," said Jackson, "but let's start by figuring out what it is we need to get on board. Let's go talk to Perez."

* * *

"We're going to be out of work by the end of the month at this rate," said Daniels. The two of them had been over the convoy and flight arrangements repeatedly without coming up with any significant ideas on improving security.

"Tell me about it," said Pritchard. "If we were looking at a purely destructive attack, then sure, there are ways to do it. But an attack where the aim is to get hold of the cash ..."

"So that's the best we've got?" asked Daniels. "A rogue pilot on the plane. Shoots the rest of the flight-crew, puts on his emergency oxygen mask and figures out a way to depressurise the aircraft in flight to render the Marines unconscious."

"Is 23,000 feet even high enough to cause hypoxia?"

"If not, there's nothing to stop him climbing. They cruise at 23k, but the ceiling will be far higher." He pulled his laptop toward him and did a quick Google search. "35k, more than enough, and the thing about hypoxia is that victims are not aware of it happening."

Pritchard nodded. "Ok, so he takes the Marines out of the equation, leaving just him, $64 million and ..."

"... two F-16s watching his every move."

"Exactly. They're not going to shoot it down, but they will certainly follow it wherever it goes, report any deviation from the flight-plan and be ready to launch missiles the moment the bad guys try to leave the aircraft with the cash."

"Ok," said Daniels, "let's say the rogue pilot depressurises the aircraft long enough to leave the Marines brain-dead. He lands the plane somewhere.

His pals are waiting for him. The F-16s are circling overhead, and calling in reinforcements. How do the bad guys make their getaway?"

"Let's give it some thought."

* * *

Perez listened carefully as Jackson and Lewis briefed him on the explosives requirements.

"We're after two things," said Jackson as he and Lewis briefed Perez. "First, we want to convince the flight crew that we can bring the aircraft down. We need a convincing story."

"Ok," said Perez, "what does it take to crash a Galaxy?"

"Not a lot, if you can place the explosives in the right place. How small a chunk of explosive would be enough to sever a metal cable with a diameter of about 3/8ths of an inch?" Jackson held out his finger and thumb, indicating the diameter.

"If you can mount it within a few inches of the cable, a completely trivial amount of C-4 or Semtex. C-4 is slightly more powerful, Semtex is easier to get hold of. But either way, the amount of explosive needed would be smaller than the detonator used to fire it. Add a radio receiver to allow us to trigger it and the whole thing could fit into a tube not much thicker than the cable, and about two inches long."

"Ok," said Jackson, "so that's the credible threat. Now we need a small demonstration. A way to show that we have explosives on board the aircraft and can trigger them at will."

"No problem," said Perez. "What could we destroy on an aircraft that would make our point without causing it to crash?"

Jackson shrugged. "Dozens of things. There are all kinds of redundant circuits on an aircraft, as well as things that are nice-to-have but not essential to maintaining safe flight."

"Such as?"

Jackson considered the question for a moment. "Weather radar would be a good choice. It'll be very visible when the screen goes blank, but will have no real impact on the aircraft unless there's a major storm system in the aircraft's path. Even then, ATC can guide them around any weather, so they'd never be in any real danger."

"Ok, I'm guessing that's just a matter of blowing a circuit-board or a few wires."

"Right."

"Simple," said Perez.

"Maybe not," said Lewis.

"Oh?" asked Jackson.

"The radio transmitter and receiver could be the tricky bits," she said. "Normally you'd be triggering at short-range, so a small, low-powered transmitter is sufficient. When you need longer-range, you typically use a cellphone, but at 23,000 feet they'd be well out of reliable range of cellular transmissions. A receiver powerful enough to pick up signals at twenty-odd thousand feet is going to have a fairly chunky antenna."

"Unless the transmitter is at a similar altitude, of course," said Jackson.

"Stick you in a plane?" asked Lewis.

"Yep. They have air corridors cleared for them, but I could get within a few miles a thousand feet above or below them."

"Clear line-of-sight up there," said Perez, "that sort of distance shouldn't be difficult."

"Right," agreed Lewis. "That gets us down to a receiver roughly cigarette pack sized."

"I'd need a jet of some kind to reach those kind of altitudes," said Jackson. "Renting one won't be cheap, but I guess we can justify the expense for this one."

"But there's only one of you and twelve of them," said Perez, "and they are all headed in different directions."

Jackson nodded. "We'd have to act fast, issue the threat the moment the last aircraft is in the air. If we deliver our our demonstration with whatever aircraft are in range, that should be enough to convince the others that we have the capability."

"Ok," said Lewis, "that sounds like it could be feasible. Let me give it some thought."

* * *

"How are we looking on the trucks?" Sullivan asked Pugh. As he had nothing to do at this stage, he'd volunteered to look into the practicalities of transporting the cash from the landing-site. He'd done some googling on freight capacities, and booked himself a trial semi-driving lesson as a way of finding out how practical it would be for the team to drive trucks. They didn't like bringing in outsiders.

"The pure carrying capacity is simple enough," said Pugh. "We have 36 pallets. With a 45-foot long trailer, we could even carry it in a single rig." He glanced over at Sullivan and grinned, "but of course we'd need a contingency in case of a problem with a rig, so we'll split it between two." The grin was because Sullivan was famed for her demand that there be a Plan B for every eventuality.

He continued: "A pallet of copier paper weighs three-quarters of a ton, so bank notes should be in the same sort of ball-park, and and that's a cargo weight of 27 tons – well within weight limits for even a single rig."

"Sounds good," said Sullivan. "How did you get on with your one-day introductory driving course?"

"Surprisingly well! I wouldn't like to try to drive one through the centre of a town, manoeuvring round parked cars and so on. And reversing one into a loading bay, well, that takes real skill. The instructor let me have a go at that, using cones to represent a bay, and the results weren't pretty. But driving along a highway, anyone who can drive a stick-shift should be able to manage that ok. We'll put a few of us through about ten hours of driving lessons across a couple of days, but it's not going to be a major problem."

"I can't see us heading through any towns," said Sullivan. "Wherever we go, it can't be far. The police roadblocks are going to be in place before we've even finished unloading the planes. The authorities will know where we are and will have every route out of there cut off."

"We still have the aircraft as hostages," said Pugh. "If we can keep them in the air, the police won't dare stop us."

"Right, but we can only do that for so long, and we're going to have a whole convoy of police cars tailing each truck and likely helicopters buzzing around overhead. At some point, the aircraft are going to be out of range and be free to land. At that point, we're dead meat."

"In the movies, they have smaller trucks inside the larger ones, and a long tunnel," observed Pugh. "The police helicopter dutifully follows the now-empty large truck out of the far end of the tunnel while the crooks do a quick U-turn and tootle off with the loot in the small ones."

"In the movies, there's only the helicopter to fool," said Sullivan. "In reality, we're going to have every squad car in the state following us into the tunnel at a respectful distance."

"Well, I guess there we're dependant on Evans coming up with a rather large-scale sleight-of-hand trick!"

* * *

Joe Rossie turned the last page of the thick mugshot book, closed it and shoved it back across the table. "Nothing. How many more of these books do I have to look through?"

Foster had started him on known Triad members, moved onto other organised crime members and was now having him work through the general mugbooks of those with a history of robberies. "All of them, if necessary," he said unsympathetically. "You come to me with a story that sounds like a complete fantasy, I'm giving you the chance to substantiate it."

"I should be getting paid for my time," complained Rossie.

"You're the one claiming to have something to sell. Prove it, and you'll get paid." Foster passed the next book across the table. "Back to work."

* * *

"So how do we and 36 pallets of cash pull off a vanishing trick?" asked Sullivan.

"Magicians have been making things disappear for centuries," said Evans. "Coins, rabbits, scantily-clad assistants. But most of those things are relatively small. Coins disappear into pockets, rabbits into false-bottomed boxes, girls into trapdoors. But when you want to make something very large vanish, you have to take a different approach."

"Go on," said Sullivan.

"Houdini had a famous trick where he made a live elephant disappear on stage. The elephant was eight feet tall and weighed 6000 pounds. He had its trainer lead it into a brightly-coloured box on-stage, closed the doors and then just seconds later flung them open again to reveal an empty box. There was nowhere for it to have gone. No trapdoor system could cope with the size or weight of an elephant, and in any case the box was on wheels and the audience could see underneath it. Houdini's assistants spun it around so the audience could see all four sides. They could see above it, they could see beneath it, they could see all round it. There was literally nowhere for the elephant to have gone.

Many magicians tried to figure out the secret, none did. The trick was only finally revealed after Houdini's death. I think we need a similar approach to making our billion dollars disappear into thin air."

"And the secret?" asked Sullivan.

"Houdini's secret was remarkably simple. Ours will need a lot more thought, but the approach is right, I'm sure of it."

* * *

"I think we can rule out a life of crime as an alternative career path," said Daniels. "We've been at this for hours. We've allowed our bad guys helicopters, speedboats and, god help us, a nuclear submarine. But we're still struggling to figure out a viable way for them to make a clean getaway."

"Well," said Pritchard, "we do at least have a concrete recommendation: low-oxygen alarms and emergency oxygen cylinders for the Marines."

"Not much to show for all this time and effort, is it?"

Pritchard frowned. "I know. Come on, we need a break, let's go grab some lunch."

* * *

"I Googled the elephant trick," said Sullivan.

"That's the trouble with magic show audiences today," replied Evans, "no willingness to allow a mystery to persist. Everyone wants to know how it's done, even though all the pleasure is in the illusion rather than the mundane reality. So, what did you learn?"

"The elephant didn't disappear at all: it remained right where it was, in the box. Or, more accurately, in one half of the box. A mirror resting face-in to one of the walls was swung into a diagonal position so that when the doors were opened and the audience thought they were looking into an empty box, they were actually looking at half the box and its reflection."

"See?" responded Evans. "So much less interesting than a disappearing elephant, don't you think?"

"You may be right," replied Sullivan, "but the elephant trick helps us how?"

"Removing the money from the landing-strip is, as we all appreciate, tricky. What is needed, as I suggested when you first outlined this rather interesting project, is a little misdirection. We need to make the authorities believe the money has gone, and to have them head off on a wild goose chase following empty trucks while the money remains right where it is."

"And how do we achieve that? I somehow don't think mirrors are going to do the trick here."

"You might be surprised," said Evans. "I have a vague idea, but need to do some research."

* * *

"I think I've figured out how we get the bombs on board," said Jackson. He'd invited Pugh to join Perez, Lewis and himself because his plan would require Pugh's skills.

"I'm all ears," said Perez. "You and I both know what airbase security is like."

"Right," said Jackson, "getting in without an invitation is all but impossible, and getting anywhere near an aircraft without a very good reason to do so is totally impossible. So we need both an invitation and a very good reason."

"And how do we acquire those?" asked Lewis.

"I was remembering a time when a planned exercise had to be postponed because the manufacturer needed to make some modifications to the C-130 Hercules I was due to fly. Even with an aircraft with a long service history, there will always be occasional issues coming to light, and improved equipment which is then retro-fitted to existing aircraft. Some swap-outs are done by the base engineers using parts and instructions supplied by the manufacturer, but if it involves delving deeper into the systems than standard maintenance procedures, the manufacturers send engineers in to do it."

"So the Galaxy manufacturer could send engineers out to fit something? And we could be those engineers?" asked Lewis.

"Lockheed Martin, right," said Jackson.

"Ok, but assuming we could pull that off, surely the USAF maintenance crews oversee the work? Or at least take a close interest in what we're doing?"

"Not if the work is in the right place," said Jackson. "The avionics bay is surprisingly spacious: you could have an audience of two or three engineers down there. But there are panels in the flight-deck footwells. I've seen engineers working with their head in there, and there's no room at all there for spectators. We'll need to show them some dummy work afterwards, a circuit-board or something, but one PCB looks very much like another, right?"

"True," said Lewis. "If you can get me photos of what's in there, I could build something that's pretty much an exact match."

"Google Images," suggested Pugh. "You'd be surprised what you can find there." There had indeed been many occasions where a Google image search had provided the template he needed to forge a document.

"Ok," said Lewis, "so how do we pass ourselves off as visiting Lockheed engineers?"

"We forge some Lockheed letters advising of a component swap-out, and letting them know someone will be in touch to arrange engineer visits. Ryan, I assume you can take care of the letters?"

"Trivial," said Pugh. "We just need a sample, which ought to be as easy as dropping them a line with an enquiry about something. Then we get samples of both the letterhead and the franking marks on the envelope."

Jackson shook his head. "No, that won't work."

"Why?"

"Because this is the military, where everything happens in triplicate. When Lockheed writes to them, someone is going to write back. At the very least, someone will pick up the phone and give Lockheed a call. We need Lockheed to confirm the arrangements."

Jackson was silent for a moment. "Then that's what we need to make happen."

"Back to our fake employee plan?" asked Lewis. "Mike didn't get anywhere with the BEP, you reckon Lockheed will make any easier a target?"

"Probably not," admitted Jackson. "Defence contractors ought to be extremely secure, but we can but try."

* * *

"So your snitch didn't recognise any faces?" asked Mather.

"Nope, swears it's none of them, Triad or otherwise," confirmed Foster.

"But he's sticking to his story?"

"Can't budge him."

"So this most unlikely of heists is being planned by a bunch of complete unknowns? This is a joke. Professionals couldn't pull off this one, and this clown – no offence, sorry, I know he's one of your informers–"

"None taken."

"He wants us to believe a bunch of amateurs are behind it? Crap."

There was silence on the line for a moment.

Mather asked: "You don't think so?"

"I did at first," said Foster, "but while Rossie is a dirt-bag, and would lie to his own grandmother to save his skin, he has nothing to gain from persisting with this."

"Except the $100 a day the Secret Service is paying him," observed Mather.

"That's the thing," said Foster. "That's good money for Foster, and you'd think he'd be trying his damnedest to convince me. All he'd have to do is pick out one of the Triad mugshots and say 'maybe that one', or claim he's seen them again and learned something else, and we'd be keen to continue paying him. But he's not doing any of that. What he's offered is thinner than a piece of cigarette paper, and he knows it: that's why I'm now leaning toward believing him."

"So what do you think is going on?"

"We're assuming that if they're not known to us, they must be amateurs. But what if the opposite is true? What if they are very professional indeed?"

"Never been caught, you mean?" asked Mather.

"Exactly. There are a lot of unsolved robberies out there, including a few major ones. Some of them we don't even admit happened. If anyone were capable of pulling off something like this, successful big-time robbers who've never been caught would be top of the suspect list, wouldn't you say?"

"Maybe so," said Mather, "but I don't see how that helps us. If they're unknowns, we have nothing to go on. And frankly, I still say this whole idea is too far-fetched for me."

"You may be right," said Foster. "I'm just putting the idea out there. What you do with it is up to you."

"Fortunately, it's not," said Mather. "I'm just the middleman here. Appreciate the call, and I'll run it upstairs."

* * *

"I do have one concern about the devices," said Perez.

"Namely?" asked Lewis.

"Anti-tampering. Marines are not specialists in explosives, but they do have basic training in ordinance. From what Jackson has said about aircraft maintenance crews, they like to know what's going on aboard what they think of as their aircraft. Almost all the electronics is found on the flight-deck; messing around anywhere else in the aircraft is likely to result in curious onlookers. The flight-deck, however, is pretty cramped. If we have two or three of us in there, they'll be no space for spectators."

"So what's the problem?"

"As soon as this whole ballgame kicks off, it wouldn't take much for one of the maintenance crew to put two and two together. Aircraft are sabotaged shortly after some external engineers have worked on them: the math isn't difficult."

Lewis nodded. "And they will report that the only place we had access to is the flight-deck."

"Right," said Perez. "The flight-crew will know the places where we could have had access to the control cables, and the Marines may well decide to try finding and removing the devices. They may well be able to satisfy themselves that there are no real devices beyond the weather radar ones."

"So we may need a plan B. A second device that persuades them we mean business."

"Without downing the aircraft."

"Right. Something significant but non-catastrophic."

"Let's go talk to Scott."

* * *

Lorrimar, Pritchard and Daniels listened carefully to Mather's report.

"So what you're telling us is that the snitch hasn't offered us word one beyond his initial report but Foster now believes him?" asked Daniels.

"That would be the executive summary, yes," said Mather. "I'm no more persuaded than you are – I'm just relaying the message."

"What do you think, Luke?" asked Lorrimar.

"Skeptical still, but Foster's reasoning is sound," replied Pritchard. "The problem is what we can do with the information, if information it is. Daniels and I have reviewed flight security and haven't found any flaws to speak of. This team has supposedly met in the club once and not been seen since. We can keep the snitch on the payroll for a while, and we could stake out the place ourselves, but for how long?"

"Lean on the owner?" suggested Mather. "The snitch says they let themselves in with a key, so the owner must know who has access."

"Maybe," said Pritchard, "but that's going to tip our hand. If there is any kind of plot here, at the moment they don't know that we're onto them."

"Even if only slightly," said Daniels.

"Well, yes. But at the moment, as far as we know, all they've done is talk. A conspiracy charge isn't going to fly with what we've got so far, which is basically zilch: the word of a small-time snitch that they're talking about something crazy. We'd be laughed out of court."

"Bug the club?" asked Daniels.

Pritchard considered it. "With what we've got so far – or rather, what we don't have – it'll be a hard sell." Both men knew that long gone were the days when the Service was a law unto itself. These days, to conduct electronic surveillance, they needed a court order just like any other law-enforcement agency. The NSA might get away with it, but those guys operated by different rules; the Secret Service was a division of law enforcement so had to obey the law. A judge was likely to want to see much better evidence than they had so far.

"Maybe the stakes would swing it?" Lorrimar asked.

"Playing on that is the best hope we have," said Pritchard. "I'm not optimistic, but there's no harm in trying."

"Ok," said Daniels, "let's give it a shot."

* * *

Chung's browser picked another anonymous proxy server, this one in Johannesburg, South Africa. Jackson was there so that, if he got into the Lockheed system, Jackson could take a look at the job titles they had and pick one that seemed a reasonable bet for managing retrofitted upgrades.

"How optimistic are you?" asked Jackson.

"Not very," said Chung, "but you'd be surprised at the security holes you sometimes find in companies you'd expect to know better. This particular approach requires a sysadmin to pro-actively protect against a risk that is there by default, so all it takes is one individual to be a little lazy."

"How long before we know?" asked Jackson.

"A few minutes," said Chung. "Here goes."

He connected to www.lockheedmartin.com, hit Employees then Careers. "That's what we're after," said Chung, clicking on Job Search. Clicking in the search box, he entered:

; Select * from sys.tables

Both men watched closely. Nothing happened for several seconds, then a list of filenames was displayed, each of them ending in .sql.

"Yes!" said Chung. "Come to papa, baby!"

Jackson looked at the listing. "That's it? It's that simple?"

"That's the first stage," said Chung. "We're looking at a list of the databases on the system. Whether we can access them is another question – it all depends whether the default SQL logins have been left intact."

Chung scanned down the list of database table names. "This one looks like it could be our baby," he said, pointing to contract_staff_temp.sql. "Contractors is safer, as they don't need to be on the payroll, so we won't run into issues with money being paid with no matching budget. Contractors only get paid when they submit an invoice."

He loaded the database and waited for the login prompt. "Here goes."

In the username field, he entered:

sa

"That stands for system administrator," he said. "It's the default login for a Microsoft SQL server, with a blank password. The moment of truth ..."

He left the password field blank and hit the enter key.

Nothing happened for a moment. Then:

Host 41.134.1.1 is not allowed to access this MySQL server

"Damn," said Chung.

"What does that mean?" asked Jackson.

"It means admin access isn't allowed from an external IP address. Which is one of those good news, bad news things."

"What's the good news?"

"The good news," said Chung, "is that the default login works – otherwise it would have given a different error message."

"And the bad news?"

"The login only works from within the Lockheed network. Which means that to add our contractor, we first have to be physically plugged in to a network port somewhere inside Lockheed's headquarters."

"Sounds like a tall order," said Jackson.

"Sounds like a challenge for Young," said Chung.

* * *

Jackson thought for a moment. "Flaps," he said. "They'd still be able to safely land the plane, but a flapless landing on an aircraft that size is ... interesting. You have to come in significantly faster. It would certainly make them think twice about what might be next if they continue to interfere."

"What do we have to cut there?" asked Perez.

"Some small cables. Similar to the main flight surface control cables, but smaller in diameter."

"No problem."

"Ok," said Lewis, "then I think we have a plan. A two-part circuit. When we trigger the transmitter, it disables the weather radar. Trigger it a second time and it cuts the flaps cables. I'll start designing the circuitry."

* * *

"You've got to be kidding me," said Judge Harry Brooks when Pritchard finished his brief summary. "You believe there's a conspiracy to steal – what, how much are we talking about?"

"It depends when and how they hit," said Daniels, "but if they somehow hit all twelve aircraft, then typically around $600-700 million."

"More than a billion if they wait for the new $50 bill," added Pritchard.

"You think someone's going to try to steal a billion dollars? A billion dollars that's probably better protected that the president."

"I appreciate that it sounds far-fetched–" began Pritchard.

"That is an understatement of truly mind-boggling proportions," interrupted Brooks.

"Frankly I don't believe it either," continued Pritchard.

Daniels gave him a hard look: this was hard enough already without telling the judge that you thought it was a fantasy.

"But our job," said Pritchard, "is to think of the worst possible case, and assume it will happen. All we're asking for here is the chance to evaluate the intelligence, nothing more."

"Intelligence," repeated the judge, picking up the single piece of paper the agents had offered him. "The word of a small-time snitch whose previous all-time record was a $26k drugs deal. You now expect me to believe he's privy to a billion dollar heist?"

"No, your honour," said Pritchard, "you don't have to believe it, you only have to consider it sufficient grounds to justify electronic surveillance."

Daniels faced the judge. "He may have been small-time so far, your honour, but he hears what he hears. Maybe it is horse-shit, but we can't afford to take the chance of assuming that. All we're asking for here is the opportunity to find out."

"And there is the Chinese hack attempt too," said Pritchard.

"The one that got nowhere," asked Brooks, "and which you have no evidence is remotely connected to your snitch's claims?"

"We're trying to gather that evidence, Judge."

"This nightclub," asked Brooks, "what's the capacity?"

Daniels referred to his notes. "According to city records, it's fire-rated for 550 people."

"And how long do you propose to have these bugs in place?"

"We don't know," said Pritchard. "However long it takes them to come back. Could be tomorrow, could be in a month's time."

"Let's assume two weeks," said Brooks. "550 people a night for 14 days ..." the judge tapped on his desk calculator, "... you're potentially bugging the conversations of nearly 8000 people."

"We're not interested in the conversations people are having while the club is open, your honour."

"Maybe not, but you'd still be intercepting them. Look, you know my record, it's why you chose me rather than some other judge. I'm a realist, and I know we can't catch the bad guys without getting our hands dirty sometimes. But this ... what you're asking for is to infringe the civil liberties of thousands of people for an unknown time-frame on the word of a piece of street trash." Brooks paused. "No, I'm sorry, you're going to have to come back to me with more than this."

"So now what?" asked Daniels as they walked down the courthouse corridor.

This was high-stakes poker, thought Pritchard. They either needed to fold – to write-off the intelligence as non-credible – or to go all-in. It wasn't an easy decision. If it did turn out to be nonsense, they could waste an enormous amount of resources on a wild-goose chase. Resources that were badly needed elsewhere. On the other hand, if it turned out to be real and they did nothing ...

But there are what-ifs in any operation. Much as you'd like to apply the precautionary principle to every possibility, it simply isn't practical. You just have to balance out risks against resources and make the most intelligent decisions you can.

"We just have to hope our snitch comes up with something concrete that we can take back to the judge, otherwise we're going to have to call the whole thing off."

* * *

Nightclubs were depressing places in daylight, thought Sullivan, as she walked in. Take away the darkness, the music, the coloured lights and of course the alcohol, and far, far fewer people would get laid.

The team arrived in ones and twos, over a 15-minute period. The mood seemed more optimistic, she thought. There was more energy in the room. They might not yet believe it, but they were fully engaged in the idea of it – and that was the all-important thing at this stage of the game.

"So," she asked, "where are we at with our six problems? Executive summaries first, then we'll go into details. Let's start with problem 1, diverting the aircraft."

Lewis spoke up: "We think we have the beginnings of a plan there. There's a lot more research to be done before we'll know how feasible it will be, but let's call it a possibility for now."

"Great!" said Sullivan. "A possibility is good progress for this stage."

She turned to Jackson. "Problem 2, a landing strip?"

"Well," said Jackson, "I can't quite reduce it to an executive summary yet, as I need to let you know my thinking."

"Go ahead."

"The landing roll for a fully-loaded C-5 is 3,600 feet," said Jackson. "The take-off roll is 8,400 feet. So, given that we do want to get them back into the air to get the Marines out of our hair, that means we need a pretty big strip. Now, C-5s are designed to land on dirt strips, so in theory we don't need an actual air-strip, just a big piece of flat ground."

"Like a chunk of desert?" asked Sullivan.

"Yep. But that idea worries me."

"Why so?"

"With unpaved runway, there's always a chance of blowing a tyre or worse, damaging the landing-gear. We're landing twelve aircraft. If one of them blows a couple of tyres on landing and can't take-off again, that leaves a bunch of Marines on the ground with us."

"That wouldn't be good."

"Not good at all," chipped in Perez.

Back in the store-room, Rossie was struggling to hear them through the tiny crack of open door. He eased the door open a touch more, and the bottom of the door knocked against something.

"What was that?" asked Lewis.

"What was what?" asked Sullivan.

"I thought I heard a noise, over there." She gesture toward the far side of the dance floor.

Perez gestured to Jackson, and the two of them began quietly making their way across the floor.

Rossie had to think fast. He eased the door shut, and looked around. There was a crate of empty beer bottles next to the door. He grabbed one of them and placed it on the floor next to a chair. He grabbed two more and put them sideways on the chair. He then crept towards the back of the storeroom.

Jackson ducked quickly behind the bar. No sign of anyone. Perez made his way toward the two doors on the far wall. One had a men's restroom sign on it, the other simply said 'No entry'. Jackson had come round from the bar. Perez pointed to the restroom door and put a finger to his lips. Jackson nodded. Perez eased back the restroom door and the two entered quietly. Perez ducked to look beneath the two cubicle doors, then stood up again. He held up three fingers to Jackson. Jackson again nodded. Two fingers. One finger. Now!

Both men hit the cubicle doors hard with their shoulders. The doors banged back against the sides. Empty.

There was no point now in stealth. They exited the restroom, walked up to the door with the 'No entry' sign. Perez turned the handle and eased it open a fraction, then let go as Jackson kicked it hard. The door flew inwards. Perez reached round, feeling for light switches. He found them and snapped the lights on. They looked around. Boxes of drinks, crates of empties, some chairs, and a set of folded tables at the back of the room. No sign of anyone.

Perez picked up the bottle on the floor, and looked at the others on the chair next to it. "Looks like that's the culprit," he said. Jackson looked round the room suspiciously, then nodded.

They switched off the lights, closed the door behind them and walked back to the others.

"False-alarm," said Perez, "just a beer bottle that rolled off a chair."

Behind the folded tables at the rear of the storeroom, Rossie couldn't hear anything but the pounding of his heart. Jesus, that had been close! With the door closed, and him right at the back of the room, he couldn't hear a thing now, but he wasn't going to move until they'd left. He had enough, anyway! He now knew their plan!

"Ok," said Sullivan, "so unpaved runway is dangerous. So we need a disused airfield?"

"Right," said Jackson. There's no shortage of those, but the runways at small airfields aren't nearly long enough. We're talking regional airport length or better, and that's much harder. There aren't too many disused regionals with their runways intact: they are by definition near population centres, so most of them have been turned into business parks or shopping centres. Our best bet is likely to be an abandoned air force base, but I need to do some web-searches to find a suitable prospect."

"If I may interject," said Evans. Sullivan nodded. "I've been giving some thought to our disappearing act, and my best idea to date has a very specific site requirement."

"Ok," said Sullivan, "then you two liaise." She continued: "Problem three: dealing with the Marines."

"That one may not be too tricky," said Perez. "Our plan to force the Galaxies down is to threaten to crash them. We'll have some devices on board, some real, some fake, to convince them we're able to do just that. So: force them to land one at a time. Offload the cash, have them take-off again. That way, we only have twelve Marines to worry about at any one time, and all the other aircraft in the air act as hostages. The Marines are going to believe that if they misbehave, we can crash the rest of the aircraft."

"Sounds reasonable," said Sullivan.

"It also takes care of the F-16s," said Lewis, "at least for a while. They can't attack us while the Galaxies are in the air."

"Right," said Jackson, "but not for long. The moment they can, they're going to get the Galaxies on the ground and the F-16s are then going to be free to strike."

"Landing the Galaxies one at a time will slow things up, won't it?" asked Lewis.

"Somewhat," said Perez, "but that can't be helped. Our escape plan has to be imaginative, we know that."

"How long do you think we have after the last Galaxy takes off?" asked Sullivan.

"Minutes," said Jackson, "no more. As soon as they're out of sight, they're going to put down on the first bit of flat desert they can find."

"Ok, so we need to make good our escape within minutes," said Sullivan. "That sounds like an ... interesting challenge!"

"Well, strictly speaking we need to disappear within minutes," said Evans. "That may not be the same thing as escaping."

"How so?" asked Perez.

"It all depends how we do the disappearing act," he said. "We may merely appear to disappear while remaining right where we are."

"Like the elephant," said Sullivan.

"Like the elephant," confirmed Evans. "Meantime, we just need to give the police something to chase."

Evans briefly outlined his thinking.

"That sounds fine as a starting-point," said Perez, "but we can't remain where we are for long. Yes, the police will go follow the trucks, but you can bet that they're also going to move in to the landing-strip and go over the place with a fine tooth-comb. If we're still there, they're going to find us."

"Ok," said Sullivan, "it sounds like the beginning of a plan, so let's leave that one with you for now. Which brings us to the small matter of problem six."

"Laundering the cash," said Young.

"A billion in sequentially-numbered fifty dollar bills," said Pugh.

"Twenty-odd million sequentially-numbered bills," said Lewis.

"Yes," said Sullivan.

"And do we have any bright ideas?" asked Chung.

"None at all," said Young, cheerfully.

"Excellent," said Lewis.

"Well, that's something for me and Young to work on," said Sullivan. "Ok, then, to summarise. Diverting the aircraft: we have a possible solution. Landing strip: Jackson and Evans will investigate options. Dealing with the Marines: we have a solid plan. Dealing with the F-16s: same thing, but only for a matter of minutes. Making good our escape: Evans has the beginnings of a plan. Laundering the cash: well, let's call it day zero on coming up with a plan for that. Alright, what details do we need to discuss at this stage?"

"Well," said Jackson, "part of our plan requires us getting access to Lockheed HQ, and doing so in such a way that we can connect to their network while we're there ..."

The rest of the discussions took quarter of an hour.

"Anything else?" asked Sullivan.

Shakes of heads.

"Ok. Then this is the stage at which we turn possible ideas into concrete plans. Let's aim for the next review in a fortnight. By that stage, I'd like us to have sufficient hard information on the feasibility of those plans that we can make a go/no-go decision."

The team filtered out of the club in ones and twos.

I am definitely not being paid enough for this, thought Rossie, as he finally decided they were gone and eased himself out from behind the folded tables. Anyone planning to steal a billion dollars wasn't going to hesitate to deal decisively with anyone eavesdropping on their plans. He was going straight to Detective Foster to tell him what he'd learned and ask for a payoff.

* * *

"Ok," said Lieutenant Mather, "now your informant really has lost it."

"He seems pretty convinced that's what he heard," said Detective Foster.

"First, they're going to hit the BEP, and now they're going to do it by hijacking military aircraft. Highly-secured military aircraft departing from a US Air Force base, filled with Marines and with F-16s for company."

"That's what he says he heard."

"And you still believe him," asked Mather, "even with this little twist?"

"Well," said Foster, "you know a lot more than I do about the security arrangements–"

"I do," said Mather, "and I'm telling you it's impossible. No, not just impossible, it's laughable."

"You don't hear me arguing," said Foster, "but I have just one question."

"What's that?"

"A hundred bucks a day is decent money to Rossie. Why would he come to me with a story he knows sounds ridiculous, rather than milk this for as long as he can with something more plausible?"

"Has he asked for a bonus for the so-called information he's delivered?" asked Mather.

"Well, yes," admitted Foster. "But he knows he's not going to get it unless this checks out."

Mather had to admit he couldn't answer that one. "Ok," he said, "leave it with me."

"Gladly," said Foster.

"Damn!" said Pritchard when Mather relayed the news. "If they'd okayed the surveillance, we'd at least know whether the meeting was fact or fantasy."

"The content of the meeting sure as hell sounds like fantasy," said Daniels.

"To me too," said Mather, "but I have to admit Foster's question is a damn good one: why would his snitch throw away a hundred bucks a day?"

"That is a bit of a mystery, I agree."

"We should at least take this to Major Timpkins," said Lorrimar.

"Have you met him?" asked Daniels.

"I have," said Lorrimar.

"Are you volunteering to make the call?" asked Daniels. "I don't imagine he's going to be too impressed."

"I'll make the call," said Pritchard. "However unlikely it seems, we have to cover all the bases, and Mather and Foster are right: the snitch's behaviour makes no sense if this is just a scam. Somehow, in some way, there has to be something behind this."

"Maybe the gang the snitch heard are just fantasists," suggested Mather.

"Maybe so," said Pritchard. "Anyway, Timpkins is in charge of the air shipment, so I'll talk with him and we'll take things from there."

Major Timpkins listened politely as Pritchard outlined the story over the phone.

"You've made the flight yourself, Mr Pritchard. You've seen the security arrangements both at the base and in the air. You also know that the aircraft are all subjected to thorough searches before the convoy arrives, the first by the aircraft engineers who know those aircraft intimately, the second by the Marines who will be flying on them. Can you see any conceivable way in which anyone can attack those aircraft?"

"No," said Pritchard frankly. He decided not to mention the rogue pilot idea: he was already tacitly suggesting that Timpkins had less than perfect security by raising the idea of a hijacking; he didn't want to compound the offence by impugning his flight crews. "But I'm in the Just Suppose business. So just suppose there's something we've all missed."

"We can suppose that aliens from outer space materialise on the flight-deck, Mr Pritchard. How does this help us?"

"I don't know," admitted Pritchard, "but this is a potential threat that we are at least starting to credit with some small possibility of turning out to be real, so I felt you had a right to know about it."

"Passing the buck," said Timpkins.

"Major Tim–" began Pritchard.

"Forgive me, Mr Pritchard," said Timpkins quickly. "A lifetime of operating in a military environment where buck-passing is a full-time occupation for all too many. You don't strike me as the kind of man who would simply shrug and hand over responsibility. I apologise."

"Gladly accepted, Major. And no: I'm not trying to hand over responsibility to you. Believe me, I'd like nothing better than to figure out some way this could be done, and to play my part in preventing it. That's why we're here."

"Understood," said Timpkins. "So ok, let's suppose that the aircraft could somehow be forced down somewhere. That doesn't address the F-16s. Those are single-seater, so no hijack potential there. And even if we assume that the hostiles could somehow take the F-16s out of the picture, that leaves the aircraft on the ground defended by a full squad of Marines. You've met them, Mr Pritchard, but let me tell you a little about Marines."

Pritchard didn't need to be told about Marines, but he allowed Timpkins to speak.

"In Afghanistan, there was an enemy contact known as the Battle of Shewan. Two squads of Marines, that's 26 men, were ambushed by over 300 Taliban fighters armed with everything from light machine-guns to rocket-propelled grenades and 82mm mortars. The Marines prevailed. Over 150 Taliban deaths, and not a single marine fatality. That was in hostile territory controlled by the enemy. Here we're talking about US soil in an operation controlled from start to finish by us."

Pritchard hesitated. Given Timpkins' contrite attitude a few moments ago, perhaps he could raise the rogue pilot idea ...

"Major," he began, "you were kind enough to apologise when you believed you had offended me. Perhaps you will allow me to do so in advance if the scenario I'm going to suggest to you causes offence?"

Timpkins chuckled. "Let's say you get a free pass. Shoot."

Pritchard succinctly outlined the rogue pilot and oxygen starvation idea for taking the Marines out of the picture.

"I'd stake my life on the integrity of any of my flight crew," said Timpkins.

"I understand. We both operate in an environment where we quite literally place our lives in the hands of our colleagues, and it's a terrible thought that any one of them might ever betray that trust. All the same, it does happen on occasion."

Timpkins sighed. "Yes," he said, "it does. So what do you propose as a safeguard?"

Pritchard outlined his proposal for low-oxygen sensors and emergency canisters for the Marines, then hesitated before adding: "The flight crew has side-arms, I saw," said Pritchard.

"They do, along with a fire-axe – but I suppose a pistol is a faster and more reliable way to take out three other crew members." Timpkins paused. "I don't like the idea of leaving any of my men unarmed–"

"I do fully appreciate that, Major. Believe me, leaving my P229 behind at the BEP was a very uncomfortable feeling."

"Usually a side-arm is a final level of protection for officers who may be downed in enemy territory, but this is a different type of operation, so perhaps that would be a reasonable precaution in these circumstances. The oxygen, I agree."

"It's all we've been able to think of to add to your incredibly thorough security arrangements, Major – and that's not flattery!"

"I appreciate the comments all the same, Mr Pritchard. Leave it with me."

* * *

"Walk me through what you need," said Young.

"I need to get inside the Lockheed Martin HQ building," said Chung. "Then, while I'm in there, I need to plug my laptop into an Ethernet port."

"For how long?" asked Young.

"Long enough to create a contractor record in the HR database. Maybe 15-20 minutes."

"And to have no Lockheed staff looking over your shoulder while you do it, presumably."

"Right," said Chung.

"You don't want much, do you?"

"Well, I could do with Jackson alongside me."

"Ok," said Young, "give me a few days."

"You can do that?" asked Chung.

"I think so."

"How?"

"I'll let you know once I've arranged it."

* * *

"So what is the special requirement you had in mind for the landing site, Aaron?" asked Jackson.

"Let me start by describing the illusion," said Evans, "what the authorities will see."

"Ok."

"When each aircraft lands, we will direct it to taxi up close to a parked semi. We'll stop the aircraft say 2-300 feet away from the truck. We use a forklift truck to transfer the pallets from the aircraft to the truck. We're in full view of the flight crew and marines: they watch us load up the truck. We can also assume that by the time the aircraft are on the ground, there will be some discreet aerial surveillance in place, who will also watch the cash go from the plane to the truck."

"Alright."

"Before the plane takes off," said Evans, "they will see the loaded truck drive to the gates and park up there ready to roll. We repeat the process with each aircraft: 12 aircraft, 12 trucks. The authorities have watched the cash get loaded into each truck, and the trucks have never left their sight. So long as the trucks remain parked in full sight, the authorities are going to imagine they know exactly where the money is."

"Since you describe this as the illusion," said Jackson, "I assume that this is not what actually happens."

"Correct. which is where my special requirement comes in: we need a landing zone with one or more tunnels running beneath it. We have Perez blow a hole down into one of these tunnels, covering it with a camouflaged sheet of some kind so it can't be detected from the air. The trucks have a large hole in the trailer bed, and are equipped with a frame and pulley system. While the forklift goes back to the aircraft to pick up the next pallet, the previous one is lowered into the tunnel. By the time the truck moves away to its parked position, it is empty."

"But semis sit pretty high," objected Jackson. "The Marines on the ground are going to be able to see underneath it. Anything lowered through the trailer bed is going to be spotted immediately."

Evans smiled. "They'll think they can see beneath the truck. Each of them will be fitted with a flip-down panel on the underside with a high-resolution photo of the view beneath the truck. We'll choose the truck parking position carefully so the background is pretty uniform."

"Can a photo really look convincing enough to be mistaken for the real thing when it's only a few hundred feet away?" asked Jackson.

"Sure. The beauty of any illusion is that your audience are willing accomplices."

"I somehow don't quite see the marines in that light."

"But they are," said Evans. "It's a human trait: people see what they expect to see. When you look at a truck, you expect to be able to see under it to whatever is on the far side, and so when we present them with the exact view they expect to see, they don't think twice about it."

Jackson could see that. "Ok, so we want an airforce base with a tunnel running underneath it somewhere."

Evans nodded. "Which I assume is not a trivial requirement? I did a bit of googling, and initially it seemed that tunnels beneath an Air Force base are not uncommon, but pretty much every website I found talking about tunnels under airbases turned out to be conspiracy theorists going on about networks of secret underground tunnels criss-crossing the country. Area 51 type stuff. So I'm assuming that tunnels beneath Air Force bases are a myth?"

"Well, most airbases have underground storage and a few service tunnels. Where the conspiracy nuts lose touch with reality is that those tunnels are purely local to the base, they don't go anywhere. None of them will go beyond the boundary of the base. So yes, we can easily find one with a shallow tunnel we could drill into to take care of the initial disappearance of the cash, but it isn't going to enable us to escape. So that leaves us and a billion dollars sitting in a tunnel with perhaps ten minutes before the aircraft are safely on the ground and the authorities come storming in. Even if they believe the money is in the trucks, they're going to take the base apart brick-by-brick in the search for clues."

"Succinctly put," said Evans. "But one problem at a time."

* * *

"The best way to follow someone," Young had explained to Sullivan earlier, "is to figure out where they're going and get there before them."

"Sounds like a neat trick if you can pull it off," said Sullivan.

"It's easier in this case, as I don't have a single target in mind – any Lockheed employee still wearing their pass will do."

"Let's hope you have more luck tonight."

This bar was Young's second attempt. He'd scouted out three bars within easy walking distance of the Lockheed building, figuring that some staff were bound to go for drinks after work. Rather than trail somebody, the idea was to hang out in the bar and wait for some employees to come to him. The first night had, however, been a bust: despite waiting in the bar from 4.30pm to 6.30pm, not a single employee wearing a pass had come in. This evening he was heading for bar number two. If that didn't work, he'd have to switch to the riskier tactic of following someone.

Young had already done the ten minutes of preparation required while wandering around a nearby shopping mall; he was all set.

He was on his third soda when two men and a woman walked in. Young could see the Lockheed Martin pass on a lanyard around the neck of the woman, and another clipped to the belt of one of the men. Easy.

He watched the three walk to the back of the bar and sit at a table. Damn: too far away. High-resolution cameras in smartphones meant you didn't need to get particularly close, you could always crop in later, but he needed to be closer than this.

There were several ways to pull this off, and Young had used all of them at one time or another. A simple but time-consuming one with a larger group was to get chatting to them, posing as a guy from out of town, there on his own and bored. Befriend them, chat for a couple of hours, then once everyone was well-lubricated, hand his cameraphone to someone and ask them to take a group photo as a souvenir. But while a stranger could attach himself to a larger group, especially after they'd had a few drinks, that wouldn't work with a group of three.

Another tactic was to go there as a couple, pretending to take a photo of his 'date' while actually focusing on the people behind her.

But he hadn't seen the need to involve anyone else on this occasion. It was a simple assignment, and he'd simply aim to take the photo discreetly. With flash and shutter sounds switched off, you could take a photo while appearing to check your email or play with an app.

Stage 1 was to buy another drink so he could move to a closer table without it being obvious that he was switching tables.

* * *

One block away, in the Lockheed building, a meeting was just starting.

"Sorry I could only meet at the end of the day," said the 50-something guy with short white hair and a military bearing. "Year-end stuff."

"I thought it was only finance staff who had year-end workloads," said the red-headed woman in her 30s, "not security staff?"

"Oh, they keep us busy too. New pass designs each financial year, for example." He passed one across the table. "The first batch had some issue with the RFID chips so we had to get replacements from the supplier. The new ones are due to be distributed on Monday and the old ones cease to work one week later, so it's been entertaining."

The woman picked one up and turned it over. "Quite a different design."

"Yeah, makes it easy for security staff to tell them apart at a glance. Anyway, to business: you wanted to talk about the launch event?"

* * *

Young pretended to play with his phone while discreetly watching the three Lockheed staff who were now just three tables away. About 15 feet.

So much of this stuff was balancing acts, he thought: in an ideal world, you always waited until they were on their second drink and had relaxed into the place. By that stage, people were less aware of the people around them. But there was always the risk that they'd only popped in for a quick drink, so the opportunity could be lost.

There were often clues. People settling in for the evening tended to spread out more: they found places to put their bags, jackets were taken off and there was a relaxed body-language to those who were there for the evening.

These three weren't giving off those signs. The woman's handbag was still on the table, the mens' jackets were still on. This was going to be a quick drink.

Young slipped his smartphone out of his pocket, selected the photo directory he wanted then opened the camera app.

He had a good view of the woman's pass hanging round her neck. Now he just needed to wait until they were engaged in close conversation and take two quick photos.

He didn't have long to wait. the woman said something and both men laughed. He held the camera at table height. Accuracy of framing wasn't important – so long as it was pointed in the right direction it would capture enough to include the three. He fired off a quick shot, made a small adjustment and then took a second one.

Acting as if he was checking his email, he then viewed the two photos. He zoomed in on the first: yes, a good enough view of the badge. He zoomed in on the second. That was good enough too. Job done. He slipped his phone back into his pocket, finished his drink and stood up.

As he turned for the exit, he felt a hand on his shoulder. It was one of the Lockheed men.

"Excuse me," he said, "my colleague said you just took a photo of us. Care to explain?" The man's tone was mild enough, and he was not showing any overt signs of aggression. All the same, he gave Young the clear impression that this wasn't something he could simply shrug off: the man wasn't going to let it go unless he got a satisfactory answer.

Young smiled at him. "Sorry," he said, "I was trying not to disturb you."

"So what's your game?"

"This." He pulled out his phone and showed it to the man. It still showed the zoomed-in view of the first photo he'd taken.

"Her bag?"

"Yeah, it's my wife's birthday next week and she has this battered old handbag she carries everywhere. I want to buy her a new one but I'm damned if I know what style. I've been looking in stores and also taking photos of other bags I see around for ideas. Look ..."

He flicked back through the photos he'd taken in the shopping mall. There were bags on display in stores, and other bags carried by shoppers.

"Oh, I see." The man had visibly relaxed.

"Sorry if I freaked you out," said Sullivan.

The man smiled. "No worries."

Young would delete the directory of bag photos later, along with the other photos he'd taken of jackets and ties.

* * *

"I've come up with an additional security measure," said Daniels.

"Wow," replied Pritchard.

"I know, it's a miracle."

"So don't keep me in suspense."

"Trackers hidden in the cash," said Daniels. "That way, if the worst happens, and someone does somehow get their hands on the cash, we'll know exactly where it is at all times."

Pritchard considered it. "I like it. Just one problem I can see: the packaging of the bills is 100% automated, so that's going to require modifications to the printing press machinery. I'm sure it can be done, but it's probably not something that can be done quickly. And I'd like it done quickly."

"This snitch business really is making you nervous, isn't it."

"Somewhat," admitted Pritchard. "I can't for the life of me see how anyone could pull it off, but at the same time I can't quite bring myself to dismiss it out of hand."

Daniels nodded. "Yeah, I know what you mean. Ok, if we can't get trackers added to the cash quickly, let's embed them in the pallets."

"But those will be dumped."

"Not quickly," argued Daniels. "We're talking about one hundred million bills here: you don't tip that into a few sports bags. The only way to transport that much cash is on trucks, and keeping the bills shrink-wrapped on their pallets is going to be the only practical way to shift it quickly. We ought to be able to follow the cash to wherever they split it, and that's going to take them time."

"Giving us time to move in on them."

"Right."

Pritchard nodded. "Ok, I'll talk to Lorrimar and get it organised."

* * *

Pugh handed over the two Lockheed Martin passes to Young. Young looked them over carefully. They looked perfect. Each bore a different photo, one bearing a superficial resemblance to Jackson, the other to Chung. That was SOP: you never used your own photo on any documentation, just in case it fell into the hands of the authorities. Nobody's pass photo looked like them anyway, you just wanted something that looked close enough. A Google images search based on the description usually did the trick.

"Remember," said Pugh, "these are visual replicas only. They'll pass a casual inspection, but with only a photo to go on, I don't know how they should feel. A detailed inspection is likely to reveal flaws."

"That's fine," Young assured him, "these will only be seen at a distance."

"I still don't see how these help. There's no RFID chip, so they won't operate the security gates to get you in."

Young smiled. "It's all in hand. I'll tell you about it afterwards." He put the passes in his bag. "Thanks for these."

* * *

Jackson had spent hours on the web, researching closed USAF bases. More than 350 bases were closed as part of the Base Realignment and Closure (BRAC) Commission set up to look into airbase needs in a post-Cold War world. Trawling through the list brought back painful memories of his own forced retirement from military flying.

Some of the bases had been converted to civilian airports. Others had been sold off to developers and were now shopping malls, business parks, industrial estates or housing. Very few of them were laying unused with their runways intact.

Jackson had been surprised to find that it was ex-WW2 airbases that were most likely to have survived largely intact. So many had been built, and in those days no attention was paid to the niceties of modern construction. Many of the sites were classified as contaminated by pollutants which would make them expensive to build on, so they sat wasting away, weeds growing through the cracks in their runways, wooden hangers slowly rotting, control towers with broken glass and rusting metal stairways.

He'd even found a website dedicated to then-and-now photos of them. He'd identified one just 20 miles outside the centre of Fort Worth. He showed the photos to Sullivan.

"Hicks Field," he said.

"I thought that was the airfield you flew from when we did the surveillance?" said Sullivan.

"Nearly. That was Hicks Airfield; the ex-WW2 base is just Hicks Field. They're just a few miles apart."

"Why did they build a new airfield when there was one there already?"

"I'm guessing contamination – that seems to be the main reason the old bases were abandoned. Lead, asbestos, you name it – no-one worried about any of that kind of stuff when these things were built, and land is not expensive there. Cheaper to start from scratch than be responsible for the safe disposal of waste from an existing base."

"Right," said Sullivan. "And you think this one might be suitable."

"It looks like it," he said, "and it does have one rather delicious irony."

"What's that?"

"It's literally four miles from the BEP. We'd be taking the money from right under their noses!"

"You're crazy," said Sullivan, "anyone ever tell you that?"

"Yep," said Jackson.

"I must say I'd feel comfortable with a more isolated location."

"It's swings and roundabouts," said Jackson. "An isolated landing site feels safer, but actually makes surveillance easier for the authorities. Something closer to a city gives us more scope to vanish."

"What about Evans' special requirements – does it meet those?"

"I'm still researching, but yes, I think it may."

* * *

"These are the trackers?" asked Lorrimar, accepting one of the matchbox-sized black boxes from Daniels.

"Yep," said Daniels. "Beautiful little things."

"They are certainly impressively small."

"But with more technology packed in there than you would believe."

"Try me," she said.

"It contains four different tracking systems," said Daniels. "GPS, GSM, Wifi and VHF."

"Go on."

"GPS is the most accurate, but the signals are weak. Really it wants line-of-sight to satellites, certainly very minimal obstructions. It sometimes works inside a curtain-sided or light-panelled truck, but definitely not a metal truck. GSM is the crudest of the four: it simply reports the signal strength of all the mobile phone masts within range, and from that we can calculate a rough triangulation of its position. Accurate only to a few hundred yards, but it will continue to pick up signals long after GPS has given up the ghost."

"Ok," said Lorrimar, "and the others?"

"Wifi is also relatively crude, again working on triangulation, but wifi signals have a much, much shorter range than cellular ones, so it narrows down the position to a much smaller area. Typically one to two hundred feet."

"I assume the government has a database of hotspots used for that?"

Daniels grinned: "Actually, it was data collected by Google's Street View cars."

"Wasn't that found to be illegal, and they had to delete it?" asked Lorrimar.

"Yes," said Daniels, "but not before the NSA grabbed a copy of the database."

"I should have guessed," said Lorrimar. "And VHF?"

"Very short range, but very accurate. It's used for direction-finding when we get close. Again, a private enterprise solution developed to track stolen cars: the company charges car owners a fee to fit the tracking devices, and an annual subscription for service, then provides police departments with free detectors for their patrol vehicles. So we use the other systems to get the SWAT teams to the right area, then the VHF system points us right to the building."

"How long will it take to prepare the finished pallets?" asked Lorrimar.

"They'll be here at 9am tomorrow," said Daniels.

"You guys don't hang around!"

"We try not to."

* * *

Lewis too had been working on designing small gadgets – the radio receivers that would be used to trigger the small explosions on board the Galaxies – and she too was very much focused on range. Building a small radio receiver with decent line-of-sight range wasn't difficult. But they wouldn't have line-of-sight. The units would be buried somewhere deep within the innards of the aircraft, and how much shielding would be created by the fuselage, insulation, other equipment and wiring was the first big unknown in the equation.

Adding greater range wasn't difficult, but each step up in range required more power. The greater the power, the bigger the battery and the larger the complete unit would be.

Which brought her to the second big unknown: how long would the unit need to remain powered? At this stage, they didn't know when they would be able to fit the units or when D-Day would be. Lewis didn't like unknowns.

Could she tap into the aircraft power, she wondered? That would solve all the power requirements, enabling a long-range receiver to be fitted into a small box. But there were two big drawbacks. The first was complexity of installation. They'd have to piggy-back off one of the existing bits of electronics, and to do so in a way that didn't interfere with it. She'd have to strip a section of power cable, wire in her feed and make the whole thing neat enough that it wouldn't be spotted. That was going to take time, and she had no wish to spend any longer on the installation than was absolutely necessary.

The second drawback was the risk of detection. If the piece of equipment she chose to piggyback off developed a fault, or was due for replacement, the additional wire leading out of it was going to be spotted as soon as they went to remove it. It was too risky. It would need to be battery-powered. She could design it to have a low-powered standby mode until woken up by a signal from their transmitter, but it was still only going to remain powered for a finite time. With that time unknown, she was simply going to have to make some guesses. She hated guesses.

* * *

"Did you fly any Lockheed Martin aircraft in your time in the USAF?" asked Young.

"Sure," said Jackson, "C-130s."

"Are they still in use in the Air Force now?"

"Hundreds of 'em," said Jackson, "and they're still in production today – why?"

Young explained what he needed.

"I think I could manage that," said Jackson.

Jackson listened and nodded.

"It doesn't need to be more than superficially convincing," said Young. "They can dismiss it immediately, we just need them to be convinced that you believe what you're saying."

"I'm sure I can manage that," said Jackson.

"Great. I'll try to get us an appointment in the next couple of days."

Young had lost count of the number of identities he'd assumed over the years. Sometimes you needed deep cover – an identity you would maintain for an extended time and which would stand up to significant scrutiny. At the other end of the scale, sometimes all you needed was a business card and an identity which would last a few minutes in the face of no scrutiny at all. This requirement was more towards the latter end of the scale. Pugh had produced a couple of business cards, Chung had created a web domain and one-page website with email address, and Young had purchased a Skype-in number with a suitable voicemail message; the whole thing had been done in one day.

He'd expected to be passed around from person to person when he called Lockheed, and he wasn't disappointed, but finally he reached a project administrator on the C-130 team.

"Good afternoon, Mr Cooper, my name is Colin Deft. Would you be the right person to talk to about a safety concern with the C-130?"

"You can certainly talk to me about your concerns, Mr Deft. You are calling from … ?"

"Deft and Wilcott. I'm a lawyer representing a serving USAF pilot who flies C-130s. There's a safety flaw in the C-130 that he and his fellow pilots have been concerned about for some time. The USAF has promised on several occasions to raise it with Lockheed, but nothing seems to have been done, and he's concerned that nothing will be done until there is a crash."

"What is the concern regarding, Mr Deft?"

"To tell you the truth, Mr Cooper, it's all a bit technical for me. I'm a lawyer, not an aircraft engineer. Give me a nice arcane piece of tort law, and I'm your man, but where aircraft are concerned my knowledge pretty much extends to being able to tell the pointy bit from the tail."

Cooper chuckled politely. "Well, I'm not an aircraft engineer either, but I should be able to follow the basics." In truth, he might understand little more than the lawyer, but his job was simply to see whether this was a crank or a credible source. If the pilot seemed credible when they met, he would pass it upstairs to one of the engineers.

"So what I'd like to do is bring my client in to see you," said Young, "to brief you on the flaw."

The C-130 had been in production since 1957 in one variant or another, mused Cooper. He was skeptical about any safety flaw that could remain undetected in an aircraft design that had remained fundamentally unchanged for decades, but when someone credible makes that kind of claim, you have to at least listen to what they have to say.

"I'd be happy to meet with him, Mr Deft, but I'm unsure why he needs a lawyer present?"

"He's concerned about bypassing the military hierarchy, Mr Cooper. That sort of thing tends to be frowned upon in the Air Force. So he would like to remain anonymous, and to have your assurance that should his identity somehow become known to you, that you will protect his confidentiality."

"Well, it's a little unusual, but I don't see any reason for that to pose any difficulties," said Cooper.

"Excellent. It's a little short notice, but would sometime tomorrow afternoon work for you?"

"Let me check my diary ... would 3pm be convenient?"

"That's perfect. I have a new associate working with me, would you mind if I brought him along?"

"No problem," said Cooper.

"That's great, we'll look forward to seeing you then."

* * *

"Hello?" said Evans, as he answered his phone.

"It's Jackson. I've been looking into the tunnel issue, and I think I've hit on something."

"Tell me."

"Mains water pipes."

"Aren't those pretty small?" asked Evans.

"Most of them, yes – between 8 and 16 inches in diameter. But high-volume feeds are up to eight feet in diameter. One of the places that get the high-volume feeds are airports and Air Force bases, partly due to their high water usage and partly to feed the fire-trucks."

"So that's a 96-inch diameter pipe, and a pallet is 48 inches x 40 inches ... so room to spare."

"Right," said Jackson. "I'm thinking we could rig up some kind of electric tow vehicles with trailers – like airport baggage carts. Possibly not even like airport baggage carts, but actual ones."

"This is sounding feasible," said Evans, "but is an old WW2 airbase big enough to qualify for that kind of high-volume feed?"

"That's the $64,000 question. Or should I say the billion dollar question. I haven't been able to find out."

"And if it is there, will it still be full of water?"

"I'm assuming not," said Jackson, "since it's currently disused, but that would be another excellent question."

"So how do we find out?"

"Got some rubber boots?"

* * *

"How long will this take?" asked the Security Supervisor in the Lockheed Martin HQ control-room.

"Oh, about two minutes," said the engineer.

"That quick?"

"Sure. At present, the security barriers are set to accept two serial number ranges: one for old passes, one for new ones. All I'm doing is deleting the old range: once that's done, the old passes will no longer work."

He studied the screen in front of him and made some edits to the code displayed on it.

"There, all done. Now only the new passes will open the security barriers."

"Right, thanks. Now I just need to issue an updated visual match sheet to the security staff so they know the old design is no longer valid."

The engineer picked up his folio. "Right, all yours."

* * *

Young and Chung – aka Colin Deft and Alan Thomas – were sat in Lockheed Martin reception with Jackson, aka Anonymous USAF pilot, as they waited to be collected by Cooper. Young and Chung smartly dressed in suit and tie, Jackson more casually attired in jeans and polo shirt. Young was carrying a briefcase, Chung was weighed down with a thick expanding case and a bulky laptop bag.

People-watching was both a hobby and a kind of continuing professional development programme for Young. When your work involved taking on other identities, you were always on the look-out for characteristics you could borrow. A particular gait when walking, a mannerism, a facial expression, even something as simple as the way someone held a phone. The harried-looking man hurrying toward the security barriers, for example, his pass on a ski-pass style retract–

"Fuck!"

"What?" whispered Chung.

Young looked around reception. "Fuck!" he repeated.

"What's wrong?" asked Jackson.

"His pass. Look at his pass."

"What about it?" asked Chung, but Jackson had already seen it.

"It's a new design," said Jackson.

"Maybe they have different designs for different departments," suggested Chung.

"No, look," said Young, nodding toward a couple of staff standing at reception. "They all have the same design. They must have changed it! Damn the timing."

"What do we do," said Chung, "make an excuse and try to re-arrange the meeting?"

Young shook his head. "No, too risky, Cooper must already have our anonymous pilot half-characterised as a nut job, if we flake out now that's simply going to confirm the diagnosis and we may not get invited back."

"But without valid passes ..." said Chung.

"I know. Scott, you're just going to have to blind him with jargon. Making it sound as convincing as possible, but make sure he doesn't understand the technicalities. We're going to need to get invited back for a meeting with an engineer."

* * *

Perez had a preference for C4, but it had almost exclusively military uses, so was not at all easy to get hold of. There were ways, but Semtex was almost as effective and was used in demolition work, so there were civilian uses. Greater supply, less control.

The most basic approach would be to break into a demolition company and steal some, but that was easier said than done. Terrorism concerns meant that Semtex thefts were a priority for police, and companies which failed to take proper precautions against theft could find themselves in hot water with the authorities – especially if they did any government work. The government viewed carelessness over the security of Semtex with a great deal of displeasure, and demolition companies were extremely careful as a result.

His old army buddies were another potential source. They all thought he'd gone into corporate security work, which was, he supposed, true after a fashion. They trusted him, and not many questions would be asked, especially when the amounts of explosive involved were small. But he didn't want to risk any of them being dragged into his various freelance projects; he wouldn't use any of them as a supplier.

What he was happy to do, though, was use them as a source of intelligence. Half of their enemies were obtaining their explosives through unofficial channels of one kind or another. Either backdoor military aid from a sympathetic nation, or merely one that had commercial interests in destabilising a region, or black-marketeers. It was a small world, and the Army knew who many of these suppliers were: surveillance operations on known terrorists frequently led to the black marketeers. There was little point in taking any of them out of the picture – new ones would rapidly spring up to replace them within days, and there was in any case a regular turnover in suppliers; disputes were not uncommon, and these were often settled in a rather decisive fashion. All Perez had needed were a few up-to-date contacts. He wasn't asked why he needed them.

He disliked dealing with black-marketeers, as he knew most of them would sell to anyone – including terrorists. Especially the Russians, they didn't care who they sold to so long as payment was in dollars. But he was a pragmatist: you had to get it where it was available. He picked up the phone to arrange a meeting.

* * *

It had been a busy 24 hours for Young and Jackson. Cooper had been sufficiently worried by Jackson's visit to have arranged for them to meet with a C-130 engineer the following day. He'd had to go straight to the third bar – the only one he had not yet visited – to repeat the photo exercise with the new pass. Jackson, now meeting with an engineer rather than an administrator, needed to make sure his story held together well enough to come across as a genuine concern. They didn't want Lockheed to act on it – modifications to two aircraft types within a short time might generate unwanted attention – merely to complete the meeting without raising any suspicion. The meeting was not the point of their visit to Lockheed.

Young had opened the meeting by asking the engineer to sign an affidavit which stated that he would protect the confidentiality of the pilot unless otherwise ordered by a court. The engineer had happily done so, and Young opened a briefcase bulging with papers and added it to the top. He'd spent the rest of the brief meeting apparently dealing with emails on his phone. His real need for the phone was to configure one simple app ready for use.

Jackson had played his part to perfection. The engineer had fully understood the reasons for his concerns, but was able to explain why the apparent risk was not a concern in reality. Jackson had allowed himself to be reassured, and the engineer was taking them back down to reception. Young reached into his jacket pocket and tapped the screen.

Just as the elevator reached the ground floor, Young's phone rang. He answered it as they stepped out.

"Oh, Dean, could I call you back in a few minutes? Oh, you're with the judge now? Just give me 20 seconds."

"Apologies, I need to take this, but we can see ourselves out, thank you."

"Ah, I'm supposed to show you out."

"No problem – could you just bear with me for one minute?" Young was holding the phone with one hand and flipped open his briefcase with the other, letting it slip from his hand as he did so. Papers went everywhere. The others scrabbled to pick them up while Young grabbed one sheet and started reading: "Clause 24, paragraph nine. Shall I read you the clause?" Young turned to the engineer. "Sorry, the judge is waiting ..."

The engineer gave in. "I understand. I'll leave you to it, just turn right and right again to get back to reception. You just need to hand your visitor badges in to the security guard and he'll let you out through the gate."

"Thanks," said Young, returning to his call. Jackson and Chung shook hands with the engineer who got back into the elevator. Young maintained his fake call long enough for the doors to close and the elevator to begin its ascent.

"Ok," said Young, "I'll wait for you at Danny's Bar." He walked around the side of the elevators, reached the barriers, handed his visitor's badge to the guard and walked out of the building.

Jackson pressed the elevator button then the two of them stood well back, apparently running through some papers together. They had to let two elevators go before they got one to themselves. As soon as the doors closed, Chung reached into his case and pulled out the two Lockheed staff badges. Both put them on in place of the visitors badges that went into the briefcase. Chung pulled out a a hard-hat and a hi-vis vest which he handed to Jackson, who quickly put them on. Chung then pulled out a clipboard. Attached to it was a small round object with adhesive already in place. Within seconds, he had it fitted.

"How does my mole look?" he asked.

Jackson examined the fake mole Chung had attached to his chin. "Looks ... like a mole," he said.

The mole was another of Young's touches. "People are lazy," he'd said. "They look for shorthand ways to remember people. If you have one distinctive feature, like a large mole, that's all they remember. Plus, it draws the eye. Put it on your chin, and they look at the mole, not your eyes."

The elevator doors opened. Forty seconds after two visitors got in, a manager and a maintenance engineer got out. All Young's work. "They are the

two real-life invisibility cloaks," he'd said. "A suit &
clipboard, and a hard-hat & hi-viz vest. With either
of those things, you can walk around anywhere you
like and everyone assumes you should be there
despite the fact that they don't know you."

Young had talked with pride of one of his earliest
cons carried out with just those costumes. He'd
turned up at large corporate offices just before 8am,
when receptionists were present but few if any
managers. He'd handed over a clipboard listing
various computer equipment on a piece of the
company's letterhead. He'd asked the receptionist to
sign, and his two associates in hi-viz vests and
trolleys had proceeded to take out about fifty
grand's worth of computer equipment, printers and
copiers in less than 15 minutes. The really clever
part was that, even if they'd been caught, it would
have been tough to prove theft: the papers that the
receptionist had signed 'for and on behalf of' the
company stated that the company was donating the
equipment. They'd hit three companies on three
successive days before deciding to quit while they
were ahead. Not a bad return for 45 minutes' work
and $100 worth of props.

Jackson smiled at the irony as the two of them
walked down the corridor: he was wandering around
wearing clothing ostensibly designed to be seen, and
yet he could see Young was right: few people even
glanced at him.

Their objective was simple: an unused network
socket in a location which would allow Chung to
work unobserved for 15-20 minutes.

There was no shortage of unused network
sockets, but most were next to occupied desks. No
use.

"Conference rooms usually have multiple
sockets," said Chung, "let's see if we can find an
empty one."

They walked through a kitchenette area and saw
a set of conference rooms on the far side. They
passed several occupied ones before spotting an

empty one on the left. It was a small room: a round table with four chairs around it. Chung opened the door and walked in while Jackson pulled a screwdriver from his pocket and pretended to be busy adjusting one of the hinges while actually serving as look-out.

Chung dumped clipboard, expanding case and laptop bag on the desk, and ducked underneath it. There were two flaps in the floor. He lifted the first: power sockets. He lifted the second: two telephone sockets and two network sockets. Perfect.

He came out from under the table and pulled out an Ethernet cable from his laptop bag, then ducked back underneath to plug in the cable. He sat down at the table, pulled out his laptop and connected it. He hit the power button. As soon as the laptop booted, he opened a spreadsheet he had saved on his desktop, then pulled up a browser and disabled the proxy server: right now he wanted the Lockheed network to see exactly where the connection was coming from. He selected the Lockheed jobs website from his bookmarks.

He clicked into the search field and typed:

*; Select * from sys.tables*

As before, the listing of filenames appeared and Chung selected contract_staff_temp.sql.

The username and password prompts appeared.

Outside the door, Jackson watched as two women walked down the corridor towards them, heavily engaged in conversation. He kicked the door – the agreed alert signal – and then walked a short distance down the corridor. Chung quickly clicked onto the spreadsheet in the task bar, which covered the browser window.

The two women walked into the conference room and stopped short.

"Oh," said the older of the two, looking at her watch, "we have this room booked from 4.30pm." It was 4.35pm.

"Sorry," said Chung, closing the laptop lid. "I was just trying to find a quiet place to work. Just give me a moment and I'll be out of your way."

He reached under the table to unplug the Ethernet cable and put the laptop into his bag, cable still plugged into it. He picked up both bags and with an apologetic smile, left the conference room, closing the door behind him. Jackson was waiting a short distance down the corridor, again pretending to adjust something. Chung set off in his direction.

"Just a moment, please."

Chung froze, then slowly turned. It was the older woman standing in the doorway.

"You forgot your clipboard," she said, holding it out to him.

"Oh, thank you!" he said, forcing a smile. "Busy day."

"No problem."

He caught up with Jackson and the two continued to the end of the corridor.

"Let's get off this floor," said Chung.

"With you there," said Jackson.

The two men took the elevator one floor down and resumed their search.

"There!" said Chung, pointing. It was row of deskettes: a single workbench with dividers, and a 'Hot-desking area' sign above them. "Different people will be using these desks all the time, no-one will bat an eyelid."

Chung headed to the end unit, closest to the wall. Jackson followed him. "I'll position myself a few yards away," said Jackson. "Anyone comes close and I'll swear loudly as if I've just hit my thumb or something."

"Great," said Chung. "Wish me luck."

* * *

Young was spending his waiting time in the nearby bar productively: mulling over the problem of laundering the cash.

There were two parts to the problem. The first was the ease with which the government could render the bills worthless. If it wanted to be ultra-cautious, it could simply withdraw the new design. He didn't think that was likely: that would involve huge logistical challenges and cost a great deal of money. But they could and most certainly would circulate the serial numbers. The bills would be brand new and sequentially-numbered. Once the numbers were circulated to banks, it would be impossible to deposit them anywhere, and equally impossible to spend in anything other than low-value transactions, a few notes at a time. You certainly weren't going to be buying any apartments or sportscars that way.

That was the problem he needed to solve first, before they even started thinking about how to launder more than twenty million bills.

* * *

When Chung had closed the laptop lid, it had simply put the laptop into sleep mode. When he re-opened it, it would be right back where he was. He simply needed to wait 10 seconds or so for the laptop to acquire a new IP address from the laptop once he reconnected it to the Ethernet port.

He yawned and stretched, holding his neck and turning it left and right as if trying to ease aching muscles. The nearest person to him was three desks away, and there was nobody else close – except for Jackson.

He opened the laptop and it resumed within a few seconds. He'd left the Ethernet cable plugged into the laptop in his haste to clear the conference room, so all he had to do was connect the far end to the Ethernet socket above the desk. He did so and waited for the crossed-out networking icon to change to a live one.

Nothing happened. It should start changing within a second or two, and be complete within ten seconds, but nothing at all was happening. The crossed-out symbol remained defiantly in place.

He checked the connection to the wall-plate: it was solid. He checked the laptop connection. Shit! The wires were half pulled out! It must have happened when he shoved it back into the laptop bag. He fiddled with it, hoping it was just slightly loose and would form a connection, but nothing he did helped. If he had a few tools with him, he could fix it, but he had nothing on him and all Jackson had was the large screwdriver brought in to complete his disguise.

What now? They couldn't possibly get back into Lockheed a third time; whatever they did, it had to be now.

Wifi! There would be a wifi connection. The only problem, and the reason he hadn't tried wifi in the first place, is that most network connections were password-protected, and the guest networks generally required a login. He could crack one or the other given time, but the process for doing so was a brute-force one: once you set the cracker software running, you just had to wait. It wasn't a quick process, and they didn't have that kind of time. His only hope now was that this wifi network was open.

Praying hard, he opened up the list of wireless networks. He quickly scanned the list. All had the lock icon indicating a protected network except for one. Lockheed Martin Visitors. If that one required a login, they were sunk. He daren't risk calling reception to ask – they'd almost certainly expect his host for the visit to do that.

He connected to it. He refreshed the browser page.

Welcome to Lockheed Martin.

To use the visitor wifi network, please ask your host or reception to provide you with a username and password.

Username:

Password:

Fuck. They were sunk.

* * *

Think, Young, think! You're the government. You've just watched a bunch of guys waltz off into the sunset with a billion dollars worth of notes. Why wouldn't you immediately get on the phone to the banks to pass on the serial numbers? What could they do to stop that happening?

Nothing. Of course that would happen. There was nothing they could do to prevent it.

Unless ...

He thought it through. Would that work? Yes! Yes, it should. The authorities simply had to be persuaded that they had not waltzed off with the cash, and that it had instead been destroyed.

The trucks held the key. The empty trucks could be more than a decoy, they could also be the means by which they convinced the authorities that the stolen cash was destroyed. Keep twelve of the Marines from the final plane on the ground. Minus their weapons, of course. Tell them the trucks were also wired with explosives, and instruct each Marine to drive one of the trucks. After a suitable time, instruct them to park the trucks next to each other and walk away. Let the Marines get a safe distance away, then detonate the trucks! A sufficiently large explosion and they could almost totally destroy the trucks. Shove in a few bank notes to be found burnt by the explosion, and it would appear that the whole lot had gone. Because all twelve trucks were parked together, it would look like a clumsy accident: the bungling robbers had managed to accidentally trigger one of their own bombs, and the whole lot had gone up in flames.

No cash out there in the wild, no need to report the serial numbers.

Which solved half the problem.

That still left the question of how they could ever bank the money. Owning a billion dollars in cash – or even an eighth of it – sounded fabulous, but cash is a very inconvenient form of wealth: you can't very well keep $125 million under your mattress. The serial numbers might not be circulated initially, but if enough bills started showing up in the system, sooner or later the fact would be detected, and then all hell would break loose.

At the very least, they needed to convert the cash into a more convenient form. That was the second half of the problem.

* * *

Maybe there was a solution, thought Chung. He unplugged the useless Ethernet cable and wandered over to Jackson.

"Excuse me," he said, as if they were strangers.

"Yes," said Jackson.

"I seem to have broken my Ethernet cable, and can't connect to the network. I only need one for a short time. Do you think you might be able to find me one I can borrow for a few minutes, maybe from an unused computer somewhere?" He gestured towards the open-plan desk area.

Jackson caught on fast: with his technician getup, nobody was going to think twice if he wandered up to an empty desk and disconnected a cable.

"Sure, give me a couple of minutes," he said.

"Thanks," said Chung, "I'll be with my laptop at the desk there."

Jackson was back with a cable in three minutes. It had felt to Chung like a very long three minutes.

"Just give me a shout when you're done with it, and I'll put it back," said Jackson.

"Will do, thanks. Appreciate it."

He connected the new cable, and almost immediately got a network connection. Thank god.

The username and password prompt was still there on the webpage. He typed in the system administrator username:

Username: sa

Password:

He left the password blank. He was fairly sure this was going to work, as the error message he'd gotten before had complained about him being outside the Lockheed network. If the login hadn't been accepted, it should have rejected it before getting that far. But you never actually knew for sure until ...

He was in!

He started by searching through the role titles. Jackson had briefed him on what to look for: a field manager or similar. Once he found something suitable, he would check it with Jackson. There: Field Technician Supervisor (Avionics). That looked like a suitable title to copy. He reached into a pocket and pulled out a pack of mints. He popped one into his mouth, then wandered over to Jackson. "Offer you a mint?" he asked. "A small thank-you."

"Oh, thanks, yes."

As Jackson leaned in to take it, Chung murmured quietly: "Field Technician Supervisor, Avionics."

Jackson took the mint. "Great," he said, "thanks."

Chung nodded and walked back to the laptop. He took a screengrab of the window and opened it up alongside the browser: an 18-inch 1920x1200 screen left plenty of room for two windows side-by-side. He selected the admin panel and selected Add Contractor. He quickly filled in the details, duplicating as much as possible from the screengrab before adding in a fictitious name, Pat Barker, and an accommodation address he'd arranged earlier.

For 'start date', he entered a date two weeks from today.

Add Photo. Chung navigated to a photo stored on the desktop. The photo he uploaded looked nothing like him – but it would look exactly like the disguise he'd be wearing when visiting the facility.

There was only one piece of info Chung couldn't supply: extension number. He put 'Use cell'. For the cellphone number, he added the number of a pay-as-you-go handset they'd purchased for the purpose.

He checked over the info and hit the Submit button.

Record added

Chung did a search on the fictitious name to make sure it was there. It was.

He shut down the laptop and unplugged the cable. He walked over to Jackson. "Thanks for that." As he handed it over, he said quietly "Meet you downstairs."

"Sure," said Jackson, taking the cable and wandering over to replace it.

Chung packed up his laptop and walked over to the elevators. He got out his cellphone and pretended to be on a call. The first elevator had people in it, so he waved them on. The second one was empty. He got in, put away the phone and quickly swapped the staff pass for his visitor's badge. He exited the elevator, walked to the barriers and handed over the visitor's pass to the guard.

He walked slowly away from the building. Jackson caught up with him a minute or two later.

"All done?" asked Jackson.

"All done," confirmed Chung. "Pat Barker is now a contractor for Lockheed Martin."

"That will definitely generate a pass for him?"

"Should do. HR systems are usually integrated, so adding a contractor should trigger a whole bunch of stuff, including security prepping a pass for him. I put the start date down as two weeks from now to allow the bureaucracy time to operate."

"Great," said Jackson, "let's go meet Young for a drink – I think we've both earned one!"

* * *

"We'll be picking up frequent flyer miles for this journey at this rate," said Jackson to Evans as they walked through Dallas Fort Worth airport to the Hertz rental desk. They'd again booked an F-150 pickup truck.

"Hopefully not," said Evans. "Even with tickets booked using different IDs, I prefer not to show up on CCTV as a regular visitor to the city."

The pickup had a GPS unit, but they were careful not to use it: they didn't want to leave any unnecessary clues. Instead, Evans used the GPS on his phone to navigate them on the 20-mile drive to Hicks Field while Jackson drove.

The landscape was very flat, and the architects seemed to have taken their cues from it, thought Evans. Outside of the city centre, most of the buildings were low-level, one or two stories high. The buildings themselves grew sparser as they drove across the increasingly rural land.

"All this farmland is my idea of hell," said Evans.

"Yeah," said Jackson, "you get agoraphobic if you get more than 200 feet from the nearest Starbucks. Not much of the rugged pioneer about you." It was a running joke between the two.

"I just like my rugged pioneering to have a few home comforts. You know, light, power, wifi, 24-hour shopping, that kind of thing." He gestured to the map on his phone. "Just look at these road names! I swear a good half of the streets are called Farm to Market Road."

"No complaints here," said Jackson. "It's good to get some farm-fresh air."

"There's nothing fresh about the air on farms. So, fill me in on Hicks Field."

"It goes back awhile," said Jackson. "It was originally a WW1 Army Corps base, and later used as a WW2 training base. Once we joined the war, most operations moved to Carswell."

"Where the BEP flights go from now."

"Right. The new airfield, confusingly called Hicks Airfield, is just over a mile away from Hicks Field, and is used today for general aviation – a flying school, a small jet charter company and private pilots making pleasure flights."

"And the original Hicks Field is now totally abandoned?"

"For the time being, anyway," said Jackson, "and personally I doubt that will change. It was used for helium production for airships back in the day. Now that helium is in demand again, though for silicon chip production and MRI scanners rather than airships, there's talk of creating a modern helium plant on the same site, but nothing has happened and as far as I can see, it's all just talk."

"So hopefully we won't be interrupted by construction workers."

"I doubt we'll be interrupted by anything larger than a passing eagle," said Jackson.

"No security?"

"There's nothing here to protect at the moment. A few run-down buildings, maybe a few pieces of rusting machinery. Likely a couple of guys with beer guts who do the occasional drive-by."

"Suits me," said Evans.

Jackson's assessment appeared accurate as he parked the pickup by the roadside and looked around. There were some white hangers and associated buildings. A mix of wood and corrugated iron. No visible control tower. Otherwise just lots of flat ground with crumbling concrete and a lot of weeds. A chain-link fence in poor condition was the only thing between them and the abandoned airfield.

"Welcome to Nowheresville," said Evans.

Jackson picked up a backpack containing head-torches and a crowbar. They locked the pickup and wandered along the fence 20 feet or so until they found a piece by a post with a small hole. Maybe created by a wild animal pushing through. Jackson bent down and pulled at it. He pulled a bit harder, and a section came away from the post. He pulled it aside and motioned for Evans to step through. Evans did so and Jackson followed him.

There was a sad feel to the place, thought Jackson. At one time, nearly a century ago, this would have been buzzing with soldiers, pilots and aircraft. And again, thirty years later, alive to the sound of a much more modern breed of aircraft. Barked orders, roaring engines, the stamping of feet. Men with a joint purpose and a determination to all play their part in something big, something important, something that changed the world. Now it was silent and empty. A ghost-town where you could almost sense the ghosts.

"So where do we start?" asked Evans, interrupting his reverie.

"We need to find the fire base," said Jackson. "That will have had a high-volume water supply. After that, we can trace the pipes back and try to find the main water supply pipes."

As they wandered between the buildings, they all looked very similar. Most of them like low hangers, a few connecting buildings with pointed roofs. Faded numbers on the hangers were all that differentiated them.

"We might have to start looking inside," said Jackson.

"No," said Evans, "there." He pointed to a hanger building that looked the same as the others but for the faded 'FIRE' lettering painted above the doors.

The 4x4 with 'Security' on the side drove slowly along the road, two uniformed guards inside.

"Pickup," said the passenger, pointing to the silver F-150 parked at the side of the road.

"We'll take a look," said the driver. He pulled up behind it. The two got out and walked one either side of the pickup.

"Locked," said Jackson, pulling at the first of several doors of varying sizes set into the front of the hanger. "You try all the shutters and doors here, I'll take a look round the back."

Evans walked up to one of the other doors, turned the rusty handle and tugged. Locked too. He walked along to the next.

One of the security guards pointed to the piece of fence Jackson had peeled away from the post. "That wasn't like that yesterday."

"Can't say I noticed," said the other, "but we'd better take a look inside. I'll just call it in." He thumbed the transmit button on his lapel radio.

"44 to base. 44 to base."

"Base, go ahead, 44."

"Possible intrusion at Hicks Field. Parked vehicle and possible disturbed fencing. Investigating."

"Roger that, 44."

Jackson had found a boarded-up door at the back. The wood was weather-beaten, and a quick shove with his shoulder had been enough to break one of the boards. He put down his backpack and pulled out one of the head-torches and the crowbar. He put the head-torch on and used the crowbar to pull away the broken board, then pulled off the ones above and below it. Behind it was a broken door. He pushed it with his foot. It didn't move. He pushed harder and it shifted a few inches. He kicked it hard and it flew open. He switched on his torch, replaced the crowbar, put the backpack on again and climbed through.

The building was completely empty inside. Some puddles of water on the concrete floor, nothing else.

He walked through to the front. Next to two large shutter doors were chains hanging from the ceiling with wooden handles at the end. The mechanism to open the doors, he thought. He pulled on one. Nothing. He looked for a locking mechanism and saw a dead-bolt at the bottom of the door. He released the bolt and tugged again on the handle. The handle descended and the shutter door lifted a few feet.

The moment it did so, Evans ducked beneath it.

"Close it, quickly!" he urged.

Jackson responded to the urgency in Evans' voice and didn't waste time asking any questions. He pulled down on the door and fastened the bolt. He also switched off the torch.

"We've got company," whispered Evans.

Both men stood motionless and listened. They could hear an engine, a car or light truck. It stopped some distance away. They looked at each other. "What's a vehicle doing on an abandoned airbase?" whispered Evans.

"I don't know," was the whispered reply, "but if you can think of a valid reason for us being here, now would be an excellent time to come up with it."

The sound of the engine got closer. They heard it pull up just the other side of the shutters. Two car doors slammed shut. Evans nearly jumped as they heard one of the door handles turning. The door rattled. "Secure," said a voice. Another door, the same result. Then the large shutter door was rattled. "All secure. Next building."

They heard the doors slam shut again and the vehicle pull away.

"That was close," said Evans. "A routine patrol, do you think?"

"I wouldn't expect that level of patrol here," said Jackson. He was thinking back to that pulled-back section of fence, with their parked pickup nearby. "I think we may have messed-up somewhat." He explained his concerns. "The problem now is if they either call in help for a more thorough search, or simply wait by the pickup."

"Do you think they'll go to that much trouble?"

"I hope not," said Jackson. "But I don't want to hang around here longer than we have to. Let's be as quick as we can."

"Works for me."

They listened out. They could no longer hear the vehicle.

"Let's start the search."

The two of them took opposite sides of the building. It didn't take long. "Here," said Evans. Jackson joined him and they both shone their torches on the large water outlet.

"That's it," confirmed Jackson. "Now we need to see if we can figure out the route of the underground pipe. Look for manhole covers – from the research I've done, they should appear at fairly regular intervals."

They shone their torches on the floor and began working out from the water outlet.

Jackson crouched down. "Got one!"

Evans came over. Jackson tapped his foot on the metal plate. "This one's no good to us, we need one out in the open, but it shows us the direction. We need to follow the trail outside."

"Do you think the guards have gone?"

"Let's take the back way out, so we can take a discreet look."

They walked to the back of the building where Jackson cautiously poked his head out.

"No sign of anyone."

He stepped through the doorway. "All clear."

Evans joined him, and they walked cautiously to the corner of the building. Jackson lay down on the ground then poked his head round the corner, at ground level. "Still clear."

They crept down the side of the building, where Jackson repeated the manoeuvre. "Clear again."

Jackson stood, and they walked around the front of the building.

"The water outlet is by that side," said Jackson, "so let's look for manhole covers leading out from there."

They walked across the front of the building and almost immediately spotted one.

"This is a little close to the building," said Evans. "We need one with a more distant background for the photo beneath the truck."

They followed an imaginary line between the manhole cover inside the building and the one outside. Around 200 yards out was another.

"Let's keep going," said Evans.

Another 150 yards took them onto the taxiway. "There," said Jackson, "the next one."

Evans looked around. "Is the taxiway big enough to accommodate the Galaxies?" he asked.

Jackson looked at the width of the taxiway and the space either side. "Yes," he said, "no problem."

Evans pointed up the taxiway to a crossway from the runway. "If we bring them in there and have them park just as they enter this taxiway, and blow the hole by the manhole cover here, parking the truck at 90 degrees, they'd be looking way off into the distance over there. That should definitely work as a background."

Jackson nodded. "Ok," he said, taking off his backpack and pulling out the crowbar, "let's check it out."

He used the crowbar to lift the cover. They could hear the running water as soon as he did so. They looked at each other: that wasn't good.

"Why would the water still be flowing to a disused airbase?" asked Evans.

"The pipe must serve other places, not just the base. Let's take a look and see how much water we're dealing with."

He put his head-torch back on. "I'll go in, you close the cover and keep an ear out for the guards. If you hear a vehicle, get back to cover. I'll rap on the manhole cover when I'm ready to come out; if you don't open it, I'll know we have company and wait."

Jackson descended the steel rungs embedded in the wall of the vertical shaft just big enough for a person. There was no way they'd get the pallets down the shaft, Perez would need to blow a bigger hole. The shaft smelled musty, and the bricks were crumbling in places. He descended about eight feet before reaching the water pipe below. His feet reached the water surface before he was fully in the pipe. He ducked down to look at it.

Yes! He could see immediately from the curvature of the visible area of pipe that it was clearly large enough to accommodate a loaded pallet, with room to spare!

The distance between the surface of the water and the top of the pipe was about five-and-a-half feet, maybe six feet. That means the water was two, two-and-a-half feet deep. That was the first piece of bad news. He studied the water surface. That was the second piece of bad news: it was fast-flowing, perhaps 15mph.

He'd seen enough.

He climbed back up and rapped on the cover. The cover lifted. "All clear," said Evans.

Jackson climbed out, and Evans lowered the cover back into place.

"Well?" asked Evans.

"Two feet or so of fairly fast-flowing water."

"Now what?" asked Evans.

"I don't know, maybe it can be switched off somewhere. But we can do that research online. Let's get the runway walk done, then we can get out of here."

Jackson needed to check the condition of the runway. The dirt-field capabilities of the Galaxies meant that a perfect surface wasn't needed, he just needed to be sure there weren't large chunks of broken-up concrete or big holes in the runway. A crash-landing could blow the whole plan.

The two men walked to the closest end of the runway. "We'll take one side each," said Jackson. "You're just looking for any debris or holes larger than your foot, say."

"Ok," said Evans, looking at the runway stretching out in front of them. "How long is the runway?"

"9000 feet: 1.7 miles. Fully loaded, a C-5 needs 8400 feet to take-off. These particular C-5s will, thanks to us, be empty but for the Marines. The take-off roll will likely be closer to 7000 feet. But that still means we need most of the runway length in reasonable condition."

The runway walk took them 45 minutes.

"What's the verdict?" asked Evans.

Jackson smiled. "It's do-able. We'll need to do a bit of a clean-up operation, and there are three holes we'll need to patch, but yes: we have ourselves a runway."

* * *

The two guards worked 12-hour shifts, and had five minutes to go when they arrived back at the base.

"Do we fill out an incident report?" asked one.

"There's not much to report," said the other. "A suspected intrusion but nothing found, and by the time we've got changed it'll be clocking-off time."

"True, but we radioed it in. We'd better just fill out a quick one."

"Guess you're right. I'll take care of it. Time for a beer after?"

"Sure thing."

The guard sat at the computer terminal, logged-in and selected the menu item for an incident report.

Nature of incident? Suspected intrusion

Enter a description of events - blank line to finish:

An empty pickup truck was spotted parked
outside the base. Close by, we found a section of
fencing which looked like it had been peeled back. A
patrol of the base found nothing. On our next pass,
the pickup truck was gone.

He hit return again for a blank line.

Number of suspects? Unknown

Description of suspects? Unknown

Number of vehicles? 1

Make, model & colour of vehicle 1? Ford F-150
Silver

Licence plate?

He consulted his notebook.

LTR 5985

He hit the Submit button and logged-off.

* * *

Karen West looked at the clock on her computer
terminal in her tiny cubicle for about the fifteenth
time that shift. Just coming up to 4am. A law
student by day, security firm administrator by
night, the hours were taking their toll. Lectures and
library work all day, finish at 5pm, home, change,
clock on at 6pm, clock off at 6am, home, shower, a
few hours' sleep and then start the cycle all over
again. It was a hell of a life, and her first few years
as a junior associate in a law firm would be no
improvement, she knew. Only the dream of one day
starting her own law practice kept her going.

The work was tedious: reading through incident
reports logged by the firm's security guards, tagging
them with appropriate keywords and dealing with
any follow-up action required. The only good thing
about it was that the pace of work expected of her
was slow. She would deal with one report, write a
paragraph of her current essay then move onto the
next.

She put down her pen and turned her attention to
the next report.

Client: USAF

Location: Hicks Field

Status: Not In Use

Nature of incident? Suspected intrusion

Enter a description of events - blank line to finish:

An empty pickup truck was spotted parked outside the base. Close by, we found a section of fencing which looked like it had been peeled back. A patrol of the base found nothing. On our next pass, the pickup truck was gone.

Number of suspects? Unknown

Description of suspects? Unknown

Number of vehicles? 1

Make, model & colour of vehicle 1? Ford F-150 Silver

Licence plate? LTR 5985

Intruders at a disused airbase? It seemed pretty unlikely. She was vaguely aware of the location, and knew there was nothing much there. But they had a licence plate, so it required a follow-up. There were strict rules about access to databases, but as a military client they were authorised to access the Texas Department of Motor Vehicles (DMV) database to run plates.

She logged-in to the DMV system and entered the plate number. Within a few seconds, the details appeared on her screen:

Make: Ford

Model: F-150

Body type: Pickup truck (open back)

Short-form colour: Silver

Long-form colour: Ford Platinum 910

Age: 4 months

Registered owner: Hertz Car Hire

As a private security company, they had no power to request the renter details from Hertz, but with the licence-plate, date and time, the police would be able to trace the vehicle if needed. She'd done all she could, and with no report of theft or damage, there was no need to notify the police.

She switched back to the Incident Reports window.

Follow-up? DMV check performed: Hertz rental

She then entered the standard abbreviation for No Further Action:

Disposition? NFA

Time for another paragraph of her essay.

* * *

Young sat up in bed with a start: that was it! That was the answer! That was how they laundered the cash!

He glanced over at the clock: 3:17am. Well, this one was worth losing sleep over. The details would require a great deal of research and exceedingly careful planning, but the idea was pure genius, even though he said so himself. A completely practical way to launder a billion dollars, and with poetic justice thrown in at no extra charge!

For a moment he considered calling Sullivan right that moment. This was worth waking her up for. But he quickly dismissed the idea: there was no urgency, and the idea would be just as good at 8am. He didn't see himself getting back to sleep, though: he needed to make a start on the research.

* * *

"Well, I guess that's us done," said Pritchard to Lorrimar. "You haven't exactly gone out of your way to make us look good to our bosses," he smiled. "Frankly we had to rack our brains to come up with the few recommendations we did manage. You guys run a tight ship here."

"Thanks," said Lorrimar, "we've been doing it a while, so we like to think we know what we're doing, but we appreciate your input. It's always good to have a fresh set of eyes look at our operation, and we'll certainly ensure that the rest of your recommendations are acted on."

"Do me a favour, would you?"

"Name it."

"If you do hear anything more about that suspected hit," said Pritchard, "would you keep me in the loop?"

"Happy to, but I doubt anything will come of it."

"Me too, but just in case."

"You got it," said Lorrimar. "Have a safe trip back to Washington."

* * *

Chung had been correct about Lockheed's integrated HR system: adding an employee or contractor triggered a cascade of actions on other systems. Each contractor on the system was assigned to a cost-centre, and any additional call on a cost-centre had to be authorised.

Holly Williams was a temp in the finance team at Lockheed. Her emails mostly comprised automated alerts from the various reporting systems. Her job was to action these as required. She looked at the next one:

From: dbase-admin-contractors@lockheedmartin.com

Subject: Missing budget entry for cost-centre

Text:

Contractor: 105973

Name: BARKER, Pat

Cost-centre: 1517

Budget entry: Null

Williams looked up cost-centre 1517. Project Taurus. The name meant nothing to her, but almost none of them did. She hadn't seen this type of report before, and wasn't sure what needed to be done. She called over to her supervisor.

"Paul ... could you spare a moment?"

Paul Price walked over. "Sure, what do you need?"

"This report," she said, "I'm not sure what I need to do about it?"

Price read the email.

"Ok," he said, "that's basically saying HR have assigned a contractor to a project but there's no corresponding entry on the budget for him. Means someone's forgotten to fill in an entry on the costing system."

"How do I handle it?" asked Williams.

"Just give the project manager a call – if you enter the name of the project into the internal directory, it will show you the project manager's name and extension. They will add the cost-centre entry at their end and that's it. If you can't reach them for any reason, just let me know and I can check it from here."

"Ok, thanks."

Williams looked up the project manager and dialled his extension. A voicemail, saying he was on leave for the next two weeks. She replaced the handset and walked over to Price's desk. "He's on vacation," she said.

"Ok, no problem, I'll sort it, thanks."

Price opened up the Accounts Payable system and tapped in cost centre 1517. He then did a search on Barker. Zero results. With no invoices received, it wouldn't cause any issues at this stage. Price looked at the time: it was bowls night, and he wanted to get away on time. They could deal with it if it still wasn't sorted by the time the first invoice arrived. He closed the system.

* * *

"So what search terms do we use, do you think?" Evans asked Jackson.

"Hmm ... water supply controls ... giant stop-cocks ... water plant valves ... who knows!"

"You're a great help!"

"I imagine they are motorised these days," said Jackson. "Probably need a key to open the control boxes, but I'm sure Pugh can take care of that."

"Well," said Evans, "let's see what we can see."

It took less than five minutes before they had their answer.

The microsite they were looking at was actually aimed at school children, but was essentially the local water company boasting about the sophistication of the technology used to direct water supplies to where they were needed. There were no manual controls, no giant hand-wheels to turn, no switch-boxes attached to valves. Everything was computerised, controlled from a central water plant control centre. There were no human-operated controls at the actual valve locations.

"Wow," said Evans.

"That does complicate things," said Jackson.

"Well, on the plus side, we have ourselves a map of the pipe network."

"Not quite the detail we're going to need, but yes, this is the one passing beneath the airbase, and it looks to come out into Eagle Lake right here. Somewhere between the two, we're going to need to create ourselves an exit point.

"Break into the control centre?" queried Evans.

"Maybe, but I don't see us having the manpower on the day. We're going to be a bit busy dealing with 12 Galaxies, 156 Marines, a chain of baggage carts and, what else? Oh yes, a billion dollars in cash. I can't see us being able to spare anyone to be miles away at a water-plant control centre, and that's assuming one person would be enough. This is going to be in the middle of the day, when the plant is presumably teeming with staff."

"Ok," said Evans, "let's just learn as much as we can about the control centre, and maybe something will occur to us."

"We also need to see what those valves actually look like in the flesh, so to speak," said Jackson.

"What does it matter what they look like?" asked Evans.

"We need to make sure the loaded baggage carts can get past them. If they are gates that slide sideways, or up and down, and fully retract, that's fine, but they could be a twist mechanism or even a venetian-blind style system."

"I guess Raul's skills might come in useful there, but underground explosions are risky, even small ones."

"And baggage carts are not exactly off-road vehicles, they won't go clambering over the remains of giant valves – they need clear passage."

"Ok, so we need to do a little scouting mission," said Evans. "Since I'd prefer to do that without scuba gear, I suggest we leave that until after we've figured out how we get control of the system."

"Let's see what we can find out."

* * *

"I have an idea about how we might launder the notes," said Young.

Sullivan looked at him. "You do?"

"This is going to sound a bit out-there."

"It's an out-there problem," said Sullivan, "so the solution isn't going to be orthodox."

Young outlined the idea in six sentences.

"Are you serious?" asked Sullivan.

"It's beautiful, isn't it? Not only do we launder the money, but we do it in a way that only the bad guys lose out. The good old American tax-payer doesn't have to pick up the tab."

"Well, I have to admit it has a certain je ne sais quoi. But really? It sounds about twice as crazy as the heist itself." She liked that she could relax with Young; she could describe the whole idea as crazy and he'd be cool with it.

"I can't deny that," said Young.

"Do you really think it could work?"

"It would take some planning, for sure. And probably some careful timing. But yes, I do think it has the potential to work."

"It would be damned dangerous," said Sullivan.

"Again, I can't disagree. But there is one very strong argument in its favour."

"What's that?"

"The fact that it's the only idea we've been able to come up with," said Young.

"Touché. You do realise that the team's going to think we've totally lost it when we present them with this idea, right?"

"I imagine there will be one or two raised eyebrows, yes."

* * *

Sullivan poured a cup of coffee from the tyre shop percolator into one of the plastic cups, took a sip and grimaced. She dropped it into the trashcan.

"So," she said, "where are we at? Problem one, divert the aircraft."

"We think we have a reasonably solid plan in place," said Perez, briefly summarising it.

"You know how you're getting into Lockheed?" she asked.

"Hopefully, we're already in," said Chung. "We have added a fictitious contractor to the HR database, and he should have a security pass waiting for him within a week or so. He should be added to the company directory, so anyone calling the Lockheed switchboard and asking for him will be put through to this cellphone." He held it up.

"So we don't even need to be there?"

"Only occasionally," said Chung. "We'll go in and grab some genuine letterheads – no sense faking them when we don't have to – and print off the letters at our leisure, then take them back in to go through Lockheed's mailroom."

"Nice," said Sullivan, "so no need to fake the origin."

Chung smiled: "None at all. The letters will quite genuinely come from Lockheed Martin."

"I love it. And the devices?"

"I have them in the VSM," said Lewis.

"VSM?" asked Sullivan.

"Sorry," said Lewis, "Virtual System Modelling. It's a system that allows me to build a virtual circuit on the PC, feed it with real inputs and get out real outputs. Essentially it acts exactly like a real circuit would but without having to physically build it, so that I can make sure everything works beforehand. Everything checks out, so now it's just a question of making the real thing. The only question-mark is over range."

"What's the issue there?"

Lewis explained the unknowns involved in the range.

"It shouldn't be a problem," said Jackson. "I can get within two thousand feet of them above or below, or three miles off to one side."

"What about the explosives?" asked Sullivan.

"I've got a meeting arranged," said Perez. "Originally the quantities required were tiny, though Sam has now made them a little larger thanks to his trucks plan! But we'll get onto that."

"Right," said Sullivan, "problem two, the landing strip."

"We think we have it," said Jackson. "A disused airbase. Long enough runway, just needs a little TLC, maybe a day's work."

"And it meets your requirements, Evans?"

Evans smiled. "In essence. There is a little challenge there, but we'll get to that in a moment."

"Good," said Sullivan. So solutions to problems one and two appear to be well in hand. Problems three and four – the Marines and the F-16s – are already covered by solution one. So that brings us to problem five: making good our escape. How's your magic coming along, Evans?"

"I'm afraid we're going to add to your explosives shopping-list," said Evans to Perez. He passed round sheets of paper with a series of colour sketches. "Beneath the airbase is a large-diameter water pipe. Large enough for the loaded pallets with room to spare. There is a manhole cover with access to the pipe at position A. The plan, in essence, is this. We blow a hole down to the water pipe, large enough to lower the pallets. The hole is thinly covered until required."

"How far beneath the surface is the pipe?" asked Perez.

"About eight feet."

"That's not a small job," said Perez. "Any inhabited areas close by?"

"A farm about a mile away," said Jackson.

"Too close," said Perez. "An explosion that big is going to be heard over quite a distance."

"I don't know that we're going to find a better location, to be honest," said Jackson. "Any way around that?"

"Maybe," said Perez. "Might need to go the non-explosive demolition route."

"Non-explosive demolition?" asked Sullivan.

"A form of demolition used when you can't use explosives for whatever reason. Essentially you drill holes into the concrete and inject chemicals which combine to expand and break up the concrete from beneath the surface. It's relatively quiet, and also neater than explosives for this type of job as you can pull out the concrete chunks as you work rather than ending up with a heap of rubble in the pipe. There are a whole bunch of different types, but Dexpan is the most common."

"Sounds good," said Sullivan. "Any drawbacks?"

"It takes time. You'll see cracking after a couple of hours, but completely breaking up the concrete typically takes 6-10 hours, sometimes even 24. We'll need to break up the surface concrete, then dig out the soil, then break up an upper section of the pipe in the same way. The pipe won't be too thick, a couple of hours will be enough for that, but even with a backhoe to take care of the heavy lifting, we're going to be looking at 12 hours plus. And given we need to give no clue that the hole is there, we also need to do a thorough job of removing all the debris. We're looking at a couple of days all-in." Perez turned to Jackson. "Any security?"

"That might be a problem," said Jackson, filling him in on the interruption to their visit.

"Ok, well, we're going to have to find a way around that."

"Let's assume we can," said Sullivan. "Talk us through the rest of your plan, Evans."

"Ok," said Evans, "so we have our access hole to the pipe and we have a semi parked very precisely above it. In the semi trailer is a hole in the floor and a lifting rig installed around it – like a bigger version of an engine-hoist. We direct each Galaxy to park at position B. It's a few hundred feet away. Beneath the semi, reaching from the floor of the trailer to the ground, is a flap covering the space between the wheels. On that flap is a photograph of the grass banking on the far side of the truck."

"I don't recall any grass banking," said Jackson, looking puzzled.

"There isn't any yet," grinned Evans, "but there will be. Half a day's work with a backhoe and some turf. It's all in the preparation, you know."

"So the folks on the Galaxy think they can see beneath the truck," said Young, smiling. "Neat."

"Exactly," said Evans. "From their perspective, the truck is fully in view the entire time. Of course, we have to assume that the authorities are going to turn up at some point to surround the airbase, so we need the grass banking to ensure there's no view beneath the truck from the perimeter fencing. We'll make it look like bunkers."

"Anyone here drive a JCB?" asked Sullivan.

There was silence.

Sullivan shrugged. "Guess one of us will be taking lessons." She nodded at Evans to continue.

"We use forklift trucks to move the pallets from the Galaxy to the truck. As each pallet goes in, we use our lifting rig to lower it down into the pipe. The Marines and flight crew see three pallets go into the truck. We then have the Galaxy take-off. As soon as it is clear, we lift the flap and position the truck close to the exit gates, ready to leave."

"The empty truck," said Sullivan.

"Right," said Evans. "Or nearly so, anyway: we'll load them up with some empty pallets, and we'll carefully transfer a small number of the bills into the back of them – I'll get to that momentarily. Rinse and repeat twelve times. Twelve empty trucks parked by the gate, one billion dollars in the water pipe."

"I assume there's no water in this water pipe?" said Pugh.

"This is where things get interesting," said Jackson.

"Yeah, 'cos so far in the plan it's been so hum-drum," said Lewis.

"There is water flowing in the pipe," said Evans. "Fairly fast-flowing water."

"We going for a swim?" asked Lewis.

"We plan to drain the water, then use airport baggage carts to transport the cash down the pipe to an exit point."

"Our disappearing act," said Sullivan, "while the authorities think the cash is sitting in the trucks."

"What happens to the trucks?" asked Young.

"The final Galaxy," said Jackson. "We ask the Marines on board if they would be so kind as to disembark and drive the trucks for us."

"Which they are going to be doubly keen to do," observed Young. "I like it."

"Very clever," said Sullivan. "Not only are we holding the airborne Galaxies hostage, but this way the Marines think they still have possession of the cash."

"There is, however, the small matter of draining the water from the pipe."

"So we need to close a valve somewhere to cut off the water flow," said Lewis.

"Right, which is the snag. The water flow is controlled remotely by the Eagle Mountain Water Plant Control Room. That is about five miles away from Hicks Field. We need to somehow gain access to that plant, with sufficient presence to either persuade them to do what we need, or to lock them out of the way while we do it ourselves. This at a time when we are likely to be rather busy."

"Maybe we don't need physical access," said Chung.

"What do you mean?" asked Evans.

"If it's controlled remotely, then there has to be a computer network to do the controlling. Maybe we can hook into it somewhere."

"You really think so?" asked Jackson.

"I have a vague memory of reading something about this somewhere," said Chung. "Let me have the details of what you've learned about it, and I'll look into it."

There was silence for a moment.

"This plan is actually coming together, isn't it?" said Pugh.

"It may not be quite as crazy as we thought," said Perez.

"Ye of little faith," said Sullivan, grinning.

"There's still the small matter of laundering the cash," said Lewis.

Sullivan nodded. "Problem six." She looked at Young and nodded.

"There are two parts to the solution," he said. "The first part is to persuade the Treasury not to circulate the serial numbers of the bills to every bank in the world."

"Well, that sounds easy enough," said Lewis sardonically.

"Actually," said Young, "we think it may be. The authorities think the cash is in the trucks, right?"

"Right."

"So, we have the Marines drive them somewhere and park them up next to each other somewhere suitably isolated. We then order them to get out, and walk say 500 yards away. At that point, something will seemingly go wrong, and we'll accidentally trigger a booby-trap on one of the trucks. That will set off a cascade of explosions that destroys all the trucks."

"Anyone think Perez is angling for a bonus here?" grinned Pugh. "This plan seems to incorporate an unusual number of explosions."

"You're the guys who keep coming to me with things you want me to blow up," said Perez in mock protest. "All I was going to do was blow up a few wires and cables."

"So we chuck a few bills into the trucks as the final evidence, and with the cash gone, there's no need to circulate the numbers," said Pugh.

"That's the thinking," said Young.

"I'm not so sure," said Pugh. "If I were the Treasury, I might believe the bills are gone, but I think I'd circulate the numbers all the same. The precautionary principle."

"It's possible," admitted Young, "but my guess is that if that happens, it happens on a much quieter scale in those circumstances. The addition of the numbers to the routine bulletins rather than urgent emails asking banks to be on the look-out for the cash. They're not expecting anything to pop up, just covering their backs."

"Which still leaves us trying to launder twenty-odd million fifty dollar bills whose serial numbers are possibly on a watch-list," said Lewis.

"Right," said Sullivan. "Now, you guys thought this whole idea was crazy at the start. So just remember that when Young tells you his idea, because it's going to sound even crazier than the heist."

"Now I'm worried," said Chung.

Young smiled, and gave a concise summary of the idea.

"You're out of your tiny mind!" said Lewis.

"You've been smoking some good stuff," agreed Perez.

"Now see, Sullivan said you'd react like that?" said Young, smiling.

"It's nuts," said Chung. "It's about as sane as ripping-off the mob."

"It would demand a certain level of care," said Young. "Intricate planning, meticulous execution. You know any teams with a track record in stuff like that?"

"How the hell would we even approach them?" asked Lewis. "Go knock on their doors and say 'Hi, we were just in the neighbourhood and wondered whether you might be interested?', perhaps?"

"I have half an idea there," said Young. "I need to work on the details."

"I'm as crazy as you are for going along with this," said Lewis.

"Ok, there's one other thing I need you and Mike to work on," said Sullivan, turning to Lewis. "From the surveillance I've done on the BEP, the convoys appear to leave at random times. So far it's always been during office hours, and my guess is that's not coincidence – probably the exact time is randomly chosen each day, but it has to be when the facility is fully-staffed – though I might be wrong. We need to know whether we might be looking at a nighttime operation. Any way you two can set up a webcam with a view of the facility, say taking a still photo once a minute and sending those back to us?"

Lewis and Chung looked at each other briefly, then nodded. "Sure," said Lewis. "A network cam hooked up to a smartphone with LTE SIM would do the trick. We just need to figure out a way to keep it powered. How long do you think we need it there?"

"At least a fortnight," said Sullivan, "preferably longer."

"I'm sure we can find a way to hook it up to city power," said Chung. "We could even tap power from phone lines."

"Just need to make it discreet enough," said Lewis.

"Any way it could be traced to us if it were to be discovered?" asked Sullivan.

"Not with me taking care of the network side," grinned Chung.

Sullivan returned the smile. "Ok, let's do it."

* * *

Chung couldn't believe what he was reading. He'd begun with a simple search on how to control water plant systems. He'd been expecting to find dusty tomes on principles or perhaps colourful water company diagrams in online brochures prepared by PR companies. Instead, one of his first hits had been this:

http://ciip.wordpress.com/2011/11/22/scada-security-evaporates-in-texas/

A hacker who thought he barely deserved the label had managed to take control of the South Houston water plant over the web!

Could that be real, he wondered? It looked it, but a Wordpress blog apparently run by a single, unknown individual wasn't exactly a credible source. He did more searches, this time specifically on that attack. Within minutes, he was persuaded: it was indeed 100% genuine. Using nothing more than Google searches and default administrator logins, a computer geek had literally taken control of the system from his home. That was why the hacker, nicknamed prOf, thought he barely deserved the label: it was so easy there was really zero hacking involved.

PrOf's way in was a system known as SCADA: Supervisory Control And Data Acquisition. SCADA was a form of real-time industrial control systems used to remotely monitor industrial equipment like motors, pumps, relays and valves. SCADA systems were used extensively in large-scale industrial operations: chemical plants, oil and gas pipelines, electricity generation and ... water distribution.

Nor was prOf's attack an isolated example:

http://www.theregister.co.uk/2001/10/31/hacke r_jailed_for_revenge_sewage/

Within fifteen minutes of searching, Chung was able to find literally dozens of similar examples spanning more than a 15-year period. He was stunned.

The reason for the vulnerability of SCADA systems was that while it sounded like very hi-tech sophisticated technology, it was in fact very elderly technology. It was developed in the old days of mainframe computing, way before the Internet and before anyone ever envisaged the idea of anyone from outside a plant location being able to gain remote access. While security protocols had been added over the years, the level of sophistication was a decade behind modern IT security, and many systems had either default manufacturer logins that nobody had ever de-activated, or low-security shared logins that were designed for convenience rather than security. You didn't want a situation where staff might be unable to switch something off because they couldn't remember the login, so extremely simple usernames and passwords were the norm.

IT sysadmins were often only vaguely aware of SCADA systems, viewing them as engineering rather than IT, and often didn't even realise that with SCADA networks plugged into computers with net access, they had effectively put their SCADA system online without being aware of it. The result was that anyone could connect to them from anywhere. Default admin logins set by the equipment manufacturers were usually left active – the equivalent of logging into someone's internet router with the username admin and a blank password.

Once in, taking control of systems was scarily easy. He hadn't known quite what form he expected water plant control systems to take, but what he hadn't anticipated was simple, pictorial representations allowing valves to be opened & closed, and pumps to be switched on & off, simply by clicking on icons on the screen. In retrospect, it made sense: the people operating the controls were not IT staff, used to typing arcane command-lines, but rather the kind of guys who once drove around a plant opening and closing valves manually. The systems had to be simple. But to have them available over the web ... !

The more he read, the more incredible it seemed. There was even a specific search-engine to search for devices – from webcams to power plants – that can be accessed & controlled over the web:

www.shodanhq.com

Could it really be this easy?

* * *

While Chung was getting excited, Jackson had been growing depressed. He'd been checking small-jet specs, looking for a rental jet able to match the C-5 for both cruising speed and altitude. The problem was that the C-5 was an extremely capable aircraft. While it might look like a lumbering great beast you'd expect to be barely able to drag itself off the runway and up into the air, the four huge General Electric turbofans each generated 43,000 pounds of thrust and gave it a maximum speed of 574mph.

Jackson had originally planned to rent a Gulfstream 450, having flown the C-37 military version and knowing it could comfortably out-perform the C-5, but that had proved impossible: the only Gulfstream charters available were with crew, and he didn't want the added complication of having to take a crew hostage. They had quite enough to deal with already.

The fastest aircraft available on a self-fly basis were Learjets, but even the fastest of them couldn't match the top speed of the C-5.

Jackson pulled out some charts and a calculator. The fastest Lear was a Learjet 55. That had a maximum speed of 540mph – a touch over 34mph below that of the Galaxies. In the climb, the Lear would hold its own, but once the C-5s reached cruising altitude, they would go out of range pretty quickly. It would be essential to gain their cooperation quickly.

* * *

Chung had spent almost two hours at www.shodanhq.com and finally found the Eagle Mountain Water Plant. It was time to make a test connection to see whether he could determine the kit they were using so that he could then Google the default manufacturer logins.

Welcome to CORE-ICS v5.3.7

Username:

Password:

He copied the system name and version, opened a new tab and Googled for default logins for that system. There were two. He tried the first:

Username: admin

Password: admin

Username and password combination not found

He tried the second:

Username: administrator

Password: 123

Username and password combination not found

Well, he thought, I guess I can't expect it to be quite that easy!

He ran the portscan he'd tried at Lockheed without success. He might have better luck here, if water plant security was as poor as it appeared. He checked the IP address from his shodan search and tapped it into his port-scan software.

Scanning …

1 open port found: 502

Port 502 was TCP, the port used by most SCADA systems. No other ports were open. To get in, he'd have to resort to a brute-force attack. He looked at the clock on his laptop; it was past 1am. Ok, time enough to pick this up tomorrow. He'd invite Evans over: assuming he did get in, the next step would be to figure out which section of pipe they were trying to control, and Evans had been there.

* * *

Perez liked to think of himself as a technical guy. In learning to defuse bombs, you learned a lot about electronic circuitry, triggering mechanisms, radio transmissions and so on. Sitting next to Lewis in her home electronics lab, however, he felt like a school physics student visiting CERN.

As he looked around the workbench and shelves above it, he recognised some of the equipment, but other things were a mystery to him.

Lewis recognised the expression on his face: it was the one most visitors wore when they first saw her lab. She gestured from left to right:

"Oscilloscope, function generator, frequency generator, frequency counter, micro controller programmer boards, bench power supply – fixed and variable, single and double polarity – digital multimeter, capacitance and inductance meters – I made those myself – LCD and LED displays, soldering station, circuit board stuff–" she made a vague wave at the boxes of solderless breadboards, circuit board holders, PCB shears, heat-shrink gun – "and then all the components boxes."

Perez looked at the multi-compartment boxes packed with LEDs, crystals, buttons, switches, capacitors, potentiometers, transistors, diodes and a few other things he didn't recognise.

"But this is my baby," she said, with obvious pride. "My VSM system."

"VSM?"

"Virtual Systems Modelling. With this, I can build any circuit simply by drawing it on-screen and selecting the appropriate components from the toolbars here, then I simply hook up my input and output devices – let's say the frequency generator – and it behaves exactly like the physical circuit would."

Perez had never needed anything so sophisticated, but he could still admire it. "It's beautiful," he said.

Lewis smiled. "I already have the radio receivers built in here, let me show you ..."

* * *

"So what's the plan?" asked Evans.

"A dictionary attack," said Chung. "Basically a piece of software that tries thousands of combinations of usernames and passwords using words taken from a dictionary together with other words and non-words known to be common choices for usernames and passwords."

"Don't you typically get only a certain number of attempts at a login before the system blocks you?" asked Evans.

"You do," said Chung. "After a certain number of attempts, the system blocks your IP address for a time-out period. It's usually not long – a few minutes – but it's enough to make dictionary attacks impractical."

"I assume from the fact that you are unfazed by this that you have a way around that?"

Chung grinned. "Naturally." He explained about the anonymous proxy servers his browser used automatically. "What the password-cracking software does is detect when it's been blocked and then switch server automatically. It slows us down slightly, but not dramatically."

"So how long does it typically take to crack a password this way?"

"Typically, hours or days."

Evans looked at his watch. "Er ..."

"But I'm expecting the SCADA system to be a much easier target than most. Maybe a few minutes, perhaps half an hour."

"Why so?" asked Evans, puzzled.

"Let me set it going, then I'll explain."

Chung opened a command window. His linux prompt appeared:

chung@laptop $

He changed to his net utilities directory, then typed:

dictac

A prompt appeared:

IP address?

He typed in the IP address again.

Port? 502

Maxchars?

The program was asking him how many characters he wanted to limit the attempts to. The higher the number, the greater the chance of success, but the longer the attempt would take. As SCADA systems were likely to have simple logins, he decided to start with four characters.

Running (^C to abort) ...

Checked 1 combination(s), 0 successful so far

He watched as the number clicked up. He was waiting for it to switch IP address to make sure all was well.

Checked 10 combination(s), 0 successful so far

Connection lost ... switching IP address

Checked 11 combination(s), 0 successful so far

Satisfied that the IP switching was working, Chung resumed his explanation.

"SCADA systems predate the Internet," he said. "In the days when they were installed, nobody ever envisaged that the systems would be accessible from outside the plant. When someone has to be physically sat in the control-room to use the system, you tend to use simple logins: you don't want someone unable to close a valve because they can't remember their login. So nobody was concerned if the username was letmein and the password was password."

"But surely they would change that when the systems were connected to the Internet?"

"That's the crazy thing about SCADA," said Chung. "In most cases, nobody ever deliberately connected them to the Internet."

"How do you accidentally connect a water plant control room to the Internet?" asked Evans. The idea sounded bizarre.

"Very much more easily than you might imagine. You have to understand that in the early days of SCADA systems, it was all hard-wired: there was a dedicated piece of wire running from the control room to each valve or pump it was controlling. Later on, that was upgraded to a local area network, where you created a single loop of Ethernet and then sent signals down it to activate particular pieces of equipment. Sometime after that, a remote control room connection would be added, so that a control room at one plant could act as a backup for one at another plant. As office IT networks sprang up, those too were hooked up to the same network. When the Internet came along, the office IT network was connected to it without anyone really stopping to realise that when the SCADA system is connected to the IT system, and the IT system is connected to the Internet, they just put their SCADA system online."

"Don't they have IT professionals whose job it is to be aware of that kind of thing?" asked Evans.

"Ah, but that's the great divide," said Chung. "The IT people look after the IT world. The industrial control system, that's the domain of industrial engineers, and never the twain shall meet."

"Except they did."

"Right, with neither side taking on board the implications." Chung explained about the South Houston water plant hack. "Which is exactly how that happened: a low-security system designed for use only within a control-room inadvertently exposed to the web. And that's just one of dozens of such cases."

Chung checked the screen:

Checked 927 combinations, 0 successful so far

"So what will we see when we get in?" asked Evans.

"I'll show you." Chung pulled up the webpage with the South Houston case that showed a screen grab of the SCADA system there.

"I've downloaded a bunch of these, and they all look very similar. Essentially a schematic of the plant, with valves, pumps, gates and so forth shown. Opening or closing a valve is as simple as clicking on it."

"Wow," said Evans, "that looks a lot simpler than I would have expected."

"Me too," said Chung, "but it makes sense. The guys in the control room aren't computer geeks, they are hardware engineers. Their language is valves and pressures and water-flow meters. So that's what the system shows them."

"So," said Evans, "all we need to do is close a valve upstream of the base to stop the flow of water into the pipe section, and open all the ones downstream of it to drain away the water that's already there."

"Right," said Chung. "In principle, it ought to be pretty simple. Let's hope it turns out to be that simple in practice. Let's grab some coffee while we wait for the dictac software to do its stuff."

* * *

John Walsh was the supervisor at the secondary control room of the Eagle Mountain Water Plant. There was maintenance scheduled for the main control room, which meant he was monitoring things remotely. The system was simple enough: a series of virtual network connections between the terminals in the primary control room and the ones here. Everything that appeared on the main screens was mirrored here, and anything he did here would take place on the terminals of the main room.

There were no operations scheduled tonight, and alarms would sound if anything needed attention, so it would be an easy shift.

* * *

Coffee in hand, Chung checked on the dictac software:

Checked 2,354 combination(s), 2 successful so far:

sys/sys

rsg/sup

"Beautiful!" he said. "What did I tell you? Sys, sys. I bet that's the login pretty much everyone uses. And I'd put money that the second one is a supervisor with the initials rsg."

"So now we can login to the system?" asked Evans.

"Yep!"

Chung hits CTRL-C to abort the dictac session and pulled up a browser window. He selected the Eagle Mountain Water Plant from his bookmarks.

Welcome to CORE-ICS v5.3.7

Username: sys

Password: sys

There was a short delay and then a pictorial was displayed. It looked very similar to the examples he'd found in his web-searches.

"That's really it," asked Evans. "That's the water plant we need to control?"

Chung smiled. "That's really it."

"And we're in? We can actually control it?"

Chung nodded. They both studied the screen. It appeared to be quite a small area. Chung looked for some way to zoom out. There was a 'map' button bottom-right. He clicked it.

The screen refreshed and displayed a large-scale schematic diagram. It appeared to be showing a very large area, but they could see no place names, just code numbers. Chung would need to see if he could Google them. But right now ...

He clicked on one of the codes and another close-up schematic appeared with valve and pump switches shown. The graphics were childishly simple: images of valves that were open or closed, gates that pointed one way or another, pumps that were on or off, and arrows showing the direction of water flow. He clicked the Back button to get back to the map and then again to get back to where they started.

* * *

John Walsh was puzzled. No-one was supposed to be using the primary control centre, yet on one of the screens someone was zooming in and out. What was going on? He considered giving them a call, but with maintenance going on they would be busy, and if they were needing to do something at the same time, he guessed they could do without interruptions.

It was odd, though. If there was something they needed to do, why didn't they ask him to do it?

He moved his chair closer to the screen in question so he could keep an eye on what they were up to.

* * *

Chung stared at the screen.

"What is it?" asked Evans.

"I'm torn," replied Chung. "I really, really want to change one of those switches, just to make sure we really can."

"But?"

"But we don't really know what any of them do. I'm reluctant to mess with something we don't yet understand. If we change the wrong thing, we could set off some alarm. And even if we don't, someone in the plant may notice what we've done."

"Not if we switch it straight back again."

"They still might," said Chung. "What we are looking at here is a copy of an actual screen in the control room. Anything we change here will change on that screen. If someone is looking at it at the time, they will see a switch change and know that they didn't do it."

The two were silent for a few seconds.

They looked at each other. Each knew the other was thinking the same thing: they had to test it. Evans said it first.

"Ok," he said, "so we're looking at the same screen the control room staff are. Anything we do appears on their screen, and anything they do appears on ours, right?"

"Right," said Chung.

"So, let's watch it carefully for say 15 minutes. If anything changes in that time, we assume there's someone there actively controlling the system. If not, we assume that nothing much is going on, anyone monitoring it likely has 20 different screens in front of them, and is probably bored. The chances of them noticing a switch change for a few seconds on one of those 20 screens has to be pretty low, right?"

Chung mulled it over. "Makes sense," he said.

"And we can't be 100% sure we really do have control until we change something. We need to know."

"Actually, we ca-" Chung stopped in mid-sentence, a look of panic on his face.

"What?"

"I'm a freaking moron, that's what!"

"What do you mean?" asked Evans.

"This is simply a remote view of the control room screen. Everything we do here happens on their screen too."

"I know," said Evans, puzzled. "You already said that."

"We've already been doing things!"

"Wha-" He stopped short. "The zooming in and out?"

"Yes. This is just a mirror of their screen. If anyone was watching it at the time, they would have seen everything I did. I'm an idiot."

"So we may have given the game away already?"

Chung nodded unhappily.

Evans said nothing for a moment, then: "In for a penny?"

"I guess so. And you're right, we did need to test it at some point, so this was an unavoidable step. And tomorrow we have to do it again."

"Why again tomorrow?"

"We need to know if our access has been detected. If it has, they'll have changed the password by tomorrow. If I can get in again tomorrow, we can be fairly sure nobody noticed our visit."

"Right," said Evans.

"There are two ways what we're doing can be detected," he said. "The first is seeing the screen change in the control centre. If that's happened, it's already too late."

"And the second?"

"By the effect of whatever change we make. If we break something or flood something or cut off someone's water supply, that may lead to an investigation which reveals the change was made remotely."

"But if it's very brief," said Evans, "switching something on and immediately off again ..."

"That will help. The other thing that will help is to try to pick something out in the sticks, rather than something central."

Chung clicked the map button to zoom back out. He looked for one of the outer areas. He navigated to a sparsely-populated screen. It had just three pipes shown on it: a pipe from the left, a Y-gate and a pipe leading off from each branch of the Y. A green arrow by the Y-gate showed that water was flowing along the upper pipeline.

"There's one more problem," said Chung. "Suppose maintenance is being carried out on the empty section of pipe. There may be a whole gang of workers in there. We could be drowning them without even knowing it."

"Not if we make it really brief," said Evans. "We just want to see the arrow change on the screen, right? As soon as it does, we flick it back. If there are workers in there, we might get their shoes damp but it won't be nearly long enough to drown anyone."

Chung hesitated, then moved the trackpad pointer to the Y-gate icon. He realised he was holding his breath. He clicked. Nothing happened.

"Damn."

"No, look!"

There had been a delay of about two seconds, but the arrow was now pointing down rather than up. It worked! By god, it worked!

Chung's elation was such that he almost forgot to switch it back immediately. He hurriedly clicked it again. Again, there was a short delay before the arrow symbol reversed.

Neither said anything. Nothing needed to be said.

For a few moments, Chung just sat there in awe of what he had just done. A geek sitting in an apartment in Brooklyn while his laptop pretended to the Internet to be in Spain had just taken control of a water system a couple of hundred miles away in Fort Worth. It was incredible.

He was about to disconnect when a sudden thought occurred to him. He pulled Evans' diagram toward him. He then hit the map button and navigated along a few screens. He stopped at a complex-looking one with half a dozen valves on it.

"What are you plotting?" asked Evans.

"Give me a moment."

He stared at the screen. Could it work? He looked at the arrangement of valves. He couldn't see any reason why it shouldn't. He wasn't going to risk further tests tonight, but he liked the idea. He liked it very much indeed.

* * *

Walsh was even more puzzled now. Someone in the main control centre had just switched the feed to zone G to the overflow bypass, yet levels in the main pipeline were perfectly normal? Why would–

The screen updated and the flow was back to normal.

Ok, he thought, they were just testing things as part of the maintenance. How boring is my job that I get so interested in someone testing a valve, he wondered?

The wind on the Brooklyn Bridge was biting, thought Chung, but it was the agreed procedure: when anyone needed to pass on an update that was particularly sensitive, they made a call arranging to meet at Phil's bar, then met instead on the Manhattan side of the bridge. It was a very safe way to talk: there was no practical way to eavesdrop on a conversation held in the open area in a noisy environment, and the combination of wind and traffic noise made the bridge the perfect place.

"So what's the big news?" asked Sullivan.

"SCADA," said Chung. "It's how water plants control the flow of water through the pipelines. It's all controlled remotely. It's intended to be controlled from a control-room at the plant, but there's a web-interface that allows it to be controlled from anywhere."

"And you think you can get in?"

"I'm already in!" said Chung, with a broad smile.

"Wow, I'm impressed!" said Sullivan.

"You shouldn't be."

"Eh? Why?"

Chung explained just how little effort it had required. "That's the reason I considered this particularly sensitive: if the authorities realised just how vulnerable these systems are, they'd move in to protect them immediately. The terrorist risk alone is huge! A terrorist could cut off water supplies, or flood an area, just by sitting in some Internet cafe somewhere and making a few mouse-clicks. Hell, they could probably dump toxic levels of fluoride into the water just as easily. It's a massive, gaping security hole."

"Christ."

"Exactly. I'm half thinking we need to alert the government to this once the project is complete."

"Guess there'll come a time when they figure out how we did it," said Sullivan, "so at that point hopefully they'll work out for themselves how easy it was."

"I hope so. It's really quite scary."

Sullivan switched back to business: "So what's the plan?"

Chung stopped walking, leant on the railing and with the pretext of enjoying the view took the opportunity to look around to make sure that nobody was close to them. Sullivan followed his cue and did the same. Nobody was showing the slightest interest in them; it was just the usual mix of commuters hurrying home and tourists taking photos. Chung reached into his pocket and pulled out a piece of paper. He held it out on the railing so both could see it.

On the paper was a diagram. Using this to illustrate, Chung talked through his idea, just as he'd done with Evans.

"We have the section of pipe running beneath the airbase. We close this valve upstream of the base to stop the water flow, and open all the ones downstream of it – these three here, here and here – to drain the water and allow the baggage-carts to drive in."

"Drive in? Doesn't it end up in a lake or something?"

"There's a large storm-drain here," said Chung, tapping the diagram. "Aaron and I went to take a look, and you could drive an SUV in there. Baggage-carts are pretty small, even with the pallets on them – there's plenty of room. The tugs we'll use are ones used to tow airliners rather than baggage carts – those can tow hundreds of tons, and they're electric, so there are no exhaust fumes to worry about."

"And they fit in the pipe?" asked Sullivan.

"With a little modification to the bodywork. We'll need to check out the route through the system to make sure there are no right-angle turns involved, but generally with water flow you want nice gentle curves so I'm not anticipating any issues there."

Sullivan nodded.

"So," continued Chung, "we drain the water, drive in the carts, collect the pallets, drive them out again well outside any police cordon, load the pallets onto trucks and away we go. Just for good measure, once we're out I'll re-open the upstream valve, close the nearest downstream one and fill the pipe so that in the unlikely event the authorities did discover our hole into the pipe it would be flooded: no way for them to follow us."

Sullivan turned to stare at him. "That's fucking amazing!"

"Elegant, isn't it?"

"It's more than elegant, it's nothing short of brilliant!"

* * *

Rossie had taken considerable persuasion and a pay-rise before he would agree to continue his daily visits to the club. He wasn't going to risk the store-room again, or anywhere else with no exit. He wanted to be far enough that he could beat a hasty retreat if any of them headed in his direction.

He'd selected a corridor leading to a fire-exit. It was further away from where the team had met on the two previous occasions, and it would be harder to hear what was being said, but frankly Foster didn't seem to believe a word of it anyway, so if he got less info it hardly seemed to matter. It was no skin off his nose if the gang pulled it off: he'd done what he was paid to do, he'd reported what he'd learned, and if he couldn't learn much more, the cops would just have to lump it.

He would at least get proof next time that the gang was meeting there: he'd switched off the flash and the shutter sound on his cameraphone and take a photo. He'd used a plane to shave off just enough wood from the bottom of the fire-door that he could see under it, and by holding the cameraphone

233

upside-down get the lens under it too. He could only do one thing at a time: watch, take a photo or listen – the latter requiring him to roll around so his ear was against the gap at the bottom of the door – but c'est la vie.

He'd started to believe the gang was never going to return when he heard the door latch go.

"I think this will be a short meeting," said Sullivan. "Problems one to four have been covered in previous meetings. Suffice it to say plans are firming-up nicely, and the details will be worked out as we proceed with the actual preparations."

There were nods at this. The team trusted each other. They knew the basics of the plans, and if those tasked with carrying them out said it was now all down to the details, that was good enough.

"We have made excellent progress with problem five: our escape-plan. Mike, would you like to briefly explain?"

Rossie had taken seven photos of the team. He flicked through them on the LCD screen. Crap! He'd angled the camera screen too far down: all he'd managed to photograph was the floor. He placed it back in position and carefully angled it up slightly.

"Love it," said Lewis.

"Very neat," agreed Pugh.

There were smiles all round.

"It's not going to be cheap," warned Sullivan. "We're going to have to buy a small fleet of semi rigs, and while some of them can be clunkers, a couple of them will need to be both mechanically perfect and presentable. It's going to require a significant investment from each of us."

She looked around. Nobody seemed to have been put off.

"Ok. We also have a more solid plan for problem six, the money laundering. Sam?"

Rossie had taken six more photos and was flicking through them. Gah! He was either getting the ceiling or the floor or the empty space to the right – and blurred ceiling or floor at that! At this rate, he'd never convince Foster that he was telling the truth. Right. This time he was going to be ultra-careful. Start low and left. Gradually tip the camera upwards in small increments, taking one photo at every step, then angle slightly right and repeat. If he did this three or four times, he had to get at least one photo of them.

It took him about two minutes. He would check them later: it was time now for some eavesdropping.

"So you think our money-laundering plan is any less crazy?" asked Young.

"It's starting to grow on me," said Perez. "The notion is a thing of beauty."

"It still seems crazy to me," said Lewis, "but I can't deny the appeal."

"You know, if we can pull that off, it would almost be even more satisfying than the heist itself," said Jackson.

Everyone looked at Chung. He threw up his hands in surrender. "The crowd has spoken. Who am I to argue?"

There was silence for a moment.

"Is it just me," said Jackson, "or do we have ourselves an operation?" Nobody said anything, but nobody disagreed.

"How long do we have?" asked Lewis, breaking the silence.

"The new bills are introduced in two months, two weeks, three days. We have to assume that they will aim to have them all delivered to the Federal Reserves at least a few days ahead of schedule, to allow time for onward delivery to commercial banks. So let's knock off the extra days to get ten weeks. That's the upper time limit for the hit. From the sums Sam and I have done, we reckon the billion-dollar shipments will continue for two weeks, so the lower time limit is eight weeks. So let's call it nine weeks from today, bang in the middle."

Sullivan looked around. "Are we all in?"

"Hell yes," said Jackson.

"Let's do it," said Perez.

"I'm in," said Lewis.

"Like I said," said Chung.

"Absolutely," said Pugh.

"You know I am," said Young.

"Then, ladies and gentlemen, in exactly nine weeks from today we shall be members of the billionaire club!"

* * *

Rossie felt elated: he knew the exact date of the hit! And he had photos! Foster couldn't give him any crap now!

He got up and crept slowly to the fire exit at the far end of the corridor. The alarm on the door was a simple contact job; easy. He pulled out a length of wire and Blu-tac'd one end to the contact on the door, the other to the contact on the doorway. He then carefully pressed down on the release bar on the door and eased it open. He ducked under the wire to exit, eased the door closed until it latched and then pulled on the middle of the wire. Bits of Blu-tac would be left on the contacts, which a particularly alert person might notice next time the doors were checked, but he didn't need to go back again – he had everything that he needed. And he expected a decent pay-off for this. His future expeditions for booze could wait a while.

He headed down onto the subway. On the train, he got out his phone and flicked through the photos. Floor. Floor. Empty space. Empty space and ceiling. Ceiling. Ceiling. Floor. Floor. There! People! Blurred people, but people at least. Blurred heads and ceiling. Ceiling. Floor. Floor. Floor. Empty space. Ceiling.

He flicked back to the first shot of the people. Four of them were in view. He zoomed in. Fuck! Blurred as hell. He flicked onto the next one. Three heads and ceiling. He zoomed in on the heads. Also blurred as hell. In the dim light, the shutter speed would have been slow, so any movement blurred the images.

Well, it wasn't what he'd hoped for, but still, he could prove it wasn't a fantasy – that there really was a gang meeting there – and most of all he knew the date of the hit! He knew what, where and when. The cops could take care of the who when they arrested them.

He got off the subway train and headed up to the street, and made straight for the precinct house. He wasn't going to let Foster have this info for a few hundred bucks. This was huge. More than huge. And he had all of the details.

* * *

"Pritchard."

"Luke, it's Kate Lorrimar."

"Hey Kate, how are you doing?"

"Well, things may be getting a little interesting."

"Oh?" asked Pritchard.

"That snitch. He's come back with something."

"What?"

"The date," said Lorrimar. "He claims to have the exact date of the hijack."

"I think that does indeed qualify as interesting!" Pritchard gestured to Daniels, then hit the conference button and dialled Daniels' extension to bring him into the call. Daniels picked up.

"I've just brought Tim into the call. Could you just repeat the news?"

"Our snitch now claims to know the exact date of the hijack," said Lorrimar.

"When?" asked Daniels.

"Nine weeks from today."

"The snitch has presumably been told he's not getting a dime unless this checks out?"

"He has."

Pritchard wasted no time in mulling it over. "We have to treat this as a solid threat. I want a conference call with you, the BEP Director and Timpkins. Are there any other decision-makers we need to get in on the call?"

"Well, it depends on what we might be deciding," she said. "If we wanted to make any radical changes to the arrangements, then the Treasury would need to approve them, but I think at this stage that's everyone we need. If the Director is on board, then we'll have the Treasury's ear."

"Ok," said Pritchard. "Can we set up the call for say one hours' time?"

"Leave it with me," said Lorrimar.

The two men hung up the phones.

"So what are you going to propose in this call?" asked Daniels.

"I have absolutely no idea," said Pritchard, "and we have exactly one hour to figure that out. Let's go grab some coffee."

* * *

Young walked into the Lockheed Martin building, looking every inch a man who belonged there. He was wearing the same disguise as in the photo Chung had uploaded into the HR system's contractor database, and carrying a drivers licence in the same name: Pat Barker. Both Young and Sullivan were great adherents to the concept that the difference between success and failure is often in the details: the exact same photo on a two-year-old driving licence and a supposedly recent photo submitted for his contractor's pass might be noticed. The photo on the driving licence was in the same disguise but with different clothes and subtle differences in hairstyle.

Young walked up to reception.

"Morning!" he said, breezily. "My name's Pat Barker, I'm due to start next week. They suggested I pick up my pass today to save time on my first morning."

"Certainly, Sir, I'll call the Security office for you." The receptionist picked up a phone and dialled a four-digit extension. "Reception here, I have a Pat Barker here to collect a pass?"

She listened to the response. "Thanks," she said, replacing the receiver and turning back to Young.

"Please take a seat and someone will be up in a few minutes."

"Thank you," said Young.

* * *

It was a little too much like something out of a bad spy movie, thought Perez. He very much doubted that Vladimir was his contact's real name, but the Russian accent seemed real enough: Semtex was manufactured in the Czech Republic, and most of the sources were East European. Well, Ortíz wasn't his real surname, though he had followed Young's advice to stick to his real first name. Unless it's an unusual one, it is of no help to anyone, and far simpler. You'll respond naturally to it, and if you bump into a friend, you can say a quick hello and be on your way. The advice had made perfect sense to him.

Meeting at the Bethesda Fountain in Central Park was a somewhat surreal touch; he'd half-expected to be asked to carry a copy of the New York Times under his arm.

The reality was rather more mundane: a phone call on his cell. "Climb the steps on the right side of the Terrace, please, Mr Ortíz."

Perez turned and walked towards the steps. "How will I recognise you?"

"When you reach the top of the steps, cross to the opposite steps and lean back against the wall." The phone clicked off.

Perez did as instructed. He was there for less than a minute before he was approached.

"Shall we walk?"

'Vladimir' at least didn't look like a character from a spy movie, thought Perez. No trench coat or wide-brimmed hat, just a very ordinary-looking guy, about 30 years old, tall, slim, goatee beard and wiry black hair.

They set off along the path.

"Remind me how you came to hear of me ... may I call you Raul?"

"Certainly," said Perez. Another lesson he'd learned from Young: lie with economy. Stick to the truth unless there's a specific reason to lie. 99% of the truth is too generic to be of any help to anyone, and unless you are a skilled liar, people can tell. Telling a harmless truth is a good way to establish trust. This truth fell into the 'too generic to be useful' category.

"I'm ex-army. I still have some contacts there, and they keep tabs on certain people. People who do business with those in your line of business."

Vladimir nodded. If the fact that he was known to the US Army was news to him, he certainly didn't show it, nor did he appear concerned about the fact.

"It is just the one order you wish to place?"

"For this project," confirmed Perez, "though I may need supplies for future projects."

"And the quantity you require?"

Perez had done the sums. Semtex was an incredibly powerful explosive, and the amounts needed for the aircraft were trivial. But blowing up the trucks with sufficient force that there would be no way to tell the bills had not been on board: that would take significant amounts.

"15kg would be ideal if you can manage it. 10kg would suffice if fifteen is a problem."

"Fifteen would not be a problem." No hesitation, Perez noted.

"We would like it without DMDB – is that possible?" Semtex itself is undetectable by both explosives sniffing machines and dogs. Since 1996, Semtex has been required to have a detection agent added – a substance which machines and dogs can detect. DMDB was the most common of these. However, the additive was mixed with the Semtex after the main production process. If Semtex could be removed from production before the DMDB was added, it remained undetectable.

Vladimir expressed no surprise. "That carries a price premium, of course, but poses no difficulty."

"That's excellent."

"When would you require delivery?" asked Vladimir.

"Sooner rather than later would be desirable," replied Perez.

"That is the case with most of my clients. Would 48 hours be agreeable?"

Perez was surprised at the speed. "Perfect," he replied. "And the price?"

"With DMDB would be $12,000. Without is $18,000. Cash, of course."

The amount seemed reasonable to Perez, but he wasn't sure whether he was expected to haggle. Vladimir quickly eliminated his uncertainty. "Firm price."

"Agreed," said Perez.

"Half today, half on delivery. You have $9,000 available cash today, I presume?"

Perez nodded. Young was sat in a car less than 15 minutes walk away with $25,000 in cash in a briefcase. "I can meet you back here in half an hour."

"The arrangements will be in place by the time you return. Handover arrangements will be confirmed by phone on the morning of delivery."

That simple, thought Perez. That simple to buy around 50 times the amount of Semtex used to bring down the Pan-Am jet at Lockerbie.

* * *

The uniformed security officer walked across the lobby carrying a folder, stopped, opened the folder and looked at it for a moment.

"I think you're probably looking for me," said Young, with a smile. "Pat Barker."

The guard studied his face and the card again. "Do you have some form of identification, Mr Barker?"

"Sure." Young pulled out his wallet and extracted the fake driving licence prepared by Pugh: it was good enough to fool even a police officer. He handed it over. The guard looked at it carefully, and made no move to return it.

"Thank you, Sir. If you'd like to come over to reception with me, I just need to get you to sign for it."

The two walked over to a clear section of the long reception desk. The guard put the folder down on the desktop and opened it. He pulled out a pen and indicated a signature line on a form in the folder. "If you could just sign and date here, please."

Young did so. The guard checked the signature against that on the driving licence. This guy was thorough, thought Young. He would have to guard against complacency in this place.

The guard accepted the pen back, and handed over the driving licence and pass. "The pass contains a standard RFID chip, just touch it on the barrier pads on entry and exit. Inside the building, please ensure that it is visible at all times."

"Will do," said Young. "Would it be ok if I pop my head round my boss's door while I'm here?

"Sure," replied the guard. "You have your pass, you're good to go."

"Thanks," said Young.

He just needed a few minutes inside the building to find a stationery cupboard, slip a few sheets of letterhead and envelopes into his bag and make one phone call from a Lockheed line. Smiling at the guard, he walked over to the barrier, touched his pass to the contact, watched the green light come on and the barrier slide aside, and walked through. He was now officially a Lockheed Martin contractor.

* * *

"First," said Pritchard, "I appreciate you all finding time in the schedule for this conference call at such short notice. I'm sure you've all had to re-arrange your schedules. I'm also sure you understand that I wouldn't have requested the call unless I felt there was good reason for it. I'd like to express particular thanks to Mr Bailey, as I realise this is coming out of the blue for you."

Peter Bailey had been Director of the BEP facility in Fort Worth for nine years, and Deputy Director for three years before that. Lorrimar had briefly brought him up to speed in requesting that he join the call.

"I've known Ms Lorrimar a long time," said Bailey. "When she tells me I need to take something seriously, I listen. But I must confess to being at something of a loss as to what you propose we do in response to this information? As I understand it, you've just completed a full external security review and recommended only – forgive me for my phrasing – a few very minor changes, all of which we have implemented. Is my understanding correct, Mr Pritchard?"

"It is, Director."

"I must say," chimed in Major Timpkins, "I'm left with the same question. I still question the reliability of this claimed intelligence. It seems quite remarkable that we are granting this much credence to the word of an informant whose own handler describes him as a nobody, and who has still delivered no evidence for his claims. If we had the identity of a known and credible gang, that would be one thing, but it seems to me we have nothing but the unsupported claims of a man being paid for his supposed information, backed up by nothing more than a couple of photos that even with enhancement could be pretty much anyone on the planet. But that aside, even if we do treat the information as credible, what would you have us do that we are not already doing? If you can suggest additional precautions, I'll gladly listen to them."

Pritchard and Daniels had been able to come up with only one idea, and Pritchard knew it was going to cause a flurry of protests. But when they already had the best possible security in place, and none of them could think of any way to improve it, it was all they had left.

"Given we know the date–" he began.

"If we know the date," corrected Timpkins.

"Ok, if. It's one day's shipment. The only thing I can suggest is that, on that date, instead of two dummy convoys, we have three. The aircraft fly with dummy bills on board."

Peter Bailey broke the two-second silence that followed. "I'm not sure whether you are aware, Mr Pritchard, but that is right in the middle of the shipments for the new $50 bills. The daily shipments at that time amount to over a billion dollars. Missing a day's shipment at any time would create headaches, but at that time in particular it would be ... non-trivial."

"We suspect the timing is not coincidental, Director," said Pritchard. "If you're going to hit a shipment, doesn't it make sense that you'd do it at that particular time?"

"Well ..." said Bailey.

"I do think the date adds credibility to the claim," said Lorrimar. "There's no way the snitch could have known there was anything special about that fortnight, so the fact that he's given a date slap bang in the middle of it is reason to take this seriously."

"The dates of new bill designs are not a secret," said Timpkins. "He could have read it in the paper."

"He could," said Daniels, "but ironically this is where the small-time nature of the informant becomes an argument in favour of the intelligence. The precinct cop who deals with him says he's not the type to read newspapers or to be able to make those kind of logical connections."

"Could you bring forward production of the new bills by 24 hours?" asked Pritchard. "That way we can remove a day's shipments and the bills are still distributed on time."

"It's not that simple, Mr Pritchard," said Bailey. "The Gantt chart for the introduction of a new bill design has literally hundreds of interlocking elements. To bring forward the introduction by even one day would have a cascade effect that would affect pretty much every step along the way. Much of it is done on a Just In Time basis, and of course the work is already underway, so there may not be a day's slack in the system."

"I'm not sure what else to say, Mr Bailey. It's the one step we can take to guard against the threat."

"Unless the gang has someone on the inside," said Timpkins. "Then if we switch to a dummy shipment for one day, they'll know about it and just change the date of the attack."

"Can we keep it to ourselves?" asked Daniels. "So that as far as everyone else is concerned, this is a day like any other, with real bills loaded onto the aircraft?"

"Impossible," said Bailey. "Don't forget that the entire BEP production system is automated. The bills get printed, cut, stacked and packaged by machines. They get taken from the print-room to the vault by robots. They get removed from the vault and loaded onto the trucks by robots. There is no human intervention at any step. To interrupt that in some way and substitute dummy bills ... well, to be perfectly frank, I don't even know offhand how we would do it, or for that matter if we could do it."

"Alright," said Pritchard, "what I suggest is this. Ms Lorrimar and Director Bailey look into the logistics of substituting dummy bills in such a way that the minimum possible number of people know about it. Major Timpkins, from your end there is no need for anyone to know: so far as the air transport is concerned, it's business as usual, with a real shipment. Everything about this operation is on a strictly need-to-know basis."

"That's not a problem from my end," said Timpkins.

"I'm not in a position to make promises," said Bailey. "As I say, I don't know for sure that what you propose is even possible. But we'll look into it and advise accordingly."

"Thank you, Director. I know you'll think carefully about who needs to be consulted to minimise those who are aware of even the idea of a dummy shipment, but please at this stage simply raise it as an additional security measure that has been proposed – for dummy shipments on random days – rather than a specific plan for a particular date."

"Understood," said Bailey.

"Thank you all for your time," said Pritchard.

* * *

Sullivan smiled at the incongruity of the sight: all eight of them stood on the apron of a disused airbase carrying out a stealth operation while dressed in hi-viz clothing and with a tipper truck, two backhoe diggers, a turf-laying roller and a mini cement-mixer all bright yellow. Two SUVs completed the ensemble.

Perez had concluded it was a safer approach than a night visit. While the Dexpan non-explosive demolition agent was a far quieter approach than explosives, the sound of the concrete cracking was something that would carry. It also required precise application, which would have meant serious amounts of lighting. Noise and lighting at night was going to attract far more attention than a work crew during the day, and sometimes hiding in plain sight was the best option. The sign-writing on the construction vehicles showed them to be a maintenance company, and the work orders they carried showed that they were there to deal with subsidence by digging out an area of the apron in preparation for later relaying. The paperwork was just a precaution: a recce had shown that the security patrols were simple drive-bys every two hours, and the hanger buildings hid them from view from the road.

"Ok," said Sullivan, "Perez, Evans and Jackson are running this operation. The rest of us are just builders' labourers. Perez?"

Perez was leaning on a hammer drill that was almost as tall as he was. "The main job is to create a hole in the taxiway here large enough to lower the pallets into the water pipe below. The pallets are 48x40 inches, and fit comfortably onto a baggage-cart with room to spare. We need to allow sufficient clearance to lower things quickly, and the trucks are eight feet wide, so the hole is going to be seven feet square."

Perez kicked his foot against one of the tubs of Dexpan lined up in front of them. "The good news is that this stuff will do the job of breaking up the concrete for us. The bad news is that there's still a lot of hard work involved. Dexpan is applied by drilling holes into the concrete and filling them with the chemical gunk. The Dexpan then expands rapidly and creates cracks between the holes. The holes have to be drilled one foot apart, so to create a seven foot square hole, we have to drill 64 holes. That's what this baby is for." He patted the hammer drill. "It's hot and heavy work, and requires two people, one to hold it steady, the other to operate it. Four of us will work the drill in shifts. Those not working the drill will be mixing up the Dexpan and pouring it into the holes already drilled."

"How long do you expect the whole thing to take?" asked Pugh.

"We have to drill down about 18 inches," replied Perez. "With a bunch of soldiers, maybe two minutes per hole. With you lot ..." He grinned. "Maybe five minutes. Call it five or six hours total to drill and fill. The Dexpan starts to work within a couple of hours. It can take up to six hours, but using the backhoe as a hammer should speed things up. Then we have to dig out enough earth to reach the pipe beneath, and insert planking to shore up the sides. It's going to be a long day, so we'll cover the hole and return tomorrow to create the hole in the pipe. That's much thinner concrete but needs to be done more precisely as we want to avoid water loss. The last thing we need is anyone investigating a leak."

"That's four of us," said Lewis. "What will the other four be doing?"

"Jackson will be taking the cement mixer out to the runway to patch three holes in the runway. You and Sullivan will create the banking and lay the turf that will keep the underside of the truck hidden from anyone viewing from the perimeter fence. Evans has managed to get himself onto light duties: taking the photographs and measurements necessary to create the boards that will hang beneath our trucks to hide the hole from the Marines. They need to think they can see beneath the trucks, so that as far as they and the rest of the world is concerned, the bills are sitting inside our trucks."

"Hey," objected Evans, less of the 'light duties' stuff – unlike you lot, I'm going to be spending whole days here once the work is complete." Since they had no way of knowing what time the flights would depart, nor what the weather would be like on the day, they needed a comprehensive set of photos covering all times of day and all weather conditions. They had established from their webcam surveillance that the convoys always departed between shortly before 10am and 5pm, but they still needed a wide variety of photos to cover all the possible combinations. Once the grass banking was in place, Evans would be spending entire days there, taking photos at all times of day and all weather conditions to ensure the photo boards on the day would be a perfect match.

"Isn't it a bit risky leaving a hole here overnight?" asked Chung. "What if a security patrol discovers it – or falls into it?"

"Evans has that, uh, covered," said Young.

"Plywood painted to look like concrete," said Evans. "It will pass at 10 feet or so, and we'd have to be very unlucky for a security patrol to get closer than that, even assuming they come inside at all routinely – as far as we can tell, they don't. Once the whole job is complete, the plywood will block the hole, but we'll lay a thin covering of concrete over the top. Just a few millimetres, so we can break through easily on the day."

"Right," said Perez, "enough chatter: let's get to work!"

Three hours later, the area behind the apron had what looked like a low bunker. It was high enough to ensure nobody from the far side would be able to see beneath the truck trailer while not hiding the truck completely from view. "The audience gets suspicious if they can tell something is hidden from them," Evans had said, "the trick is to show them enough that they mentally fill in the gaps for themselves."

The work he was doing now was crucial.

The key to their escape was that the authorities be convinced the cash was in the trucks. Any hint of the truth, and the authorities would move in to block all tracks and roads leading from the path of the water pipe. In principle, it was a trivial illusion: the grass banking of the fake bunkers was essentially bland and featureless. But photos are two-dimensional and the world is three-dimensional, so the illusion would work only from a limited range of angles. A vital part of the planning would be to control not only where the Galaxies parked, but also the route they took while taxiing in.

Evans had spent the entire three hours on the first part of the exercise: walking across the apron with camera, chalk and a folded satellite photo printed from Google Earth. At over 90 separate points, he carefully marked the position on the satellite photo and made a corresponding chalk-mark on the apron. Now he was carefully retracing his steps and taking a photo at each point. The camera was fitted with a 50mm lens, known as a 'standard lens' because it replicated the perspective of the human eye.

Having the Galaxies park several hundred feet away and in a specific place meant that the illusion would be taking place in a well-controlled environment, but the flight crew and anyone else in the cockpit would be able to see the truck as they taxied-in towards it. It was essential that he constrain the route the Galaxies took so as to keep the viewing angles to as narrow a range as possible.

Jackson frowned as he surveyed the hole he'd just filled with concrete and smoothed-down. His concern was not the quality of the work – it was rough-and-ready but more than good enough for an aircraft designed for dirt field landings – but rather all the smaller holes he'd earlier decided they didn't need to worry about.

Each of the 28 wheels on the landing-gear of a C-5 is four feet in diameter, more than enough to bridge small holes in a runway, but it was the sheer number of them that concerned Scott. Even small holes would cause some degree of impact to the tyres. Could enough small bumps cause a blow-out? The answer had to be yes, but he didn't know the aircraft well enough to know what the limits might be, and it was the sort of thing unlikely to be found by googling: it was the sort of thing flight crews knew by experience rather than a number written in a manual.

"Christ!" exclaimed Pugh.

Perez laughed. "Loud, isn't it?"

The first section of concrete to crack had done so with what sounded like an enormous bang.

"I can certainly appreciate now why doing this at night wouldn't have been a good plan," said Sullivan. "A sound like that would carry a long way across flat ground."

"Do you think we need worry about visitors?" asked Chung.

Perez shook his head. "I don't think so. This is Texas, where there are more guns than people. By the time the sound reaches the nearest houses, it's going to sound like someone doing a bit of target practice. But the paperwork will cover us if anyone does get inquisitive."

"It still makes me a little nervous," said Chung. "If our cover is blown here, that's the entire operation down the pan."

"I know," said Sullivan, "but it's a small risk, and we all know you can only minimise them, not eliminate them."

Chung nodded.

Evans allowed himself a smile of satisfaction as he replaced the last of his chalk-marks with paint ones. He'd walked the route three times now, once from the centreline, once each from a position around fifteen feet either side, stopping at regular intervals to check the view through the camera. He was satisfied that the illusion would work for the entire path of the aircraft, even allowing for them deviating a little from the direct route from the runway.

The one remaining complication was the weather. The Dallas-Fort Worth area of Texas had a humid subtropical climate, and the weather could vary from hot and clear to heavy rain. He would have to make several visits to the airfield to take photos in different weather conditions, allowing them to prepare several alternative sets of photos for each truck. The actual set would be applied the night before, based on the short-range weather forecast. That was usually reliable in the area, so the chances of them needing to do a last-minute swap on the day were low. Close to nil, he hoped: they were going to be very busy on the day.

Well, decided Scott, there wasn't much they could do about it: it wasn't practical to fill all of the holes. He wasn't concerned about an aircraft crashing on the runway: the risk was a blown tyre preventing one or more of the aircraft taking-off again. Their escape plan very much depended on ensuring there were no Marines left behind.

But the risk really only concerned the final aircraft. If any of the others were unable to depart, they could instruct the Marines to transfer to one of the other C-5s. In that eventuality, they would need to count them very carefully during the transfer!

* * *

It had been a long, hard, hot two days, thought Sullivan, but you couldn't beat the feeling of such a visible step forward in their plans. Looked at from ten feet away, you'd never know they'd been there. The concrete surface looked exactly the same as it had before: rough, dirty, dusty. Thanks to the careful photos they'd taken beforehand, even the oil stains were back in the same place.

But what had once been solid concrete was now a hole in the ground covered by a sheet of ply and over that a wafer-thin layer of concrete just to match the appearance. She felt like she had a similar layer of concrete on her overalls.

"I can't wait to get back to the hotel and spend about a week soaking in a hot bath," she said as she climbed back into the SUV.

"Hot?" asked Jackson. "You're crazy. I'm going to put the aircon on full whack and then stand under a very cold shower."

"Men don't understand bubble-baths, eh, Lewis?"

Lewis smiled and said nothing. Bubble baths were not her thing.

Sullivan turned to Chung. "What's the state of play with our exit point?"

"The drainage ramp looks good," replied Chung. "The ramp is plenty wide enough, and the slope is gentle. Looks like it was designed with some kind of inspection vehicles in mind – the tugs will easily cope. There's a track leading out to the nearest road, it was fine with the SUV, we just need to test it out with one of the rigs. Jackson and Pugh will take care of that while I do some more research on the valves we need to control."

"Sounds like all is in hand."

* * *

Chung sighed and decided he needed something stronger than coffee. He'd been googling the location codes found on the water plant schematics for more than an hour without success. The problem was, they were too generic. A code like S-456/2 brought up hundreds of hits, representing parts numbers for everything from kitchen blenders to motor yacht engines. Not a single one was a location in a water pipe system.

He walked over to the minibar, opened the door and pulled out a couple of whisky miniatures. This, he thought, was going to take some time and patience.

* * *

Jackson was rather enjoying himself as he guided the big-rig down a back-road running east from Hicks Field. He guessed there was a little of the trucker fantasy in everyone, no matter how mundane the reality of the job might be. The scenery was certainly lacking in excitement: corn, grass, dirt, a few scrubland trees, some farm buildings dotted about here and there, a few houses and not a lot else.

Pugh was monitoring the GPS for the location of the track. Jackson had marked it as a waypoint on his previous visit, noting that the area was distinctly lacking in landmarks.

"Coming up on the left," said Pugh. "Three hundred yards."

Jackson eased off the gas and started taking the rig down through the gears.

"I got it," he said, spotting the anonymous-looking track.

He indicated more from habit than need – there was no-one around to see the signal – and braked almost to a halt. The track surface looked a little rougher than he'd remembered, but he didn't think it would be a problem: the rig had big wheels and plenty of ground clearance. He checked his wing mirrors, swung out wide and turned in.

The only part that concerned him was turning the rig around. There was a wide open area close to the drainage ramp, but reversing an articulated rig was harder than it looked. It was easy to point the trailer the wrong way or back yourself into a jack-knife if you weren't careful. He intended to be careful.

* * *

Perez was studying the simulated circuit on the VSM monitor in Lewis's home electronics lab.

"I have tested it all, you know," said Lewis. It was a little early in the morning for her; Perez still seemed to favour military hours.

Perez smiled apologetically. "I know, and I know how annoying it is to have someone re-checking something you already know is fine. But in ordinance work you don't do a single thing without getting a colleague to confirm each step before you take it."

"You must do sometimes. What about defusing a bomb? You surely don't have a colleague standing next to you?"

"Not next to you," said Perez, "but on the radio, and where possible watching a head-cam feed too. You tell your colleague what you are about to do, they confirm, then you do. Ordinance is an unforgiving trade, and this stuff -" he indicated the red-coloured slabs of Semtex sitting on the bench- "might look like plasticine, but it only takes a very small amount of it to make what is technically known as a very big bang. Something goes wrong with this much Semtex and they won't be identifying us by our dental records because there won't be enough left of us to even find our teeth."

"Fair enough," said Lewis.

"All I'm doing is making sure the circuit will be open when we connect the detonator, and that only the correct coded transmission can trigger it. I won't connect the Semtex until after the detonator in any case, but even a detonator firing in the same room as Semtex is not something you want happening."

"Consider my indignation officially withdrawn."

Perez traced the circuits with his finger for several minutes, using the mouse to zoom in and out.

"And this chip here is the addition I asked for?"

"Right."

"Ok," he said, finally, scooting his chair away from the PC and over to the workbench. In front of him sat the Semtex, the twenty-four circuit-boards Lewis had prepared, a plastic box containing twenty-four detonators, a cutting-board, a pot of paint, a small paintbrush and a soldering station. He picked up the first board, and carefully locked it into the clamps on the bench. He picked one of the detonators out of the box. It was a plain silver-coloured cylinder around an inch-and-a-half in length, with two short wires emerging from it: one red, one black. Perez positioned it on the circuit-board and picked up the soldering-iron. "Device one," he said.

Lewis watched closely. Perez didn't take his eyes off the board but grinned. "Now who's double-checking."

Lewis grinned back. "Just following your motto."

Perez finished soldering the black wire to the pin on the circuit-board. He positioned the red wire against another pin. He soldered that, waited for it to cool then gently tugged at it.

"Happy?" asked Perez.

"Happy," confirmed Lewis.

Perez removed the board from the clamps and laid it to one side. "I'll connect the detonators to all the boards, then add the Semtex."

Lewis nodded. Perez picked up the second circuit-board.

* * *

Jackson grinned as he finally got the rig pointed back out toward the track leading to the road.

"I won't claim it was the most elegant manoeuvre in the history of truck-driving, but it did the job."

"Yep," said Pugh, "and the rig has no problems on this surface. Even if it rains, it's all flat ground – no issue with traction, and the surface is compacted enough that we're not going to sink into it."

"Looks like we have ourselves an exit point," agreed Jackson.

* * *

Jackson had volunteered to write the letter to Lockheed as he was familiar with the military-style language used by defense contractors, as well as the correct designations of the aircraft. While civilians referred to it as the Galaxy and the military as the

C-5, the full Lockheed designation of the specific model in question was the L500/C-5B/AMP.

Young had called Carswell Air Force Base while he was inside the Lockheed Martin building to find out the name of the maintenance chief in charge of the C-5 fleet, one Lt. Jack Boulder.

Dear Lt. Boulder

L500/C-5B/AMP RETROFIT NOTICE: WEATHER RADAR MICROPROCESSOR CIRCUIT

Analysis of parts requests has revealed an issue with the weather radar microprocessor circuit fitted to L500/C-5B/AMP aircraft which can result in premature failure of the system. As a precaution, Lockheed Martin is carrying out a retrofit program to replace these components.

The retrofit will be carried out in situ on the base by Lockheed Martin engineers at our expense. It is recommended that this replacement be carried out at your earliest convenience. The work will require access to the flight deck of each aircraft for no more than 10-15 minutes.

Please telephone me on the main switchboard number at Lockheed Martin HQ, above, to arrange a convenient time for the engineers to visit.

Thank you for your attention to this matter.

Yours sincerely

Pat Barker

Field Technician Supervisor, Avionics

C-5 Maintenance Support

"That's it?" asked Young, reading it on-screen.

"That's it," confirmed Jackson.

"It seems too simple."

Jackson laughed. "I know what you mean. But that's the beauty of the military mindset. Everything happens by the book. No maintenance chief wants things failing on his watch. They get a letter like this, they call Lockheed, ask for Mr Barker, the receptionist looks him up in the internal telephone directory, sees that calls should be put through to his cell and the call comes through right here." Jackson held up the PAYG handset bought for the purpose with cash and no trace to them. "My guess is we'll get the call the same day the letter arrives and the appointment will be set for no more than a week later."

"Fantastic," said Young, sliding a piece of Lockheed Martin letterhead into the printer. "Print it out and I'll go back into Lockheed tomorrow to put it in a post tray."

"Lovely, isn't it?" asked Jackson. "Lockheed not only provides our credentials, but even pays the postage!"

* * *

Finally! It had taken Chung another hour and a second glass of whisky, but he had his match: the page he was looking at was a municipal planning site for the Dallas Fort Worth area. Several of the codes matched, and were in locations that made sense. Now what he needed to do was match up the codes to plans of the airbase. That was going to require some more old-fashioned research, and could wait for the morning. He would, though, need a little help from Pugh.

* * *

"Halfway there," said Perez, unclasping the twelfth board. "Now for the Semtex."

Lewis eyed the Semtex slabs nervously. "I've just become a convert to your ultra-cautious approach. I know the circuit is good, you know the circuit is good, but adding that ... Well, it makes it kind of real, doesn't it?"

Perez nodded. "The good news is that the Semtex is purely passive here: there's no electronic connection. The Semtex explodes only if the detonator does, and as we can see ..."

"Right."

Perez picked up a Stanley knife and pulled the first slab of Semtex toward him. He cut off a small section. He reached into his pocket and pulled out a tiny plastic box around two inches long by half an inch wide and half an inch deep.

"Now for the clever bit," he said.

Lewis smiled. The clever bit was indeed a touch of genius.

* * *

"So," said Sullivan, "where the hell do we begin? I feel like we need an Advanced Money Laundering course for this one."

"The numbers," said Young, with a smile, "always with the numbers. Shouldn't have to tell you that!"

"The biggest ... markets."

"Right. I figure ten at a hundred million each. We don't know how many of those will work out, so I guess we want 20 or 30 targets. So we start by ranking them by size, then things get a bit more subjective. We'll just have to decide between us the risk level involved with each. By the end of it, we end up with a list of possibles, each of which can handle that kind of cash and which we feel represents an acceptable level of risk."

"None of these guys are exactly going to be cuddly characters," said Sullivan. "Especially not with what we plan to do to them."

"Quite. Risks are always relative. But while they are scary people for sure, their reach is mostly within their own countries. Provided we can get in and out before they realise what's going on, we shouldn't have too much to worry about."

"I wish I shared your confidence."

"Come on," said Young, "let's do some research."

* * *

"Twelve of twelve." Perez set the last completed circuit board aside. "I think a coffee now, before we move onto the truck explosives, don't you?"

The two of them walked through to the kitchen where Lewis had a bean-to-cup coffee machine on the counter.

"You like your coffee," observed Perez.

"Truth be told, I like my gadgets." She grinned. "The fact that it makes great coffee is a bonus."

Perez smiled, as he pressed the button for a latte.

"So onto the easy bit next," he said. "No need for subtlety for the trucks. A mobile phone to serve as trigger, and a fuckton of explosives to blow them to rather small pieces."

"Oh, there's still some subtlety to the circuits," said Lewis.

"Oh?"

"We want the trucks to explode in close succession, so that it will look like one accidental explosion triggered the rest," said Lewis. "If we have to call each phone in turn to trigger them, that's at least two or three seconds per call – a suspiciously long gap."

Perez picked up his latte.

"Way too long. Sympathetic detonation is measured in hundredths of a second. So what happens instead?"

Lewis pressed the button for a cappuccino.

"Chung wrote a small app for the phones and another piece of code running on a server. The apps continually poll the server once per second. When we call the first phone to trigger it, it changes a value on the server from 00 to 01. Then it fires the detonator. Phone 2 sees that value change, updates it to 02 and fires its own detonator. Phone 3 sees that change, updates it to 03 and fires. And so on, each one a few hundredths of a second apart, as you say. From the outside, it will look like each truck exploding sets off the next one."

"Nice," said Perez.

"Glad you like."

"Right," said Perez, "let's go make some truck-disposal devices."

* * *

"Any more changes?" asked Young.

Sullivan shook her head.

"So we're happy that this is the final version of our list? We have twenty-five."

"Happy might be over-stating things," replied Sullivan, "but yes, I think those are our best shots."

"Right, so that's the easy bit done. Now we need to make a credible approach. That's the tricky part."

"Now you've switched to under-statement."

Young grinned at her. "Where's Ms 'Never happier than when faced with a challenge' Sullivan gone?"

"She's taking a small leave of absence. I'm starting to doubt our sanity with this one. Pugh can create all the documentation we need, but we're not going to get that far without them already believing that we are who we claim to be."

"Do I have to quote the old adage again?" asked Young.

"I know, I know ... The bigger the con, the easier it gets."

"That's the one."

It was one of the counter-intuitive lessons of the confidence trickster's trade. Try to con people out of a small amount of money, and they'll ask all kinds of questions. Make the sting big enough, however, and people assume it has to be for real. Like the guy who held a secret conference of the top scrap metal companies in France and convinced them the Eiffel Tower was dangerously corroded and would have to be pulled down and the metal sold. It was so big a story they didn't question it.

"Like the loans game," said Sullivan. It was a truism in banking that it was easier to borrow a million dollars than it was to borrow a thousand.

"Right. And we have the advantage that the money is completely, 100%, verifiably real. They can carry out any tests they like, it'll pass all of them."

"Once we get that far," said Sullivan. "But we're a ways from that. I have a feeling we need to talk to Chung."

* * *

Chung was, just at that moment, introducing himself to the woman at the Information Desk in the Fort Worth Planning and Development Dept.

"Morning!" he said, handing over the business card created for him by Pugh which said that he was Vincent Choi, Senior Surveyor with DFW Developments. A short-term contract with a telephone answering service meant that the phone number on the card would, if it proved necessary, be answered in the name of the fake company. "Vincent Choi." He looked down at the name-plate on the desk. "And you're Beverley Crane?"

The woman accepted the card, glanced at it and handed it back. "I am. How can I help you, Mr Choi?"

Chung laid out on the counter a large-scale map of the Hicks Field area.

"We're doing some development in a couple of areas, one by Hicks Field and another out by Eagle Mountain. In both cases, we need to run some network cabling between buildings which will cross land owned by several other companies. We'll need to negotiate permissions from them, but first we need to figure out a feasible route, using existing underground infrastructure as much as possible. I need plans showing the routes of the underground water system, sewage pipes and so forth."

Crane nodded. "That area isn't computerised yet, it's all paper plans, but the index is computerised and I can photocopy anything you need." She pointed to the tatty leaflet taped to the wall showing the schedule of copying charges. "Let me show you to the terminal, you can identify the plans you need then just bring me the reference numbers for the ones you want copied."

Crane led him over to a computer terminal. She logged in. Chung watched with amusement as she typed Planning in the username field and watched her fingers on the keyboard as she typed, yes, Department for the password. There was, he supposed, no reason to have security on the system at all, but he objected to token security on principle. You either have proper security, or none at all. If no security at all is considered an unacceptable risk, that tells you that you need proper security.

Crane double-clicked on a large-scale map to zoom into the Hicks Field area. "The mapping system at this level is just a Google Maps feed," she said. "So you scroll around it and use the plus and minus keys to zoom in and out in the usual way." She zoomed in several times. "Once you have the area you want, zooming in will display an overlay like this one–" she pointed to a blue rectangle bordering an area of the map, with a reference number in the bottom left corner. "That's the reference number for that sheet." She zoomed out and pointed out a larger rectangle encompassing eight or nine of the smaller ones. "That's the schematic for the wide-area utilities schematics, but those are just schematics, they don't show precise locations, you need the large-scale plans for that. Just make a note of each reference number and I can pull out the paper plans and copy them for you."

"Got it," said Chung, "thank you."

"You're welcome," said Crane, standing up. "If I'm not at the desk when you're done, just ring the bell."

"I'll do that."

Chung was almost done when his phone buzzed with a text message from Sullivan.

Can you check your email then give me a call?

He quickly tapped out a reply:

Sure, give me a few minutes.

He hit Send then returned his attention to the plans on the screen in front of him.

In all, it had taken less than fifteen minutes to identify the sheets he needed. He needed the large-scale plans for the airfield, as well as possible exit points close to Eagle Mountain, plus the larger-scale schematics showing the water pipe routes between the two. He jotted down the last reference number and wandered back to the desk.

"Found what you need?" asked Crane, with a smile.

"Yes, thank you," replied Chung, pushing the notepaper with the reference numbers across the desk.

The clerk looked at them. "That's quite a few sets."

"I hope that's ok?"

"Yes, of course, it will just take me around 20 minutes to locate and copy them all."

"No problem."

"I'll be as quick as I can," said Crane.

"No rush," said Chung, "I have a phone call I need to make anyway."

Chung opened the email app on his phone and tapped on the email from Sullivan. They used PGP encrypted emails and a secure server to enable them to communicate freely without having to worry about interception. Several high-profile prosecutions had failed when the government was unable to break PGP encryption, and while some of the more paranoid geeks had suggested that the authorities were willing to sacrifice a few big-time cases to protect the fact that they had in fact broken the system, Chung didn't consider it likely.

He read the email, and examined the list of ten names and countries. Interesting.

While email was secure, cellphone calls weren't. Intercepting calls was relatively trivial, so they refrained from discussing specifics on the phone. Chung wandered out of the building before calling Sullivan.

* * *

There are many clerks who do mundane tasks like copying without giving much thought or attention to the content of the documents. Beverly Crane was not one of those people. Naturally curious, she was puzzled as she looked at the plans she was copying.

Choi had said he needed to run cables between buildings. That made sense of some of the large-scale plans he'd requested, which showed the exact locations of underground infrastructure: water and sewage pipes, electricity cables, gas pipes, cable and telephone cables and so forth. But he'd also requested small-scale plans providing only outline routes of pipes across large areas. He'd mentioned two areas, but hadn't said anything about needing to connect the two, and to do so would surely be prohibitively expensive? She was also puzzled at the detailed plans he'd requested of Hicks Field. As far as she was aware, that was still government-owned, with no commercial property on the airfield itself.

It didn't matter why Choi wanted the plans – they were a matter of public record, and anyone who wanted them was entitled to see them – but that didn't stop her wondering. Once she'd finished copying the documents, she'd do a little digging, just to satisfy her curiosity.

* * *

"Hey," he said.

"How's it going?" asked Sullivan.

Chung kept it vague. "Just getting copies of the plans. Should have everything in 20 minutes."

"Excellent," said Sullivan. "You got my email?"

"Yes."

"So we need to establish contact in a manner which persuades them of our claimed identities."

Sullivan's language was potentially incriminating should anyone be listening in, but the lack of any specifics made any risk a tiny one.

"That's really two tasks," replied Chung. "The second should be relatively easy," replied Chung. "The former not so much."

"Let's start with the easy bit."

"I can make our emails appear to have originated from an appropriate source. We instruct them not to reply to the emails, but to await contact from someone using a named codeword. That much is trivial."

"And the non-trivial part?" asked Sullivan.

"Establishing who to contact. We need to identify someone who is (a) senior enough to be able to strike a deal of that magnitude, and (b) part of the inner circle privy to the, ah, private financial arrangements of the head honcho."

"I suspect that's not as difficult as you might think."

"Oh?" asked Chung.

"I think it's a reasonably safe bet that the two or three most senior names in each country are in on the game. They wouldn't hold the positions they do were that not the case. If they are greedy and brave, they'll want to do the deal personally; otherwise they're going to take it to the boss-man."

"Hmmm."

"I can hear the cogs turning from here," said Sullivan. "What are you thinking?"

"I'm thinking that if we had access to their email accounts, we could probably find enough evidence to confirm our suspicions, and identify the best candidate from the several candidates in each country."

"And I'm guessing you have a plan for that."

"Depends how paranoid and tech-savvy they are," said Chung. "But an email from a different credible source with a link to a webserver could be enough if we can get them to click it. Leave it with me."

* * *

Jackson froze. The phone that was ringing was not his main one, and the number was listed in only one place: the contractor database entry for Pat Barker.

He froze because this was the phone call that would determine everything. Either the call was from Carswell to arrange the engineer visit, in which case the operation really was a go, or it was from someone at Lockheed who had somehow caught onto the contractor in the database who ought not to exist, and wanted to know what was going on – in which case the operation was over. There was no possibility of anything between the two: this was triumph or disaster. He took a deep breath and answered the call.

"C-5 Maintenance Support, Pat Barker speaking."

"Mr Barker, Lt Boulder, Carswell. I got your letter about the retrofit."

"Oh yes, thanks for calling, Lieutenant. Sorry for the inconvenience, but these things happen, and at least this one's a quick fit."

"No problem," said Boulder, "got to expect a few of these along the way."

"Appreciate your understanding. What would be the best day for us to visit?"

"A question of both day and time. Mission schedules vary, and it sounds like you guys will need about four hours total to cover all twelve aircraft."

"That would be safe," replied Jackson. "It's just a question of disconnecting two spade connectors, unscrewing the existing box, screwing in the new one and refastening the connectors."

"Sure you don't want us to handle it for you?" asked Boulder. "Save you the visit?"

"To be honest, the main reason I joined the field team is that I get to spend most of my time out of the office," said Jackson with a chuckle. "Nothing worse than being stuck behind a desk or in a workshop all day."

Boulder returned the laugh. "Yeah, know what you mean. Ok, how does Thursday look, 2pm to 6pm?"

"Let me check the diary," said Jackson. He counted to ten then continued: "Yep, looks good. It'll be myself and Katrina Shaw," he said, following Young's advice that using real first names was usually the safest course any time two or more members of the team would be working together. Too much risk of accidentally using the wrong name otherwise. They'd decided his first name was a bit too unusual to risk it, especially if the authorities realised he had a military background. But no reason not to use Katrina's first name.

"Barker and Shaw," repeated Boulder. "I'll send out a letter of acknowledgement, and make sure the gate is expecting you. I'll be on duty then, so I'll see you on Thursday."

"Looking forward to it, Lieutenant."

* * *

Beverly Crane logged into the land ownership database and carried out a search for Hicks Field. Yes, as she'd thought: the land owner was still listed as the United States Department of Defense. Why was a private developer looking at plans for a government-owned property?

She noted the property reference number and logged into a separate database of planning applications. She entered the property reference and hit Search.

There was one application on file, dated five years earlier. She clicked on it to bring up the details.

A pro-forma application had been made for possible use of the disused airfield for helium production. The application noted that it has previously been used in that role during WW2, and referred to the potential construction of a modern plant on the site. The pro-forma status meant that there were no immediate plans: it was effectively a holding tactic, aimed at enabling a final application to be decided quickly should one be made. The records indicated that an initial site survey had been completed, declaring the site suitable, and that there were no objections on the part of the municipality. Should the application be finalised, the plans would be published, enabling members of the public to object should they wish. There were, though, no notes indicating that plans had been taken any further forward since then.

Crane pushed the keyboard away. It was odd. The government of course used private contractors for construction work, but then why would Choi lie about the purpose of his visit? And why was he looking at wide-area plans? Could helium be piped from the plant like natural gas? She'd have to research that. But right now, it was time for lunch. She logged out of the system.

* * *

"So," asked Young, "how do we do this?"

"There are several possible approaches," said Chung.

Young grinned. "With you, there always are."

"The simplest, and least likely to work, is to send them an HTML email with spoofed headers."

"Spoofed headers?"

"Makes it seem like it's come from a legitimate source. We then try to get them to click on a link in the email. That link leads to a webserver which looks like an e-commerce site, so it'll look like a clever piece of spam. As soon as they arrive on the webpage, a piece of Java will silently install a key-logger on their PC. With that, we have access to their email and anything else they access on their PC."

"But most won't click on the link, hence the least likely bit," commented Young.

"Right. If they think they know the sender, they may do it, but technically-literate people are wise to that these days and won't click on a link even from a known source unless they are expecting the email. But you'd be surprised how many will do it, even today."

"Won't we raise the suspicions of the others?"

Chung shook his head. "Those who are wise to it will simply mouse-over the link to see where it really goes. The link will appear to be a Chinese site selling cellphone covers. They'll just dismiss it as spam and delete it."

"Ok," said Young, "and for them?"

"Strike two is to target the mail servers, in a similar way we did for the BEP and Lockheed."

"But the BEP attack didn't work, and the Lockheed one worked only because we were able to gain physical access to the building. That isn't going to be practical here."

"True, but those were both high-security facilities in the USA. Our targets are likely to operate in, shall we say, less developed IT environments."

"And if that doesn't work?" asked Young.

"Then things get tricker," said Chung. "But we have a list of 25 targets, and we're only after 10, so let's see how we get on."

* * *

Beverley Crane could now add helium production to her list of random and largely useless areas of knowledge. She joked that she was a 'two-minute expert' on hundreds of topics, able to give a two-minute overview to an interested audience while sounding knowledgeable, but not knowing enough to hit two minutes and 15 seconds.

Helium could indeed be transported by pipeline, explaining Choi's interest in the wide-area plans. But why lie about it? She shrugged. Private developers! They were always secretive. Pointlessly so, as far as she could see, since all plans had to become public at the planning application stage. She'd just keep an eye out for planning applications for the base – her curiosity would be satisfied at that point.

* * *

"Ready?" asked Jackson, as he drove the Lockheed Martin-liveried truck slowly down the Carwell Air Force Base access road.

"As I'll ever be," replied Lewis. "It's ok for you, you have the military experience, this is familiar territory for you. For me, this is a scary place."

"I know. But remember, we're supposed to be here. And this is just a routine and rather boring day for two Lockheed engineers who spend their lives doing this. Just look bored and you'll be fine."

Both were dressed in coveralls with Lockheed Martin logos, and had Lockheed Martin passes round their necks, exact copies prepared by Pugh of the genuine pass held by Young. Lewis had a clipboard with the perfectly genuine USAF acknowledgement of the Lockheed appointment letter.

"Showtime," said Jackson as he pulled up at the barrier and an armed gate guard walked toward them.

"Good morning, Sir, Ma'am."

"Morning," said Jackson, "I believe Lieutenant Boulder is expecting us." Lewis pulled off her pass and handed it to Jackson. Jackson handed over the clipboard and both passes to the guard.

The guard flicked through the paperwork on the clipboard, then checked the visitor's list on his own clipboard. He studied Jackson's pass before giving Jackson a long, careful look. Expressionless, he did the same with Lewis's pass and face. It felt to Lewis like he'd been staring at her for hours. Another guard, meantime, was checking under the truck with a mirror on a long stick.

Finally, he nodded and handed everything back to Jackson. "Drive through the first barrier and park up in the spaces on the right, Sir, just past the guardhouse. Once you're parked, leave the truck unlocked and come to the desk, bringing with you anything you need to take onto the base. We'll give you your visitor's passes and give the maintenance hanger a call to make sure they're ready for you, then you'll be taken in by Jeep."

"You got it," said Jackson. They parked up and both exited the truck, paperwork in hand. Jackson picked up the briefcase with the explosive devices, while Lewis picked up a small toolkit. They walked up the guardhouse steps to a stern-looking Sergeant at the desk.

The Sergeant too studied both passes and their faces. He took a leisurely look through the paperwork on the clipboard, then held each pass against the visitor list on a clipboard in front of him. Satisfied, he picked up a numbered visitor's badge from the tray in front of him. He carefully copied the badge number onto the visitor list against Jackson's name. He handed Jackson the Lockheed Martin pass and visitor's badge. "You know the drill with these, keep both passes visible at all times while on the base, and return the visitor's badge here on your way out." Jackson nodded.

"That's all the kit you need to take in with you?" asked the sergeant.

Jackson nodded. "One case of components, one toolkit, that's it."

"Open the first case, please."

Jackson did. This was another make-or-break moment. If the explosives were detected, not only would the operation be at an end, but he and Lewis would find themselves arrested as terrorists within 30 seconds. Perez had assured them that untagged Semtex was impossible to detect by sniffer, but there remained the possibility that they'd be required to open one or more of the boxes. Perez was confident his precautions would suffice, but he wasn't the one stood here surrounded by lots of men with guns.

"What are they?" asked the sergeant as he looked at the twelve pairs of black boxes neatly held in place with foam cutouts. Each box was about three inches long by an inch in diameter, with a compact two-pin terminal on one end.

"Replacement weather radar microprocessors and display drivers," said Jackson. "We've been getting some premature failures, so are doing a precautionary swap-out."

The sergeant pointed to one of the boxes at random. "Remove this one, please."

Jackson complied, handing it to the sergeant. Chung had fitted the boxes with special security screws that could be removed only with a special screwdriver Lewis carried as part of her toolkit.

"Open it, please."

This was the moment.

"It requires a special tool," said Lewis.

The sergeant's face remained impassive. He said nothing. Lewis hesitated a moment, then opened her toolkit and pulled out the screwdriver with star-shaped head. She turned the box face-down. On the rear, in the centre, was a self-adhesive pad. At each corner was a small torx screw. Slowly, she unscrewed the first one, placing the screw carefully on the desk. She unscrewed the second, placing the screw next to the first one. She repeated this for the third, then fourth screws.

She lifted the back of the case off and handed the open box to the sergeant.

The sergeant peered inside. It was a single circuit-board with several microchips, and a 9v battery disguised as a capacitor. Lewis was not concerned about the battery: she was confident that would pass any inspection bar peeling it open. She was concerned about the Semtex.

The sergeant held the box up to the light and tilted it first one way then the other. The Semtex was right in front of him.

Semtex is orangey-red in colour, intended to be immediately visible, and to be unmistakeable to anyone familiar with high explosives. This Semtex wasn't, not any longer. Lewis and Perez had spent hours painstakingly cutting it into a thin, perfectly even rectangle, painting it gloss black and embedding a dummy microchip into it. With the gloss black finish, and chip pins emerging from it, it was intended to look like just another chip on a circuit board.

When she'd created it, she'd wondered if all the work had been necessary. The chances were, she'd thought, that the box would never be opened, that nobody would ever see inside it. Spending so much time, and taking so much care, had seemed like overkill. It didn't any longer. Right now she was wishing she'd taken three times as long on it.

The sergeant put the box down on the desk and reached into a drawer. He pulled out a piece of wood about a foot long with a plastic bag wrapped around the end. He opened the bag to reveal a small, white piece of lint-like cloth on the end of the stick. Both Jackson and Lewis knew exactly what it was: a piece of sterile cloth used to swab equipment and clothing, and then inserted into an explosives sniffer. The sergeant swabbed the inside of the box thoroughly.

"Won't take a moment," he said. He passed the swab to a private, who took it into a side-room.

Perez had assured them the Semtex had been supplied without the tagging agent. If so, the machine would detect nothing. But if the supplier had let them down ...

The private seemed to be away for a very long time. Jackson and Lewis each concentrated on maintaining bored expressions. Lewis felt it was taking every ounce of her concentration. With the open box in front of them, and the Semtex in plain sight, the disguise seemed less and less convincing by the second. She was sure that at any moment the Sergeant was going to frown, lean forward and prod it with a 'Hey, wait a moment!'.

Finally, the private returned. He nodded at the sergeant.

There was one further small risk here: if the sergeant wanted to search the case itself. Hidden behind the foam lining were a further twenty-four boxes. These ones were empty: as they were installing twenty-four 'replacement' boxes, they might need to show the ones that had supposedly been removed. If the boxes were discovered, they would be explained as simply spare casings in case any were found to be damaged, but Jackson didn't think it a very convincing explanation. He hoped it wouldn't be needed.

"Thank you," said the sergeant. "You can close it up now."

Lewis focused all her attention on maintaining a neutral expression as she replaced the back of the casing, and carefully inserted and screwed up each of the four screws. She then replaced the box in its foam slot in the case. Jackson closed the case.

The sergeant had meantime picked up the phone and dialled a four digit number. "Gatehouse. Two visitors from Lockheed for Lieutenant Boulder." There was a short pause, then: "Thanks."

The sergeant replaced the handset, turned his head and yelled: "Transport!"

A private appeared within seconds, nodded to the sergeant – only officers got salutes – and then turned to Lewis and Jackson.

"If you'd like to follow me, Sir, Ma'am."

Jackson picked up the case and the pair of them followed the private back outside to a Jeep. They got in the back, the private got into the driver's seat and started it up.

The two finally risked a look at each other. The first big danger point was behind them. Now they were being driven swiftly and efficiently to an even bigger one. Jackson cracked a small smile. Lewis didn't dare return it; she nodded, solemnly.

* * *

"We're on," said Chung.

"We have our ten targets?" asked Young.

"Seventeen, actually!"

"Fantastic. Though I think we'll target ten of them first, with the rest as reserves: we don't want to complicate the operation any more than we have to. So was it done via spoof emails or mailserver hacking in the end?"

"A mix of the two," said Chung. "The spoof emails got seven clicks, and the key logger was successfully installed on six of them. The other one must have some unusually good security software. Of those six, three of the email accounts were obviously operated by underlings."

"PA type underlings, or henchmen type underlings?" asked Young.

"More the latter, I'd say, from their activities. It's quite possible that they have enough clout to pull off the deal themselves, but if they're doing it behind their boss's back, that obviously increases the risks."

"Yeah, I don't think we want to stick ourselves in the middle of a mess like that. This thing is risky enough as it is."

"Agreed," said Chung. "The other three, they are the main men, and boy do they qualify."

"So we have those three plus fourteen more targets from the mailserver hacks?"

"Right. Once I had access to the mailserver, I could read all of their stored emails, incoming and outgoing. That gave me more than enough to go on."

"Ok," said Young, "so now we're ready to send the approach emails."

"Yep. Just need you to write the text, then I'll take care of making it look like they came from the claimed senders."

"Receiving an email from those apparent sources will doubtless cause a few hearts to beat a little faster," said Young with a smile. "It can't be every day of the week they have direct personal contact – at least, not via email."

"I imagine not," replied Chung.

"You'll have the text of the emails today."

* * *

The Jeep drove around several low buildings and one hanger before they got sight of the C-5 Galaxies sat on the apron. Jackson had warned her about this moment. They'll blow your mind when you first see them up close, he'd said. The sheer scale of them leaves people open-mouthed. But you need to make sure you keep your jaw firmly closed. You're a Lockheed engineer on the C-5 team. These things are like Fords to you.

The warning had been necessary. As they approached one and drove within 20 yards of the right wing, it was hard to believe the thing could even move under its own power, let alone be capable of flight. It looked more like a building than an aircraft. And there were five of them in a line, with six more behind.

To Jackson, the sight was too familiar to be impressive. His focus was on just one thing: eleven aircraft rather than twelve. Where was the twelfth?

The Jeep drove on and pulled up just outside the hanger. Jackson momentarily relaxed: the missing C-5 was inside.

The private jumped out. "This way, Sir, Ma'am." Jackson allowed himself a nostalgic smile. As a graduate of the Officer Training School, he'd never been a private, but he remembered even as a newly-qualified 2nd Lieutenant he'd been tempted to think of everyone he met as either Sir or Ma'am.

The private led them into a two-storey portacabin structure within the hanger. He saluted the 2nd Lieutenant behind the desk. "The Lockheed engineers, Sir!"

"Thank you, Lawson." The private saluted again, turned and left. The lieutenant came out from behind the desk.

"Lieutenant Boulder?" asked Jackson, offering his hand.

"Dan, please," said Boulder, shaking first Jackson's hand then Lewis's.

"I'm Pat, and this is Katrina," said Jackson.

"Want some coffee?"

"Sure," said Jackson. In truth, they wanted to be out of there as quickly as possible, but it would have been out of character to refuse: no field engineer is ever in any great hurry to get back to the office.

They wandered through to a kitchen where they each grabbed a coffee.

"Ex-Forces yourself?" asked Boulder.

The last thing Jackson wanted was to get into a discussion about his service record, but there were too many small ways he could have given himself away to want to risk it. "A long time ago," he said, simply, trying to adopt a tone which suggested it wasn't a topic he wanted to revisit without actually sounding unfriendly.

Boulder nodded. "Can always tell."

He didn't ask the same question of Lewis, noted Jackson. Either he really could tell, or it was the casual sexism still present in many in the Forces.

"So, been having some trouble with the weather radar systems, I gather," said Boulder. "I checked our maintenance logs and we haven't experienced any problems here."

Jackson nodded. "Yeah, it's not a major problem, just had an unusual number of premature failures which led us to identify a weakness, and we know what a PITA it is when equipment fails in flight, so we're just doing a precautionary swap-out."

"You got that right. You need any help with the swap-outs? No shortage of wrench monkeys round here."

Jackson grinned. "Thanks, but we got it covered. Five-minute job. Take longer to show them what to do than to do it ourselves."

Boulder shrugged. "No worries. Well, when you're done with your coffee, we've got one aircraft in here, the rest on the apron. This one's got a few guys in the cargo hold fitting it out for a drop, but the flight-deck is clear. The rest are empty."

"Great," said Jackson, "we'll make a start."

"Right." Boulder poked his head round the door at the end of the kitchen. "West! Get your ass in here."

A private appeared, snapped to attention and saluted. Jackson smiled at the contrast between the casual order and formality of the response.

"West here will be your escort. Just let him know if there's anything you need."

"Thanks," said Jackson. He'd been afraid of this, but tried not to let it show in his expression. SOP on a military base was for visitors to be accompanied at all times, but he wasn't sure whether that would apply to Lockheed engineers. Clearly it did. Worse, the fact that the private had been in the hanger suggested that he was one of the maintenance staff. They'd need to be very careful.

As soon as they left the portacabin, West visibly relaxed. "Guess you know your way round these things," he said, conversationally. No Sirring and Ma'aming from him, Jackson noted.

"Just a bit," said Jackson. "I could probably draw you a wiring diagram from memory."

"Heh," said West.

Jackson looked at Lewis. She hadn't said a single word since they'd entered the hanger. He knew this was much harder for her, not having his long familiarity with airbases. "Coffee woken you up any?" he asked with a grin. Lewis managed to smile weakly in return. She was as tough as they came when required, but they couldn't be out of here a moment too soon for her tastes.

They climbed the ramp and followed West up the stairs to the flight-deck. West sat down in one of the two flight engineer seats. "All yours," he said, gesturing to the front of the cockpit.

Jackson was pleased to see where West was sitting: it was far enough back that there would be no way for him to see what they were doing behind the weather radar display.

Sleight of hand was definitely Evans' territory, but they needed Jackson for his familiarity with the aircraft and Lewis for her electronics expertise, and thought turning up with three engineers for a simple swap-out would just look too odd. Evans had worked out the play, tutored them and made them practice endlessly, but this was the real thing, and they would be breaking one of the cardinal rules of magic: never let the same audience watch you perform the same sleight of hand more than once. They would be performing this particular trick twelve times in twelve different aircraft in front of the same audience of one.

Step one: control the audience's view. Jackson reached down to the left-hand pilot's seat and pulled up the lever allowing the seat to be adjusted fore and aft. He slid the seat all the way to the rear position. He then carefully placed the case containing the black boxes onto the seat, crouched down and opened the case. With the lid and the seatback towards West, there would be no way for the private to see exactly what he was doing. Lewis set her toolkit down in the same way on the observer's seat, ensuring that West couldn't come and sit closer if he decided to take an interest in what they were doing. Step one complete.

Jackson yawned, using the opportunity to glance over at West, who was looking in his direction but without any great signs of interest. Lewis reached into the toolkit and extracted several screwdrivers, a pair of wire-crimps and a magnetic dish. She very carefully laid these out on the centre console. As she did this, Jackson pulled out one pair of the black boxes and carefully laid them on the console next to the tools. Lewis pulled a sheaf of papers out of one of the pockets of her overalls and held them out, pretending to check the serial number of the two boxes against the list on the top sheet. The position in which she held the papers blocked Private West's view of Jackson, who quickly extracted the two dummy boxes. These would be the boxes that Lewis would 'remove' from the aircraft.

Step two: misdirection. Lewis pulled out a pen and initialled a space on the top sheet. She then passed both paper and pen to Jackson. Jackson likewise pretended to check the numbers, and added his initials before passing the papers back to Lewis. Behind the papers was one of the two dummy boxes. Shielded by the papers, she took this and slipped it into her sleeve, reaching up to scratch her nose so that it fell right down the sleeve as far as her elbow.

Jackson picked up a large cross-head screwdriver and undid the first of the six screws holding the weather radar display unit in place in the console. He handed the screw to Lewis, who placed it in the magnetic dish. They repeated this for each of the remaining five screws. Jackson carefully pulled the weather screen toward him. Lewis leaned forward to hold it as Jackson ensured that none of the attached wires snagged. Lewis rested it on the console in a way that completely blocked West's view of the hole from which it had been removed. Equally importantly, it blocked West's view of the magnetic dish.

Jackson eased himself out past the pilot's chair, and Lewis took his place kneeling in front of the now open hole in the console.

Step three: pulling a rabbit from a hat. Lewis picked up a much smaller cross-head screwdriver and reached in, peering closely before pretending to undo a screw. Her hand closed around a non-existent screw, she reached out to the magnetic dish hidden from West's view. She reached to the sloping underside of the dish on the side facing away from West, pulled off one of the four small screws clinging to the side and held it above the dish before dropping it in from a height of several centimetres so it landed with an audible clink.

She repeated the trick, removing a second fictitious screws from inside the void.

Step four: a bigger rabbit. Reaching in through the hole once more, she tilted her elbow up so that the dummy black box travelled down her sleeve and into her hand. She then extracted the box 'removed' from the aircraft, then eased herself to her feet and backed out of the way. She reached into the toolkit, peeled off a 'Removed from service' sticker from a roll in the toolkit and applied it to the front of the box. She then placed it into one of the empty slots in the case.

Step four: the vanishing trick. Jackson picked up the first of their real black boxes. He peeled off the self-adhesive pad, and reached into the void with the box. This part required his expertise. He needed to attach the box to a flat surface in a position where the tiny explosion would cut the wires to the weather radar without destroying anything vital. Perez had done the calculations carefully, and assured them that the explosion would be sufficient only to destroy anything within an inch or so of the box, but Jackson didn't want to take any chances. Aside from their no-violence rule, there was an unspoken bond between pilots. They all shared the knowledge that all that stood between them and death was a thin aluminium tube, a small number of mechanical linkages and a lot of electronics. In war, pilots would shoot each other down if the mission called for it, but it was not something they did lightly even with enemy pilots, and the thought of putting USAF crew in harm's way was anathema to all of them. Jackson wanted to ensure that the pilots of this aircraft would get the message but without affecting their ability to keep the plane in the air.

In a large aircraft like the C-5, it wasn't terribly difficult: there was a lot of empty space behind the panel. But he also needed to pull off the vanishing-trick: position the box somewhere where it wouldn't draw attention to itself. The terminal connectors on the end of the box were dummies: the box wouldn't actually be connected to anything. The connectors had to be there, otherwise their absence might have been questioned when searched, but now they were a liability. If the box were placed somewhere too visible, or too close to a component that might require maintenance, an overly curious maintenance engineer might wonder why there was a black box with no wiring running to or from it.

Jackson's plan was to attach it to the underside of the power supply unit for the radar unit. The power supply box was extremely simple; the chances of it failing, and thus needing to be removed, were extremely slim. The chances of that happening between now and D-day were almost non-existent. The supply was held in place in a bracket by a simple pair of spring-loaded clips. There was plenty of space beneath it for the small box.

He first carefully placed the box on top of a wiring loom, pressing it very lightly so that the adhesive pad would hold it safely in place long enough for him to unclip the PSU but not firmly enough that it would reduce the effectiveness of the adhesive when the box was put in place.

He reached down and felt for the spring clip at the closest end of the PSU bracket. It took a few seconds, but he felt it give, and he was able to lift one end of the power supply. With that end released, the second end was easy. He turned it upside-down. He reached over for the black box, freed it from the loom with a tiny tug and then pressed it firmly to the underside of the power supply. He held it in place for several seconds. He then reached out to the magnetic dish and picked up one of the screws. He repeated Lewis's sleight of hand in reverse to move the screw from the bowl to the underside of the dish while pretending to hold it in his hand. He picked up the small screwdriver, peered into the void and pretended to position and do up the screw. He repeated the sequence with the second screw.

One box done on one aircraft. Second box to go, the one for the flaps, then eleven more aircraft.

* * *

Luke Pritchard was still on his first cup of coffee of the day when his phone rang. He glanced at the clock display on it: 09:04. He hoped it wasn't going to be one of those days. He picked up the handset.

"Pritchard."

"It's Kate Lorrimar."

"Kate," he said, warmly. "Good to hear from you."

"And with good news even," said Lorrimar.

"Oh?"

"We've managed to figure out a mechanism for the dummy shipment, and Bailey has approved it."

"Fantastic!" said Pritchard. "So that's it? It's a done deal?"

"Not quite," replied Lorrimar. "The Treasury department has the final say."

"How long before they make a decision?"

"Who knows? The wheels of the bureaucratic machine turn at their own pace."

"Just so long as they don't leave it too late to implement," said Pritchard in a worried tone. "How much notice do you need?"

"Not more than a couple of days. The main thing is ensuring they do actually make a decision before the day."

Pritchard looked startled. "You really think there's a chance they won't?"

"Bureaucrats are not overly fond of making decisions, and a favourite avoidance tactic is simply to leave a decision until it's too late. But Bailey has given them a strong recommendation, and he seems confident it will be accepted."

"So for now, we wait."

"For now we wait," confirmed Lorrimar.

* * *

This was it, thought Jackson, with a feeling of relief: the last aircraft. All he had to do was attach this, pretend to screw it up, do the same with the box for the flaps, and they would be done. Within the hour, they'd be back at their hotel downing a cold one. Many cold ones, he decided.

He removed the backing from the adhesive pad, reached into the void and placed it lightly on the wiring loom. As he moved his hand across ready to unclip the power supply from its bracket, he caught the box with the edge of his hand. The adhesive was barely touching the loom and the slight adhesion wasn't enough to keep it in place. It fell from the wiring loom, bounced off a cable junction beneath and fell to the floor panel below, close to the rudder pedal linkages.

"Damn!"

"What's up?" asked Lewis. Private West also looked over at him.

Jackson forced an embarrassed grin. "Oh, just dropped the box. No big deal: they're not fragile, all solid-state."

He reached down for it, but it was out of reach. He hesitated for a moment. The last thing he wanted to do was spend more time here. Even with his easy familiarity with aircraft and airbases, the strain of installing explosive devices in twelve USAF aircraft was beginning to tell. If he pretended to retrieve it, could he just leave it there? He dismissed the idea as soon as it occurred to him. No, definitely not. First, it was right by the rudder linkages. The tiny explosion shouldn't be powerful enough to damage them – they were pretty solid metal things – but they couldn't take the chance: an aircraft with no rudder control could be landed by a skilled pilot given good weather, enough time and some luck, but it was a non-trivial endeavour in an aircraft of this size. They couldn't risk it. Second, a loose box rattling around in an aircraft was going to attract attention sooner or later, and it might well be sooner rather than later. The box had to be retrieved.

He leant back and turned to Lewis: "Can't quite reach it, can you try?"

They swapped places and Lewis reached down. No: it was well beyond her reach.

"No, can't reach it."

"Ok," said Jackson, "no worries, we'll just pull off the panel behind the rudder pedals and retrieve it from there."

West stood up and approached them. "That's a fiddly job," he said, "so many damn screws and clips in that thing. Here, let me see if I can reach it first."

The last thing Jackson wanted was a USAF engineer rooting around where they were working, but one electronics box looks much like another. There was no reason for him to suspect anything, and he couldn't see any way to refuse the offer of help.

"Thanks," he smiled. "Maybe you have longer arms than us."

Jackson stepped back to allow West access. West looked inside, then reached in with his arm. After a few seconds, he adjusted his position to give himself a better angle. "Al-most ..." He twisted his shoulder. "Got it!" He pulled his arm out and handed the box to Jackson with a grin. "See, you should have let us do the installation, you Lockheed monkeys are all thumbs."

Jackson grinned back. "Yeah, yeah, we know the kind of lash-ups you guys do to our beautiful aircraft out in the field."

West stepped out. "You ain't made nothing yet that can't be fixed by enough duct tape and determination by a true USAF engineer."

"Heh," replied Jackson, returning to work.

Three minutes later, they were done. Twelve USAF C-5 Galaxy aircraft were booby-trapped. They could disable the weather radar to make their point, and take the flaps out of commission if the flight crews didn't take the hint. For their part, the operation was a go.

* * *

The ten emails were sent out within the space of a few minutes. The body of each email was identical, but the headers varied. Each appeared to have been sent from a very particular office located in the city of each recipient. The text of each email was short and to the point.

SUBJECT: Confidential briefing

PRIORITY: High

EYES-ONLY.

We wish to arrange a meeting to discuss substantial matters of potential mutual interest. I regret that I am unable to be more specific in an email, but you will appreciate the reasons for this when we meet.

Please treat this meeting as confidential TO YOU PERSONALLY. I understand that you would of course normally wish to have junior staff present at any meeting between us, but on this occasion we would prefer that the matters we need to discuss be known to as few people as possible, and we believe that you will find such discretion to be personally advantageous.

Please advise a personal mobile number on which you may be reached, and then await contact from a representative who will identify himself with the code-phrase 'American Cleaning Services'.

The code-phrase had been Young's idea: he enjoyed amusing himself with such things.

The email was signed on behalf of the alleged sender, and ended with a PGP signature block.

Now it was just a question of waiting. If the targets replied with a contact number, it was a near-certainty they would be open to the proposition.

* * *

The first email was opened within minutes. Young was wrong: the recipient, a heavily-built man in his late 50s, was not as surprised at the purported source of the email as Young had predicted. Young could not have known it, but it was not the first time such unofficial contacts had been established to discuss confidential matters of mutual interest.

The recipient read the email carefully. He then read it a second time. The man would not have made it to his present position without a decided talent for reading between the lines, and the email seemed unusually transparent. It was clear that his cooperation was being sought for some clandestine endeavour, that his compatriots might not approve and that he could be expected to be suitably rewarded for his assistance.

He could recall several such contacts over the years. Often the objective would be one that would be of mutual benefit, other times it would be a matter of no consequence to him one way or the other. Usually the cooperation requested amounted to little more than looking the other way whilst certain activities took place. Occasionally more direct assistance was needed.

He was a pragmatic man. If the assistance needed could be provided with little or no risk of discovery, and the personal rewards were sufficient to justify such risks as existed, he would agree. When a request arrived from this particular source, the rewards were usually more than sufficient. He hit reply, typed a phone number and hit Send.

* * *

"Pritchard."

"More good news," said Lorrimar, not bothering to introduce herself.

"The Treasury has approved the plan?" asked Pritchard, surprised to hear back from her so soon.

"They didn't take too much persuasion, it seems."

"Really?" said Pritchard, with genuine surprise. "You made it sound like it was touch-and-go whether they'd make a decision at all."

"According to Bailey, nobody there wanted to be the person responsible for making a decision that could result in the loss of a billion dollars! Each of them passed the buck until it landed on the desk of the Secretary of State."

"You're kidding me."

"I'm not. Bailey said you'd think the email was a hand-grenade, such was the speed with which each of them passed it on. From first request to approval was three days."

Pritchard laughed. "For a government agency, that's practically the speed of light. Bureaucratic cowardice does have its benefits sometimes."

"Quite so," said Lorrimar.

"So, that's it? On the day the heist is supposed to take place, all three convoys will be dummy ones?"

"That's it. If this hit is real, they're going to get nothing more than 36 pallets of blank paper."

"Beautiful," said Pritchard. "Blank paper on 36 pallets fitted with trackers, in fact, which allows us to take one step back in terms of the additional security. We'd obviously like to catch these guys if they do attempt the hit, but I don't want to do anything to look out of the ordinary on the day. I'm going to arrange for Secret Service agents to be positioned in helicopters and rapid-response vehicles in some discreet locations so we can remain invisible but move in quickly if needed in case the informant is right about the hit but wrong about it being in the air. In the unlikely event it is in the air, we have extra fighters ready to scramble from every airbase along each of the routes."

"Sounds great."

"One way or another, this gang, if it exists, is going to get one hell of a surprise!"

* * *

"We're on," said Chung, the moment he walked into Sullivan's apartment.

"Ten replies?" asked Young, surprised. He'd expected most of the targets to at least be sufficiently intrigued to proceed to the next step, but he hadn't dared hope for positive responses from all ten.

"Ten phone numbers," confirmed Chung. "Looks like you're going to be earning some air miles."

"I have to make the calls first. There's no guarantee they'll agree to meet."

"They'll meet," said Sullivan.

"Why so confident?" asked Young.

"The fact that they replied at all tells us they're at least intrigued, and they're not going to learn much more from your call. All you're doing is arranging a discreet meeting. But more than that, these are greedy men. They wouldn't have gotten to be where they are otherwise. They'll agree."

Young tilted his head in tentative agreement. It was a truism in the confidence game that you could only ever con a greedy person. Someone who wanted something for nothing, or thought they were getting an unbeatable deal. Ordinary people, faced with a deal too good to be true, would dismiss it as such.

"When will you make the calls?" asked Chung.

"Various times, depending on time-zone," said Young. "More chance they can speak freely in the evening, without too many staff around, so we'll time them to be in their evening."

"You making all the calls yourself, or splitting them between you?"

Sullivan shook her head. "Young will make all the calls, and all the visits. These men are not used to negotiating with women, and some of them would find an approach by a woman to be insulting."

"Not the most enlightened of individuals, eh?"

"Exceedingly unenlightened, I should think. These are not pleasant gentlemen."

"Or gentlemen at all," added Young.

"Not who we'd choose to do business with under normal circumstances," agreed Sullivan, "but we can take comfort from the fact that hooking up with us is going to prove a very expensive experience indeed!"

* * *

Young looked again at the moving map on the screen in front of him. It had been a very long flight, but he could see they were finally approaching the African coast. The Time to Destination field on the display read 27 minutes.

He was terrified.

What the hell had he been thinking, he wondered? This crazy money-laundering idea of his had felt like genius when he'd pitched it to the team back in the safety of a tyre shop in New York City. Then, it had been a concept: a beautiful, joyous concept. He remembered the excitement and smugness he'd felt presenting it to the team ...

"Right," said Sullivan. "Now, you guys thought this whole idea was crazy at the start. So just remember that when Young tells you his idea, because it's going to sound even crazier than the heist."

"Now I'm worried," said Chung.

"Laundering the money presents two problems," said Young. "First, the list of criminal organisations that could handle a billion dollars is a very short one."

"I'm surprised there's a list at all," said Lewis. "I'd have thought there was the Mafia and that's it."

"That is indeed the entire list," said Young. "They have an estimated annual turnover of around $200 billion a year, so laundering a billion dollars wouldn't be beyond their capabilities. But the second problem is that while the authorities may initially believe the bills have been destroyed in the truck explosion, they're not going to continue to believe that once the bills start showing up in the banking system. The moment that happens, the serial numbers make the cash the hottest property outside of the surface of the sun, and the bills become worthless in any quantity. Spending them quietly in small quantities just isn't an option with that much cash. So that means whoever launders the cash is going to get stiffed."

"Please tell me you're not suggesting we stitch-up the mob," said Chung.

"No," said Young. "Too many risks."

"I'd agree with that," said Lewis. "I don't look good in concrete. So who else do you have in mind?"

"Dictators," replied Young. "To be more precise, the regimes of Chad, Nigeria, Iran, Haiti, Sudan, Uzbekistan, Syria, Turkmenistan, Equatorial Guinea and Venezuala."

There was silence for a few seconds.

"Um," said Evans, "if I'm totally honest, those regimes don't sound a vast improvement on the Mafia when it comes to the list of people you'd rather not piss off."

"They have the benefit of being a little further away, but the plan relies on them being convinced that they are in fact dealing with the US Government. By the time they realise they've been taken, it is the White House they will believe has done the dirty on them. They're going to be mightily pissed-off, but even a crazed dictator is going to realise there isn't a whole lot they can do about it."

"You don't think we risk encouraging terrorism?" asked Jackson.

"Only if they are willing to argue for it by admitting to their fellow countrymen that they just tried to trouser a hundred million dollars for themselves," said Young. "I think that's something they're going to want to keep to themselves."

"So what's the plan, exactly?" asked Lewis.

"We inform them that we have a need to exchange dollars for something less traceable in order to conduct certain unspecified black ops. Diamonds, ideally."

"The most portable form of wealth," added Sullivan.

Young nodded. "The notes will be genuine, so will pass any tests they conduct. Sequential numbers will make perfect sense given that the bills supposedly come from the US Treasury. Best of all, instead of settling for the ten or twenty percent we'd get from conventional money-laundering, we will exchange the cash for diamonds at more-or-less face-value."

"So we get the diamonds, and the dictators get a bunch of cash that will be worthless the moment they attempt to bank it," said Perez.

"Right," agreed Young. "It doesn't matter where in the world they deposit it – Switzerland, the Cayman Islands, wherever – the moment the cash hits the banking system, it will be immediately flagged as cancelled currency. The US government and our fellow Americans lose nothing. We're basically stealing diamonds from dictators."

"We're the good guys after all," smiled Lewis.

"The dictators lose a lot of wealth," said Sullivan. "Who knows, maybe even enough to topple one or two of them."

"Always nice to play our part in creating a better world, don't you think?" asked Young.

"We're regular Robin Hoods," said Lewis.

"Apart from the giving to the poor part," said Jackson.

"Well, yeah, apart from that," agreed Lewis.

"Do all those regimes have diamonds?" asked Pugh.

Young nodded. "I've been doing some reading up on the matter – investigative reporting, UN reports and so on – and it appears diamonds are a dictator's best friend. Some of the countries are diamond exporters, so have them to hand any way. For the rest, it's a near certainty. Swiss bank accounts are no longer the safe option they used to be since the global financial clampdown, and heading up a volatile regime, you have to assume you may need to get out of the country quickly if it all falls apart. Diamonds are by far the more portable form of wealth. Even if they don't have them, they'll be able to get hold of them."

"Use cash to buy diamonds to sell to us for cash? Why would they do that?" asked Evans.

"We're offering them a two percent commission for their trouble," said Young. "Around two million bucks for a bit of shopping."

"I can see that doing the job," said Evans.

"So you think our money-laundering plan is any less crazy?" asked Young.

"It's starting to grow on me," said Perez. "The notion is a thing of beauty."

"It still seems crazy to me," said Lewis, "but I can't deny the appeal."

"You know, if we can pull that off, it would be even more satisfying than the heist itself," said Jackson.

Everyone looked at Chung. He threw up his hands in surrender. "The crowd has spoken. Who am I to argue?"

Now all he had to do was turn a great idea into a done deal ...

He'd sounded so calm and self-assured back then. Tomorrow evening, it was going to be a reality. He was going to be face-to-face with one of the most dangerous men in the world, selling the biggest sting in the history of the game.

A real-life dictator. Christ. The head of one of the most brutal and corrupt regimes in the world. And Young was there to sell him a bill of goods. To pitch a con to a man who could have him killed as easily and as casually as Young might order a pizza back in NYC.

And this was just the first leg of the trip. After this one, he had nine more countries to visit, nine more dictators to meet, nine more pitches to make.

Jessica Sullivan was, he knew, two rows behind him. The two had not spoken or acknowledged each other in any way at any point during the 13-hour flight. Their tickets had been booked separately. Different credit cards, different laptops, different locations. On arrival, they would take different taxis to different hotels. They would not exchange a single word at any point during the trip. So far as the airline and anyone else who might take an interest was concerned, there was nothing to connect the two of them.

They had one other thing in common besides their flight. A quite unremarkable thing: they both had the same carry-on bag. It was nothing anyone would notice: the bag was the standard anonymous black roller-bag used by business travellers the world over. Once they cleared Immigration, they would happen to find themselves next to each other in the taxi queue. At some point, when nobody was looking, he would pick up her bag and she would pick up his. Everything that identified him as Sam Young – passport, wallet, plane ticket, phone – would be in the bag Sullivan took. In the replacement bag would be everything needed to assume his new identity: passport, credit cards, plane tickets, a phone with contact and calendar entries to match his new persona, the works. A very thorough job designed to stand up to the closest scrutiny, a scrutiny he fully expected to occur.

He looked again at the screen. Time to destination: 24 minutes.

* * *

Back in Fort Worth, Chung too was feeling nervous. Although he had been over the water plant schematics a dozen times, and was confident that his plan would work, theoretical confidence was not enough: he had to actually test it. They had to actually take control of the stretch of water pipe running beneath the base, and watch each of the three phases actually happen on-site: watch the water level fall after they closed the inlet valve, watch it cease flowing when they closed the outlet valve, watch it resume its downstream flow as they re-opened both valves.

The danger, of course, was that they risked the test being detected. Everything they did on the SCADA system would be reflected on the monitors in the water plant control-room. All it took was an operator glancing at the screen at the wrong time, and the whole escape plan was dead. Worse, they had no idea what chaos they might cause elsewhere by messing with the valves, or what alarms might be activated if they did something that shouldn't ever happen.

But while testing it was risky, not testing it was riskier still: it had to be done.

They would be taking two precautions. First, the test would be as brief as possible. While he controlled the SCADA system, Evans would be at the airbase monitoring the water levels and flow. The moment Evans saw a sufficient change in level, he would call Chung. If all went well, the test would take only ten minutes or so.

Second, the test would be conducted at 4am. The plant was likely to have only a skeleton crew then, and physiologically 4am was the low-point in the human circadian rhythm. No matter how used we were to shift work, 4am was the time when we were likely to be most tired, least alert.

Tonight he and Evans would run through the test, step by step, ensuring that they both knew exactly what they had to do. The following night, at 4am, they would conduct the test.

* * *

Young put the finishing touches to his minimal disguise – not enough for anyone already tailing him to notice a difference, but just enough to throw off a description – and examined himself closely in the mirror. He was satisfied. He checked his wallet. Nothing was being left to chance: he fully expected to be searched, and he would have nothing on him that wasn't consistent with his claimed identity. Everything from credit cards to gym membership card would confirm he was who he claimed to be. Pugh had been busy!

Every possession in his hotel room too was consistent with his assumed identity. He had to assume it would be searched: such a precaution would be well within the capabilities of the people with whom he was dealing. That was the reason for Sullivan shadowing him on the trip: he must have nothing on his person or in his hotel room that didn't match his persona.

Young checked every pocket in his suit. Nothing was present that shouldn't be present. Even the carefully-crumpled ticket receipt from an upmarket pole-dancing club in his claimed home city stuffed into a jacket pocket in his wardrobe was there quite deliberately. Men with flexible morals tended to feel more comfortable dealing with others they perceived to be in some way flawed. The laptop left out on his hotel room desk would, if examined, be found to contain several ... interesting ... videos that would again suggest a man not unduly troubled by a conscience.

He looked at his watch – a watch whose back was inscribed with a message from his 'wife'. 6.53pm. He had been told a car would be picking him from the hotel at 7pm precisely, and he didn't intend to be late. He looked around the room one last time to ensure everything was as it should be, picked up his hotel keycard and set off for the lobby.

* * *

"I know it's simple in principle," said Chung to Evans as they drank coffee, "but conducting this test scares me to death. I want to be messing with the system for the absolute minimum time necessary to confirm that everything works, and that means being ultra-slick in the way we do it."

"No need to explain that to a magician," said Evans with a smile which took any sting out of the admonishment. "Illusion is 1% idea, 99% practice."

"Makes sense."

"So," said Evans, "let's go over the steps."

"Ok," said Chung, "it's just three steps. First thing is for you to go down and report the initial water level so that I can put it back to the same level afterwards. You needn't be precise, just empty, low or high. You won't be able to get a phone signal while below ground, so as soon as you have the info, you climb back up to ground level and call me with the level."

"No problem," said Evans.

"At the risk of being all cloak-and-dagger-ish about it, let's agree one-word reports, both for security and to make things as fast as possible. So just say say the single word empty, low or high."

"Ok," said Evans.

"Step two," said Chung, "is draining the water. I'm going to close the nearest upstream valve and open all three downstream valves. You just go back down and wait until the water is completely drained, so you can stand on the bottom of the pipe. Once that's done, you come back up to ground level and report empty."

"Clear," said Evans.

"Step three is returning the water to its previous level. I'll open the upstream valve and close the furthest downstream valve. Once the level is back where it was, I'll reset all the valves to their initial state. With that one, you'll need to anticipate slightly, and climb the rungs to give me a 'Task complete' report just before the water reaches the correct level so that it will be at the correct level by the time you make the call."

"No problem."

"Great," said Chung, "then we're all set."

* * *

The journey from the hotel had taken just seven minutes. There had been no audible siren, and Young hadn't noticed the reflections of any blue lights, but the black sedan with state flags had been able to cut through the traffic with ease. Neither driver nor front-seat passenger had introduced themselves nor said a single word to him after the initial polite 'Mr Collins?' as he'd approached the car and a brief "If you wouldn't mind, Sir" as they quickly and efficiently frisked him before allowing him into the car.

They approached the gates of a large compound. Soldiers immediately opened the gates and the car passed through without stopping. Ahead was a curved drive leading to a palatial home occupying about the same space as an entire block in NYC. Young had done his research, and recognised it as the private residence of the man he was to meet. A good sign, he thought, suggesting that the meeting was indeed being held in confidence.

The car pulled up at the foot of the steps leading up to a large portico. Two more soldiers flanked the steps.

The driver stayed put, the passenger came out and opened the door for him. As Young stepped out, both soldiers stared wordlessly at him, their fingers inside the trigger-guards of the MP-5 assault rifles. The passenger gestured for him to climb the steps. As Young stepped forward, the soldiers turned.

Their MP-5s were pointed toward the ground, but they tracked his movements. Young glanced round, expecting the car's passenger to be alongside him, but he was getting back into the car.

Young climbed the twelve steps to some extremely heavy-looking double doors, about twelve feet high and eight feet wide. Two more soldiers were positioned either side of the doors. They too were staring directly at him. None of the politeness of the US military, Young thought: Marines would have been staring directly ahead, pretending to be oblivious to him.

He was about five steps away from the doors when they swung silently open. A caucasian man dressed like a butler from a period drama stood a few feet inside. As he walked through, the butler said in clipped English tones: "If you would like to follow me, Sir."

In other circumstances, Young would have smiled at the incongruity; he felt no such temptation there.

More double doors opened as they approached, revealing an enormous living-room. Like the butler, it looked like a scene from 19th Century England. Chandeliers, chaises longues, polished tables, standard lamps, over-stuffed sofas and padded dining chairs with floral patterns. The only concession to the heat was the marble flooring and ceiling fans.

As he entered, he recognised the man who immediately stood to greet him with a broad smile.

"Mr Collins, delighted you could make it." The man strode toward him and held out his hand as he spoke with a perfect upper-class English accent. He knew from his research that the man had been educated at Eton and then King's College, Cambridge.

Young smiled inwardly at the irony as he shook hands: when you had an invitation to meet this man, there was no question of being unable to keep the appointment.

"Your Excellency."

"No need for such formality. Mr President will suffice."

For a moment, Young thought the man was being ironic, but quickly stifled a laugh: it seemed the man was serious. This was his idea of informality.

"Mr President."

The President gestured for Young to sit in an uncomfortable-looking chair, while he sat in a much grander chair opposite.

"May I offer you some refreshment? A gin and tonic, perhaps?"

"Thank you," said Young.

It seemed his acceptance had been assumed: no sooner had he answered than the butler placed the drink on the table at his side. The butler bowed, turned and left the room, bowing again as he closed the double doors behind him.

"I trust you had a pleasant flight?"

"I did, thank you."

"From Washington, I presume?"

Young was ready for the trap: he assumed the President would be well aware that there were no direct flights from Washington.

"Via New York," he said.

"Of course, of course. And your hotel? Comfortable?"

"Perfectly, thank you, Mr President."

"I'm pleased to hear it. If there is anything they can do to make your stay more comfortable, please feel free to let me know."

"That's very kind," said Young, glad of the small-talk: it delayed the moment he was going to have to begin the biggest hustle of his life.

"Have you visited my country before, Mr Collins?"

"I have not had that honour, Mr President."

"I hope you will have time to see a little of what modest entertainments the city can afford a visitor?"

"Sadly not," replied Young. "My schedule is a little tight: I leave tomorrow."

"I see, I see. Well, then, perhaps we should address ourselves to business affairs. I believe there was a matter you wished to discuss?"

Young swallowed. Show-time.

"You will appreciate that this is a delicate matter, Mr President."

"I assumed as much from the manner of your approach." The expression and tone were pleasant. "You may rest assured that whatever you have to say will not go beyond this room."

"Thank you, Mr President. I'm sure you will appreciate that there are times when any government may find there to be some variance between its public policies and private actions."

"I am given to understand that may sometimes be the case."

"My government wishes to carry out certain transactions which we would not wish to be traced back to their source. The operatives responsible for these transactions are, shall we say, representing themselves as being from some other part of the world."

"Not my part of the world, I trust, Mr Collins?"

"No, indeed not, Mr President."

"Then how may I assist these ... transactions?"

"It would aid the credibility of the representations if the operatives were able to conduct the transaction in diamonds rather than dollars. Rough diamonds."

"I see."

"The transactions are quite large, and there would be no way for the US Government to purchase the required quantity of diamonds on the open market without drawing unwanted attention. We are thus seeking to purchase the diamonds in a private and strictly confidential capacity." Young gave a slight emphasis to the words.

"I can see that would be advantageous, Mr Collins. What size of transaction had you in mind?"

"There are two possible sums," said Young. "Either $96 million, or $128 million, as you prefer." The team didn't want to have to waste time splitting pallets. Splitting 36 pallets between ten ... outlets ... meant some would receive three pallets, others four.

If the President was surprised, neither his face nor tone revealed it.

"I see."

Young said nothing. This was the moment. The offer was hanging there in the air. The biggest mistake a conman could make at this point was to keep talking. To push. To seek to persuade. You had to let the mark reach the decision on their own, or at least make them believe that was the case.

There was silence for around ten seconds. It felt much, much longer.

"Did you have a timeframe in mind for this transaction?" asked the President, in a conversational tone, as if there had been no pause at all.

"We do," said Young. "The transaction in question needs to be completed in around six weeks' time."

"And my interest in this transaction would be ... ?"

"We thought it possible you might have access to diamonds that you would like to convert to dollars. And we propose a two percent commission to cover any inconvenience on your part – you simply supply diamonds to ninety-eight percent of the value of the cash."

"The diamonds would need to be delivered where?"

"To the port," said Young. "They will be leaving by sea."

"And the matter of settlement?" asked the President.

"We were hoping that cash might prove acceptable."

There was just the slightest slip in the President's neutral facial expression at that moment; a momentary hint of surprise.

"One hundred and twenty eight million dollars in cash."

Young held out his hands in a gesture of apology. "We appreciate that electronic transfer to a suitable off-shore bank would be more convenient. Unfortunately we have to be careful not to leave an audit-trail, and it is difficult to hide an electronic transfer of that magnitude. Cash leaves no traces." Young silently noted that the President immediately opted for the higher of the two numbers.

The President was again silent, his face again expressionless.

Young took a sip of his drink as a means of occupying a few seconds.

The President remained silent. For Young to do the same felt like an almost physical effort. He made a point of studying one of the paintings on the wall behind the President. He had little interest in paintings, but occasionally in his career it had been necessary to take a temporary interest. The painting was familiar – the original was supposed to be in the Met Museum, yet this didn't seem the sort of man to go in for reproductions.

Still the President was silent.

Young took another sip of his G&T, now wondering whether he had been overly optimistic in his assessment of the ease with which the man would be able to obtain such a large quantity of diamonds. Did he have a hundred lieutenants, each eager to take his place and watching his every move in an attempt to gather material to assist them in their ambitions? Was the president in fact a prisoner of his own position, no more able to lay his hands personally on the gems mined in his country than the President of the USA would be able to wander into Fort Knox and help himself to the country's gold reserves?

Finally, the President spoke. He said only six words, and then stood to signal that the meeting was at an end. Three minutes later, Young was back in the car, being driven back to his hotel.

* * *

Chung checked the clock display in the corner of his laptop screen. 3am. One hour to go. He wanted at least 45 minutes of observing the system to ensure nobody was using it. He logged into the SCADA system using the sys/sys credentials. That was the first good news: if anyone had detected his previous intrusion, the login should have failed.

At his side was the schematic he'd drawn up from a combination of the water plant website and the plans he'd obtained from the planning dept. He studied the screen in front of him and identified the section it was displaying. He worked out which way he needed to navigate from there. He estimated four or five screens to the right then one or two up.

Evans too was taking no chances. He'd reached the road alongside the disused airbase almost an hour early, then turned onto a dirt track. He wanted to ensure the pickup could not be seen from the road. He started driving down the track, aiming to get at least a mile down it. The moonlight was pretty bright, so he'd turned off his lights.

3.45am. Chung allowed himself a small moment of satisfaction: in 45 minutes of staring at the screen, he'd seen no activity at all. Nobody seemed to be actively controlling anything. Probably just a single operator on duty overnight in case of emergencies. So far, so good.

Evans had walked back down the dirt track and slipped through the fence into the base. The moonlight was bright enough that he didn't need his head-torch above ground. He walked quickly to the manhole cover, slipped the crowbar out of the small sports bag he carried and levered it open and to one side. He switched on the head torch, peered down into the hole and then started climbing down the rungs.

* * *

Jack Grant was on the graveyard shift in the water plant control room: 6pm to 6am. Most of the operators hated it: there was usually nothing to do, the only job was monitoring.

In theory, there were screens to watch and occasional tests to run, but in practice the systems were almost 100% automatic, and alarms would sound if anything went wrong: water levels too low or too high, or a valve stuck open or closed. He'd been doing the job for 16 years, and it was rare he had to intervene. Mostly he dozed and watched recorded movies and TV shows on his tablet. It was a pretty good gig.

* * *

3.55am. Still no signs of life on the SCADA system. This was the first dangerous bit. Chung clicked the right arrow to move the display one screen to the right. The new section of schematic came up, and the new location codes matched the plans. He clicked right again. Again. Twice more. Yes, he just needed to go up from here. He clicked the up arrow, checked the display and clicked up again. He was looking at the schematic of the section of pipe running beneath the airbase. On the left, the inlet valve. On the right, the outlet valve. Both were set to open. He clicked right again. The next outlet valve was also open. Right again. Also open.

Anyone looking at this particular screen in the control centre would have been able to observe him moving around the schematic. That was the first danger, but not the greatest one. Being observed would require someone to be looking at the screen in the control centre at the time, or at least being observant enough to notice that the display had changed. It was a relatively small risk at 4am. The far greater danger was actually operating the valves.

While it looked innocuous enough – temporarily draining a section of pipe – he couldn't be sure what the knock-on effects might be. By closing the inlet valve, they would be raising the level of the water upstream of that valve as well as draining the downstream section. That might result in water reaching overflows, or alarms being activated. There was simply no way to know: the plans he'd obtained only showed the layout, they gave no clue as to the water levels expected in any given section. All he could do was pray.

Evans pointed his head-torch at the water surface. The level was pretty much at the halfway point, but they'd agreed that to keep the calls as short as possible he would choose either High or Low as the level report. He couldn't say one way or the other, so picked High. He set off up the ladder.

Chung gave an involuntary glance at the phone on his desk as the laptop clock changed to 04:00. He didn't have long to wait: the phone rang within five or so seconds.

"High."

"Acknowledged. Step 2 underway."

He hung up. This was it. He clicked on the upstream valve to close it. As with his initial test, it took a few seconds before the display changed to show the valve in the closed position. The three downstream valves were already open: there was no need to do anything at that end. Now all he could do was wait.

In the pipe, the signal to close the upstream valve was transmitted from the control-room computer to the remote valve via a network of Cat-5 Ethernet cables running through the pipes in waterproof housings. At the valve itself was a simple circuit-board which triggered a relay when an open or close signal was received.

The 'close' signal triggered the relay to operate the valve. The valve was effectively a thick steel disc which emerged from a slot on the left and rolled across until it sealed the pipe. On its own, the closer the gate got to closing, the greater the water pressure forced through the closing gap. Eventually, the pressure would be so great it would prevent the gate from fully closing. To address this, a much smaller valve in a bypass pipe opened to allow some water to continue flowing until the main gate was fully closed. The butterfly valve in the bypass valve simply spun on a vertical axis, so the pressure exerted on one side was balanced by equal pressure on the other side. Once that valve was closed, the water flow would cease.

The complete process of closing both main gate and bypass valve took 18 seconds. Nine seconds had elapsed so far.

Evans slipped the phone back into the side pocket of his fleece jacket and started climbing back down the ladder.

The success or failure of a plan often rested on the tiniest of details. The team all knew this. They did their very best to think of every eventuality, every detail, and had an enviable record of success. Evans in particular knew that it took only the slightest slip to spoil an illusion, to reveal the secret. But he was human. The detail he forgot was a trivial one: he failed to rezip the pocket after putting the phone back into it.

* * *

Young didn't dare show any sign of emotion until he was back in the hotel room. Even there, he had to allow for the possibility that surveillance equipment had been fitted during his absence: he would do and say nothing out of character.

It would be expected that he would report back to his superiors, of course, so sat at the laptop which also matched his borrowed identity in every respect, logged in and and opened a new email apparently to a US Treasury department address. In reality, the hosts file of the laptop had been edited such that the email would in fact be received by Chung.

He typed the short codeword which signalled the outcome of the meeting and hit Send.

Even if were being observed, it would be reasonable at this point for him to show the emotion that might be expected given the outcome of the meeting. He walked to the minibar, pulled out a whisky miniature, poured it into a glass, sat back in an easy chair, took a small sip and allowed himself a smile of satisfaction as he replayed in his mind the six words that indicated a successful sting: "I believe that can be arranged."

* * *

The automated water plant systems were crude but effective. Water sensors were placed towards the top and bottom of the pipes at regular intervals. The bottom sensor should normally be covered by water, so its default state was on. If the level dropped too low, it would be uncovered and set to off. That would send a 'Too low' signal back to the computer system in the control room.

The top sensor was normally not covered by water, so its default state was off. If water levels rose too high, it would be covered and set to on. A 'Too high' signal was sent to the computer.

In many cases, the automated systems could open and close valves to deal with the problem without requiring human intervention. But sometimes there would be knock-on consequences, and a human being needed to make the call as to the best way to resolve it. In those cases, an alarm would be sounded at the monitoring station in the control room, and the relevant section displayed on the main monitor. The affected stretch of pipe would flash yellow for a too-low water level and red for a too-high level. A supervisor could then take manual control to remedy the problem.

Sensitivity was controlled by the simple method of sensor placement: if a wide variation was acceptable in a particular section of pipe, the sensors were located close to the bottom and top of the pipe; if only a smaller variance was acceptable, the sensors were placed close together, ensuring that the level would remain near-constant.

In the section of pipe beneath the disused airbase, the sensitivity was low: both upper and lower sensors were placed at the 5% mark.

As the water level slowly fell, it came closer and closer to the lower sensor. When the sensor was uncovered, the system would kick into action.

Evans watched the water level fall. Chung had said it would happen pretty quickly, but it didn't look that way to him: the level was visibly dropping, but the large pipe diameter meant that the level was creeping down rather than falling rapidly.

He decided to time the water as it reduced by one row of bricks. Since the water level was roughly at the halfway point, he could then count the remaining bricks to the top, know that there had to be roughly the same number of rows to the bottom and get a rough estimate of the time it was going to take.

Jack Grant pressed pause on his tablet halfway through the episode of Lost. The older he got, the lower his bladder capacity seemed to be. He put down the tablet and headed towards the rest-room.

Why was it taking so long, wondered Chung? Was the water level not falling? Had he missed something? Had he messed up?

Or had Evans been caught? There shouldn't be any discernible level of security at a disused base, and in cover of darkness this ought to be as safe as it gets, but you never knew.

Should he play safe and re-open the upstream valve? Abandon the test and run it another night?

Evans had calculated it was going to take around 2m 40s to reach a level close to the bottom of the pipe. He shone his head torch on his watch. He felt nervous. There were so many unknowns. Chung had seemed worried about the test, and there was always the chance of a random security patrol. Well, there was nothing he could do about it, only wait.

The Dallas Fort Worth Police cruiser turned off the road and onto the dirt track. Sergeant Kevin Booth was a 29-year veteran, but still hated the graveyard shift almost as much as when he'd been a raw recruit. 4am to 6am was the worst. His patrol area was pretty much entirely rural, and a occasional stolen truck or small-time theft was about as exciting as it ever got in the early hours.

He couldn't complain about community support, though. If anything did happen, he could be sure someone would let the Police Dept know about it, even if it was as innocuous as an unknown vehicle parked on a farmer's track, and even at 4am - farmers rose early in these parts.

He'd driven over a mile down the track before his headlights picked up the gleaming black pickup. He had to agree it did look out of place here: most of the local vehicles had more visible rust and dirt than paintwork. There were no buildings anywhere near, no obvious reason at all for anything to be parked here in the middle of the night.

"Control from one seven."

"One seven, go ahead."

"One seven is ten-twenty three. Black Ford F-150, licence LTS 1384. Checking it out now."

"Copy that. Standby."

Booth clicked his transmit button on and off in acknowledgement and climbed out of the cruiser, unclipping the flashlight from the dash as he did so. The truck was dark - no exterior or interior lights on. He approached cautiously from behind the driver side, shining the flashlight into the interior. He kept his right hand close to his belt holster, but he hadn't drawn his service weapon in almost seven years and didn't expect to do so tonight.

"One seven, control."

Booth finished covering the truck interior with the flashlight, then thumbed his radio.

"One seven."

"Vehicle is a black current year Ford Foxtrot 150 pickup registered to Hertz rental. No reports."

"Roger that. No sign of any occupants, standby."

"Acknowledged."

Satisfied the vehicle was empty, and the moon providing enough light to see by, Booth switched off his flashlight and walked to the hood, placing his hand on top of it. It was still somewhat warm: the vehicle hadn't been there too long.

Booth scanned the surrounding fields. He couldn't see any sign of anyone. He switched the flashlight back on and did a 360-degree survey with that. Still nothing.

Booth stood there for a moment. There was no evidence of any crime in progress, but it was odd. There was no reason for a rental truck to be parked out in the middle of nowhere like that. Booth didn't like odd. Odd bothered him. He'd take a little drive around, see if he could spot anyone.

Evans too was nervous at how long the water was taking to drop. He was staring intently at the edge of the water in the torchlight as it slowly fell.

He caught a glimpse of something metallic as the water receded. He stared at it. It was a small, metal rectangle with a black pad in the centre. The water fell a little more and uncovered a rubber-coated wire. The level reduced further and he saw a second, identical metal rectangle.

A sensor! A water-level sensor! It had to be. Fuck!

He had to let Chung know immediately, tell him to start refilling the pipe. He quickly began climbing the rungs to the top.

It was a damp environment, the metal rungs were greasy and Evans was hurrying. As he climbed, his right hand slipped off the rung as he stepped up. Instinctively, he threw his arm backwards to the brick wall just behind him. His hand slapped against the wall and he came to a halt. The phone, close to the mouth of his fleece jacket, didn't: it was jerked out of the pocket, bounced off the wall as it fell before landing in the remaining water with a splash.

Evans stared down at it. Beneath him, the second rectangle was now fully uncovered. If he was right, and it was a water-level sensor, an alarm was likely now sounding.

Evans was correct. With the sensor uncovered, a signal was sent back to the control-room computer. The software controlling the automatic adjustments was designed to be fail-safe. It was able to regulate water flow where an over-level or under-level resulted from failures in the system, but it was not allowed to over-ride manual inputs by control-room staff – otherwise you could end up with the plant staff and computer system battling each other. Where a problem resulted from operator input, it was passed back to the operator for resolution. The alarm circuit was triggered.

The affected section of pipe was automatically displayed on the main screen, flashing yellow to indicate a too-low condition. An audio alarm started blaring.

In the rest-room, Grant heard the alarm sounding. Alarms weren't common, but they were not so unusual or urgent that they required him to propel his bulk into rapid action, and he was too old and fat to start running. He'd leave that kind of thing to the young guys. He zipped up his pants and started walking back toward the control room.

Evans silently thanked Sullivan and her insistence on belt-and-braces planning at every stage. The spare phone was zipped into his interior pocket. He would take no chances this time: he would climb out of the manhole before he opened the pocket and made the call.

Sergeant Booth had driven up the rest of the dirt-track to the farm, accompanied the farmer on a quick look around without seeing anything. The only other sign of civilisation within walking distance was the disused airbase. He swung the cruiser around and headed back towards the road.

Chung didn't need Evans' call to tell him what had happened: he could see for himself on the SCADA system screen that a red box had popped up with a flashing white UNDER-LEVEL message in red capitals. Beneath it was an ACK link. He clicked it, and the popup message vanished. Chung opened the upstream valve and closed the nearest downstream valve so that water would flow back into the section of pipe as quickly as possible. That done, he checked the time on his screen: two minutes, 27 seconds. That was how long it had taken to drain the pipe. Perfect.

Evans pulled himself out of the manhole, reached inside his jacket and unzipped the spare cellphone. Spare phones were kept fully-charged and switched off. He powered it up and waited the ten seconds or so it took to boot. That ten seconds felt like a very long time.

He called Chung.

"Refill it! Refill it!" he urged.

"Don't worry, I got it. Just get back down and tell me when the level is nearly back where it was."

Evans didn't waste time asking how Chung knew about it. "On my way."

As Grant reached the end of the corridor, the blaring alarm getting louder with every step, he turned into the control room. Almost simultaneously, the alarm ceased. The flashing yellow section of pipe on the main screen ceased its flashing and returned to its previous overview display.

Grant walked over and quickly scanned each of the screens in turn. Everything looked normal, no flashing alerts. Just some glitch somewhere, or some temporary issue that the automatics managed to resolve. He eased himself back into his chair, picked up his tablet and resumed watching Lost.

Sgt Booth reached the end of the track and could see the airbase fence ahead of him. He turned the patrol car to the left, the lights on main-beam to illuminate the whole stretch of road. No sign of anyone or anything. He swung the car around in a U-turn to illuminate the road in the opposite direction. Also nothing.

If whoever parked the pickup truck on the track did go into the disused base, he reasoned, they likely entered somewhere close to where the track emerged. It was likely nothing, but checking it out gave him something to do. He pulled over at the side of the road, grabbed his flashlight and climbed out for a look.

Had there been an audible alarm as well as a visual one, wondered Chung?

How long had it been between the message popping up and him cancelling it? Not more than ten seconds, he was pretty sure, but if an alarm had been blaring even for a few seconds in a control room in the dead of night, it could hardly have gone unnoticed.

Well, he thought, nothing he could do about that now other than make sure he still had access tomorrow night. If he did, then it meant nobody had worked out what had happened.

Chung suddenly realised: he'd been so focused on the alarm that he hadn't taken a moment to fully appreciate that the test had worked! It was no longer theoretical: he really had taken control of the water system!

It didn't take Sgt Booth long to spot the section of fence that had been pulled back. He knelt down and examined it closely. Looking at the rust on the exposed edges, this wasn't a recent break: it must have been like that for years. But still, it was the logical entry point. He reached for his radio and clicked the transmit button.

"Control from one seven."

"Go ahead, one seven."

"No sign of anyone so far, I'm going to check out the airbase. I'm parked close to a break in the fence and heading in for a quick look-see."

"Acknowledged."

"One seven out."

Booth pulled back the fence carefully: last time he'd gone through a fence like this, he'd managed to tear the sleeve of his jacket. He ducked through, stood up and shone his flashlight in a wide arc.

Chung picked up the phone on the first ring.

"Mission complete," said Evans.

"Thanks," replied Chung, hanging up.

Chung re-opened the downstream valve so that the water flow would resume. The test was complete, there was nothing further for him to do tonight.

But there was one other thing that caused him major concern. Their test was at night, when the plant likely had a skeleton staff. For the real thing, they had no control over the timings, and their webcam surveillance had shown that the convoys always set off during office hours – presumably when the BEP was fully staffed. In the day, the water plant control room would likewise be fully staffed. As soon as he started moving around the system, everything he did would be mirrored on the control room screens, and the chance of someone there seeing what he was doing had to be high.

He very much doubted that anyone on-site would have the IT skills needed to lock him out of the system, but they wouldn't need to: all they had to do was undo everything he did. When he opened a valve, they could immediately close it again. When he closed one, they could re-open it. They could end up in a tit-for-tat battle for control of the system, like two kids fighting over a toy.

But the stakes here would be rather higher: if he couldn't retain control of the water flow, the escape plan would fail – and most of the team would be trapped with the cash on the disused base.

But he was pretty sure he had a way to stop that. He wouldn't risk anything further tonight, but tomorrow night he'd login again, this time using the suspected supervisor account he'd identified. If his theory was correct, there would be no battling over the controls.

Sgt Booth was doubtful anyone would be on the base. There was nothing here of any value now. They got kids entering from time to time. A little graffiti. The occasional photographer with a passion for abandoned buildings – the ghost-town thing. And the odd amorous couple, usually married and usually not to each other. Maybe that was the deal here, he thought. A rental truck, so someone from out of town. Someone on a business trip engaging in a little extra-curricular activity, perhaps. But usually they had perfectly comfortable hotel rooms at their disposal. Still, tastes varied, the thrill of the open air and all that.

He wasn't particularly interested if that was the case. They were miles from anywhere, and if there was no-one else around to witness proceedings, then he didn't see the harm. Technically, they were trespassing on government property, but he wasn't going to bust his ass for a misdemeanour. Still, he was here now, he'd take a quick look around.

Evans carefully replaced the spare phone back into the inside pocket of his jacket and made sure it was zipped-up. He manhandled the manhole cover back into place, then kicked a bit of dirt over the tell-tale marks where it had been slid back and forth. He looked it over. All looked fine.

He started walking back towards the hangers, ready to head back to the pickup, when his bladder made its presence known. He needed a leak.

Even though he was on a deserted base in the middle of the night, with likely no-one around for miles, he felt exposed. Instinct compelled him to seek cover, even though logically he felt silly doing it. He walked towards one of the hanger walls.

Sgt Booth came around the side of the old control tower and shone his flashlight in an arc again. Nothing.

He waited for a second, then shrugged and turned. He'd check on the pickup again on his next pass in an hour or so, and if it was still there then, he could consider whether it merited further investigation.

Evans didn't even see the flashlight. The moonlight provided enough light that there hadn't been sufficient contrast to catch his eye, hidden as he was around the corner of the hanger. By the time he zipped up his pants and started making his way back to the fence, the patrol car was gone, neither man having been aware of the presence of the other.

* * *

The tyre shop was starting to feel almost like home, thought Sullivan, as the last of them arrived. There was a palpable feeling of jubilation in the air. Sullivan intended to change that.

Most of the time, her role was that of cheerleader, encouraging them to go for it. Tonight, she had the opposite job. Tonight, she had to deliver her famous anti-pep talk: what Young had termed The Speech. They'd all heard it before, but they were going to hear it again tonight.

This was the shoot-down meeting. All the preparations were complete, and they were, in principle, now ready to roll - with almost six weeks left before D-Day. Each team member was confident they had their own elements handled. Their job now was to adopt their most pessimistic attitudes and look for any holes they could find in both plan and preparations.

"Ok," said Sullivan. "You all know the drill. Nobody gets precious about their work being challenged. Nobody is afraid to call bullshit on anything that doesn't sound right. There is no objection too dumb or too minor to raise. If you can see even the tiniest glimmer of a problem, you yell. If you have even the slightest doubt about any aspect of the operation, you speak up. If someone questions your most carefully-planned approach, the one you sweated night and day to make sure there's no possible way it could go wrong, you listen with an open mind to what they have to say and consider whether there is any conceivable way in which the concern could be justified. If somebody asks a question too dumb to be worthy of a response, you think very carefully about whether you could be the one being dumb. And if, in listening to an objection, or just thinking things through again yourself, you realise you've been an idiot and screwed-up somewhere, you say so. Nobody-" she looked around as she said this, with an expression which implied that there would be no disagreement on this point- "is going to scream and shout at you. Nobody is going to rip you a new one. We're just going to be very, very glad the problem was identified. This is the meeting that keeps us all out of Attica doing life without."

The Attica Correctional Facility was a Federal Supermax prison: a level above even Federal high security prisons. Conditions were grim, and the authorities prioritised security over all else. Back in 1971, when prisoners rioted and took guards hostage, the authorities took an uncompromising approach. State Troopers went in guns blazing. There was no discrimination in the hail of gunfire. Ring-leader, innocent bystander, even guard. Lives, even those of the staff, were less important than security. Twenty-nine inmates were killed in the gunfire, along with nine guards.

Nobody liked to think about what could happen if things went wrong, but it was vital to ensure that they each thought about the stark reality of what was at stake here.

None of the team was hurting financially. They could all live out their lives perfectly comfortably on the proceeds of their previous escapades. While more money is always better than less, money wasn't the primary motivation here for Sullivan, and she was pretty sure it wasn't for any of the others. This was about the challenge. The game. Most of the time, viewing it as a game worked. It took off the pressure, enabled them to think creatively, gave them a can-do attitude when they encountered obstacles along the way.

But they couldn't afford to get complacent. The stakes were very, very real. In the shoot-down meeting, you couldn't afford to have any of them going through the motions – she needed each of them doing their damnedest to find any flaws that might exist.

"This is a Federal crime," she continued, "and for something this big, there is only one possible sentence: life without the possibility of parole in a Supermax. And that assumes we survive long enough to be arrested in the first place. We're going up against very serious people with very serious weaponry, and no compunction about using it. A single mistake, one forgotten element, one tiny flaw, is all it takes to end up dead. Our job tonight is to look for those mistakes like our lives depend on it, because they do."

Sullivan looked each of them in the eye. The smiles were gone, and she got a nod from each.

"Ok, then," she said. "Let's begin. Task one: diverting the aircraft."

"Well," said Jackson, without hesitation, "the first possibility we need to address is that of technical failure. Do we have enough redundancy built-in?"

Sullivan nodded. "Lewis? Perez?"

Katrina Lewis was the first to speak. "Technical failure is always a possibility, but the risk here is near-zero. The circuitry is solid-state, no moving parts. Not immune to failure – nothing is – but very, very reliable. The design of the circuit has been extensively tested on the VSM system, with every conceivable variable thrown at it. The physical circuits were all individually tested after construction, and again the day before they were fitted. So far as the circuits are concerned, I don't think there's anything more we could have done to ensure they do their job."

Raul Perez was next. "The Semtex, well, there's really nothing to fail, it's a simple and inevitable chemical reaction. Fire the detonator and the Semtex goes bang. You can conceivably get a duff batch, and of course buying through unofficial channels there's always the risk of being sold fake material, but I've tested a small sample and it works. The risk comes with the detonators. No detonator is 100% reliable. They are very simple devices, with very little to go wrong, but they can and do fail.

There's frankly nothing you can do about that other than ensure the integrity of them when they are fitted. But the stats are very much on our side: the failure rate is less than 0.01%. Where the risk of failure does increase markedly is in the remote triggering. You can never state with confidence the range of any radio transmission because radio wave propagation is subject to a whole bunch of factors, from weather conditions through interference to the shielding effects of other nearby components. The transmitter we're using has a theoretical range of 50 miles, but a combination of factors could reduce the effective range to ten miles or increase it to 200."

"So we could be working with a range of ten miles," said Pugh.

"It's not likely," said Perez, "but it's possible, yes."

"Supposing it was ten on the day," asked Young, "how long are we within range?"

Scott Jackson took that one. "We'll be in a Learjet 55. That can match the climb-rate of the C-5s, so we're fine for the first ten minutes or so. Once the C-5s reach cruising altitude, they top out at 574mph while the Lear is limited to 540mph. If we assume a worst-case scenario of them flying at V-Max – unlikely but we're being pessimistic here, so let's say they do – then they pull ahead by 34 miles in an hour. If we assume a reduced range of ten miles, then that puts them out of range 20 minutes after they reach cruising altitude, or around 30 minutes after take-off. We plan to hit them within minutes of take-off, so we don't have time to mess around, but we do have enough time to get the job done."

"Ok," said Young. "The equipment is as reliable as we can make it, and we can work with significantly reduced range, but suppose the equipment does fail – what then?"

"We don't need all twelve devices to work in order to have a viable threat," said Perez. "In principle, even one working would be enough to make our point. With even two or three of the devices working, the argument for them to cooperate becomes unassailable."

"Well," said Young, "we're considering worst-case scenarios here. What if all twelve devices failed?"

"If they all failed," said Perez, "we'd be in trouble. We'd have drawn attention to ourselves by issuing the threats, and would have no way to prevent them coming after us."

"But that's statistically impossible," said Lewis. "One failure, already very, very unlikely but possible. Two failures, vanishingly small odds – my calculator probably doesn't have enough zeroes before the decimal to calculate them. All twelve devices failing, forget it, it's not going to happen."

"Supposing the transmitter itself fails?" asked Pugh.

"The standard aviation approach," said Jackson: "triple redundancy. We'll have three of them on board."

"And I'll have stripped them down and tested every component of all three beforehand," added Lewis. "Nothing is being left to chance."

The room was silent for several seconds while they all tried to think of something else.

"What if something goes wrong with the Lear?" asked Young.

"If we don't get off the ground, then the mission is postponed with no harm done. If we get close enough to fire the transmitters, then the job is done and any problem with the Lear after that is something for me and Perez to worry about."

More silence.

"Ok," said Sullivan, "we're all racking our brains to think of other objections, but you three are the experts in this phase – what else could possibly go wrong? Don't forget the dumb stuff: you all know it's the stupid stuff that often causes plans to fail."

"Weather," said Jackson, "but if the Lear can't fly, no harm is done. And the Lear can fly in most weathers the C-5s can manage."

"Ok," said Sullivan, "what if they call our bluff?"

Jackson fielded that one. "Initially, I expect them to. We'll need to blow the weather radars on a couple of aircraft before they start to pay attention to us."

"Do you think that will be enough?"

"Hard to say," said Jackson, "but I suspect not. I think we're going to have to take out the flaps on either one or two aircraft before they accept we can do what we say we can do."

"And you're sure we're not going to risk crashing a plane by doing that?"

"Yep," said Jackson. "C-5s are designed for short field landings. A flap-less landing means coming in 35 knots faster - plenty of room to stop on the runway."

"What about take-off?" asked Lewis. "We need to get them back into the air afterwards."

"Again, not a problem at all on that length of runway."

"What if they still won't cooperate after we blow their flaps?" asked Lewis.

"I can't see it happening. By that stage, we've successfully demonstrated that we have placed explosives aboard their aircraft, and that we have the capability to detonate them at will. There is no reason at all for them to doubt our ability to sever the control cables too, and no way for them to definitively rule that out while the aircraft is airborne. It just wouldn't make sense to run what they will believe is the near-certain risk of losing an aircraft and its crew."

"Not even to save a billion dollars?" asked Pugh.

"It would be a pretty major sacrifice even then, but it's not going to look like they're doing that. They will have every confidence that as soon as they have the Galaxies back on terra firma, they will regain control of the situation. They have F-16s up there, and can have helicopters stuffed full of Marines airborne within minutes and on-scene in maybe 15 minutes. They don't know at that stage that we're going to effectively take some of them hostage by having them drive trucks full of explosives, of course."

"Nor that the trucks are empty," added Perez.

"Indeed."

"What happens if the Air Force works out it's the Lear doing the transmitting?"

Jackson answered that one too. "We expect them to figure it out eventually, but not immediately – by that time we expect to be out of the Lear and using the handheld transmitter on the ground. Even if they do figure it out at the time, I can't see them taking the chance of blowing us out of the air when they can't be sure there isn't a second transmitter somewhere else."

"Anything else that could go wrong with phase one?" asked Sullivan.

Silence.

"Positive?" she persisted. "Remember the rules: nothing too trivial or silly to mention."

Sullivan looked at each of them in turn. Each shook their head.

"Ok," she said, "let's move on to phase two ..."

Two hours and forty-three minutes later, Sullivan was satisfied. There wasn't a single aspect of the mission they hadn't questioned, and all of the answers had been satisfactory. She'd known the team were pros, and everything tonight had confirmed it. Each team member had clearly thought through all of the possible failure modes, and had put in place contingencies for each. Where no contingency plan was possible, the odds were so low as to make the matter academic.

"Anything else?" she asked. "Anything at all?"

None of them had anything.

"So the plan is a go, and we're fully prepared."

Again, the ritual of looking at each in turn and awaiting confirmation.

"Ok, then."

That was it. Two utterly mundane words to declare the go-ahead for the biggest and most audacious robbery the world had ever seen. Likely the biggest robbery it would ever see.

There was just one eventuality the team hadn't considered: that the authorities were already onto them, and that on D-day there would be no money to steal. Not a billion dollars. Not a million. Not a hundred thousand. Not even a thousand. Just 36 pallets loaded with over 20 million pieces of blank, worthless paper.

* * *

7pm, the day before D-day

The team had made their way to Sullivan's hotel room one at a time over the past twenty minutes. There would be no gathering in the morning: this was it, the final briefing before they set off to steal a billion dollars.

The hotel room was cramped with all eight of them in it. Jessica Sullivan herself was standing, leaning back against the desk. Katrina Lewis and Aaron Evans were sat in the only two chairs. Sam Young and Mike Chung were sat on the two-seater sofa, Ryan Pugh perched on one of the arms. Scott Jackson and Raul Perez were sat on the edge of the bed.

"We all know our jobs tomorrow," said Sullivan without pre-amble, "so all I'm going to do here is cover the final elements of the logistics. If anyone has any questions at all, any last-minute concerns, speak up."

She paused, the only sound in the room the whirr of the air-conditioner.

"The main vehicles are in the parking garage, backup vehicles in the parking garage of the Hilton, at the opposite end of the block."

Young smiled. When Sullivan thought contingencies, she didn't take any half-measures. She'd not only considered the possibility of breakdown, she'd also thought about the possibility of the entire parking garage going up in flames or a security alert closing off the hotel and its surrounds: that was why the backup vehicles were a block away.

"The trucks have been prepped, and we have drivers delivering them to the airbase at 7am. They think the trucks contain technical equipment for a hush-hush movie shoot, and that's why they won't be told the destination until the morning. They also think the movie doesn't start shooting until next week, just in case they decide to tell their friends to show up to catch a glimpse of the stars arriving. I'm sure word will get around, and there'll be a bunch of paparazzi and autograph-hunters there next week, but we'll be long gone by then. The local police have also received the same notification, so there won't be any questions about signs of activity there, and we've of course got keys for the padlocks."

"What happens to the drivers once they've parked the trucks?" asked Jackson.

"There's a bus collecting them. And a backup bus, of course, along with the two backup trucks."

"Naturally." Jackson smiled too. They sometimes teased Sullivan about her layers of contingency, but they were all glad of it.

"Jackson and Perez drive straight to the airport to pick up the Lear. They will be pre-flighted and ready for take-off by 8am. Chung will remain here to monitor the BEP webcam and call us when the convoy departs, and of course to connect to the water-plant system. As soon as the convoy departs, Chung will start emptying the pipe so that we can get the baggage carts in. Pugh and Lewis will be standing-by at the exit point, ready to drive the baggage carts in."

The two of them nodded.

Evans, Young and myself will go direct to the base to set up our little truck illusion and to prepare for some manual labour. Jackson and Perez land the Lear here as soon as the Galaxies are where we want them and within ground range. Chung will meet us at the airport afterwards. Any questions?"

There were none: everyone knew their role.

Sullivan nodded. "Ok. Let's all get an early night: tomorrow is going to be a very busy day."

* * *

D-Day. 8am. BEP.

It was the waiting. Always the waiting that was worst, reflected Luke Pritchard as he accepted Kate Lorrimar's invitation to take a seat in her office.

He had that familiar yet hard-to-describe feeling he got back when they had a piece of intelligence at the White House suggesting some kind of an attack might be attempted. You knew that it was almost certainly a false alarm, but there was that tiny chance that it was for real.

You knew that even if it was for real, you had layers upon layers of protection, and that the measures you had in place would almost certainly defeat any attack that was attempted.

Almost certainly.

Presidents had been assassinated. Not on his watch, not in his time, but it had happened, and there was always that chance. Once you'd put in place all the extra protective measures practical, all you could do was wait. The best you could do was find distractions.

"So how did you manage it?" he asked. "You said before that everything's automated and that you weren't sure how it would even be possible to substitute blank paper for the real thing."

Lorrimar gave a tired smile. "You wouldn't believe how much work was involved."

"Try me."

"The first thing we looked at was whether we could somehow intercept the SARVs between printroom and vault, and swap the pallets. No surprise that was a complete non-starter."

"No," said Pritchard. "No-one allowed anywhere on the path between printroom and vault while the SARVs are on the move."

"Right. Same deal with intercepting them between vault and loading bay. No go. So idea two was to put the SARVs into manual mode and load dummy bills into the vault."

Pritchard nodded.

Lorrimar shook her head. "That was also a bust. Manual mode is there in case we have to do something like use one SARV to tow out another, broken-down one. That much we can do. But the system knows what bills have been loaded in what locations in the vault. There's just no way to manually interfere with that process without completely screwing up the entire system."

"Right," said Pritchard.

"So eventually we hit on the idea of loading the print machines with dummy paper and dummy ink. Basically ordinary copier paper instead of the proper stuff, and transparent ink, so the machines would think they were printing real bills but wouldn't be."

"And?"

"About a million and one headaches. Production isn't the only thing that's automated: quality-control is too. There are checks that the paper meets about a dozen different criteria. Copier paper meets none of them. We looked at disabling the checks, so the machines would accept any paper we gave to them, but that was essentially impossible without reprogramming the entire system. The tech guys eventually said we'd have to use the real paper."

"Ouch."

"Yes. I was adamant I didn't want that to happen - even if all they got was the blank paper, that would be a counterfeiter's dream."

"For sure."

"But eventually I had to accept it. We did manage to add an extra dye to the paper that will make detection easy, but that was the best we could do."

"And the transparent ink?"

"The ink, as you know, is metallic and is checked electronically. It's also ultra-low-spread. So we had to create a dummy ink that had the same metallic content and the same ultra-low-spread characteristics yet was totally transparent. That kept a lot of guys in a chemical lab working very long hours for about a fortnight."

"But they did it?"

"They did it."

"What about the real bills on top?"

Lorrimar shook her head. "No way to do it. I can't see any way in the world the bad guys could get close enough to see through the saran wrap prior to their hit, but as a precaution we switched to black opaque saran wrap as soon as the dummy shipment plan was agreed. If the team is somehow watching in a way that lets them get direct sight of the pallets, they will have seen it, but they'll also have seen the same thing happens every day. It's routine by now."

Pritchard nodded.

"So what we have sat in the vault right now," continued Lorrimar, "is one day's batch of completely blank bills. We keep ten days' worth of bills in the vault, and the SARVs operate on a first-in, first-out basis. The printroom operates every other day, so the blank bills had to be produced nineteen days ago. Those are the bills that get loaded today."

"Quite the operation," said Pritchard.

"There were a lot of late nights," confirmed Lorrimar, "and the 19-day lead-time added to the pressure. But it did at least mean there was no last-minute panic: it's all done-and-dusted, so there's nothing to do today but business as usual."

"Let's hope it really is."

"Amen to that."

* * *

D-Day. 6.30am. Hicks Field.

"Pretty spectacular sunrise, huh?" remarked Sam Young as the three of them surveyed the landscape around the disused airbase. Young, Sullivan and Evans.

"Certainly is," said Young, "good thing the convoys operate office hours or you'd have had a lot of different sunrises and sunsets to match, Evans!"

"Yeah, that might have meant moving into one of those buildings for a few weeks for the photography."

"Ok," said Sullivan, "you're in charge here, Evans – this is your illusion. Take us through it one last time."

By this point, any one of them could probably have recited the briefing word-for-word, but all knew Sullivan's view that you could never over-plan, and no-one could argue with the idea that it was better to hear the same thing twenty times than to forget some vital detail.

"It's pretty simple," said Evans. "The original concept was to have some fold-down photo boards attached to the undersides of the trucks with the appropriate backgrounds for the weather and time of day, but I decided that was too risky: if they were noticed by the Marines we get to drive them, it would give an immediate clue that all was not what it appeared. We need the authorities to have all their attention on the trucks rather than the base. If the boards were spotted and they put two-and-two together quickly enough, they might divert their resources back to the base before we've had a chance to complete our disappearing-act."

Sullivan nodded.

"So instead," continued Evans, "the boards will lay flat on the ground – with photos of the concrete surface on the reverse – and flip up on supports when the truck is positioned. That way, no-one from the opposition ever gets closer to the photo boards than a few hundred yards. As soon as each truck is loaded, we wait for the Galaxy to take-off before we move it to the parking area, and we have the next one positioned before the next Galaxy lands."

"Sounds good," said Young.

"Sullivan, as you know, you proved the most accurate driver with both the trucks and the forklift, so you'll be responsible for positioning each truck exactly as per the practice runs. You can see here on the concrete I've painted markings showing the tire tracks for the trucks, and marking the stop position. The markings are deliberately faint – clear enough from up close, but not visible from any distance. We don't want any clue that the truck has been parked precisely. So long as you approach along these tire tracks, and stop with the driver's window level with these markings, the truck will be at the correct position and angle for the illusion."

Sullivan merely nodded: she'd practiced the manoeuvre on waste ground, with Evans watching her every move, literally hundreds of times.

"We've got the yellow container 400 yards away." Evans nodded toward it. "The Galaxies will be instructed to park with their nose-wheel a hundred feet short of it. Jackson tells me those things can turn on a dime despite their size, so they can clear it as they turn back to the runway after we've relieved them of their cargo. Young and I will be in the trailer of the truck. So far as our audience is concerned, you are the only person here. As soon as the first truck is parked, we nip out through the hole in the trailer, flip up the photo boards then slide back the cover over the hole leading down to the pipe. Young will climb down the rope ladder to await the arrival of the baggage carts trains being driven in by Lewis and Pugh. I'll operate the hoist. Everything just as we practiced it back at the warehouse. All you have to do is make sure the pallet is square-on to each cart as I lower it in. Remember, you never, ever, get underneath the pallet, always off to the side: we don't want anyone getting hurt."

Young nodded. He, Pugh and Lewis too had practiced their part over and over in a disused warehouse; it wasn't difficult with three of them.

"As soon as the pallet is seated on the cart, the straps go over and ratchet down tight, just like the rehearsal. Remember, if a pallet falls off the cart, we don't just lose that pallet, we block the pipe and lose the lot. So a cart doesn't move until all three of you independently check the straps and give them the ok. Remember, there's no rush here. Sullivan will be taking her time driving back to the Galaxy with the fork-lift truck to collect the next one, so slow and sure is the order of the day."

Sullivan listened with approval. Evans was merely repeating what he'd told them on every practice run, but she was glad to hear him do so. Better to be told too many times than too few. They had put in too much blood, sweat and tears to have the mission fail because of a stupid mistake.

"Once we have all three pallets from one Galaxy loaded onto carts and the empty Galaxy has taken off, I'll drop through the hole to lower the photo boards, you'll drive the truck to the parking area and return with the next one. Rinse and repeat. The only variation is the final truck: the radio-controlled one."

If Lewis had been there, she'd have smiled at that, he was sure: she was proud of this bit. The one remaining problem they'd faced was that once Sullivan had driven the final truck to the parking area, she was exposed. They had to assume there would be air surveillance in place by then. The authorities might even be able to task a satellite to photograph the base, so there was nothing visible in the air. If Sullivan was seen walking back to the loading point and disappearing down into the hole, the whole escape plan was blown.

Lewis had thus modified the twelfth truck so that it became a giant radio-controlled toy. Because a Marine would be driving it later, nothing could be visible in the cab: everything had to be under the hood. As soon as the final pallet was lowered, Sullivan would follow it down into the hole, pull the covering boards back into place over her head and then use the remote-control system to 'drive' the truck to the parking area.

The truck was fitted with hidden cameras in the right headlight, with the video relayed to an iPad. Chung had written the app. It looked pretty much identical to any driving game, but this one was live and real. She would park the truck over a manhole cover leading into a sewerage system. They had earlier loosened the cover so the authorities would later 'figure out' that's how she'd escaped. Inside the sewerage pipe, they'd left a subtle trail leading to a second manhole cover outside the base, half a mile away. It would look exactly like Sullivan – apparently the only gang member on the base – had left that way, and hopefully the authorities would waste a considerable proportion of their resources conducting a fruitless air and ground search for her.

Of course, the authorities would eventually go over the airbase inch-by-inch in the hunt for clues, and they'd discover the hole. But by that time, the pipe would be filled with water again and they'd be looking for boats. Maybe they'd figure out the truth eventually, but by that time they'd be long gone, and so would the cash.

"Ok," said Evans, "any last-minute questions?"

There were none.

"Right, let's get the first truck set up. Once that's done, we can all relax for a while until we get the call from Mike to say the convoy is en-route."

Lewis and Pugh pulled back the grill from the mouth of the overflow ramp and lent it up against the wall. They'd undone most of the bolts the previous evening so that they could open it quickly. They already had the truck backed-up to the mouth of the overflow, with metal ramps extended to enable them to drive the baggage cart trains into the mouth of the pipe. As soon as the baggage carts were inside, they'd pull the grill back into place in case anyone happened by, but only fasten two bolts to facilitate a quick exit. The ramps would go back in the truck, which would be parked a short distance away.

"Just like a real-life Italian Job," grinned Pugh.

"A little slower and less glamorous," replied Lewis, with a smile. "These things are limited to 18mph."

"I'll still imagine I'm driving a Mini."

"I'll whistle the theme-tune for you."

The pair of them started walking up the ramp to position the baggage trains ready to enter the pipe as soon as the water was turned off.

* * *

Pritchard and Lorrimar stood at the back of the control room, not daring to take their eyes from the screens showing the CCTV feeds from the loading bay. Pritchard knew it was irrational, but he watched intently as the SARVs loaded the trucks. He still didn't really believe the hit would be happening at all, and if it was, it was supposed to be happening in the air, not here inside the BEP, but all the same, his senses were tingling.

"Almost comical, isn't it?" asked Lorrimar.

"What's that?" he asked.

"Us. Watching like hawks as the most secure transport operation in the world loads and transports twenty million blank pieces of paper."

He laughed, the tension broken. "Put like that ..." he said.

"You think it'll happen?" asked Lorrimar.

Pritchard had asked himself the same question hundreds of times, but still hesitated before answering. "No," he said, finally. "You?"

"I'd like to say no, but ..."

"But we're both trained to expect the worst."

"Exactly."

"But if you were betting a hundred bucks on it?"

Lorrimar smiled. "Then I'd say no."

* * *

"Scared?" asked Jackson, looking over at Perez in the rented pickup as he turned into the airfield.

"Yep," said Perez, simply.

It was the one of the benefits of having shared a military history. Whatever kind of a front they might put up in front of others, with each other there was no bullshit. They'd both been there, done that: they had nothing to prove to one another.

"Hard to believe it's really happening, isn't it?" asked Jackson as he parked the truck.

"Yeah," said Perez. "After all that planning, all the rehearsals, this is finally it."

"Would that half the military missions we carried out were as carefully planned, hey?"

Perez nodded.

They climbed out of the truck, closed the doors and Jackson touched the blipper to lock it. "Ok," he said, as they started walking towards the office buildings, "let's go pick ourselves up a Lear."

* * *

On the airfield apron, the BP Jet-A fuel truck was parked next to the Lear 55. The driver-operator disconnected the fuel-hose, slotted it back into its holder and switched the pump to Off. He disconnected the grounding cable and placed that back into its clip, then walked over to the steps, climbed up, poked his head through the open doorway and called out: "Both tanks topped-off."

The aircraft engineer sat in the cockpit called back. "Ok, thanks."

There were three remaining unchecked boxes on the checklist on the clipboard on his lap. He checked the gauge for tank 1, in the left wing: it read full. 3,500 pounds. He ran his pen along the line marked 'Fuel - Tank 1 - full' and ticked the box next to it. He checked the gauge for tank 2, in the right wing. That too read full. He ticked the penultimate box next to 'Fuel - Tank 2 - full'. One final step, then he'd be done.

Theft was not a major concern in the executive jet rental business. There was a limited market for high-end exec jets, and both the airframe and most of the major components were registered. It wasn't the sort of thing you could stick up on eBay. All the same, no chances were taken. Each aircraft in their small fleet was fitted with a tracker. That tracker sent back GPS position and altitude information once a minute to a monitoring system in the office. Software on a PC there monitored position against the flight-plan submitted by the client, and any deviation would trigger an alert.

The engineer peered round to ensure the gas truck had pulled away: radios could not be used while the truck was present, whether or not it was fuelling. The truck had gone. He thumbed the transmit button on his radio.

"Base, hanger."

"Go ahead, Tom."

"Tracker signal up?"

"One sec ... Yep, tracker active."

"Roger. Lear checks complete. Hanger out."

He checked the last box on the sheet, signed it then reached into his pocket for his self-inking stamp. He applied the stamp. It still gave him a small thrill to do that: he'd finally qualified as a certification engineer eighteen months ago, meaning that he could sign-off his own work, declaring that the aircraft had been prepped according to manufacturer and operator requirements, and that it was safe to fly. The thrill was tinged with just the slightest touch of anxiety: in the event of the worst happening, he was legally responsible for any fault found with the aircraft.

He eased himself out of the captain's seat, exited the Lear and headed over to the office to hand over the paperwork.

* * *

Chung was watching the webcam stream from the BEP facility intently. To ensure his attention didn't wander, he'd programmed a timer to bleep every 30 seconds as a prompt to check the feed, but it hadn't proven necessary: he hadn't been able to bring himself to stop staring at it. Finally, there was movement. He leaned in closer to the screen. Yes! It was the convoy arriving!

Chung checked the time on the clock on the laptop screen: 09:47. An early departure.

He knew from his daily reviewing of the webcam recordings that it was a matter of minutes from the army convoy assembling outside the BEP facility to the trucks emerging and the convoy heading out, but he still waited for the first truck to actually emerge before he picked up the cellphone and hit the speed-dial button for Sullivan.

The phone rang twice before it was answered. The conversation comprised three words in total.

"Yes?"

"Action."

"Understood."

* * *

Jackson and Perez adjusted their seat positions and fastened the five-point harnesses. Both were wearing thin leather gloves to avoid leaving fingerprints: with their military backgrounds, their prints would be on file.

Although Jackson had tens of thousands of hours of flying time on a wide range of aircraft, he had limited time on the Lear. He'd flown larger and more complex aircraft, so his limited practical experience on type didn't greatly concern him, but he didn't want to take any chances.

He'd starting by spending dozens of hours practicing on X-Plane, a PC game similar to Microsoft Flight Simulator, but with far more accurate physics: the performance and handling of the simulated Lear closely mirrored that of the real thing.

Once he felt he was familiar with the theoretical handling characteristics, he booked twelve hours in a full moving-axis commercial simulator. These are so close to the real thing, a commercial pilot can actually get a type rating in a simulator without a single hour in the actual aircraft.

He specifically didn't want to actually *achieve* the type rating: that would be logged in the FAA records, and could only draw attention to himself when the authorities went looking for qualified Lear 55 pilots. He just wanted to be certain he knew how to fly it.

One of the things he'd practiced over and over in X-Plane was the procedures from initial switch-on to take-off. They'd timed everything. They'd checked these timings on the recce flight, and knew that from strapping-in to taxi took six minutes. Taxi to threshold took four minutes. Subject to clearance, they'd be airborne two minutes after that.

Perez picked up the laminated Pre-flight Checklist card and began reading out the items.

* * *

Chung connected to the SCADA system, but this time used the supervisor login his hack had uncovered back when he first gained access.

Username: rsg

Password: sup

He'd tested the login the day after the test-run, and knew that it gave him access to an admin panel. One of the things he could do in that panel was add and remove other users, as well as change their passwords. He knew there were four users in all. He clicked the Edit users link.

Admins:

rsg

dev

Users:

sys

rem

Click account to edit / Add account / Back

He was using the rsg admin account. There was a second one named dev which he suspected was used by the developer during testing. The sys one was, he was sure, the one used by the control room staff. The final one – rem – was likely short for 'remote'. Maybe for use from a backup facility, or perhaps over the Internet as he was doing now. It didn't matter: the account wouldn't exist for long.

He clicked first on the rsg username – the one he was using.

Edit / Delete / Back

Chung clicked on Edit.

Username: [rsg]

Password: [sup]

Level: [Admin]

He clicked into the password field. He deleted sup and replaced it with hg781&%e@hz451. That would lock anyone else out of the supervisor account.

He suspected no-one would be using the developer account, but he wasn't going to take any chances. He clicked on the dev account and clicked Edit.

Username: [dev]

Password: [admin123]

Level: [Admin]

He smiled at the easily-guessed password. It confirmed his theory that nobody ever expected the system to be accessible from outside the plant when it was first created. He changed the password on that to 483hyq&*y6&r3-z]8.

Next, he clicked on rem. For this account – the one he suspected was used for remote access – he wasn't just going to change the password, he was going to actually delete the account so there would be no possibility of it being used.

Account 'rem' will be deleted and this user will no longer be able to access the system. Are you sure? Yes / No

Chung clicked Yes.

Account deleted. Undo / Continue

Chung clicked Continue and the revised user list was displayed.

Admins:

rsg

dev

Users:

sys

He had deliberately left the sys account – the one he suspected was used by control room staff – intact for now. The moment he locked out this account, the water plant staff would know something was wrong: their screens would blank and return to the login screen. When they attempted to log back in, they'd get an Invalid password message.

At this point, a supervisor would be called and they would attempt to login with the supervisor account. That would also fail, of course, as he'd changed the password on that account too.

How long it would take them to solve that was an unknown. There would, somewhere, be a backup of the server files. Restoring the backup would undo the changes he'd made and allow the water company to retake control. He didn't imagine that was something anyone at the plant would know how to do. It would require an IT specialist, likely one that had to be called in from elsewhere.

It was just about possible they would know about the developer account, and would attempt a remote login with that. That too would now fail, of course. At that stage, they would need to locate the backup and would need physical access to the server to carry out the restore. It was something that had probably never been needed before, and his best guess would be that it would take several hours to get hold of the right person, for that person to locate the backup, get to the plant and carry out the restore.

But there was no sense in taking any chances. He would change the password on the sys account only at the moment he needed to take control of the plant. Draining the section of pipe had taken less than two-and-a-half minutes in the test. Evans had told him the initial water level had been around half-full. Even allowing for the possibility that the level might be right up to the top, that suggested a maximum time of five minutes to drain the pipe. He would change the password on the sys account and begin draining the pipe only once he got word from Sullivan that their remote-controlled hijack was underway. Five minutes to drain the pipe, eleven minutes to drive the baggage carts from the entry point to the base: 16 minutes. Jackson and Perez would give the final landing instructions to the first Galaxy only once Sullivan confirmed that the baggage carts were in place.

Until then, the water plant account would remain operational and nobody would know that anything was amiss.

* * *

Major Timpkins acknowledged the radio call advising him the convoy approaching was the live one – though today he guessed this one counted as a dummy too, being filled with blank paper – and watched closely as it entered the base. He didn't believe there was a chance in hell that anyone was going to attempt to take on the most heavily-guarded convoy in the world, much less that it was possible to attack it while in the air, but he was too old and experienced to think anything was totally impossible. Everything they did was meticulously planned, but he was mindful of the famous adage: no battle plan survives contact with the enemy.

He watched as the Bradley led the convoy onto the apron where the twelve C-5s were waiting. The Bradley peeled off to the left and one of his Marines signalled to the first truck to position it for unloading.

Timpkins waited for confirmation over the radio that the base gates were secured behind the last vehicle in the convoy before taking out his phone.

Lorrimar jumped as the phone on her desk rang.

"Lorrimar."

She listened for a moment, then said "Thank you, Major. Please let us know when the convoy is in the air."

She replaced the handset.

"So far so good, then," said Pritchard.

Lorrimar nodded. "Though it's when it's in the air that the hit is supposed to happen."

"That will be the nerve-wracking part," said Pritchard. "Forty-seven minutes before the first Galaxy touches down at Kansas City, and a little over three hours before the last one lands at La Guardia."

"You think they plan to hit one flight, or all twelve?"

"All twelve seems to be stretching credibility beyond breaking-point," said Pritchard, slowly, "but then, to be honest, so does hitting even one of them."

"Yet here we are," said Lorrimar.

"Yet here we are," echoed Pritchard.

* * *

On the flight deck of the lead C5 Galaxy, First Officer Neil Gill flipped over the laminated page in the ring-binder on his lap.

"Startup checklist complete."

"Taxi checklist, please," said Captain Turner.

"Ramp and crew doors."

Turner pointed to each of the indicator lights in turn, and Gill checked them with him. In aviation, a single missed check could spell disaster in the air, so standard operating procedures called for both pilots to check each other.

"Closed and locked," said Turner.

"Nav lights."

Turner again pointed to the indicators.

"On."

"Taxi lights."

"On."

"Fuel dump."

"Off."

The two men had been through the procedure hundreds of times, but everything was done by the book.

"Heading indicator."

"Set."

"Altimeter."

"Set local."

"Standby instruments."

The two men scanned all of them.

"Operational."

Twelve more items on the list, then they would be ready to taxi out to the runway.

* * *

In the Lear, the pre-flight checklists were complete, but there was one additional item not on any of the laminated cards. During taxi, Perez walked back to make one final check that all three transmitters were securely strapped down. It would only take a single loose strap to send one of the transmitters tumbling back through the cabin on take-off, and that might be the end of the mission right there. He tugged at each of the straps then shoved the transmitters, trying to move them. None gave. Satisfied, he returned to the co-pilot's seat and strapped back in.

Jackson pushed the transmit button on his radio: "Hicks Tower, November Eight Fife Niner Foxtrot Delta."

"Foxtrot Delta, Hicks Tower," came the response from the air traffic controller.

"Hicks Tower, Foxtrot Delta requesting permission for take-off," said Jackson.

"Foxtrot Delta, winds 300 at 10 gusting 15, runway 32, cleared for takeoff."

"Foxtrot Delta rolling."

Jackson taxied onto the runway and lined-up with the centre-line. He placed both feet on the brakes, pushed the throttles forward to TOGA power – shorthand for Take-Off/Go-Around – and waited for the engine to reach take-off revs before releasing the brakes. The aircraft lurched forward and almost leapt down the runway: the Lear was a powerful aircraft, and today it was lightly loaded with just the two crew and the three small but powerful radio transmitters. It was going to be a sheer delight to fly.

With larger aircraft, the first speed called out would be V1 – the point at which there was no longer enough runway to abort the take-off and come to a halt. Once that speed was reached, the aircraft had to take-off even in the most drastic emergency of an engine-fire. Usually VR, the speed at which the pilot would ease back the yoke to rotate the aircraft and lift it into the air, would come a few seconds later. But with a lengthy runway and a powerful, lightly-loaded jet, that was not the case today: the Lear would reach rotation speed long before it reached V1.

"VR," said Perez as the speed reached the bug set on the airspeed indicator.

"Rotating," acknowledged Jackson.

The Lear lifted off the runway and climbed rapidly into the air.

* * *

The take-off roll of the C5 was a far more lumbering affair. Major Timpkins, watching through binoculars, knew that each of the four TF-39 high-bypass turbofan engines that had just been spooled-up to TOGA power were generating a massive 41,000 pounds of thrust, yet such was the size of the craft that it initially appeared to be barely moving.

It was partly real – the sheer weight of the aircraft meant that nothing happened quickly – and partly illusion. The brain judges the speed of an object by the time it takes to move one length forwards. Since it's hard to grasp the true size of the aircraft, it appears to be moving much more slowly than it is. Even its flight-crew, who loved the aircraft, joked that they were surprised every time it managed to lift its huge bulk off the ground.

But finally, it did, and the undercarriage slowly folded away as the first of the twelve C5s climbed into the clear blue skies. Its two F-16 escorts were already circling overhead, waiting for the C5 to join them.

Timpkins lowered the binoculars, took the phone from his pocket and hit redial. The call was answered immediately.

"First C5 airborne," he reported.

* * *

"What the fuck?" exclaimed Perez as the Lear cockpit was filled with the sound of an alarm bell, the bright yellow Master Caution light lit up and the jet veered suddenly to the right.

Jackson had seen a brief flash of something black in front of the cockpit windscreen and knew exactly what it was.

"Bird-strike," he said, not wasting any words.

A flock of birds had crossed in front of them, and one or more had been sucked into the right engine. The engine had stalled, and with that engine inoperative and the left engine still at full power, the result was the sudden veer to the right.

Jackson punched the alarm cancel as he corrected the yaw with left rudder. He then closed the throttle on the right engine. The engine-fire warning light was on. He knew Perez wasn't qualified to check him on this, but the ingrained habit was too strong to ignore. Jackson pointed to the warning light.

"Fire in right engine," he said with the calm tone that comes with thousands of hours of flying experience and numerous emergency scenario sessions in simulators.

Perez wasn't a pilot, but military training meant he too remained cool in stressful situations. He hadn't been briefed on engine fire procedures, but the intention seemed obvious: to verify that Jackson had identified the correct engine. There were two indicators next to each other, and the one on the right was lit with a red LED.

"Yes, right."

Jackson hit the fuel cutoff and then turned the fire-suppression handle before pressing the transmit button on his headset.

"Mayday, mayday, mayday. Foxtrot Delta, Foxtrot Delta, Foxtrot Delta. Position two miles south of Hicks Airfield, heading 320 at 140 knots, altitude 1900 feet. Lear 55 with two souls on board. Bird strike, right engine out. Request immediate return to Hicks."

Air traffic controllers too are trained to respond swiftly and calmly to emergencies. The response was immediate.

"Mayday Foxtrot Delta, Hicks. Acknowledged. All runways available. Cleared to land at your discretion." Jackson knew that, in the background, they would be issuing any instructions necessary to other arriving or departing aircraft to clear a path for them.

The aircraft could fly perfectly well on one engine, albeit with reduced performance, but there was no possibility of continuing with the mission. Even if Jackson was willing to ignore the safety rules, with only one engine they couldn't hope to match the climb-rate of the Galaxies. The plan was at an end. Fuck! Jackson levelled-off at 2000 feet and began a turn to the left.

Jackson turned to Perez. "We need the engine-out checklist – will be in the red-tabbed section."

Perez flipped the tab in the binder of laminated cards and flicked through to the Engine Out Checklist.

"Got it."

"Mayday Foxtrot Delta, Hicks. Say your status when able."

"Hicks, Mayday Foxtrot Delta, standby."

Jackson would talk to ATC when he was ready to. A mantra had been developed to ensure that pilots got their priorities right, both in routine flying and most especially in an emergency situation: aviate, navigate, communicate. In other words, keep the aircraft flying first, then worry about where you are and where you need to get to, and then talk to ATC. While a busy controller might demonstrate impatience with a slow-responding pilot in routine flight, no-one hassled the crew of an aircraft in distress: ATC would monitor what the mayday aircraft was doing and get other traffic out of its way.

Jackson worked his way efficiently through most of the checklist before turning his attention to ATC.

"Hicks, Mayday Foxtrot Delta. Heading now 140, altitude 2000 feet, airspeed 135 knots. What's the current weather, please?"

"Mayday Foxtrot Delta, winds now 280 at 10 gusting 15, all runways available, emergency equipment rolling."

"Hicks, Mayday Foxtrot Delta, roger. Intention is visual landing runway 32 but need to dump fuel first. ETA around 20 minutes, looking to circle to the south-east of the airfield."

"Mayday Foxtrot Delta, understand intend visual landing runway 32, all other runways available. Understand your intention to circle to the south-east of the airfield for fuel-dump."

Aircraft had two different maximum weights, one for take-off, a lower one for landing. On a normal flight, an aircraft would burn off the majority of the fuel on board, leaving enough for the landing plus a reserve sufficient to divert to two alternative airports plus 30 minutes. With an emergency landing shortly after take-off, the aircraft would be too heavy for a safe landing and would need to dump fuel through a system which allowed fuel to flow from the tanks to nozzles in the trailing edge of the wing. Emptying sufficient fuel to allow the aircraft to reach the maximum weight for landing was going to take about 20 minutes.

"Hicks, Mayday Foxtrot Delta, descending to one thousand feet."

"Mayday Foxtrot Delta, Hicks. Understand descending to one thousand feet. Emergency equipment is in position for your landing on runway 32, please advise any change in plan."

"Hicks, Mayday Foxtrot Delta, wilco."

Jackson and Perez completed the remainder of the checklist.

"Call Sullivan," said Jackson.

"Is it safe to call while we're flying?" asked Perez.

"Don't believe the bullshit you hear in the airline announcements. That's the reason I've dropped to a thousand feet – you should get a signal now."

Perez reached into his pocket for his cellphone and hit the speed-dial for Sullivan.

"Missioned abandoned, repeat mission abandoned," he said, as soon as the call was answered. "I'll explain later, aircraft problem."

"Shit!"

"I know."

"You're ok?"

"We're ok. I'll call you when we're on the ground."

"Fuck."

"Yep."

Sullivan hesitated for a moment, scarcely daring to ask The Question. The question that could almost four months of planning had come to nothing, and very possibly a jail cell. But she had to know.

"Are we expecting any Galaxies?"

If Jackson and Perez had gotten as far as instructing the first of the Galaxies to land at the disused base, that meant the authorities would be closing in. Not only would the entire operation be exposed, without the Lear to keep the Galaxies hostage, their chances of making good their escape were slim to none.

"No," said Perez. "I'll call later."

He hung up.

* * *

Young and Evans had only heard the words from Sullivan's end of the conversation: shit, you ok, fuck and The Question. They didn't need to be told the news wasn't good.

"It's off," said Sullivan. "They have a problem with the jet."

"And the Galaxies ... ?" asked Young. He'd always accepted the risk of ending up in jail one day: it was an occupational hazard if you chose to take possession of other people's money by unconventional means. But for it to happen like this ... after all their careful planning, and without so much as sniffing the money ...

Sullivan shook her head.

"Thank god."

"Yep. Ok, let's get this thing closed down."

She had a contingency plan for this, but never imagined she'd actually have to use it. The drivers who had delivered the truck had been hired for the day, and right now were either still on the bus or at the diner they'd picked as the standby location in case they were needed again. She picked up the phone to make the call to the agency to get the drivers back to get the trucks off the base.

That was item one on the cancellation checklist. There were another 27 items.

* * *

To anyone who didn't know what was going on, Lorrimar and Pritchard had been enjoying a morning of light conversation punctuated by occasional phone calls. In reality, the lightness was forced through the tension that had been their ever-present companion throughout the day. Neither had eaten their packed lunches.

The final call they were awaiting was already ten minutes overdue. It wasn't looking good.

Both jumped when the phone rang.

Pritchard listened to Lorrimar's side of the conversation.

"Lorrimar."

...

"You're sure?"

...

"Nothing out of the ordinary?"

...

"Ok, thank you."

Pritchard raised an eyebrow. "So that's it? The last plane safely on the ground?"

"Twelve for twelve," confirmed Lorrimar.

"So the tip was a bust after all."

"Thankfully. I have quite a lot of extra security costs to justify at the monthly review, but hopefully everyone will be too relieved to give me a hard time over it."

Pritchard gave Lorrimar a slightly puzzled look. "You know, as crazy as it sounded, I really had half-convinced myself this was real."

"Yeah, me too. But I sure am glad it wasn't. Anyway, it wasn't entirely for nothing."

"Oh?"

"We proved that even creaking government machinery can jump through hoops when the occasion demands it."

"Or not, as it turned out."

"Well, yeah."

Lorrimar looked at her watch. "You know, I don't usually drink during the day, but today ..."

Pritchard grinned. "Yeah, I may make an exception too."

"There's a decent Italian round the corner, I could see if we could get a late table?"

"Sounds like a plan."

* * *

6pm on the day of the aborted heist

It was early evening by the time the team had completed all the tasks needed to postpone the operation, and the eight of them were gathered together in the hotel suite. They'd expected to be drinking chilled champagne by now; instead, the room was littered with dirty coffee cups.

"That was way, way, way too close a call," said Chung.

"Yes it was," said Sullivan, "and a long day sorting everything out. But no harm has been done. We allowed for this."

"You allowed for it," said Lewis. There had been times during the project when she'd expressed impatience at Sullivan's belt-and-braces approach to everything, and felt she owed it to her to express appreciation now.

Sullivan gave her a grateful smile. "Well, the important thing is there's no great drama. The charter company is getting another Lear flown in, so we're still in business. Everything happens exactly as per plan, just two days later, when the next shipment goes out."

'No drama' was under-playing it somewhat. There had been a lot of frantic work, and the calls to the dictators had been especially tense after Young's earlier insistence that the dates were absolutely fixed. But some smooth talking, and in two cases a little sweetener, had ensured that things were back on track.

"Lewis is right," said Young. "I used to think I was the ultimate contingency planner until I met you. We could easily have been left scrabbling around trying to figure out how to dig ourselves out of the mess. But you, you had a fucking spreadsheet for it."

Sullivan laughed. "As I recall, you once accused me of having a spreadsheet for making love."

Young looked momentarily embarrassed, and Lewis gave him a questioning look which Young ignored.

"I don't know about you guys," said Perez, "but after today's excitement, I think we've earned a drink, and I don't mean a miniature. What say I call room service and get a bottle of Jacks sent up?"

"Nothing to do tomorrow except twiddle our thumbs," said Jackson. "We can afford a hangover." With the two BEP facilities shipping bills on alternate days, the new D-Day was the day after tomorrow – they would get a day off.

"Well, if we're going for a hangover," said Lewis, "we'd better make it two bottles."

"I'll vote for that," said Pugh.

Sullivan picked up the phone and pressed the room service speed-dial button. "I'd like to order two bottles of Jack Daniels, and food for eight." ... "We don't care, just food. But don't wait around for that: send the Jacks up now."

* * *

Morning, two days later

Charlie Mason had been the the supervisor in the aircraft rental office for the last 18 months. He habitually kept a scanner tuned in to the local ATC channels. It auto-hopped between Ground, Arrivals and Departures channels dependent on radio traffic: when one channel went quiet, it skipped to the next. The Arrivals channel gave him a heads-up on aircraft being returned, but mostly it provided a bit of welcome background chatter to ease the boredom of the job. There wasn't that much to do when all the rentals were out.

"Hotel Tango, winds 280 at 15, runway 32, cleared for take-off."

"Hotel Tango rolling."

Mason glanced out of the window. From his position, he couldn't see the aircraft at the start of its take-off roll, but would see it as it started its climb-out from about halfway down the runway.

He knew most of the call-signs by heart: Hotel Tango was an S2 Pitts Special, a twin-seat aerobatic biplane powered by a 260 hp flat-6 Lycoming. His shop did the maintenance on it. The aircraft was jointly owned by two Delta airline pilots. Pilots were crazy people: they flew big jets for a living, and then in their time off they flew old-school biplanes for fun.

The S2 was designed and built with one thing in mind: aerobatic competitions. The powerful engine enabled the aircraft to climb vertically: it didn't need much of a take-off roll to get off the ground. He watched as it came into view already in a steep climb.

"Hicks Tower, Hotel Tango."

"Go ahead, Hotel Tango."

"Yeah, we're going to be in our usual aerobatics area to the north-east. Operating between 500 AGL and three thousand. Any traffic we should be aware of, over?"

"Hotel Tango, Hicks. We have an inbound Bell 44 helicopter to your seven o'clock, currently ten miles out at 1500 feet. There's a Lear 55 currently in a holding pattern 12 miles north at three thousand feet. Other than that, and the usual Carswell corridors covered in the NOTAMs, it's all clear for now."

"Hicks Tower, Hotel Tango, all received with thanks. Hotel Tango out."

Mason looked at the scanner in surprise. The Lear had filed a flight-plan to LAX. What was it doing in a holding pattern just outside the airfield?

All the rental aircraft were fitted with ACARS equipment: Aircraft Communications Addressing and Reporting System. It was a simple system that transmitted data on speed, position and altitude, enabling the rental company to track their aircraft in flight. Mason pulled up the ACARS screen on his

PC. He clicked on the 12-digit code for the Lear and then clicked the History tab, showing its track for the last five minutes.

Yep, it was indeed in an oval holding pattern just 12 miles away from the airfield. That made no sense at all. At $3600 an hour, it was a hell of an expensive way to kill time. If they were waiting for something, why on Earth hadn't they waited on the ground? Be a hell of a lot cheaper for them.

Mason picked up the walkie-talkie that connected him to the mechanics in the hanger.

"Hanger, Base."

"Go ahead, Charlie."

"Tom, the guys in the Lear, they say anything to you about needing to hold?"

"Negative, why?"

"Just curious. They're in a holding pattern just outside the TMA." The Terminal Manoeuvring Area was the controlled airspace around the airfield in which all movements had to be approved by ATC. Outside the TAM and other restricted areas, aircraft flying visually were free to navigate at their own discretion.

"Weird."

"Yeah."

"Think we should file an SAR?"

An SAR was a Suspicious Activity Report. Aircraft rental companies were required by law to report any suspicious activity they felt might be related to either drugs-running or terrorism. Drugs smugglers frequently used rental aircraft to avoid the same aircraft being seen repeatedly doing the same runs, and with the Mexican border just a few hundred miles south, it was a constant concern. If they were waiting until the coast was clear at the landing zone, that could explain a hold.

But a Lear made no sense for a drugs operation. They couldn't land at the dirt strips the drugs gangs preferred, and Lears attracted attention wherever they landed. Drug smugglers liked low-key aircraft

with unpaved landing capabilities. The Cessna 172 –
a 4-seater Lycoming piston-engined aircraft used
the world over by flying schools and private owners
– was a favourite. No-one looked twice at those.

Terrorists? Mason looked again at the holding
tracks. He clicked the transmit button of the walkie-
talkie.

"No," he said. "They aren't anywhere close to
either the city or DFW, and Carswell can look after
itself, so nothing to worry about for now. Just a bit
odd. I'll keep an eye on them."

"10-4."

* * *

"There!" said Perez, pointing down to the Carswell
Air Force Base. "The last C-5 is off the ground with F-
16 escorts in tow."

"Game on," said Jackson, calmly.

They knew that five of the Galaxies followed the
same air corridor east for the first part of their
journeys, so the plan was to track the corridor ten
miles to the south to keep them comfortably in
range. That course ought to keep three more,
heading in a south-easterly corridor, also within
range for 10-15 minutes. They might get lucky with
some of the others, but they didn't think it mattered:
so long as they could hit enough to get cooperation,
the others could be instructed to turn around, at
which point they could carry out the same
demonstrations with those.

Perez moved back to the passenger cabin where
the main data transmitter and two reserves were
strapped down. They had practiced the next bit
dozens of times. The logistics were simple. Making
the initial voice call was the nerve-wracking bit.

Jackson already had the secondary radio set to
243.0 – the military guard/distress frequency. The
secondary radio in all military aircraft was set to
that frequency throughout an operation, so they

didn't have to worry about different aircraft being on different ATC frequencies on their primary sets. He selected the secondary and took a few seconds to compose himself before pressing Transmit. It was a carefully-rehearsed script.

"All BEP C-5s, priority transmission. Please switch immediately to Air Tanker Common frequency. I say again, all BEP C-5 aircraft, switch immediately to Air Tanker Common frequency for priority message."

He could imagine the confused faces in the C-5s right at that moment. An unidentified source telling them to switch to a frequency typically used only by air tankers on in-flight refuelling duties. It would make no sense to them, but military training was to act first, ask questions afterwards. He expected them to comply.

Specifying the frequency by name rather than number was deliberate. They wanted to minimise the number of eavesdroppers. There would be kids with scanners listening in to the distress frequencies in case they heard something exciting, but they likely wouldn't know most frequencies by name. It was nothing that a bit of Googling wouldn't tell them, but it would at least reduce the numbers a little. Every additional eavesdropper increased the likelihood of someone calling a TV station, and they didn't want any more media choppers up there than they could help.

Jackson dialled in 281.0. He planned to wait a few seconds for everyone to get on frequency – he guessed they might have to look up the frequency on their frequency cards – but the first response was immediate.

"Unidentified source from BEP 1. Identify yourself."

Jackson thumbed the transmit button. "I will do so imminently, BEP 1. I just want to wait a few seconds to ensure all your colleagues are on-frequency."

"Unidentified source, I say again, identify yourself immediately." It was the voice of a man who expected instant obedience when he issued an instruction.

"BEP C-5s, please watch your weather radar screens closely."

Jackson counted to three to ensure they were all watching, then reached out with his right hand and waved it. Perez, watching the open cockpit doorway from the passenger cabin, immediately reached out to the main data transmitter. On the top surface was a dial marked 1-12, a green button and a red button. The dial was set to 1. He pressed the green button, moved the dial to 2, pressed the green button again, moved the dial to three and repeated the process until he had pressed the green button on 12. He returned to the cockpit and nodded to Jackson.

"BEP C-5s, I am now ready to identify myself. We are the team who just took out your weather radar sets. You can call me Thunderbird 7."

The call sign was a deliberate insult. It was the call sign of the Operations Officer of the world-famous Thunderbirds USAF display team. The idea of the call sign being appropriated by an attacker would be highly offensive, he knew. USAF pilots are chosen and trained as people who remain calm under pressure, so any small step he could take to irritate them could only help in establishing dominance.

On the flight-deck of the C-5 bound for New York, call-sign BEP 1, Captain Dave Turner stared at the weather radar screen. Sure enough, he had watched it go blank.

"What the fuck?"

His co-pilot, Neil Gill, rapped the screen with his knuckles. The aircraft were not in the first flush of youth, and equipment failures were not too uncommon, but a failure that happened to order was no coincidence.

Turner switched back to the primary frequency and hit transmit.

"BEP team from BEP 1. Switch primary sets to reserve frequency."

He waited two seconds for them to comply.

"BEP 2 from BEP 1, sitrep."

"BEP 1, BEP 2, weather radar went out."

"BEP 3, sitrep."

"BEP 1, BEP 3 ditto."

"BEP team from BEP 1, any aircraft with functional weather radar, report."

"BEP 9, BEP 1. Weather radar functional."

"BEP 7, BEP 1, functional."

"BEP 10, BEP 1, also functional."

Silence followed.

Turner and Gill looked at each other. That was nine of the twelve aircraft whose weather radar had just been taken out by an unknown enemy. How the fuck could that happen? These were highly-protected military aircraft which spent their entire lives in secure military airbases. How the hell does anyone get to sabotage them?

Turner reached out to the transponder and set it to 7500: the code indicating a hijacked aircraft. On both military and civilian ATC radar screens, the Galaxy would now be clearly highlighted as a hijacked aircraft. He thumbed the transmitter.

"BEP team from BEP 1, all C-5s set transponder code 7500 whether or not affected. F-16s, remain as set for now. No need for acknowledgement."

With all twelve of the C-5s now flashing up as hijacked, that was going to cause one hell of a stir on the ground.

Aboard the Lear, Jackson didn't know what the BEP reserve frequency was, nor did he particularly care. It was pretty obvious what they would be doing: verifying the threat. He left them to it for 30 seconds before thumbing the transmit button on the secondary radio.

"BEP 1 from Thunderbird 7, I take it I have your attention?"

There was silence for several seconds.

"Seven, BEP 1. You'd better have a damn good explanation for this."

Jackson smiled. The pilot couldn't bring himself to use the Thunderbird call sign, he noted. That was good: it had obviously done its job.

"BEP 1, Thunderbird 7." Jackson placed a little emphasis on 'Thunderbird.' "We do indeed have a good explanation. We require your cooperation. The weather radar was merely a trivial demonstration. We have additional devices on board your aircraft that can sever the main control cables. We would prefer not to have to demonstrate, but can do so if desired. Would you like us to do so, or are you ready to cooperate?"

There was silence for a second or two before the response.

"Seven, do you have the faintest idea who you are fucking with here?"

Jackson smiled.

"Affirmative, BEP 1. We know exactly who we are fucking with, and you are indeed going to get fucked if you don't do exactly what you are told. Do I make myself clear?"

On the flight-deck of BEP 1, Gill looked at Turner.

"Is this for real?" he asked, incredulously.

Turner shook his head. "I have no fucking idea. But there's a hell of a difference between taking out a weather radar set and having the ability to crash us."

"True," said Gill, "but it's not a theory I'm overly keen to put to the test."

"Get hold of the base," said Turner, "get them up to speed."

While Gill called the base on the primary radio, Turner transmitted on the secondary.

"Standby, Seven."

Jackson knew this was the key moment. The moment at which he had to take immediate and total control. He indicated with his thumb back to the cabin. Perez nodded and walked back. Jackson hits the transmit button again.

"Negative, BEP 1, there will be no standing by. I see I need to get you to take me more seriously. I am now going to select one of your aircraft at random and take out their flaps." The random part was a bluff: although they had devices aboard each of the twelve Galaxies, with discreet frequencies for each, they had no way of telling which was which by call sign.

Back in the cabin, Perez set the dial to 1 then pressed the red button. He returned to the cockpit.

"BEP 1, I suggest you each try your flaps."

He knew they could only begin deploying flap at 190 knots or slower, which was a side benefit of choosing the flaps for the secondary demonstration: all the C-5s would have to slow down, keeping them in range longer.

Turner reduced the speed of his C-5 to 190 knots. Gill, watching the airspeed indicator, then activated the flap lever, setting it to 5 degrees. The flaps deployed. He retracted them. Turner pressed the transmit button on the primary set.

"BEP team, BEP 1. Report in if your flaps are non-operational."

"BEP 4, BEP 1, confirm flaps non-operational."

Fuck! This was for real. He turned to Gill.

"What did base have to say?"

"One guess."

"Standby," said Turner and Gill in unison.

"Ok," said Turner, "we need to take this seriously and see what these fuckers want." He selected the secondary radio.

"Seven from BEP 1. Pass your request."

Jackson smiled at the phrasing. He knew it would have been too humiliating for the captain of a USAF C-5 protected by two F-16 fighters to request 'instructions.' But the job was done: the C-5s were going to comply.

"BEP 1, Thunderbird 7. Kindly instruct all your aircraft to return to the base area and enter a nice neat holding pattern at thousand-foot intervals in sequence, you at the bottom of the heap, BEP 12 at the top. I don't want any other aircraft, military or civilian, in the air within a 30-mile radius. Advise when in position, Thunderbird 7 out."

Turner, like all USAF pilots, had been trained in negotiating with hijackers. Rule 1 was to appear compliant and bide your time until an opportunity arose to retake control. He selected the ATC frequency first.

"Carswell TMA from BEP 1."

"BEP 1, Carswell, pass your message."

"Carswell, BEP 1. I need you to clear holding area Delta of all traffic, military and civilian. We need the complete stack to ourselves. Once you've done that, we need a no-fly zone established in a 30-mile radius around Delta."

"BEP 1, Carswell, understood. There is no traffic in the pattern right now, will advise civilian ATC, Delta is all yours; we'll need a little time to get the no-fly zone in place."

"Carswell, BEP 1, thank you."

Turner switched back to the BEP reserve frequency.

"BEP team from BEP 1. Return to base operations area, enter holding pattern Delta. BEP 1 will be at one thousand feet, BEP 2 two thousand, BEP 3 three thousand and so on up to BEP 12 at twelve thousand. Acknowledge in sequence, please."

"BEP 2, Wilco."

"BEP 3, Wilco"

"BEP 4 ..."

Jackson had put the Lear into a gentle left-hand turn to position himself ten miles south of the disused airbase. He knew the authorities were going to identify the Lear as the attacker at some stage, but he hoped that was going to be several hours later. With the C-5s all safely within data transmission range of the disused airbase, they could safely land the Lear and tuck it out of sight. Should any further demonstrations prove necessary, those could be carried out from the ground.

Perez, meantime, picked up his smartphone and hit the speed-dial for Sullivan. She picked-up on the first ring.

"Operation is a go," he said. "We're on our way."

"Confirm go," said Sullivan.

"Confirmed."

* * *

Major Timpkins had completed four of the five calls in the Emergency Response Plan. The CAA would be keeping all civilian traffic well away from the area; airbases across neighbouring states would be preparing to launch additional fighters; the State Police would be mobilising to the area ready to set up cordons as soon as the first C-5s were given a destination, assuming it was within Texas; the FBI were briefing the State Police in neighbouring states, and would be ready to deploy their own agents. The final call was to the Secret Service, who had a watching brief on all currency-related crime. There was a central number for him to call, but in this case it made more sense to call the man who was already up to speed on the specific scenario they faced here: Luke Pritchard. He looked up Pritchard's cell number in his cellphone.

Pritchard and Daniels were at that moment sat in the gate lounge at Dallas-Fort Worth, awaiting their return flight to Washington.

"Pritchard."

"It's Major Timpkins."

Pritchard could hear the tension in the man's voice, and knew immediately.

"It's happened."

"Yes. Or more precisely, it's happening. The hijacks are underway as we speak."

"How?"

"They somehow managed to sabotage the aircraft remotely. They've already demonstrated an ability to bring down the aircraft at will."

"They haven't ... ?"

"Not yet, no, but they've done enough that we know this is for real. Anyway, you can appreciate I have a lot to do, but I wanted you to know it's underway. I haven't yet called the Liaison Center – you want me to do that or will you?"

"I'll take care of it, then we'll get straight over to Carswell to join you if we may?" said Pritchard.

"Yes, of course."

"Thank you, Major."

Pritchard put down the phone.

"Fuck," said Daniels, having overheard Pritchard's side of the conversation.

"Fuck indeed." Pritchard was already selecting the contact card for the USAF Liaison Officer within the Secret Service. He hit the call button.

"USAF Liaison."

Pritchard identified himself, and succinctly outlined the situation. The duty officer calmly acknowledged the report and promised to alert the local office in Dallas. Daniels, meantime, was making another call.

"I've just arranged a chopper flight from the GA terminal," said Daniels.

"We have a service chopper here?" asked Pritchard, surprised.

Daniels shook his head. "Nope - I just chartered a civilian one."

"That's going to make for an interesting expenses claim."

"Yep, but I didn't think you'd want us sitting in a taxi."

"Too right."

The two men were walking back to security. The General Aviation terminal required them to go back Landside first. Getting back the wrong way through Security was normally a non-trivial business, but a Secret Service badge opened a lot of doors.

* * *

Chung also answered his mobile on the first ring.

"Operation is a go," said Sullivan.

"Water level?" asked Chung.

"Maybe a third full."

"Got it," said Chung, hanging up.

Chung had already deleted the rem account, to lock out remote access by the backup control centre, as that was unlikely to be in use and could thus safely be taken out in advance to save time without alerting anyone. He had left the sys account – the one used by the main water plant control room – intact until it was time to empty the water pipe. That time had now arrived. Chung called up the user list again.

Admins:

rsg

dev

Users:

sys

He clicked first on the sys username – the one the water plant staff were using.

Edit / Delete / Back

Chung clicked on Edit.

Username: [sys]

Password: [sys]

Level: [User]

He clicked into the password field. He deleted *sys* and replaced it with *75hf;&^gz@(2145.*

Warning: account 'sys' is currently logged-in. Changing the password will end their session & logout user – are you sure? Yes / No

This confirmed that the sys account was indeed the one being used by the plant workers. He clicked Yes.

Password changed – user sys logged-out. Undo / Continue

Chung clicked Continue.

That was it. The water plant control room screens would now have blanked and returned to the login screen. Any attempt to log back in would fail as he had changed the password. He alone had complete control of the water system.

"Hey!" exclaimed Chloe Watts, the water plant operator, as the main screen in front of her suddenly switched to a login screen. She quickly scanned the monitors above and alongside it. All blank.

"Problem?" asked her colleague, Martin Day, looking up from his magazine. There wasn't much to do in a typical shift, so they all brought in stuff to read. You couldn't get away with watching movies on the day-shift, but nobody minded you reading.

"Looks like a computer crash. I'll login again."

Watts typed sys into the Username box, tabbed into the Password box, typed sys again and hit the Submit button.

Invalid login

"What the hell?" she asked.

"What's up?"

Watts tried again with the same result.

"The login isn't working."

"Let me try."

Day eased his bulk out of the chair and walked over to the main workstation. Watts scooted her chair over to let him get at the keyboard. Day also tried it twice without success.

"I'll call the backup centre," said Watts.

Chung switched to the main screen. He'd mentally rehearsed this so many times it felt almost second nature now.

He clicked on the upstream valve to close it. The click of his trackpad in his hotel room sent a signal via the Internet to the computer system in the water plant control room. From there, a two-part numeric code was sent along Ethernet cables running along the pipe system in waterproof conduits. The first number was an identifier. At each valve was a control box. When the numeric signal arrived, the control box ignored it unless the identifier matched the code programmed into that box. When the signal reached the correct box, the second part of the code was a 1 or a 0. A 1 told the control box to open the valve, a 0 told it to close it.

The control box at the valve upstream of the airbase read the 0 and activated a relay. It transmitted another 0 back to the control room computer to acknowledge the instruction. The thick steel disc forming the valve began to roll into the closed position.

Chung knew from the test that it took a few seconds for the graphic on the SCADA system to update to show the valve as closed, but this time it felt like hours. Finally, the screen refreshed and the valve graphic changed to one representing a closed valve. He scrolled right to check the two further downstream valves. As before, both were already open. There was nothing more to do until the team and the cash were safely out. Until then, all he could do was wait.

As the disc rolled across the opening, reducing it to a smaller and smaller gap, a switch triggered when it was 80% closed. This opened the butterfly valve in the bypass pipe, relieving the pressure and allowing the disc to close fully. Both valves closed. The water flow ceased.

With the upstream valve closed and the downstream ones all open, the water was rapidly draining away.

Chung looked at the clock on his laptop. In the test, it had taken 2 minutes and 27 seconds to drain the section, but that had been with a higher water level: this time Sullivan had said the pipe was only around a third full, so it should be faster.

19 seconds had elapsed.

"Backup."

"Watts here, in the main plant."

"Hi Chloe, it's Michael."

"Hey," she said. Michael Saunders had worked in the main plant before transferring out to the backup centre when his kid started school and they moved house to be closer to a good school. "Our system just went down and won't let me log back in. Can you try from your end?"

"Give me a minute," said Saunders.

"Sure."

She waited.

"That's odd," he said, thirty seconds later. "The reserve login doesn't work either."

"Try the main one – sys, sys."

"One sec."

Silence again for a few seconds.

"Nope," said Saunders.

"Shit. Ok," she said, "I'll call it in."

"Let me know," said Saunders.

"You got it."

Watts replaced the handset and picked up a battered ring-binder. She'd worked there nearly two years and had never needed to call her Area Manager before. Just for good measure, she tried the login once more before making the call. Nothing. She looked up the number and dialled it.

Chung's phone rang. Sullivan. He hit the call button.

"All clear," said Sullivan.

She was telling him the section of pipe was now drained. Chung checked the clock. Two minutes, four seconds.

"Great."

"Will call again when ready."

"I'll be here."

Chung hung up. The next call he got would be when all of the pallets had been transported through the pipe to the exit point and loaded onto the trucks. At that point, he would re-open the valve to restore the water flow. It wasn't strictly necessary, but would help throw the authorities off the scent when they discovered the pipe.

* * *

Daniels had made it clear he wanted the helicopter sitting with rotors turning awaiting their arrival, and he wasn't disappointed: he could see the Sikorsky S-76 chopper sitting outside with blades spinning as he handed his credit card to the smartly-dressed man at the charter company desk.

"The pilot has already been in contact with Carswell," said the charter agent. "You know about the no-fly zone?"

Daniels shook his head. "No, but it's not a surprise."

"It was to us. Don't suppose you can tell me ... ?"

"No," said Daniels, simply.

"Ok. Well, when the pilot explained who you were he got clearance for a low-level flight, but you're going to be skimming the deck."

"Fine," said Daniels.

"There's your card and your receipt. Straight through the blue door where my colleague will take you to your aircraft. Have a good flight, gentlemen."

Major Timpkins replaced the receiver after receiving the initial report from the Tower and wasted no time. He walked to the connecting door to the office where three of his senior officers were based, opened it and wasted no words.

"Captain Price, suspected attack on BEP flights. Get the SEPs underway. I'll be in the Tower."

There were Standard Emergency Procedures for everything in the military, from the base commander being taken ill to global thermonuclear war. The exact steps to be taken might vary with the circumstances, but there were laid-down protocols that at least specified the ways in which information was gathered, situations were assessed, decisions were made, procedures were considered and people were informed. Step one in the SEPs was to place all the relevant authorities on alert. For an attack on the BEP flights, that included every military base in the country, the FBI, Secret Service and the White House.

"Lieutenants Morris and Mason, you're with me."

The two men – known throughout the base as 'the two Ms' – scrambled to their feet as Timpkins strode directly through the office toward the exit.

Timpkins could have coordinated things from his desk, with radio comms patched through to his phone, but Timpkins was a great believer in removing unnecessary variables from an equation wherever possible, and putting himself in the tower gave him immediate contact with both the BEP flights and all other USAF assets. He took the stairs two at a time.

"Any further communication?" he asked the 2nd Lieutenant in charge of the control tower as he walked into the room.

"Negative, Sir."

There were two unused positions in the Tower, and Timpkins strode straight over to one of them and put on the headset.

"Frequency?" he asked.

"We're using the BEP reserve frequency, Sir."

Timpkins selected it, using his own call-sign, CAG, short for Commander Air Group.

"BEP 1, CAG. Sitrep."

"CAG, BEP 1. Nine aircraft with weather radar out. BEP 4 with flaps out. We consider attacker has convincingly demonstrated the capability to down the flights. Attacker has ordered us to holding point Delta, stacked from one to twelve thousand feet, we are complying for the moment. They have ordered no other air traffic within 30 miles, understand ATC is in the process of organising. Sitrep complete."

Timpkins was taken back to his promotion interview. He was asked what skills he felt differentiated a base commander from other senior ranks. He'd answered that there were three things. First, the ability to rapidly assimilate changing situations. Second, the discipline to prioritise and, in particular, to distinguish between actions needed immediately and actions that could wait. Third, the determination to remain pro-active rather than reactive even when the enemy appeared to have the upper-hand. He needed every last ounce of each one of these qualities right now.

He desperately wanted to understand how the hell this would have happened, but that could wait. The priority now was to figure out the game-plan of the attacker, and position themselves one or two steps ahead. He turned to the two Lieutenants who were standing directly behind him.

"Morris, I want you to identify potential LZs. The attackers clearly have to get the aircraft on the ground before they can do anything else, and I want every potential landing site within a 100-mile radius checked for signs of activity. I know that could include every flat stretch of desert and quiet highway, so start with disused airfields and low-traffic civilian airfields in current use. If they plan to get their hands on the money, they're going to need transport, so I want each potential site checked out for large cargo aircraft, transport helicopters and trucks. Ships too, if they are by water."

"Sir!"

"Mason, I want any aircraft that doesn't immediately comply with the no-fly zone flagged as a potential hostile and tracked. The moment the E-3 is on station, let me know. I'm going to order Turner to act up in the hope of getting another flaps demo so we can identify the frequency used and see whether the E-3 can block it."

"Sir."

The Boeing E-3 Sentry was probably the most immediately recognisable aircraft in the world, even if most people didn't know what it was called. Based on the Boeing 707, the aircraft is an Airborne Early Warning And Control aircraft designed to provide total air, ground and communications surveillance of a wide-scale operational area. The large rotating radar dome above the fuselage is what makes it so distinctive.

Designed in the Cold War days with nuclear war a real prospect, the aircraft was designed to remain permanently in flight for several days, having both air-to-air refuelling capabilities and two complete crews, with rest areas for the off-duty crew. It was intended to provide the broadest possible intelligence, plotting and tracking the movements of hundreds of aircraft at once, while simultaneously plotting ground movements and enemy assets. It was equipped with a highly detailed mapping database of everything from military bases to the smallest civilian airfield, and was capable of integrating live satellite images of areas beyond its own surveillance range. Its radio capabilities allowed it to intercept both voice and radar transmissions on every frequency from military aircraft to cellphones. It was the ultimate eye-in-the-sky: nothing could move within its operating range without being seen.

Sullivan watched from the truck cab as the Lear touched down, a small puff of smoke from the tyres. The Lear did a high-speed taxi to a hanger about half a mile away. The jet was still moving as its door opened and the steps started to unfold: the fly-boys weren't hanging around.

This was no modern hanger, with metal sliding doors: the doors were wooden, with paint flaking off, and the doors hinged open concertina-style. Perez pulled them open, and the Lear taxied in, the steps still hanging down.

The hanger hadn't been chosen at random: it had a manhole cover leading down to the water-pipe. Once they were done with radio comms with the Galaxies, after the last one took off, the two would climb down into the pipe and travel with the baggage carts.

It was time for Sullivan to don what the team had termed her tactical gear: a black jumpsuit fitted with padding to disguise her trim figure, a balaclava leaving only her eyes visible and mirrored ski-goggles. As the only team member who would be in clear view, she needed to be completely unrecognisable.

Timpkins looked up from his station in the control tower as Lt Mason approached him.

"What have you learned?" asked Timpkins.

"We have three aircraft of interest at present, Sir. A Cessna 152 failed to respond to the all-aircraft call establishing the no-fly zone. An F-16 was sent up to intercept it, and it's now being directed to follow the F-16 to Carswell where we'll have a full reception waiting."

Timpkins nodded; the Cessna, its occupants and baggage would all be subject to a thorough search before the pilot and anyone else on board would be interrogated. Detailed background checks would also be made on all on board.

Mason continued: "There was a media chopper that ignored all-aircraft requests to clear the area, and only responded when addressed directly by call-sign. It returned to its base. We've asked local police to detain the occupants and got a crew on the way."

"And the third aircraft?" asked Timpkins.

"A Lear 55. It complied as soon as the no-fly zone call went out, but landed at Hicks, a disused USAF base, when its home field was actually closer. Since then, ATC has been unable to establish radio contact with it."

"Sounds like it could be the men we're looking for."

"That's what I thought, Sir. I've tasked the E-3 to carry out a detailed scan of Hicks and ground forces are on the way to secure the perimeter. The runway is still listed as available in an emergency, so right now it looks a very good candidate for our LZ."

"Have you informed Morris?" Lt Morris was tasked with checking out potential landing-zones.

"Yes, Sir. He'd already identified it as a possible, and the detailed plans are being faxed over – they're only available in paper form."

Fax might be an extremely elderly technology, but there was a lot of that in use in the military.

"Good work, Lieutenant."

"Thank you, Sir."

Timpkins picked up the headset, checked the radio was still set to the BEP flight reserve frequency and thumbed the transmit.

"BEP 1, CAG."

"CAG, BEP 1."

"Turner, we have a possible LZ. The disused base at Hicks." As an emergency runway within close proximity to Carswell, he knew Captain Turner would have at least a passing familiarity with it. "We're sealing the perimeter and we should have full coverage from an E-3 within the next few minutes."

On board the Galaxy, Turner looked across at his co-pilot. "Pull up the emergency landing info for the disused base at Hicks." Gill nodded, and reached for the ring-binder containing diagrams and data for emergency runways.

"CAG, we're pulling up the details. Do we have any intelligence on the hostiles?"

"BEP 1, negative, but once the E-3 is on station … practiced a flapless landing in that thing recently?"

Turner smiled. "On the simulator on my last check. Not had to do one for real yet, but it's not a problem given sufficient runway. What's the plan?"

"When the hostiles next call, we want you to play up a little, not enough to piss them off in a major way, just being a little slow and reluctant to respond. We want to force them to provide another demonstration. The E-3 will be doing a full frequency scan, and from that we hope to get at least an initial steer on the location of the transmitter. We may need two or three demos to achieve it – the rest of your boys up to it?"

"You can count on it, Sir. I'll let everyone know they should expect to lose their flaps."

"Roger."

Perez picked up his mobile to call Sullivan.

"All set?" he asked.

"We're ready."

"Ok, let's go get ourselves a Galaxy."

He hung up.

Jackson hit transmit on the radio.

"BEP 1 from Thunderbird 7."

"We're listening, 7."

"You are familiar with the disused base at Hicks, I take it?" He knew they would be: as a nearby disused runway, it would be on their list of emergency landing sites.

"Affirm."

"We'd like you to pay a little visit. Just you, for now."

"I don't think so, 7."

Jackson looked at Perez, a concerned look on his face. "They can't have figured out it's a bluff, surely?"

"Perhaps they think they've managed to jam our transmissions."

"Is that possible?"

Perez shook his head. "Highly unlikely. Each transmission is a fraction of a second long, so pretty near impossible for them to have even identified it from the thirteen transmissions we've made so far."

"Perhaps we've underestimated them?" asked Jackson.

"Only one way to find out."

Jackson nodded, and thumbed the transmit button again.

"BEP 1, do we really have to take out one of your aircraft to make a point?"

"We think we have your transmissions blocked. But you don't have to crash an aircraft to prove us wrong, just take out my flaps."

Jackson felt a pulse of fear. If they really had managed to block the transmissions, it was game over, and all this would have been for nothing.

He turned to Perez. "Well, no point wondering: let's find out."

"There is the small problem that we can't target a particular aircraft by call-sign."

"Let's take them all out. They may just be playing for time. I want to put an end to any games right now." With all aircraft now back within range, they ought to be able to take out the flaps on all the aircraft.

"You got it," said Perez. He flipped the dial to position 2. "Ready when you are."

Jackson pressed transmit. "BEP 1, you want another demo, you've got it. But we're not playing games here. I'm not just going to take out your flaps, I'm going to do the same for all of you."

He waved at Perez who pressed the red button before flicking the dial to position 3, and doing the same thing again. Within 15 seconds, he had completed the complete set. None of the Galaxies should now have functioning flaps.

"I sure as hell hope they take the hint now," said Perez, "because we're now out of ammo. We've done all that we can do to them."

"I'm confident they won't risk downing an aircraft," replied Jackson.

"I hope you're right."

"Time to find out." Jackson thumbed the transmit button. "BEP 1, Thunderbird 7, are you satisfied now, or do I need to start crashing aircraft?"

On board the Galaxy, Gill had just finished checking in on the rest of the flight. "Confirmed," said Gill to Turner: "flaps out on all aircraft."

"Ok, I'd better respond, you check whether the E-3 had any luck."

Turner hit the red button. "Seven, BEP 1. You've made your point."

"Glad to hear it," said Jackson. "We have no desire to hurt anyone. So, get your aircraft down onto the runway at Hicks. And please advise your base that if we so much as see a jet contrail anywhere in the sky, we will consider it a hostile act and respond accordingly."

"You got it."

Turner peeled out of the holding pattern and set the aircraft up for a visual downwind leg: flying parallel with the runway in the opposite direction to the landing. For a civilian landing, this would be followed by a 90-degree left turn onto base leg followed by a second 90-degree left onto final approach. Military landings were normally done in a single sweeping 180-degree turn, making their path less predictable in hostile environments.

Gill ended his conversation with Major Timpkins with a "Wilco, Sir."

He looked across at Turner and shook his head. "No joy so far, the E-3 boffins are now replaying the cross-spectrum recordings but say it's going to take time. Timpkins says to offer full cooperation in the meantime but to take any safe opportunity to play for time."

"Ok," said Turner. "Pre-landing checklist for a flapless landing, please."

Gill hadn't been idle during his conversation with Timpkins: he already had the laminated card in front of him, together with the airfield briefing sheet for Hicks. The latter was a diagram showing the layout of the base. With only one runway and one main taxiway, it was a simple one, but showed the height of the runway above sea level and the runway heading so they could plan their approach.

"Checklist ready," he said.

"I'm going to do a minimum-speed approach with an extended downwind leg and turn to final about two miles further out. Can you think of anything else we can do to play for time?"

Gill shook his head. "Only a slow taxi once we're down."

"Ok, brief the Marines – I want them in defensive positions, but no engagement without my say-so unless we come under fire."

"Wilco."

Gill picked up the intercom and relayed the instructions.

"All done."

"Ok, as soon as we complete the landing checklist, get the short take-off card out: I want to be ready for an immediate take-off just in case."

"You got it."

"Ok, item one ..."

The S-76 pilot was ex-military, and clearly enjoying himself as he expertly guided the helicopter across the flat desert terrain no more than thirty feet off the deck at around 110 knots.

"Be there in two minutes," he said, though the headset intercom.

"Thanks," said Daniels.

"My pleasure," said the pilot, "haven't had this much fun in years."

Perez had exited the Lear and was standing with a pair of powerful field binoculars, the hanger door ajar just enough to give him a view of the lead Galaxy. He watched it fly past the airfield, around a mile away. He raised the walkie-talkie to his face.

"He's on downwind."

"Acknowledged," came the reply from Jackson.

In the tower, Timpkins called the E-3.

"Eye-sky from CAG, come in please."

"CAG, Eye-sky."

"Eye-sky, sitrep, please."

"CAG, negative match so far, we're still running the tapes."

"Eye-sky, hostile is jumpy, we need you to stay out of visual range of Hicks."

"CAG, not a problem."

"Eye-sky, any ETA on the scan?"

"CAG, six minutes."

"Eye-sky, understood. CAG."

Timpkins turned his attention to Lt Morris, who was standing at his side.

"Report, Lieutenant."

"We've had the civilian police do a drive-by at the base in an unmarked vehicle, Sir. There are a bunch of trucks sat out there, close to the main exit gates."

"Ok, let's make sure we have every route out of there fully covered, backroad tracks as well as surfaced roads. We have to assume they have some plan to stop us following the trucks in choppers, and we also have to assume they may split up and head in a dozen different directions. I want the whole damn county locked down tighter than a duck's ass."

"Understood, Sir."

Morris saluted and headed for the stairs, passing Pritchard and Daniels, who were striding up them two steps at a time.

"Landing checklist complete," said Gill.

Through the cockpit windscreen, they could see the runway at the disused airbase. It looked ropey, but nothing the C-5 couldn't handle.

The intercom buzzed and Gill picked up the handset. He listened for a moment then said "Standby."

"Sergeant Walsh wants permission to slip two Marines out of the aircraft as soon as we get down to taxiing speed. Says it could be useful to have men on the ground on the inside."

"Negative," said Turner, "not until we can see the lay of the land. But tell him to have them ready and let him know that starboard will be the blind side of the aircraft if the hostiles are watching from the buildings or taxiway."

"Negative, Sergeant, but be ready. Starboard side will be the one to go for if we clear it later." He replaced the handset. Ahead of them, the runway threshold was approaching fast.

Perez let the binoculars hang from the strap and raised the walkie-talkie.

"Short finals." The signal that the Galaxy was in the last stages of final approach, and would be landing imminently.

"Acknowledged."

In the Lear, Jackson hit the speed-dial for Sullivan.

"Just landing now."

"We're set," said Sullivan.

In the massive cargo bay, Sergeant Walsh was not a happy man. As far as he could see, the hostiles were calling all the shots here, and that wasn't a position in which a Marine liked to find himself. Dropping a couple of his men out the back of the aircraft as it taxied-in would at least give them a small edge, something the bad guys weren't expecting. He would never dream of bucking the chain of command, and the fly-boys upstairs were in charge, but he didn't have to be happy about it, and he could at least be prepared in case permission were granted.

"Ross, Pearson, grab a surveillance kit, then I want you at the starboard rear door ready for a stealthy exit. If I give the order, you exit swiftly and get to cover, right side of the runway. Report in on the tactical channel anything you see. Ross, you are Ground 1, Pearson Ground 2."

"Sarge."

The two men moved immediately to the small door on the right-hand side at the rear of the aircraft. Two other Marines moved into position, ready to open and close the door. Seamless teamwork was their trademark.

"Fifty."

The Galaxy was fitted with a radio altimeter, providing a height-above-ground reading that was far more accurate than the altimeter, which estimated height above sea level by measuring air-pressure. In a large aircraft, a radio altimeter was a valuable aid to landing – all the more so on a military aircraft that was sometimes required to do low-level air-drops, over-flying a drop-zone at a height of as little as 30 feet to throw supplies out the back of the aircraft. An automated voice called out the heights as Turner eased the lumbering beast down toward the runway.

"Forty ... thirty ... twenty ... ten ... five."

It was a perfect landing, with barely a shudder as the main landing gear made contact with the concrete runway. The smoothness didn't last long: despite the repairs carried out by Jackson and Perez, the surface was old and uneven, and the Galaxy rumbled across it as Turner applied full reverse-thrust. The C-5 was designed for short landings, and Turner wanted to maximise the time they had to respond to whatever awaited them. He eased the aircraft down to just a few knots. Even without flaps, they'd used only around a quarter of the runway.

"See anything?" asked Turner. Both men were scanning the runway ahead and the taxiway to the left.

"Nothing before the buildings."

"Nor me."

Turner picked up the intercom that connected the flight-deck to the cargo-bay.

"Walsh."

"Sergeant Walsh, go ahead and drop off your men if you're confident you can do it without being spotted. We have to assume the hostiles have high-powered binoculars on us."

"My men won't be seen, Sir."

* * *

"BEP 1, Thunderbird Seven."

"Seven, BEP 1."

"Taxi to the end of the runway – and not at your current speed, I want to see a fast taxi. You still have eleven other aircraft in the air, and we can turn off the power to any and all of them at the flick of a switch, do I make myself clear."

"Understood," said Turner. He turned to Gill: "Tell Walsh it's now or never."

Gill picked up the intercom. "Go go go."

At the rear of the aircraft, a door to the right – the side hidden from view of the buildings and apron area – briefly opened and closed. Two figures dropped, rolled and ran swiftly into the long grass to the right of the runway, disappearing from view.

A second later, the engines spooled up as the C-5 increased speed to its maximum taxi speed of 30 knots. A short time later, it was approaching the far end of the runway.

"BEP 1, Seven–" Jackson had decided the 'Thunderbird' prefix had served its purpose – "turn left onto the taxiway then right onto the apron."

"Left then right," acknowledged Turner.

There was no longer any need for binoculars: Perez had a perfect view of the massive aircraft as it turned right onto the apron. He raised the walkie-talkie to his mouth.

"On the apron."

In the Lear, Jackson continued his instructions to the C-5.

"BEP 1, as you clear the buildings, turn left. Ahead of you, in the centre of the apron, you will see a yellow container. Advise when you have it in sight."

Perez watched as the Galaxy made a slow left turn.

"Seven, BEP 1, I have the container in sight."

"You will park parallel to the building to your left, your nose-wheel 100 feet or so short of the container. Once we are ready for you to depart, you will be making a right 180 back to the runway, so allow clearance for your landing gear to clear the container, over."

"BEP 1."

Gill pointed to the truck a few hundred feet away. "Seen that?"

Turner nodded. "Update Major Timpkins while I park us."

Gill got on the radio as Turner slowly eased the Galaxy toward the yellow container.

"CAG, BEP 1."

In the tower at Carswell, Major Timpkins had instructed the team that he would handle all comms with the BEP flights until he advised otherwise. He was in the middle of discussions with his two Lieutenants when the call came in. One of the ATC staff alerted him. Timpkins slipped his headset back on.

"BEP 1, CAG."

"CAG, BEP 1, we're on the ground, being instructed to park up on the apron. We can see a truck off to our right. No prizes for guessing what happens next, over."

"BEP 1, copied. We're going to continue to cooperate for now. We're working on the basis that they will want to keep your aircraft in the air for as long as possible to keep you all hostage while the trucks head out, but we have a plan to defeat that. Once I've finished briefing you, I want you to relay everything to the rest of the BEP flights, over."

"CAG, wilco."

"BEP 1, here's what we're going to do ..."

Perez radioed up to Jackson that the Galaxy was parked.

"BEP 1, Seven, listen carefully. First, only one of your men will be exiting the aircraft. We see anyone else put so much as a single toe out of the aircraft, we'll assume you need a graphic illustration of the consequences. Clear, over?"

"Clear, Seven."

"You will lower your rear ramp, and use your forklift to bring out one of the pallets. You will drop the pallet directly underneath your right wing-tip, then the forklift will return to the C-5. The forklift will remain on-board the C-5 until our forklift has picked up the pallet and is headed toward the truck. At that point, you will drop the next pallet under the wing-tip. Rinse and repeat for the third and final pallet. Everything clear?"

"Affirm."

"Good. Begin."

Back across the far side of the runway, the two Marines were carefully making their way through the long grass toward the end of the runway. It was a long way, and they had to do all of it on their elbows and knees. Nothing they hadn't done hundreds of times before, but it never got any easier or more comfortable, you just got faster.

Sergeant Walsh hung up the intercom handset and briefed his men.

"I'll drive the forklift myself."

"With respect, Sarge," said a red-haired Marine with a matching scar running down the right side of his face, "I'm qualified on forklifts, you're not."

"I've done the basic training, Fletcher." One of the perks of belonging to the elite regiment was that they could get training to drive any vehicle they liked, on the basis that you never knew when the skill might come in handy.

"But Sarge–"

Walsh cut him off. "This is not a precision exercise, Fletcher, I just need to put the pallet on the ground in roughly the right place. I want to get the best view I can of their setup, and the forklift provides that view. You can pick up each pallet and position the forklift by the ramp, I'll take it from there.

"Sarge." Fletcher knew better than to argue further.

"Ok, let's get things underway. Fletcher, you load the first pallet. The rest of you, take turns to grab a view from the flight-deck. Right now, this is an intelligence-gathering operation, and I'll expect a full report on everything you can see of the setup of the hostiles, along with suggestions for action, when I'm down to the last pallet."

Fletcher climbed onto the forklift and went to load the first pallet, while the rest of the men dispersed. Walsh picked up the intercom.

"Ready to lift the nose, Sir."

Sullivan watched from the rear of the semi as the huge nose of the Galaxy slowly lifted into the air, and the ramp extended beneath it. Despite the tension of the operation, she couldn't help but be awed by the sight. The aircraft itself was impressive enough, but as the nose lifted it looked like half the aircraft was climbing into the air. It was like some massively-oversized, highly improbable child's toy.

For around 30 seconds, nothing happened, then she saw the forklift – dwarfed by the scale of the Galaxy – make its way down the ramp, the pallet in the air. Now she felt a different awe. The pallet looked like such an insignificant thing against the scale of the massive aircraft, but she knew she was looking at $32 million dollars. Thirty-two million dollars now at the bottom of the ramp and turning towards her.

She didn't even dare to blink: she felt that if she did, it might have vanished when she re-opened her eyes.

The forklift tracked back to the wing. She knew from Jackson's briefing that the wingspan was 222 feet and 9 inches. Such a crazy thing to remember at such a moment. Half of that, less the fuselage, and the forklift probably had to travel less than 100 feet to reach the wing-tip, yet it seemed to be crawling along, inch by inch.

A delaying tactic? She almost picked up the phone to ask Jackson to warn them against playing stupid games when she realised she could feel her heart pumping. It should be racing right now, but instead it felt incredibly slow, almost languid. She was paying such close attention, she realised, that time was almost standing still. Neither the forklift nor her heartbeat were operating in slow-motion, it simply felt that way, like watching a car crash.

She hoped that wasn't what she was doing. She'd planned this operation to the nth degree, tried to cover absolutely every aspect, with a plan, alternative and emergency contingency for everything, but there was always that nagging doubt, that small, quiet voice at the back of her head asking the question What if you've forgotten something? What if the authorities respond in a way you failed to predict? What if ... What if ... What if ...

Aloud, she told the voice to shut the fuck up. There was nothing she could do now. She needed to focus on the operation.

Finally, the forklift reached the wing-tip. She desperately wanted to be looking through field glasses, but she'd ruled it too dangerous: she had to assume the opposition had both powerful field glasses and telephoto lenses trained on her face. If she lifted the goggles even for a moment, that might be enough to get a photo from which she could later be identified.

The forklift slowly lowered the pallet to the ground, backed up, did a U-turn and headed back toward the ramp. Now she would wait. She wanted to be sure the forklift was completely back inside the cargo hold before she began the long, lonely drive of their own forklift to collect the pallet.

She watched as the forklift drove up the ramp and disappeared from sight. She counted to ten, then jumped down from the back of the truck and walked to her own forklift. It was propane-powered, and the ignition was already on. She settled herself in the uncomfortable metal seat and eased the tiny vehicle forward, toward the Galaxy.

This was the scary moment. She was completely exposed. A single shot from any of the Marines aboard the Galaxy would kill her instantly. Perez had tried to persuade her to wear a bullet-proof jacket beneath the jump-suit, arguing that she needed padding as disguise anyway so it might as well be useful padding. She'd refused. A headshot would take her out just as easily, and she didn't want the weight or constriction of the unwieldy jacket. Right now, she wasn't sure she'd made the right choice. The closer she got to the massive aircraft, the more stubborn her decision felt.

It felt like half an hour before she finally reached the pallet. This was the tricky bit. The height of the forks was simple: you lowered them to the minimum height, then up just a touch. But you had to approach the pallet absolutely square-on. Come in at an angle and the forks would foul in the frame of the pallet. Do that with any force and you risked breaking the fragile wood, rendering it impossible to lift. One small mistake, and she'd be leaving behind thirty-two million dollars.

She'd practiced it over and over and over. So many times that she knew when this operation was complete she didn't ever want to sit in a forklift truck again so long as she lived. She'd practiced it approaching from 90 degrees on. She'd practiced it approaching from the left. She'd practiced it approaching from the right. She'd practiced it until she could do it perfectly, first try, every time.

But all that was practice. No pressure. Nothing at stake. This was the real thing. A billion dollars was at stake.

Thirty-two million of it at a time, she thought, managing at least a small smile at the craziness of it.

It's like landing an aircraft, Jackson had said: it's all in the approach. What he'd meant was that if you set up your final approach correctly, the perfect speed, the perfect glide-slope, perfectly aligned with the runway, the touch-down was virtually automatic. Good landings were created in the approach. Same here. Get the forklift perfectly aligned while you were still ten feet away. Get the angle perfect. Then just hold it steady. Nice and slowly. Slowly. Slowly.

The tips of the forks disappeared into the frame of the pallet. The angle looked perfect. Slowly. Slowly. Just the gentlest of taps to confirm that the forks are all the way in, the frame resting against the rear stays. A gentle lift, just until you felt the forks start to take the weight. Then tilt back. Then lift. Not far, just enough to be sure of clearing any obstacles. The lower the pallet, the lower the centre of gravity, the more stable it was. She raised the load a couple of feet. Enough.

Then she looked at it. She'd been so focused on the pallet itself, that she'd scarcely looked at the load. Under that coloured plastic wrap was 640,000 fifty dollar bills, fresh from the printing presses. 640,000 sequentially-numbered bills, but they'd planned for that. It wasn't going to be a problem.

Carefully, she rotated the forklift. They were almost like dodgem cars, able to turn in their own footprint. She was now facing the semi, her back to the Galaxy. A single shot in the back of her head ...

But they had eleven other Galaxies hostage in the air. Even if the reality was that they couldn't do a thing to them. She was being kept alive by a bluff. It wasn't a comforting thought.

She stared at the truck, looking for any clue that the ground visible beneath the truck was photographic rather than real. Even knowing how it was done, it looked 100 percent convincing to her. She accelerated forward and began the long journey of 400 yards back to the semi. She kept her eye out for obstacles. They'd surveyed it carefully, but a single unnoticed pothole could damage the forklift. They had a backup on-site, of course, but the point of backups was to keep them in reserve, not to have to use them.

Every now and then, when she was certain her immediate path was clear, she'd look up again at the photo boards, trying to spot any sign of the illusion. It was only when she got within 30 feet or so that she could see something odd, and even then it was hard to tell exactly what. If the Galaxy crew had powerful enough field glasses, perhaps they would spot something, but they wouldn't know to look for it. Evans had done an amazing job.

Finally, she reached the back of the semi. This part also required care. She again wanted to be absolutely square-on. Inside the trailer were motorised rollers. She had to position the pallet onto those centrally and square, so that it would roll neatly back to the hoist platform, ready to be lowered through the hole to the waiting baggage cart below. From here, she could see nothing: the interior of the trailer looked black against the bright sunlit surrounds.

First the lift. Get the pallet high enough for the bottom of it to clear the floor of the trailer, not so high that the top of it would come anywhere near the roof. She eased it slowly upwards. Careful now: with the centre of gravity higher, the vehicle was less stable – no violent movements.

Again, the approach. Get it square on at a good distance, then keep it straight. She drove slowly forward. The height was right. She kept moving slowly forwards. The shadow of the side of the truck passed over the load as the pallet passed into the rear of the trailer. Very slowly now: failing to stop in time, and driving the forklift into the rear of the trailer could damage either or both. Even pushing it forward harmlessly could spoil the illusion of the photo boards. Carefully now.

Finally she could see the pallet was completely inside the truck. As her eyes adjusted, she could see Evans standing inside the trailer, off to one side, giving her a hands-down signal.

She carefully lowered the pallet until it was hovering a few inches above the trailer floor. It was still tilted back, now she needed to cancel the tilt, bring the pallet upright. There. Now, gently lower it to the floor. Gently. There was a dull thud as the pallet made contact with the rollers. Evans gave her a thumbs-up. Just two more steps now.

She eased the forks down just a tiny amount, to relieve them of the weight of the pallet. Evans crouched down and gave a push-back signal. She eased the forklift slowly back to pull the forks clear of the pallet.

Done! Inside the trailer, she knew, Evans would be using a wired remote control to run the pallet along the motorised rollers until it was on the hoist platform, but as her eyes adjusted back to the bright sunlight she could no longer see inside the trailer.

One pallet down, two more to go. After that, eleven more Galaxies, each with three pallets. It seemed like a Herculean task, but she couldn't think like that. One pallet at a time.

* * *

Major Timpkins acknowledged the sitrep from the C-5 on the ground at Hicks, then removed the headset and passed it to one of the tower staff.

"I've instructed Captain Turner to contact me if there are any developments – just call me if you hear from him."

"Sir!"

Timpkins wheeled his chair across to a small table he'd had brought up. Sat around it, crammed into a space far too small for four people let alone five, were Lieutenants Morris and Mason, Luke Pritchard and Tim Daniels.

"Well, gentlemen," said Timpkins, "the theft is underway. We have two Marines on the field, so we're not entirely helpless, but so far the hostiles are in control. That's something I intend to change. So, two immediate questions: how the hell do they intend to escape, and how – to use the technical military term – do we fuck up their plans?"

Pritchard spoke first. "I've just spoken with the joint-forces liaison officer. Police are getting all the exit routes from the base covered, right down to the smallest dirt-track. They'll have both inner and outer perimeters established within 20 minutes. The bad guys aren't going anywhere without one hell of a lot of police in pursuit. The army has troops on standby, with light and heavy armoured divisions ready to lend whatever support the police may require. Your boys have both choppers and F-16s positioned ready to provide air cover. The only problem is we can't make a move while the Galaxies are still in the air. We have to assume they intend to keep them there long enough to reach some kind of safe haven, but god knows what or where."

"The Galaxies won't be in the air for long," said Morris. "We know they have nothing in the air locally, the E-3 has eyes on everything within a 50 mile radius. That means they have no way to know what the Galaxies do once they are beyond the horizon. If we keep them low, that's less than five minutes. C-5s are designed for dirt-field landings, so as soon as the last one is in the air we'll instruct them to get the hell out and drop them onto the ground at the earliest opportunity."

"What if they instruct the Galaxies to remain in sight?" asked Daniels. "Or if they can read the flight data? If they can plant bombs on the planes and detonate them at will, tapping into the instruments has to be within their capabilities."

"This has clearly been a carefully-planned operation," agreed Pritchard, "so we have to assume their escape plan has also been well thought through."

"But what's their end-game?" asked Mason. "We'll assume they can delay our response, but sooner or later the trucks have to reach their destination."

Major Timpkins nodded. "That's what I want us to figure out, gentlemen, and we haven't got long to do it. Morris, let's have another look at those maps ..."

* * *

"Here," said Lewis, handing an airport-style metal-detector wand to Evans as the two of them stood next to the pallet in the water pipe. "I'll use the spectrum analyser to check for radio transmissions and you'll check for metal if I get anything."

"You really expect to find a tracker unit?" asked Evans.

"Expect? No. Think it possible? Yes. You know the drill: almost every eventuality we plan for won't happen, but we plan for it all the same."

Lewis began her scan. The device she was holding looked like an overly-clunky tablet: a thick grey box with a colour screen on which was displayed a green grid. Capable of reading the complete radio spectrum, it would detect signals from anything that used radio as a means of transmission: wifi, 3G, LTE, VHF, you name it.

Bzzzzz!

Lewis looked at the screen, and continued looking at it as she pressed one of the buttons several times in succession.

"Well," she said, "I'm impressed. GSM, wifi and VHF."

Evans began running the metal-detector wand along the pallet.

Bleeeep!

"I've got something," said Evans.

Lewis walked over to the corner of the pallet, where Evans waved the wand, which again bleeped and a red LED illuminated.

"Seems to be right in the corner," he said.

Lewis shone a powerful flashlight over the wood, looking for any sign of a break where something might have been embedded.

"There!" she said.

Evans peered over her shoulder.

"I can't see anything."

Lewis pointed with her finger to two tiny lines crossing the grain of the wood, each around an inch long.

"It's beautifully done," she said, "there's no way anyone would ever have spotted it without detecting it first. Hold the flashlight for me."

She put the scanner down and pulled out the multi-tool from the pouch on her belt. She unfolded a knife with a blade of 2-3 inches, pressed it against one of the horizontal lines and then levered it outward. The wood splintered and a square of wood about an inch square popped out. She then hooked out a featureless black plastic box.

"You check with the detector for any more metal – there may be more than one tracker."

"Ok," said Evans.

Five minutes later, they were confident there was only one tracker.

"This is great news," said Evans.

"Yep," said Lewis, "we'd have been in trouble if we hadn't checked for trackers."

"No," said Evans, "it's great news that they are there in the first place."

"Why?"

"Because it reinforces the illusion. We'll put the trackers into the empty semis. Not only did they see the cash go into them with their own eyes, but their own trackers will confirm that's where they are."

* * *

It had taken Ross and Pearson almost ten minutes to work their way on knees and elbows through the long grass on the far side of the runway. They were now positioned directly across from the wide apron where the Galaxy stood. From there, they had a view of both the Galaxy and the trucks – kind of. The overgrown grass on the far side of the runway didn't make for the clearest of views.

Ross reached for the tactical radio. The encryption system it used ought to be safe from eavesdropping by the hostiles, enabling him to speak freely.

"BEP 1 from Ground 1."

"Ground 1, BEP 1. Sitrep, and make it quick."

"BEP 1, Ground 1 is opposite apron. Eyes on both C-5 and truck. Unable to get any closer without being seen, so you have a much better view than we do. We've spotted more trucks close to the gates. Nothing else seen so far. Sitrep complete."

"Ground 1, understood. Use your own initiative to gather intelligence, but do not, I say again, do not under any circumstances risk being seen. We still have eleven vulnerable aircraft up there. Maintain radio silence unless you have information. If I haven't heard from you by the time we depart, I'll alert BEP 2 to expect a report from you, and suggest that they also drop off two Marines. By the time all 12 are down, we'll have 24 of you on the ground. BEP 1."

* * *

Positioning the pallets on the baggage carts was going perfectly. With all the practice they'd had beforehand, it took nothing more than a light touch here and there to align each pallet with the cart.

After each pallet was loaded, Lewis needed to drive the tug forward just enough to position the next cart. Pugh used painted marks on the front right tyre to determine the correct distance: 3.25 turns. They didn't need it quite inch-perfect – they could swing the pallet a few inches either way on the hoist – but it had to be close. So far they'd loaded two pallets. The third – the last from the first Galaxy – was on its way down.

With the semi just a short distance above them, they'd decided it was safer to simply yell up to Evans when they needed the hoist to slow and stop: they had no cellphone signal in the pipe, and didn't want to risk any walkie-talkie transmissions being overheard. The only way they could make good their escape was if the authorities had no clue where they were. Sullivan had already closed the trailer doors: so far as anyone observing from the Galaxy was concerned, the money was now aboard the semi.

Pugh yelled up: "Slow!"

The pallet was about a foot above the cart. At the hoist controls in the semi, Evans switched the motor to slow. It was now descending toward the cart at about an inch per second. Pugh waited until it was two or three inches above the cart.

"Hold!"

Evans stopped the motor and the pallet came to a halt about an inch above the cart. Pugh's job now was to swing the pallet forward or back to drop it in the centre of the cart, while Lewis stopped the pallet from rotating. Timing was all. No harm was done if a pallet landed askew – it could be lifted again and the manoeuvre repeated – but that would take time. Right first time, every time, was their aim. So far it was two for two.

"Drop!"

Evans hit the brake lever to allow the steel cable to drop freely, and the pallet thumped into place. Perfectly. Three for three. Pugh unhooked the cable.

"Clear!"

Evans switched the motor to Lift and retracted the cable until it was fully back into the cab. He then phoned Jackson.

"Galaxy one complete."

"Understood."

Evans hung up and climbed down through the hole until he was underneath the semi trailer, ready to flip the photo boards flat as soon as the Galaxy had departed.

In the Lear, Jackson pressed the transmit button.

"BEP 1, Seven."

"Go ahead."

"You are now cleared for take-off, to resume your slot in the holding-pattern. No delaying tactics: I want to see a fast taxi and immediate take-off. As soon as you are wheels-up, send in BEP 2."

"BEP 1."

Jackson smiled at the brusque response. In aviation, there were three ways for a pilot to acknowledge an instruction. For something critical, like a landing clearance, protocol called for a 'read-back': a repetition of the instruction. The controller would listen to the read-back, and ensure that it was correct. That gave everyone confidence that an instruction had been heard properly, and that the pilot was going to do exactly as instructed.

The second approach was a 'Wilco', shorthand for "Will comply." This was used to acknowledge receipt of a simple, non-critical instruction. The third approach, the most brusque, and generally used only for the most trivial of instructions, was a simple transmission of the aircraft's call-sign. Clearly the captain couldn't bring himself to acknowledge that he was doing as instructed. Jackson didn't mind at all. So long as the pilot did in fact comply, he could be as rude as he liked about it.

The Galaxy did a slow about-turn. Sullivan watched nervously. The manoeuvre would bring the flight-deck just that little bit closer to the truck. She knew from her own observations from the forklift that the Galaxy wouldn't come anywhere even vaguely close enough to see through the photo-board illusion, but she'd still be happier when it had completed its turn and was headed back to the runway.

The aircraft seemed to take an age to complete its turn, but it did indeed almost turn in its own length as Jackson had advised it could. She heard the engines spool-up as it began a rapid taxi back toward the runway.

Walsh hadn't wasted any time with the intercom: as soon as he was back on board the Galaxy, he'd run straight up the stairs to the flight-deck and asked to use the radio to report in to Major Timpkins. Gill gestured to the empty seat in the centre of the cockpit: while the flight was being operated with two pilots and two flight engineers, there was provision for a third pilot. Gill reached back to dial in the correct frequency.

"Carswell, BEP 1 for CAG."

"Stand by."

There was a short delay before Gill heard Timpkins' voice.

"CAG."

"BEP 1, Sir. Sergeant Walsh. The hostiles have offloaded the cargo into a semi rig. We only spotted one hostile on site. We managed to drop two Marines on the ground with surveillance kit, codenames Ground 1 and 2. They have a partial view of operations but no intervention opportunity spotted as yet. I've asked them to report in to BEP 2 when it lands. Suggest we drop two Marines from each flight. BEP 1."

In the tower, Timpkins thought for a moment. Dropping more Marines onto the field was the obvious thing to do, but that was what decided him against it. Whatever the hostiles had planned, it didn't involve hanging around at the airfield, and until all the C-5s were on the ground there was nothing they could do. Having a large group of Marines sat in a field once the hostiles were on the move wasn't going to help.

No, two were enough. Walsh had said they had surveillance kit, and that included four tiny GPS trackers. He wanted twelve. He still hadn't figured out how the hostiles planned to make their getaway, but they clearly had some plan and Timpkins intended to stay one step ahead, whatever that plan might be.

In the cab of the semi, Sullivan watched as the Galaxy gathered speed as it headed back toward her on the runway. It looked like it was travelling so slowly. Then, at what seemed an impossibly low speed, the nose wheels lifted off the ground, the main gear followed and suddenly it was gone. She revved the engine twice: the signal to Evans to drop through the hole in the floor of the truck, crawl across to the boards and flip them flat.

In the semi trailer, Evans was already crouched by the hole. As soon as he heard the signal, he eased himself down through the hole in the floor, reached the concrete apron and quickly flipped the photo boards flat. He then positioned himself at the edge of the hole into the pipe, felt with his foot for the rope ladder and eased himself in. Once half into the hole, he pulled the fake concrete board over his head to cover the hole. He needed to remain hidden until Sullivan returned with the next truck, so would take the opportunity to clamber down the rope ladder to see how the baggage cart team was doing down in the pipe.

With the radio still set to the reserve channel being used for comms with the BEP flights, Major Timpkins hit the transmit button on his headset.

"BEP 2, CAG."

"CAG, BEP 2."

"BEP 2, there are two Marines on the ground at Hicks, codenames Ground 1 and 2. When you land, I want you to run wide, to the far side of the runway, and instruct the Marine sergeant to drop three surveillance kits, activating one of the GPS trackers. Instruct him to make contact with Ground One and ask them to pick up the kits. Once they have them, they are to make their way to the area where the trucks are parked and attach one GPS tracker to each truck. Once that's done, they are to revert to intelligence-gathering. CAG."

"CAG, all copied, Major. Three surveillance kits, one GPS tracker active, Ground 1 to collect and attach a GPS tracker to each truck. BEP 2."

Sullivan engaged first gear and eased her foot on the gas and began the short half-mile drive to where the rest of the trucks were parked by the gates. Once there, she would park this truck and return in the next one. Perez, meantime, was making his way to the door at the rear of the hanger to use his field glasses to double-check that all was well with the parked trucks before Sullivan reached them.

One load down, eleven to go.

* * *

Timpkins put the headset down and rolled his chair back to the table.

"Ok, gentlemen, how are you getting on with figuring out where the hostiles plan to take the trucks."

"We've been discussing it," said Pritchard. "They have to have a plan for getting the cash out of the area, if not out of the country, and there are only two theories that make sense. Airports or ports."

"Not much ocean around these parts, Mr Pritchard," observed Timpkins.

Pritchard looked across at Lieutenant Morris, who looked embarrassed.

"Well, spit it out, man!" said Timpkins impatiently.

"This is going to sound a little like a movie plot, Sir, but there are lakes."

"What good does it do them to get the cash onto a boat on a lake, Lieutenant? They just have to return to land. And what's all this about a movie plot?"

"A submarine, Sir."

Timpkins looked at him like he was about to call for MPs to have the man restrained.

"I know how it sounds, Sir, but we have to remember this team managed to sabotage military aircraft that spend their life either in the air or on military airbases. That's a Big Deal. We can't underestimate their capabilities."

Timpkins looked expressionless for a couple of seconds, then nodded.

"You're right," he said, "we can't afford to rule anything out. Ok, so an airport or a loading dock at a lake." He gestured to the maps. "Which?"

Daniels spoke up: "Somewhere close. Has to be. They're not going to want to turn this into an OJ convoy, with every squad car and military vehicle in the country following them, and they have to know that at some stage we're going to be able to put those Galaxies down on the ground, at which point they've got no leverage. Whatever they plan to do, they're going to want to do it quickly."

"Agreed," said Timpkins, "so where does that leave us."

"Assuming they're not planning to catch a scheduled flight from Dallas-Fort Worth," said Daniels with a tight smile, "there are eight other airports within half an hour's driving distance for a semi with enough runway length for large cargo aircraft." He pointed to the circles they'd marked on the maps. "There are any number of smaller airstrips, but they're going to end up with 36 pallets: you'd need a hell of a lot of light aircraft to carry that."

"Perhaps that's the plan," said Timpkins, "lots of aircraft doing low-level runs below radar surveillance in lots of different directions at once. Be a hell of a job to try to track them all, even with the

E-3 up there. Some of them would likely make it through. Even one of the 36 pallets is, what?"

"$32 million," said Daniels. "But tracking them isn't a problem if they stay low: we have trackers embedded in the pallets that transmit their location via GSM. I've confirmed with the BEP that the tracker signals are active, and we can login to the system from here."

"Ok," said Timpkins, "that makes life easier. And perhaps we'll only have one pallet to track: $32 million is not a bad haul. Perhaps one is all they're aiming for."

Pritchard shook his head. "It's possible, but I don't think so. Partly because the logistics would be massively complicated – it would need an army of pilots, for example – and most of them would inevitably be caught – but mostly because these guys have gone to a great deal of trouble to steal a billion dollars. I think they intend to keep it all."

"Ok," said Timpkins, "let's assume you're right." He turned to Morris. "Your submarine theory isn't absolutely impossible, but sooner or later it has to surface, and we can always set up blanket surveillance of the lake for as long as it takes, if it comes to that, so for now I'm going with the airport theory."

Morris nodded.

"Ok, said Timpkins, "eight airports. Morris, get a squad of Marines and some heavy armour to each. Mason, retask the BEP flight F-16s. We have 24 in total, so task three per airport. Rotate the three: two to remain overhead at all times while the third refuels. Mr Pritchard, can I leave you to arrange a suitable Police presence at each?"

"On it," said Pritchard, reaching for his phone.

Timpkins looked thoughtful, reached for a phone and dialled an internal extension.

"Timpkins here. How many pallets can a 747 freighter carry?" He listened for a moment, then: "Do so, and call me straight back on this extension."

He turned to Pritchard. "Let's see how many aircraft they need. A 747 freighter is not difficult to lease, there are hundreds of them available."

The phone rang almost immediately.

"Timpkins." He listened. "Thank you." He hung up. "Forty-five."

"So one aircraft would do it," said Pritchard.

"I'll ask the controllers here to get copies of all inbound and outbound flight plans for each of the airports, as well as alerting them to advise us immediately if they have any unexpected heavy cargo traffic. I want to know what the hostiles are planning long before they get a chance to do it."

* * *

The second Galaxy touched down and the captain immediately put the engines into full reverse. He wanted the aircraft at taxiing speed as far up the runway as possible so the Marine sergeant could drop the surveillance kits as far as possible from the hostiles. The sergeant was ready to throw them into the grass at the far side of the runway. The one active GPS tracker would enable the Marines on the ground to home in on the package.

Jackson and Perez had been slowly and carefully working their way toward the parked trucks for the past ten minutes. Now that the Galaxies were cooperating, there was no need to monitor things so closely. Jackson carried an ICOM handheld aviation transceiver that would enable him to remain in contact with the BEP flights without needing to be aboard the Lear. Their plan was to get under the trucks without being seen by any aerial surveillance that might be in place, jump up through the hole in the floor of one of the 'empty' trucks and then be carried in it back to the hole into the water pipe. They too could then disappear as soon as the last Galaxy was in the air.

The pair of them paused for Jackson to relay the same taxiing and parking instructions to the Galaxy he had to the first. That done, they resumed their stealthy approach toward the trucks.

The two Marines were also slowly working their way through the grass, using a smartphone to home in on the position of the active GPS tracker. The trackers were military spec. These used a combination of dual-frequency receivers that could compensate for atmospheric interference and a Differential GPS system. Differential GPS supplemented satellite signals with those from ground-based transmitters whose precise locations were of course known. By combining data from both satellite and ground-based transmitters, D-GPS systems were sufficiently accurate to provide a typical accuracy of a few inches. Right now, they were 422 feet from the tracker.

Sullivan watched as the forklift with the first pallet rolled down the ramp. Galaxy two of twelve. Pallet one of three. She would be very, very glad when this operation was over.

"Got it," said Ross, as he pointed to the surveillance packs laying in the grass about fifteen feet away.

Pearson nodded, and the two quickly crawled the last few feet to the packs.

"You think we can risk crossing the runway?" he asked. "We're about one-and-a-half clicks from the apron, and there's no reason for the hostiles to be staring at an empty runway. Be a hell of a lot quicker than working our way all the way around the threshold."

Ross considered it. It was a risk, but then so was working their way through the grass if the hostiles were in fact keeping a close eye on the runway. Greater exposure for a short time versus lesser exposure for a longer time.

"Ok," he said, "let's do it. Fast and low."

Campbell Field, the most isolated of the eight airports identified by Major Timpkins and his team, had never seen so much activity. The approach road was a mass of blue-and-red flashing lights, with more squad cars than civilian vehicles. Just inside the gates forming the cargo entrance to the airside area of the airport, more police were coning-off a large rectangular area.

Barriers had been erected, and every vehicle approaching the airport was being stopped and searched. While the semis were at this time still safely parked at Hicks Field, and the idea of the hostiles transferring the cash to anything smaller than a truck seemed inconceivable, the authorities weren't taking any chances. Better to inconvenience a few more people with a brief search than risk a breakdown in communications triggering searches after they were needed.

A similar scene was unfolding at each of the seven other target airports.

In the Carswell control tower, Pritchard hit the end-call button on his cellphone and slipped it back into his jacket pocket.

"Everything in place at the police end of things?" asked Timpkins.

"All set," confirmed Pritchard. "The roadblocks at both inner and outer perimeters covering all of the exit routes from the disused airbase have all been set up, from dirt track to major highway. The airport reception committees are all in place. Every airport has either a local or FBI SWAT team present. Every police helicopter in the county is on standby for aerial surveillance." Pritchard pointed to a laptop he'd set up on the table. "And that's the tracking data from the pallets, so we can see exactly where each one is."

"Good," said Timpkins, simply. He turned to Lieutenants Morris.

"Air Force assets?"

"The F-16s are overhead each airport, two each, rotating with a third for refuelling as per your instructions, Sir. The Apache helicopters are refuelled and on hot standby, crews on board, with a scramble time of 45 seconds."

Timpkins nodded, and looked at Lieutenant Mason, who had taken over US Army liaison duties.

"All the convoy vehicles have been retasked, Sir. Six of the airports are getting an M2 Bradley tank, the remaining two a couple of Stryker armoured vehicles apiece. The thirty-six M1114s – the Armoured Humvees," he added for the benefit of the two Secret Service agents, "are being dispatched to the outer permitter road-blocks."

"Why outer?" asked Daniels. "Don't we want to contain things as tightly as possible."

"We do, but we can't use force until the C-5s are safely on the ground. Covering the outer perimeters gives us more time."

"Not even a Presidential visit gets a ring of steel like this," observed Daniels.

"Let's hope it's enough," said Pritchard.

Jackson felt himself tackled from behind and thrown to the ground. He turned, ready to fight, when he found it was Perez who was pinning him to the ground.

"What is it?" he asked quietly, willing his heart-rate to return to normal.

"Company," whispered Perez. "Two Marines, right there, by the trucks."

"Shit."

"Indeed."

"Now what do we do? We can't get across the open apron without being seen, and now we can't get to the trucks either."

"Watch and wait," said Perez. "It's all we can do for now."

"How far away are they?" asked Jackson.

"Thirty or forty feet from the trucks, about 200 feet from us."

"Then we can't wait here – as soon as this load is complete, we need to get on the radio to order the next C-5 in. With a couple of Marines 200 feet away, they could easily overhear us."

"Ok. Let's pull back. But slowly."

The two Marines in question, Ross and Pearson, were now just thirty feet from the closest of the semis.

"That's odd," said Ross.

"What's that?"

"There are twelve semis here. Eleven parked together, plus that one over there." He indicated a rig sat around half a mile away.

"So wha-" Pearson stopped. "Oh. Right. Twelve aircraft, twelve semis here, plus the one being loaded. Thirteen in all. Must be a spare."

"We only have twelve trackers."

"Well, the chances are we wouldn't get a chance to attach one to the final semi without being seen, anyway. Twelve out of thirteen will have to be good enough," said Pearson.

"Cab wheel arches?"

"Yep."

"Let's do it," said Ross. "No messing: In and out, meet back at the post over there." He gestured back to a fading speed limit sign twenty feet behind them.

"Let's go," said Pearson.

"You look worried," observed Daniels.

"I am," said Pritchard.

"You think we've forgotten something?"

"We're missing something."

"Ok," said Daniels, "let's be the bad guys. We've got twelve truckloads of cash on a disused airbase. We have to know the police will have sealed off all the exit routes. We have to know air surveillance will follow our every move. What's our exit plan?"

Pritchard turned to Timpkins.

"How long could the hostiles keep those Galaxies in the air?"

"Well, my plan is to get them on the ground fast."

"If they can disable circuits on the aircraft, they can certainly detect the wheels going down or read the altimeters," said Pritchard. "We have to assume the bad guys can keep those aircraft in the air until they're running on fumes. How long is that?"

"Maximum endurance once empty is a little over five hours," said Timpkins.

"Ok," said Daniels, "so the bad guys are safe for five hours."

"Long enough to get to any of the eight airports, transfer the cash to cargo aircraft and get the hell out of Dodge," said Pritchard with a frown.

"Long enough to get out of US airspace," said Daniels.

"Fuck," said Pritchard.

"Yeah."

"None of our roadblocks do us the slightest bit of good if they can just smile and wave as we're forced to let them through."

Pritchard turned back to Timpkins. He hesitated.

Timpkins was a practical man, and had had to make many tough decisions in his career. He didn't need to wait for Pritchard to ask the question.

"You're wondering whether we have to consider the Galaxies and their crews expendable." His face was expressionless, his tone neutral.

Pritchard said nothing. There was silence for several seconds.

Ross and Pearson ran quickly to the parked semis. With well-practiced ease, they each reached into a pouch, grabbed one of the tiny GPS trackers and attached the magnet side to the inside of a

wheel arch before moving swiftly to the next truck.
Slapping the trackers onto each truck and
withdrawing back to their previous position took
less than two minutes.

"It's not my call," said Pritchard, finally. "But my
recommendation will be no: these are brand-new,
sequentially-numbered bills. Worst-case, we can
cancel them."

"I still hate to think of the bad guys getting clean
away," said Daniels.

"I think we've overlooked something else," said
Timpkins. "The blindingly obvious, in fact."

Pritchard stared at him.

"The hostiles are already sat at an airfield suitable
for flying cargo aircraft in and out," said Timpkins.
"Why not simply bring their aircraft into Hicks?
Why the semis?"

Again, there was silence for a moment.

"You're right," said Pritchard. "Those trucks aren't
heading for an airport. They have to have something
else planned."

"Morris's submarine theory?" asked Daniels. "If
we leave aside the small matter of how you get a
submarine into a lake in the first place without being
noticed. Would also get around the trackers: we
wouldn't receive any signals through a submarine
hull, even if it were only just beneath the surface."

"I don't get the submarine theory," said Pritchard.
"It buys them time, sure, but as the Major says,
sooner or later they have to surface." He turned to
Timpkins. "How long can a submarine stay
submerged?"

"I'm an Air Force man–" began Timpkins, before
Morris caught his eye, "but I believe the Lieutenant
may have been doing a little research?"

"It depends just how far-fetched we want to go ..."

"Go on," said Timpkins.

"It wouldn't be that difficult to get hold of an
electric or diesel submarine. Say a decommissioned

WW2 one. Those have to run on battery-power when submerged, and rely on carbon dioxide scrubbers to clean the air. Fully-crewed, they could stay submerged for three or four days. A skeleton crew might stretch it to a week, perhaps even two." He paused, and looked embarrassed. Timpkins gestured for him to continue. "A nuclear submarine, well, indefinitely, basically. They of course remain powered while submerged and can generate their own oxygen as well as remove CO_2. The only real limitation there is food supply. Several months with ease."

Timpkins coughed. "I think if a nuclear submarine had gone missing, even an ex Soviet one, we'd have heard about it."

"Sir," said Morris, in a small voice.

"How large are the lakes around here?" asked Pritchard.

"Lake Ray Hubbard is the largest," said Morris, who had clearly been researching his pet theory, "over 22,000 acres. Plenty of shoreline and quite a few access roads large enough to get truck access. But only 40 feet deep."

"Well, that makes your theory very easy to test," said Timpkins. "The E-3's radar is easily capable of detecting a submarine in water that shallow." Timpkins gestured to the tower manager. "Get the E-3 on the line and tell them we'd like to check Lake Ray Hubbard, and all other lakes within a 30-mile radius, for the presence of a submerged submarine."

The tower manager nodded like this was a perfectly ordinary request and turned away.

"Ok," said Timpkins. "We have the submarine theory covered. Right now, we have a hell of a lot of resources committed to those airports. The question is whether we should re-deploy them."

Pritchard frowned. "The next question, and one to which I don't think we yet have an answer, being 'To where?'. Until we can answer that, I vote we leave them where they are."

"I still can't see any rationale to using trucks to take the cash to another airport when they could fly directly from here," said Timpkins, "but in the absence to any answer to your question, and with all the exit routes already covered, I must confess that repositioning them randomly makes even less sense."

Daniels spoke for the first time in a couple of minutes.

"Could a helicopter lift those trailers?"

"A sufficiently large one, certainly," replied Timpkins. "What are you thinking?"

"I don't know," admitted Daniels. "I mean, maybe that's how they evade ground pursuit – helicopters swoop in to scoop up the trailers – but that still leaves air pursuit and the question of the end destination. We're still not seeing the end-game here."

The five men looked at each other glumly.

Sullivan would have smiled if she could have overheard the conversation. While the authorities were speculating about submarines and helicopters, their much lower-tech transport – two aircraft tow trucks and a lot of baggage carts – was slowly taking on board its cargo. They'd just loaded the last pallet from the second Galaxy. Everything was going to plan.

"Major Timpkins," said the tower manager, holding out a headset. "BEP 2 with a patch-through to Ground 1."

Timpkins put on the headset and pressed transmit.

"Ground 1, CAG."

"Sir, GPS trackers fitted. We don't think we're going to learn any more by watching them load the rest of the trucks, but we do have an opportunity to try to slip aboard the first semi – the one already loaded with the cash. Would mean a welcome party wherever the trucks get taken to, Sir. Ground 1."

Timpkins considered the proposal for a couple of seconds. Trackers were one thing, but a couple of Marines on board would make for a handy backup.

"Ok," said Jackson, "we're far enough away."

"Not a moment too soon," commented Perez, pointing his head toward the semi that was pulling away and heading for the apron.

Jackson raised the transceiver to his face and repeated the same instructions he'd given to the first Galaxy, ordering BEP 2 back to its holding pattern and instructing it to send in BEP 3. That done, he turned back to Perez.

"Explosives, do you think?" asked Perez. He was referring to the devices they'd watched the Marines attach to the cab of each truck.

Jackson considered the idea. "Could be. The bills are replaceable – they just print some more – and I'm sure they consider us dispensable too."

"Hmm," said Perez. "Well, if they do plan to blow up the convoy, there are three possibilities. One, they do it the moment the last truck is loaded. Two, they plan to do it somewhere en-route. Three, it's just a contingency plan in the event that they see the trucks somehow making good their escape."

"Only the first of those would concern us."

"Indeed. Though so long as we can make sure they don't blow any of us up with them, that could play right into our hands: there's nothing suspicious at all about the explosions if they initiate them."

"So, you're our resident explosives expert: how would you do it?" asked Jackson.

"Most likely, it's just a fallback plan. I think they'd prefer to catch us than kill us, and they're going to want to hush the whole thing up if they can. That gets harder when there are big explosions involved. But if I did want to blow up the trucks, I'd wait until they were all parked together: it ensures maximum destructive power, and if any of the devices fail to detonate, the chances are the rest would do the job."

"Makes sense, but I don't like the idea of gambling lives on it."

"Nor me," agreed Perez. "Ok, let's think this through logically. If they wanted to destroy the trucks before they were even loaded, they could have detonated them as soon as they'd retreated to a safe distance. They haven't done that. So that leaves the outside chance they plan to do it the moment the last pallet is loaded. And at that point, we have Aaron in the back of the trailer and Jessica alongside it."

"So what do we do?"

"We have to get to that twelfth rig, and pull off the explosives device."

"Without being seen," observed Jackson.

"Right."

"Which is a little problematic given that we have two Marines positioned about a hundred yards away from them."

"Well," said Perez, "we have time. Sometimes the most effective plan of action – and the hardest one to do – is to go into wait-and-see mode."

Timpkins shook his head. No, Marines boarding a truck was too risky. If they were discovered, he'd have eleven or twelve crashed Galaxies and a lot of dead airmen and Marines. They had all exit routes covered, they had GPS trackers in place on the trucks, and multi-frequency trackers embedded in the pallets, there was no need to take chances.

"Ground 1, CAG. Negative. You've done what we needed done. Withdraw to drop-off point, report when in position and I'll have the next Galaxy pick you up as it taxies."

Ross looked at Pearson. This wasn't what either of them wanted to hear. If they couldn't get the go-ahead to get aboard a truck, they at least wanted to be on the ground.

But you only questioned orders when you had a solid reason to do so, and right now Ross couldn't think of any other solid proposal.

"Sir. Ground 1 out."

Jackson pointed to the Marines as he watched the two of them head quickly back in the direction of the runway.

"I see them," said Perez. "Let's give them five minutes. I want to make sure they're not pulling back far enough to detonate the trucks."

"Let's wait ten," said Jackson.

The tower manager called across to Timpkins.

"I have the E-3 for you, Major."

Timpkins walked over and accepted the headset.

"Eye-sky, CAG."

"CAG, Eye-sky. We've checked out all of the lakes. There's definitely no submarine in any of them, Sir."

"Degree of certainty?"

"Four nines, Sir."

That meant 99.99%. Essentially a certainty.

"Anything else to report?"

"Negative, Major. No unauthorised air traffic in the no-fly zone, and nothing is getting in or out without our tracking it."

"Thank you. CAG."

Timpkins removed the headset and walked back to the table.

"No submarine," he said.

"So what the hell have we missed?" asked Lieutenant Morris.

"Fucked if I know," said Pritchard, with feeling.

"Ok," said Perez, "let's go."

The two men kept low as they worked their way around to the trucks. They had numbered the trucks with stickers on the driver's doors, 1 to 13. Number

13 was the one earmarked for the demonstration explosion, kept well away from the others. Number 12 was the tricked-up one with the remote controls, which Sullivan would pick up last.

"There," said Jackson, pointing to the '12' sticker.

"You duck under the trailer and climb in," said Perez. "I'll grab the device and join you in 30 seconds."

"Ok."

Jackson pulled himself up through the hole in the trailer and waited for Perez.

"That was more like 25," he said, as Perez's head appeared.

"I'm a motivated team member," he said.

"What did you do with the explosives?"

Perez opened his hand to reveal a small black cube."

"Oh great," said Jackson, "you brought it in here with us. Just the company I wanted."

Perez grinned. "Well, I wanted to check it out, and didn't fancy sitting exposed out there studying it."

He turned it over in his hand, then tossed it across to Jackson: "Catch!"

Jackson did so, instinctively.

"Hey! You might have a casual attitude to things that go bang, but I don't."

Perez smiled. "You can relax. It's not explosives, it's a tracker unit."

"You're sure?"

"Yep, standard issue for reconn units. Accurate to within inches."

"You'd better put it back, then," said Jackson. "We are quite content to have them track the trucks. And best let Sullivan know we're in the truck – don't want to scare the life out of her or Evans."

"True enough. Be right back."

Sullivan waited for the signal from Evans before pulling away. Two loads down, ten to go.

The drive across the apron to their impromptu truck park took just two minutes. Switching off the engine but leaving the keys in the ignition, she clambered down from the truck and into truck 3. She started it up, and swung it round with what now felt like practiced ease.

In the trailer, Jackson commented on it. "Smooth ride."

Perez nodded. "I reckon she has an alternative career path if the money ever runs out."

Two minutes later, the semi came to a halt and Evans popped his head through the hole in the floor.

"Morning, gents. Be back in a mo."

Evans raised the photo boards into position, then pulled himself up into the trailer.

"Any news from your end of things?"

"We have a couple of Marines on the airfield," said Jackson.

"Marines?" asked Evans, a worried expression on his face.

"We don't think they're a problem," said Perez. "They attached trackers to the trucks then withdrew."

"Maybe they're not alone," said Evans, not looking any less worried.

"Always possible," said Jackson, "but they're not a threat to us unless they get close enough to see through your illusion, and with a wide open apron all around us, I can't see that happening."

"All the same, they're not the kind of company I like to keep in the present circumstances."

"Wouldn't be top of my invitation list today either," said Perez with studied casualness, "but nothing we can do about it, so let's just stick to the plan."

Major Timpkins had 747 freighter data sheets in front of him. He checked the take-off roll figure against the runway length marked on the Hicks chart.

"Even fully-loaded, they could take-off from here."

"So maybe the trucks are just intended to throw us off the scent? You think they intend to fly the cash right out of Hicks?"

Timpkins nodded. "The more I think about it, the more sense it makes. They can keep the C-5s in the air long enough to get the 747 into international airspace, and then we're in very tricky legal territory."

"Could they drive the trucks directly into the 747?" asked Pritchard.

"No," said Timpkins, "I've checked the dimensions and the bottleneck is the lifting nose entryway. Pallets slide in with room to spare, but not trucks."

"So they're loading them onto the trucks only to offload them again?" asked Lieutenant Morris. "That makes no sense."

"Yes it does," said Timpkins. "Offloading doesn't take much longer than if they'd simply stacked the pallets on the ground. Both trailers and 747 freighters have roller-systems for the pallets, so the transfer can be done quickly enough. Meantime, they have us thinking they intend departing by road. We tie up massive resources blocking every dirt track in the county while they simply fly out, waving to us from the flight-deck."

Timpkins turned to the tower manager.

"Contact the E-3 and tell them we're looking for a 747 freighter, maybe in the air outside the exclusion zone, maybe on the ground inside it. Tell them to look for other large cargo aircraft too, but a 747 is number one on the suspect list."

"Sir!"

"Ok," said Pritchard, "so now we know how the bad guys plan to escape; the question is, how do we stop them?"

"That is indeed the question," said Timpkins, slowly. "And I think the answer is as much political as military."

"Oh?"

"We have to assume they can keep the C-5s in the air long enough to leave US airspace. Once they reach another country's airspace, we can do nothing other than prevail on that nation's government to intervene, and there is no shortage of destinations where payments to the right people will ensure that such cooperation fails."

"They're not exactly short of cash for those payments, either," said Pritchard.

"Right," said Timpkins. "So if we can't touch them inside US territory because they have the C-5s hostage, and we can't touch them once they reach their destination country, wherever that may be, that leaves international airspace."

"I can't claim any familiarity with airspace law," said Pritchard.

"It's messy, but the bottom line is that the repercussions of shooting down aircraft in international airspace involve a whole world of pain. United Nations Security Council resolutions, Senate debates, that kind of thing."

"But surely," argued Pritchard, "if it's a US aircraft shooting down another US aircraft, that's nobody else's business but ours?"

"That would be my view, but the aircraft may not be US-registered, and there may well be foreign nationals aboard. It's a decision well above my pay-grade."

"So who can make that call?"

"Only your former boss," replied Timpkins.

* * *

There aren't many things that justify interrupting a meeting in the Oval Office, but the hijacking of a dozen USAF aircraft with a billion dollars on board will do it. President Michael Grant had been informed within minutes of the first call to the BEP flight, and had ordered his National Security Advisor to the Oval Office and the Joint Chiefs of

Staff to the Situation Room. He'd given instructions that he was to be advised immediately of any developments.

One of the few positive legacies of 9/11 was the flattening of lines of communication between the officer on the ground dealing with a threat and the White House: it was now fully understood that minutes mattered, and the request from Timpkins to the White House passed through only one intermediate level in the hierarchy – a four-star General. It was an efficiency that would have been unimaginable before that infamous day.

Grant did not look or sound like the movie image of a President. If you'd had to guess his profession before he became a household face, you'd have said professor of English literature, or perhaps the kind of high school teacher you remembered fondly years after you'd graduated. At 5'9" and rather lightly built, with a kindly face, and a careful, precise manner of speech, he was anything but the imposing figure we have come to expect from the most powerful man in the world.

Grant had gotten the Republican nomination as the compromise candidate at a time when the conservative and liberal wings of the party were threatening to tear it apart. Many had doubted he had what it took to make the tough calls, but his quiet but determined performance on the campaign trail had changed hearts and minds.

His NSA Emily Lloyd did not have a kindly face. Grant couldn't ever recall hearing her laugh, and even her smiles were tight and brief. But she combined a photographic memory with a fierce intelligence and an unswerving determination to protect her country and its way of life from any and all threats. Grant found her a little humourless and hard work at a times, but perhaps those were the character traits demanded of the role, he'd decided.

It was Lloyd who took the call.

"I'll inform the President immediately. You'll have a decision shortly, General." Lloyd replaced the receiver and turned to Grant. "We should go to the Situation Room, Mr President. I'll brief you on the way."

Grant nodded, stood and the two of them walked the short distance to the stairs leading down to the underground Situation Room, two Secret Service agents accompanying them. Lloyd's en-route briefing was succinct.

"Mr President, the USAF believes the hostiles intend to fly the bills directly out of Hicks on board a cargo aircraft. They believe the C-5s will remain hostage until that aircraft reached international airspace. The two questions are: one, do we sacrifice the Galaxies and their crews to prevent them getting that far? Two, do we shoot them down whilst in international airspace? Considerations: we don't yet know the registry of the aircraft, nor the nationality of the hostiles on board them. It's possible that none of them are American, Sir."

"Thank you," said Grant.

The third Galaxy touched down and the captain threw the massive jets into full reverse to slow the aircraft to walking pace while it was still in the first quarter of the runway. As soon as he felt the aircraft touch down, the Marine Sergeant in the rear motioned to one of his Marines to crack open the rear right passenger door and hit the transmit button on his tactical radio set.

"Ground 1 from BEP 3."

"BEP 3, Ground 1 in position."

"Board by right rear door asap."

"Ground 1."

A matter of seconds passed before the two men were on board. Another Marine, intercom in hand, informed the flight deck, and the Galaxy accelerated back up to fast taxi speed.

Movies always show the President placing his palm-print on a pad to unlock the doors. The reality was far less hi-tech: a nod from a third Secret Service agent as he held the door open. There was no need of electronic gadgetry to access the room: nobody who shouldn't be here would have been allowed to get this far.

The Joint Chiefs stood as Grant and Lloyd entered the room, but Grant quickly motioned for them to take their seats. He repeated what Lloyd had told him, almost word for word.

"Views, gentlemen?"

General Harry Ross, Chief of Staff of the Air Force, spoke first.

"On question one, no. It's not justified or necessary. We get the Galaxies on the ground, then deal with the hostiles."

"Opposing views?" asked Grant.

There was silence.

"Ok," said Grant: "do we shoot them down, even if they have reached international air-space?"

"Yes, Mr President, we certainly do shoot them down. Under international law, we are entitled to engage an aircraft which we believe poses an immediate threat to the security of the United States. I'd say that threatening to blow USAF aircraft out of the sky qualifies. We order the aircraft to return to US airspace, where we land them at the nearest airbase. If they fail to comply, we shoot them down."

"Views to the contrary?" asked Grant.

Admiral James Price coughed. "Well, in principle I agree with General Ross, but if we're going to wait until the C-5s are on the ground, we may be on more difficult ground claiming an immediate threat."

"I disagree," said Ross. "The hostiles have already triggered explosive devices on board the aircraft, that makes them terrorists. The audacity and planning behind the attack suggests they may even be foreign military. Terrorists or hostile powers in possession of a billion dollars of US currency pose a huge risk to our security."

"Admiral?" asked Grant, turning back to Price.

"There's certainly merit in that argument," said Price. "I have no moral qualms with the General's view, and agree with his assessment that they are terrorists. My concern is purely how such an act might play out on the international stage. From a pragmatic perspective, these are brand-new, sequentially-numbered bills. If the hostiles succeed in escaping with the bills, we simply cancel them."

"And let the hostiles get away scot free?" asked Ross.

"Less than ideal, I agree," said Price, "but effectively getting away empty-handed seems a hollow victory."

"Mrs Lloyd?" asked Grant.

"It makes us look weak, and could encourage other attempts. I'm with General Ross."

Grant did what he always did when making a difficult decision: reached a provisional decision in his mind and asked himself The Question: thirty years from now, when scholars were studying the events in college, would the decision be viewed as commendable or regrettable? Satisfied by the answer, he nodded.

"I'm authorising the shooting down of the aircraft."

* * *

Timpkins had arranged for all radio transmissions to and from the BEP aircraft to be relayed to the tower by the E-3, monitored by Lieutenant Mason, but so far they'd learned nothing useful. The routine had been unchanged as each Galaxy had been landed in turn. The unloading of the final aircraft was now almost complete.

Timpkins picked up the headset set to the channel used for communication with the E-3.

"Eye-Sky, CAG."

"CAG, Eye-Sky 1."

"Eye-Sky, confirm still negative on any inbound aircraft, over."

"CAG, confirmed. Nothing in the air, nothing matching spotted on the ground, over."

"Eye-Sky, thanks. Assuming that situation remains unchanged, your primary mission is surveillance of the semis, over."

"CAG, understood, over."

"Eye-Sky, CAG out."

Timpkins turned to the others at the table.

"Well," he said, "that's four forms of surveillance in place: trackers in the pallets, trackers on the semis, infra-red from the satellites and radar from the E-3. Now, any more theories about where they are headed?"

Everyone shook their heads.

"Well, whatever they have planned, I guess we're about to find out." Timpkins turned to the tower chief. "Put the relay comms on speaker." With the controllers having no other air traffic to deal with, they could put the radio transmissions onto the speaker system without risk of distracting anyone.

"I can hardly believe it," said Sullivan, as Lewis climbed back down after her, having transferred the tracker from the final pallet in the twelfth Galaxy back up into the semi.

"I know," said Lewis. "A billion dollars!"

"It's not ours yet," said Evans, as he joined them, having just lowered the photo boards and pulled the fake concrete panel across the top of both photo boards and hole. "We still have to get it out of here."

"I know," said Sullivan, "but allow a girl a few seconds to savour the moment, would you?"

"No time to savour right now," said Evans. "You've got a truck to drive."

Lewis handed the iPad to her. "All yours."

Sullivan looked at the screen. Chung had kept the app simple. The entire screen showed her the view from the camera in the right headlight. There was another camera in the left headlight, which Sullivan could switch to should the first one fail. Overlaid on the live video image was a head-up display showing speed and gear. The only visible controls were buttons for up/down gear-shifts and a toggle for the ignition, which was currently showing 'On.' Steering was achieved by tilting the iPad left or right, acceleration by tilting it forward, braking by tilting it back. Sweet and simple, and she'd had great fun practicing in a parking-lot while Young sat in the cab pretending to drive.

Jackson was alongside her, looking across at the iPad screen. He waited until he saw Sullivan remotely park the semi with the others and switch off the ignition, then picked up the air band radio.

"BEP 12, Seven."

"BEP 12."

"BEP 12, you have a dozen Marines on board. Off-load them onto the apron via the rear ramp, please. Without their weapons, naturally."

There was silence for a moment. Jackson was expecting that. He could imagine the 'What the–' exchange on the flight-deck. He was also well aware that they would slip their backup handguns from their holsters into pockets, but that wasn't a concern.

"Seven, anything else you'd like besides our Marines? Pizza and ice-cream, maybe?"

Jackson smiled. Sarcasm was as much a military tradition as close order drill.

"A small pepperoni would be nice, but I'll settle for the Marines."

His pizza request was deliberate: he was trying to give the impression there was only one of them at the base.

"Do we get to know why you want the Marines, over?"

Jackson smiled again. This was a question he was happy to answer.

"Affirmative, BEP 12: I thought they might like to drive our trucks for us. They will find the keys in the ignition and satellite navigation systems fitted."

Jackson again could almost hear the conversation taking place on the flight-deck.

"Why the hell not?" came the response.

"BEP 12, I'm confident your men will offer their cooperation freely, but I wouldn't want there to be any misunderstandings – any of them deciding to do a little freelance delivery work, that sort of thing. I trust you'll forgive a small demonstration of a simple precaution. Do you have sight of the trucks?"

"We do."

"You'll notice that there is one of them parked some considerable distance from the others. Please keep your eye on that one."

Jackson turned and nodded to Perez, who was holding a small transmitter with one switch and one push-button. Perez flicked the switch to the down position. He then pressed the push-button.

There was a large fireball and loud bang where the semi used to be. Jackson pressed transmit again.

"BEP 12, apologies for the drama, but they say actions speak louder than words. Please advise your men that all twelve remaining trucks are similarly outfitted. You can appreciate that given the rather valuable cargo, we would be loathe to have to destroy any of the loaded rigs, but we would not hesitate to do so in the event that any of the Marines fail to follow our instructions. Seven."

"You've made your point," came the terse response. "Standby."

There was a pause of around 20 seconds.

"Seven, the Marines are on the apron."

"BEP 12, thank you. Please instruct the Marines to walk to the rigs and climb into the cabs. Once they are on board and you've relayed their instructions, you'll be free to depart and to resume your position in the holding pattern. Seven."

"BEP 12."

Jackson replaced the transceiver in his pocket. They could at this point allow the Galaxies to land, but they wanted to keep the authorities guessing so, for now, he wanted them in the air.

Timpkins looked at Pritchard as they listened to the exchange on the tower speaker system.

"Well, I guess that partially answers the question."

Pritchard nodded: "So, they have the rigs doubly protected from interference – holding both the trucks and the C-5s hostage, and making it impossible to intercept the rigs anyway. We're still no nearer to figuring out their end-game, though. The only logical plan is to fly the cash out of the country, but if they're going to do that, why didn't they do it direct from Hicks? We're still missing something fundamental here."

"I wish I could disagree. But I'm damned if I can see what it is."

"We may have one slight edge here," said Daniels.

"Slight or not, I'll take anything going," said Pritchard.

"It looks like only one of the hostiles is on the base, but he has to still be in one of the semis. We have the airfield surrounded, so he's not going to hang around waiting to be picked up, which means he has to be on one of those rigs. Most likely the last one he drove there. If we can figure out which one for sure, that's one rig he's definitely not going to want to blow up."

"That's true," said Pritchard. "I'm guessing he's no longer in the cab, though, so not sure how we figure that out."

"I have a thought."

"Let's hear it."

"Once the rigs are underway, we instruct the Marines to do an emergency stop then set off again. We stagger that at ten-second intervals. If our man complains and asks what the hell we're playing at, that's the rig he's in," said Daniels.

"Smart."

"Smart but unnecessary," said Timpkins, with a smile. "Morris here had the bright idea of tasking a KH-12 satellite to add to our surveillance capabilities. The KH-12 has infra-red cameras that can check the semis for a heat signature."

"They can detect a man inside a big rig from a satellite?" asked Daniels, surprised.

"Keep it to yourself," said Timpkins. "Those things were designed to provi-"

Their conversation was interrupted by the speakers.

"Seven, BEP 12, the Marines are in the cabs."

"BEP 12, excellent. They will find each cab fitted with a satellite navigation system with a pre-programmed direction. All they have to do is follow the directions to their destination. One of them will find a key to the padlock on the gates attached to the ignition key, so they can let themselves out of the airfield. Once they reach the destination, they walk away. Well away. As in, a mile away, remaining in clear view. Are the instructions clear?"

"BEP 12."

Timpkins wasted in no time in giving orders at the tower chief.

"Tell the satellite station to check for heat signatures in the trailers – we believe there's a hostile in one of them. Then ask BEP 12 to instruct one of the Marines to check the GPS for the route and final destination, so that we can put a reception committee in place. Let me know as soon as."

"Sir!"

Timpkins turned back to the group at the table.

"Lieutenant Morris, as soon as we have that destination, mobilise the ground teams. We won't assume the destination is genuine – it's a pretty obvious thing for us to check – but it's likely the true destination is somewhere en-route so that the hostiles can just order them to pull over once they reach it. Get a decent force to the final destination anyway, tucked away nicely out of sight, but spread the rest at intervals along the route. No matter where they stop, I want suitable assets in place."

"Major."

"I'll arrange the same with police and Secret Service teams," said Pritchard.

"Thanks. They're bound to still have the C-5s in the air at that point, so it's going to be a surveillance operation initially."

"Ok," said Daniels, "we have Presidential authority to shoot down any aircraft used in the escape, so I propose that we consider that avenue covered and focus on the alternatives."

"A great idea bar our complete inability to theorise any credible alternatives," said Pritchard.

"My only thought is that making one semi disappear has to be easier than doing the same with a dozen of them. So maybe once the hostiles take over the semi driving, those rigs are heading in twelve different directions," said Daniels.

"Well," said Pritchard, "whatever the end-game, that's the trickiest scenario from our perspective and thus a good possibility to cover."

"Ross," said Timpkins, "once we have the route, I want you to study maps and figure out the best place or places for them to head off in lots of different directions."

"Sir."

"Seven, BEP 12."

"Go ahead, BEP 12."

"The Marines are on board the rigs."

"BEP 12, instruct them to depart, then resume your place in the holding pattern. We will now be maintaining radio silence until the semis reach their destination. Any questions until then, over?"

"Negative, Seven."

"Very well. I hardly need point out that attempting to land any of the C-5s before we ok it would not be a good idea. Seven out."

Jackson's final words were a bluff, but given that the crews had cooperated in handing over the cash, there was no reason to suppose they would take any chances afterwards. Jackson switched off the transceiver.

"Let's go."

Sullivan and Jackson quickly clambered down the rope ladder into the pipe, where the others were waiting for them. They climbed onto the back of the lead aircraft tug and Sullivan slapped the roof twice. Perez, at the wheel of the tug, eased it forward slowly. The weight load was nothing for the tugs – they were designed to pull 200 tons of aircraft, so 12 tons of cash was light work – but it would only take one broken link to significantly delay them. They had contingency plans in place, of course, in the form of heavy-duty chains and clasps, but they didn't want to be hanging around here playing repair man.

Perez eased the tug forward at a crawl until he was confident that all of the slack had been taken up, then accelerated away down the pipeline. The journey to the exit point should take nine minutes.

The convoy of trucks pulled out of the airfield, heading down the main road in the direction of Dallas.

In the tower at Carswell, Timpkins had just received word that the convoy was underway when a second message came in.

"The E-3 wants to talk to you urgently, Major."

Timpkins took the offered headset.

"CAG here, pass your message."

"Sir, we spotted something odd when we were looking for the heat signature in the trailers. That was the first surprise: there was nothing there, definitely no-one in any of the trailers. But we did pick up two faint heat signatures on the apron, right by where the semis were loaded. A visual check revealed nothing – just an empty piece of concrete – and the heat signatures disappeared after a few seconds."

"Residual heat from the loading process."

"Negative, Sir, the signatures were faint but too strong to have been residual heat so long after loading completed. We're not sure where or how, Sir, but we believe there are two hostiles still on the apron, under some kind of cover."

Timpkins gestured to Lieutenant Pearson. Pearson approached.

"Two hostiles still at the loading area on the apron, under some kind of cover. Get forces over there, don't approach but make sure we have the apron surrounded."

"Sir."

Timpkins hit transmit on the headset.

"Eye-Sky, CAG, maintain surveillance and advise any update."

Oblivious to the fact that their cover was blown, the two baggage trains continued their surreal journey through the water pipe towards the exit point. Sullivan looked at her watch. One minute to go to the valve, four minutes to go to the exit point, then the slow process of transferring the pallets to their shiny new trucks.

In the tower at Carswell, Lieutenant Morris was pointing out a major intersection he'd circled on the map laid out on the table with the GPS route marked with a highlighter.

"It's here, Major, I'd stake a month's salary on it. They can go two different directions on the freeway, two different directions on the road they came in on, and they only have to drive to the intersections here, here and here, and they can head in another six different directions. There are any number of permutations from there, but this is the obvious scattering point."

Timpkins studied the map for 30 seconds in silence, then nodded.

"Very well, let's have that be the main interception point. Let's get assets in place along each of the likely escape routes from there."

"Sir."

Perez brought the tug to a brief halt just beyond the valve, and Jackson hopped off. He clambered onto the fixed steel-rung ladder leading up to a manhole cover. He waved to Perez, who saw him in the mirror and pulled away. They needed to get both trains clear of the valve, and their method for communicating this was simple but effective: a football whistle. As soon as the rear train was clear, Jackson would blow the whistle. Inside the pipe, the sound would carry for a mile or more. Perez would take that as the signal to halt. Right now, Jackson just needed to be high enough on the ladder to avoid any risk of being squashed by the pallets.

Each train comprised 18 carts. Two trains, 36 carts. Jackson watched in fascination as more than a billion dollars in cash slowly made its way past him. It seemed to take days.

Finally, the last cart cleared the valve and Jackson reached for the whistle slung round his neck and blew it as loudly as he could, almost deafening himself in the process. He hoped the sound would carry – he didn't want to be left behind.

He needn't have worried: the sound, bouncing around the inside of the pipe, was still almost painfully loud when it reached Perez.

As soon as the train came to a halt, Jackson clambered up the ladder and pushed on the underside of the manhole cover. He looked around to make sure no-one was in sight, then eased the cover to one side before pulling himself up onto the ground outside: he didn't want to risk another dropped phone moment.

As soon as he was sitting on the ground clear of the hole, he hit the speed-dial button to call Chung.

"All set?"

"Go for valve close."

"Confirm clear."

"Confirmed."

"Valve closing."

Chung had been logged into the SCADA system from the outset, and only had to click on the valve icon to close it. It seemed to take an age, but finally the image changed to the closed graphic.

"Valve closed. Definitely no-one left behind? Because I'm about the flood the section with water."

"Everyone accounted for," confirmed Jackson.

"Standby."

Chung clicked open on the valve at the upstream end of the section of pipe. Again, it seemed to take far, far longer than in the practice run. Just adrenaline, he told himself. Then that too changed status to show the valve was open. With the build up of water behind the upstream valve, and the section they had been using completely empty, the water would be rushing in at an incredible rate. In a matter of minutes, the whole section would be completely filled with water.

"Water in, clear to proceed," said Chung.

"On our way," said Jackson.

"Good luck!"

"Thanks."

Aboard the E-4, two visual analysis technicians were studying the video of the two faint infra-red signals they'd detected. Instead of the clear white outlines you'd expect of people in the open, the images were gray and fuzzy.

"If I didn't know better, I'd say they were inside a wooden shed," said one.

"It does have that look," said the other, flicking back to the visible light view, "but there's definitely no structure there – just empty concrete."

"I wonder ..." The technician walked over to the radio operator in contact with Carswell. "Can you see if Carswell can check the plans of the base – see if there's anything beneath the ground?"

"Wilco."

In the headlights of the tug, Perez could make out the Y-split in the pipe. The right pipe was the main feed, supplying water to several communities beyond before leading eventually to a relief valve at a lake, where any excess water could be dumped. The left pipe led up a gentle ramp to a drainage culvert. Perez eased the tug toward the left side.

He glanced at his watch. It would take the semis around 90 minutes to reach their destination, at which point they'd be expecting the next communication. They would instruct the Marines to exit the trucks and withdraw by at least a mile. At that point, it would be time to detonate the trucks.

At Carswell, the team in the tower were studying the plans of the Hicks base.

"There!" said Lieutenant Mason. "A water pipe! It looks to run directly beneath the point where the rigs were loaded."

"But there's no access point marked," said Timpkins. "You can see manhole entrances marked here, here, here ..." He pointed to several points some distance away, "but nothing very close to this point."

"Maybe there's an access point missing from the plans," suggested Pritchard.

"Could be."

Timpkins turned to the tower manager. "Get hold of the troops on the ground at the base, reiterate that they are to hold their distance, I don't like trigger-happy hostiles with the ability to blow my C-

5s out of the sky, but use field glasses to really study the ground, report anything they spot."

"Major."

Timpkins turned back to the others.

"I think we may have been had."

Pritchard nodded, slowly. "I think you may be right. Where does the pipe lead to?"

"Mason, we need wide area plans for the water system."

"Sir!"

Perez brought the tug to a halt as it reached the barred exit at the top of the ramp. They had replaced the padlock with one of their own the previous day. He jumped out, unlocked the padlock and pulled the gate open. Hopping back into the tug, he continued forward into the open-air culvert.

The first section had sides about 12 feet deep. As they progressed along it, the slope continued gently upwards, the sides of the culvert getting gradually lower. In about two minutes, they would reach an access road. One more gate, a short drive along the access road in the scrubland, and then they would reach their parked semis.

The aircraft tugs had masses of torque, designed to push 200-ton aircraft around from a standing start, but were not built for speed. Inside the pipe, the proximity of the walls had given some sense of speed, but here, out in the open, they seemed to be crawling along.

Finally, though, they passed through the final gate into the clearing where two 40-foot semi rigs awaited them. The livery of each trailer was different. One claimed to be a Fedex truck, one UPS. Travelling individually, rather than in convoy, each would be an everyday sight and shouldn't attract a second glance from anyone. Alongside the two rigs was an SUV: two of them would travel in each rig, the rest in the SUV.

To ship the cash to ten different countries, they would need to split it into ten different containers, but none of them liked the idea of hanging around anywhere even remotely close to the scene of the crime any longer than they had to. They had thus opted for a two-stage process. Stage one, get the cash loaded and out of there in a hurry. That meant loading it as quickly as possible into one of the two semis. Stage two – transferring the pallets to the individual shipping containers – would be done 320 miles away, in Galveston, the port from which the containers would make their onward journeys.

But it was the immediate part of the operation that worried Perez: transferring the pallets to the trailer unit of the Fedex semi. The 45-foot trailer was large enough to accommodate all of the pallets – the second rig was just a backup – and it had a motorised roller system to speed up loading. In repeated practice sessions they'd got it down to 90 seconds per pallet. But with 36 pallets to load, that was still 54 minutes. That was 54 minutes the authorities had to figure things out. If they did, the team would be sitting ducks.

Lieutenant Morris was checking in with the E-3 regularly to get position updates on the trucks. He used a yellow highlighter to mark the progress on a paper map. He grimaced slightly at the low-tech nature of it, but that was the nature of military operations sometimes, he reflected. When you planned an operation, you could have all your technology sorted in advance; when you were responding rather than instigating, you had to do the best you could.

The latest position put the semis about halfway toward what they believed the split-up point to be. They had no direct contact with the Marines driving the rigs, but BEP 12 was relaying comms. So far, the drivers had nothing to report.

The moment the second tug was clear of the ramp, Sullivan called Chung.

"We're out."

"Confirm everyone clear."

"Confirmed."

"Ok, thanks."

As she spoke, Perez pulled up alongside the first truck and everyone leapt into action. As soon as the first batch of three pallets was offloaded, he would move the train forward to line up the next batch. He checked his watch. They were on schedule, but he really, really didn't like this part. Not one little bit.

Chung reopened the closed valve. The water flow would now return to normal, and within two or three minutes it would be back to normal levels and speeds, once the initial deluge had flooded the empty sections.

Smiling, he changed each of the three passwords back to their originals. The water plant staff would now be able to login at their next attempt and all would be back to normal.

Chung just had one more thing to take care of: a completely unrelated system he'd gained access to a few weeks back. He needed to add ten records to a database, backdating the entries to a week ago. It would take just a few minutes.

"I have the Hicks ground commander, Major."

Timpkins took the headset.

"CAG. Sitrep."

"Sir, we've studied the ground area with field glasses. There is something on the ground there, we can't tell exactly what, but we can see a slight ridge, like a sheet of something sitting flat on the ground. We can also see a change in the grass line in the banking beyond. It looks newer than the rest of the grass, Sir."

"Standby," said Timpkins. He needed to think carefully before he made a decision. On the one hand, he had a dozen C-5s in the air, and hostiles with the proven ability to blow them out of the skies. There could be a hostile with eyes on the apron ready to give the word to detonate the explosives on board the aircraft.

On the other hand, he was now pretty certain the hostiles were gone. They'd given no instructions not to enter the apron area in any case. He made a decision.

"Sergeant, I want you to move in very visibly and at a leisurely pace. If there are any hostiles present, I want them to see you. Be ready to come to an immediate halt the moment you hear the word. Once you reach the target, let us know but do nothing without further instructions."

"Wilco, Sir."

Timpkins addressed the tower manager.

"Get me BEP 12."

A few seconds later, the tower manager nodded to him.

"BEP 12, monitor the hostile's channel carefully. We may get an instruction from them to halt some troops we have on the ground. Stay in contact with the tower and if you receive such an instruction, inform us instantly."

"Wilco, Major."

"Control room, Watts speaking."

"Hey, it's Eric Lane from IT support here, we had a report that you couldn't login."

"Yeah, that's right – we got dropped out and now can't log back in," said Chloe Watts.

"What login were you using?" asked Lane.

"Sys slash sys."

"Hmm, that's what I see on the admin screen, and we've been able to connect fine from here with that login."

"That's odd," said Watts, "the remote login didn't work either."

"Ok, I know this is IT response 101, but could you try it one more time for me?"

"We've tried it a bunch of times already, but sure, one more time can't hurt."

Watts typed sys into the username field then the same thing into the password field.

"Weird!" she said.

"You're in?" asked Lane.

"Yep."

"Ok, looks like some transient glitch somewhere along the line, I'll give Backup a call and make sure they can login with the remote credentials, as that login also works fine from here."

"Ok," said Watts, "thanks for your help."

"No worries."

Watts replaced the receiver and checked the display. She scrolled through the main pipe sections they controlled. Everything looked absolutely fine, no alerts, water levels right where they should be. She called across to Martin Day.

"We're back up, everything's fine."

"Cool," said Day, returning to his paper.

Chung did one last check, comparing each of the ten serial numbers he had entered into the database with those supplied by Pugh. All was correct. He hit Save and exited the database. All was now in place for the next phase of the plan.

* * *

At Hicks, the squad of 13 Marines advanced across the apron at a most unmilitary-like stroll. The Sergeant kept his eyes on the target while those around him scanned all around them.

As they got closer, he could see that there was definitely a sheet or board of some kind on the ground, and he could see from disturbed dirt that it had been recently moved. He could also see some painted marks on the concrete.

Finally, he reached it. It was painted to look like concrete, but it was actually wood. He radioed in to Carswell and was immediately passed to Major Timpkins.

"Sitrep," said Timpkins, without pre-amble.

"Major, there's a wooden board that's been recently moved. There are also some painted marks on the concrete that are much newer than the base. Ok to check it out, Sir?"

"Proceed," said Timpkins. He didn't need to warn the Marine to assume booby-traps and to proceed with appropriate caution: they were all combat veterans, and the fact that they were still alive was evidence enough that they knew how to look after themselves.

"Wilco."

The Sergeant gave orders to two of his men. One unravelled a line of tough but thin cord, the other applied some instant glue to attach about a foot of one end of the cord to the board. The Sergeant nodded his approval as they stood, and gave the order for everyone to withdraw.

The Marine with the cord unrolled it swiftly as they backed off. Once the end of the cord was reached, he held it up.

"Ready, Sarge."

The Sergeant looked around. The rest of the squad had already dropped flat on the concrete without needing to be told.

"Let's do it," said the Sergeant.

The Marine eased in the slack then gently pulled in about a foot's worth of cord. He paused, then pulled in some more. He'd estimated the size of the board at around 12 feet in diameter. He kept pulling until he was confident he'd pulled in more than 12 feet's worth. Whatever was beneath the board should now be exposed.

"You and you."

Two of the Marines walked toward the board in a crouch, then dropped to their stomachs to advance on elbows and knees the last 20 feet or so. They peered into the hole. One pulled out a flashlight and shone it slowly around the complete perimeter.

"Clear, Sarge."

The others joined them.

"No obvious booby-trap, Sarge, but the rope ladder is how I'd trigger it."

The Sergeant looked down into the hole as several Marines played flashlights into it. The rope ladder led down to a pool of water.

"Same procedure, let's pull the ladder up a few feet."

"Sarge."

The Marine with the cord cut the end of it from the board, leant into the hole and carefully tied it around one of the rungs.

The squad dropped back once more and again hit the deck. Marines were known for their courage, but avoiding pointless risks was part of what kept them alive.

The cord was again pulled in, lifting the rope-ladder up several feet, then letting it drop suddenly. Nothing.

"Check it out, Sarge?"

The Sergeant shook his head.

"I'll go."

The Sergeant walked back to the hole and lowered his feet onto rungs of the ladder. He tested it, then transferred his weight. He stepped down, gingerly at first, then more confidently. Within 30 seconds, he was at the water surface. The bottom section of the rope ladder was floating on the surface, the wooden rungs making it buoyant. There was a strong water flow through the pipe.

He climbed back out, signalled the others that it was safe to approach then got on the radio.

Seven pallets loaded. Twenty-nine to go.

Perez wasn't the only one feeling nervous, Sullivan too couldn't help glancing over her shoulder at regular intervals. The authorities didn't know their identities, but the team was now officially responsible for the biggest robbery the world had ever seen, and the biggest manhunt in history would be underway.

All that was protecting them was that the authorities would be following the decoy trucks, and had absolutely no idea where the team and the cash really were. They had chosen the exit point not just because it was secluded, but also because it would be outside the realistic radius of any cordon the police set up. They should be able to quietly set off onto the nearest freeway, and from there be far away within a matter of minutes. But there were twenty-five pallets left to load yet. It was time for their little diversion.

Jackson picked up the air band transceiver and pressed the transmit button.

"BEP 12, Seven."

"Seven, BEP 12."

"Please instruct your Marines to pull over at the side of the road where they are."

"Standby."

The 15 second delay seemed longer.

"Seven, BEP 12. The trucks are stopped."

"Instruct your men to exit the tractor units and double-time, as a group, half a mile upwind of the rigs. Please advise them that their lives depend on the distance: the trucks are fitted with toxic gas generators as well as explosives, and we are about to activate the gas. If there are any civilians nearby, get them away too. Seven."

"Standby."

The toxic gas was another bluff: the team simply wanted to ensure that the Marines were clear of the trucks when they detonated the explosives fitted to them. A pause of just a few seconds this time.

"The Marines are exiting. We'll advise you when they are half a mile away."

"Tell them not to hang around, please."

"BEP 12."

Marines pride themselves on their physical fitness. With minimal kit, and with significant motivation, Jackson knew it wouldn't take long for them to get clear. He was right: it was a little over three minutes before the call came in.

"Seven, BEP 12."

"Go ahead, BEP 12."

"The Marines are clear."

"BEP 12, please confirm: we are about to release the toxic gas and have absolutely no desire to hurt anyone unnecessarily."

Fifteen seconds went by.

"Seven, that is affirmative: the Marines are clear."

"Very well."

The next part was going to require some brief acting skills on Jackson's part. He looked at Perez, and nodded.

Perez had a transmitter in his hand with a switch and a button. He flicked the switch. A green LED lit up. He pressed and held the button. A red LED lit up.

At the side of the road, the Marines were debating what the hostiles had planned. Toxic gas to keep them clear, fair enough: if the hostiles had NCB suits, they could move in, but all around was flat, open ground. There was nowhere for them to come from. And with the C-5s still in the air as hostages, why did they need toxic–

WHOOSH!

There was a huge fireball as one of the rigs exploded! Almost instantly, another as the second rig went up. In less than a second, one explosion after another, all twelve rigs were little more than burning wreckage.

"What the hell?" asked one of them.

Jackson hit the transmit button. He adopted a hysterical-sounding voice.

"What the fuck did you do?" he screamed. "What the fuck, what the fuck!"

He released the transmit button.

The captain on board BEP 12 had no idea what the question referred to until his co-pilot relayed the news from the Marines on the ground.

"Seven, BEP 12, we're informed you just detonated the trucks."

Jackson gave a thumbs-up sign to Perez: that was the confirmation they wanted to hear.

Hysterical voice time again.

"Fuck no!" he yelled. "We activated the gas, not the explosives. What the hell did your guys do? Fuck, fuck, fuck!"

He released the transmit button.

Perez grinned at him. "Hollywood's loss is our gain."

"Seven, BEP 12, our men were half a mile away when the rigs went up. We had nothing to do with the explosions. BEP 12."

Jackson hit transmit: "Fuuuuuuuck!" He released the button.

"Not sure about the scriptwriter, though – it's pretty basic dialogue."

"Hey, it does the job."

"I hope so."

Major Timpkins pulled off the headset after the second of the two pieces of news in close succession: the explosions, and the discovery of the hole beneath the apron.

"What's up?" asked Pritchard, noting the expression on his face.

"I think we've been had."

"How so?"

Timpkins quickly relayed both pieces of information.

"Fuck," said Daniels.

Lieutenant Mason pushed back his chair and stood up.

"Which way is the water flowing?" he asked.

"The team said east to west," replied Timpkins.

"I'll grab the wide-area plans for the water system, and see where it exits."

"So the trucks were just a decoy?" asked Lieutenant Morris. "They just blew up empty trucks?"

"Looks that way, said Timpkins.

"But the pallet trackers – the pallets were in the trucks," said Morris.

"Maybe the pallets were, but the cash wasn't."

"We have a forensics team waiting right outside Hicks," said Daniels, "I'm thinking we send them in now, to see what they can learn."

"I agree," said Pritchard.

Timpkins merely nodded. Daniels got on his cellphone.

"Boats, then," said Pritchard.

"Has to be," agreed Timpkins. "They send us haring off with half the armed forces and police following a bunch of empty trucks while they float gently downstream to wherever the hell the water comes out. Morris, looks like your damn submarine theory was almost right."

Mason spread out the wide area water system plans on the table. Pritchard turned the plans around to face him.

"If the water's flowing west from Hicks, then it's almost certainly going to exit into Eagle Mountain Lake." He tapped the lake on the map. "Lake Worth is less likely, and Marine Creek Reservoir will be an inflow rather than an outflow. It has to be one of these two, and Eagle Mountain seems by far the more likely."

"Morris, get the bulk of our forces headed that way, Pritchard you do the same with the police." Timpkins called across to the tower manager. "Get the E-3 and KH-12 tasked to Eagle Mountain Lake, give them the grid reference of the outflow and tell them to zoom right in. I want to know about any signs of activity close to the outfall, I want to know any trucks parked nearby and I want details of every boat on that lake, go!"

"Sir!"

The tower manager picked up his headset and spoke urgently into the mic.

"I've just thought of something," said Daniels.

Pritchard and Timpkins turned to him.

"The water flow," continued Daniels, "there must be a way to control it. Maybe we can stop the flow before they exit and leave them stranded in the pipes."

Timpkins gestured to the tower manager.

"Get the ground team back on the radio and ask them to estimate the speed of the water flow."

Daniels got his cellphone out again.

"I'll find out where the control room is and ask them to stop the flow."

Sullivan looked at her watch for about the tenth time since they started transferring the pallets to their fake-branded trucks. Fourteen pallets loaded, and they were slightly ahead of schedule.

"Control room, Watts speaking."

"My name is Tim Daniels, I'm with the Secret Service."

"Yeah, right. Who is this?"

"I don't expect you to believe me, Ms Watts, so please call Information, ask for the main Secret Service office in Washington DC and ask them to patch you through to agent Tim Daniels on his cell.

Give them the codeword 'Moonlight' and they'll connect you immediately. Please do this right away."

"You're a funny man. Who is this?"

"Ms Watts, I don't have time to be nice about this: either I hear from you in the next minute or you're going to be facing Federal charges of obstructing an agent in the execution of his duties. Make the call."

"Ookay." The skepticism in her voice was clear. Daniels hung up and looked at his watch.

Fifty-three seconds later, his phone rang.

"Daniels."

"This is Chloe Watts, from the water plant control room. Look, I'm sorry about that, it's just–"

"It's ok," said Daniels, interrupting. "Now, please listen carefully. I need to know about the section of water pipe that runs beneath the disused airbase at Hicks."

"Do you know the marker numbers of the section you're interested in?"

Daniels studied the plans. There were a number of references numbers marked. He read one of them to her.

"That's not a marker number," said Watts, "it should be two letters, a dash and four digits."

Daniels looked again.

"There's nothing like that, these are all 8-digit numbers."

"Ok," said Watts, "you must be looking at the municipal plans, not the water system ones – they use a different numbering system."

Daniels swore.

"It's ok," said Watts, "Let me see if I can find any reference to Hicks on my system."

"Thanks, as quickly as you can, please."

There was silence on the line. More silence. Yet more silence. Come on, thought Daniels.

"Mr Daniels?"

"Have you found it?"

"I think so. You said it was a disused airbase?"

"That's right."

"Well, there's a location tag reading USAF HK MF, that sounds about right, don't you think?"

"It certainly sounds plausible," said Daniels. "In the section of pipeline I'm interested in, water is flowing east to west, does that tally?"

"One moment ... Yes, yes it does."

"Great, and does that have an outflow somewhere, somewhere where it exits into a lake or river or something?"

"Yes, of course," said Watts, "it's a main feed, so there's always an overflow. Eventually it flows into Eagle Mountain Lake."

"Fantastic, I think that's exactly what we're after. Can you see the speed of the flow?"

"Sure, one second." There was silence for a couple of seconds. "Ok, looks about 3mph right at the moment."

Daniels looked at his watch. The decoy trucks had departed the base one hour and 12 minutes ago. Three miles per hour for 1.2 hours ... they should have travelled 3.6 miles by now.

"Can you tell me the distance from the base to the outflow?" he asked.

"I'll need to move through the screens and total up the section distances. Give me a minute or two," said Watts.

"As quickly as you can, please."

The silence seemed to last forever. Several times, Daniels wanted to ask what was taking so long, or to tell her to hurry, but he knew this would only slow her down. He waited.

"Ok, it's approximately 5.8 miles to the lake."

Fantastic! Thought Daniels. They would still be in the pipe. Some of them, at least.

"That's great, Ms Watts. Are you able to stop the flow from there?"

Watts hesitated.

"Well, I can, sure, but I'd need to get clearance. Any flow cutoff can leave areas without water."

"The Secret Service is giving you clearance. I take full responsibility, and will confirm you were acting under my direct instructions on a matter of national security. Now, please, do it."

"Ok. Give me a moment."

Daniels waited.

"Ok, it's stopped."

"Great job, Ms Watts. I need you to ensure that the flow doesn't restart for any reason. Anyone starts yelling about water supplies, you just refer them to the Secret Service office in DC, ok?"

"You got it."

Daniels thought for a second.

"Actually, are you able to reverse the flow? Make it flow west to east?"

"Hmm, let me see ..."

Chloe Watts tracked the pipeline back.

"We-ll," she said, "it could be done, but not for long – the water level is relatively low, so if we divert water from the upstream section then it'll flow backwards but only until it empties, which wouldn't take long."

"You can empty it? That's even better, go right ahead, please."

"You're sure you're taking the rap for this? Diverting water out of the upstream section is going to have some knock-on effects, it's going to get kinda messy."

"One hundred percent my responsibility," confirmed Daniels, "please go right ahead."

"Ok, this will take a few minutes."

"I'll stay on the line until it's done."

Twenty-four pallets loaded, thought Sullivan. Twelve to go. They were still ahead of schedule.

Daniels waved at the others around the table to get their attention. He cupped his hand over the mouthpiece.

"I think we've got them," he said, with a broad smile. "Based on the water flow, the last of their boats should be less than four miles downstream from Hicks, and the outflow is 5.8 miles away. I'm getting the section drained, so any minute now their boats are going to come to a sudden halt as they find themselves sitting in an empty pipe."

"Brilliant!" said Pritchard. He pulled the plans round. "Ok, four miles downstream is somewhere around here." He circled a small area on the plans. There are three access holes in that area, we'll get teams to each of those first, then expand out from there."

"As soon as the pipe is empty, we'll get Marines in at the Hicks end," said Timpkins. He turned to Lieutenant Mason. "Mark the path of the pipeline on the emapping system and get it uploaded to the E-3 and the satellite monitoring station. Mark off the area Pritchard has circled and tell them we want close visual and thermal imaging coverage of that section. They are to maintain visual of the outflow too, but I want to know if anyone pops their head up from one of the access covers."

"Major." Mason pulled the plan around and cross-referenced it with the above-ground map. He then zoomed-in on the area on the emapping system on the laptop before uploading it to the E-3. He then hurried over to grab a headset to bring them up to speed on what was required.

Timpkins, meantime, was briefing Lieutenant Morris.

"We don't know the strength of the opposition we might face. It's now clear that the rest of the team was underground, in the pipeline, so we don't know how many of them or how they might be armed. As soon as the pipeline is drained, we have them trapped, so there's no need for any heroics. I don't want a firefight in the confines of a pipe if it can possibly be avoided."

"Plus we'd like to take them alive," interjected Pritchard. "I'd really like to know how the hell they were able to pull this off. We have a very long list of unanswered questions right now."

"Understood," said Morris, "I'll get our teams briefed."

"I'll do the same for the civil authorities," said Pritchard.

Thirty-two pallets on board, thought Sullivan, just four to go. A few more minutes, then they'd be out of here.

To the traffic held up at each of the six airports the authorities had been covering, it was a very puzzling sight: one minute, the tightest security they'd ever seen at their modest airports, with a scary-looking array of military vehicles and more police than they thought existed in the county; the next minute, the entire mass of vehicles and personnel had departed, leaving only two local security guards to wave the cars on through.

In the tower at Carswell, Lieutenant Mason was checking the distances the convoys would have to travel. He put down the pen and rule.

"They're obviously very scattered," he reported, "but we'll have the first of the teams on scene in around 20 minutes. It'll be over an hour before we have everything, but we shouldn't need more than one of them."

Pritchard chipped in: "We'll have the first police officers on scene in two or three minutes, with many more on the way. They can obviously travel rather faster than the military vehicles."

Timpkins nodded.

"Please ask the police to hold back until we have military personnel on-scene. We want to ensure we're prepared for all eventualities."

"Agreed," said Pritchard, "they'll simply act as perimeter guards until then."

Two pallets left to load, noted Sullivan, with satisfaction. They were making good time. They'd soon be on their way.

If anyone had been able to observe the scene from the air, it would have looked like an invading army as almost every military vehicle in the operation started converging on the same tiny area, just half a mile long.

They had no way to know that they were all converging on the wrong section. The cash, and the team, was less than two miles away.

* * *

"Sirens!" exclaimed Perez.

The sound of multiple sirens could clearly be heard, getting closer.

"Everyone, stop!" called Sullivan. "Get behind the trucks."

The team rapidly assembled behind one of the trucks. The road was less than a quarter of a mile from the clearing they were in. It was surrounded by bushes, and in theory protected from view, but if the authorities had already worked out where they were ...

"What the hell?" asked Jackson. "You think they know where we are?"

"Could be coincidence," said Perez. "It might be for something unrelated."

"That's not one or two cars," said Sullivan. "Just listen to them."

They listened as the sound increased. She was right: this was more like half a dozen sirens.

"Ok," said Sullivan, "let's stay calm. I don't like it, but either they're onto us, in which case there's little we can do other than a pointless chase across the desert, or they're not, in which case we don't want to do anything stupid to give ourselves away."

The sirens reached a peak in volume, and they could see flashes of red and blue lights through the bushes, but couldn't see any of the vehicles themselves. The sirens started decreasing in volume. Before they had entirely faded, however, they heard a new sound: helicopter blades!

The helicopters were apparently flying low: none of the team caught sight of them through the tree cover. Like the sirens, they just heard the sound of the choppers getting louder then quieter.

"Ok," said Sullivan, "back to work. Wherever they're headed, it isn't here, and that's all the matters. But it seems like we don't have long."

There was one pallet left to load.

Lieutenant Mason put down the headset and walked quickly back to the table.

"We have two choppers at the site. Both have landed and offloaded the troops, they're setting up a perimeter around the three access points. They won't move in until we have backup from the first of the ground forces."

Timpkins turned to Morris.

"How long?"

"They were about four minutes out ..." he glanced at his watch ... "two minutes ago."

"We already have seven police patrols on-scene," added Pritchard.

"Ok," said Timpkins. "I don't want any fuck-ups here, and I especially don't want any friendly fire incidents. Nobody is to do anything other than monitor unless fired on."

Morris, Mason and Pritchard each relayed the message.

About a minute, thought Timpkins. About a minute before they'd have heavy firepower in place.

As of that moment, there was not a chance in hell the hostiles were going to get out of there.

Sullivan eased the forklift forward, to position the last pallet in the trailer. Once that was done, they simply had to load the two forklifts onto the back of each trailer and they'd be out of here. Less than five minutes, and they'd be gone.

The five M1114s – Armoured Humvees – pulled up alongside the two Apache helicopters. A Sergeant jumped out of the lead vehicle and approached the two pilots.

"Who's in charge here?" he asked.

"Lieutenant Berry is coordinating things. Orders were that no-one was to advance until you boys arrived with your toys. Not sure why," he added, "we could take out a medium-sized town with the armaments we have on board. But you can reach Berry on channel niner."

"You fly-boys know you can't be trusted to do anything without real soldiers to take charge," said the sergeant, taking the radio.

"That's it, Major," confirmed Lieutenant Mason, "we have M1114s in place. Two Bradleys are a few minutes away, but there's plenty of firepower there."

"Ok," said Timpkins. "Give the go ahead for two Marines apiece to advance to each of the three access points. If the cover is undisturbed, crack it open and get an inspection camera in. If that's clear, one of them descends to get a visual on the hostiles from inside the pipe, the other provides cover."

"Sir."

They were done! Sullivan watched as Perez and Jackson pulled over the tarpaulin disguise. It had been Evans' idea: a piece of black-coloured canvas and a net, to which they'd attached several layers of scrap metal. To anyone looking inside the back of the trucks, it would look like a massive pile of scrap metal.

Sullivan wasn't ready to breathe a sigh of relief, not with police and helicopters so close, but the trucks were loaded and all that remained was to quickly change into their various uniforms then they could set off for Galvaston.

The two Marines advanced cautiously on the access cover. One crouched down, his M16 assault rifle pointed at the cover. He nodded.

The second Marine, laying on his stomach, slid the blade of his OKC-3S bayonet under the edge of the cover and carefully levered it up. Once he had a small gap, he eased the head of the inspection camera into the hole. He studied the 2-inch LCD screen. Black. He switched to infra-red, which would show any heat sources. Again, nothing. He looked up at his colleague, who nodded again. Marines needed little in the way of verbal communication when working on stealth operations. He flicked back to visible light and hit the switch for the light.

There was no response from the access hole, and he looked again at the screen. The light was a small but powerful Cree LED. He could see the access ladder was clear, but nothing was visible below. He switched off the light, withdrew the camera, tucked it away in a pocket and the two of them together lifted the access cover off.

The Marine with the M16 stood over the access hole, covering it with his assault rifle. The other slipped feet first into the hole and began slowly and silently to descend the metal rungs embedded in the concrete walls of the hole.

Sullivan was driving the lead semi. There was no sense in attempting to be stealthy about it, she'd decided: you can't sneak past someone in a 40-ton rig powered by a noisy 450hp engine.

There was no traffic in sight to the left. Evans, sat along side her, looked to the right.

"Clear right," he said.

Sullivan pulled onto the road. She turned onto the road, watching the trailer carefully in her mirrors, then gunned the tractor unit. She would be sticking strictly to speed limits all the way, but otherwise would not be hanging around.

Jackson was number two behind her. He would wait one minute, just enough separation that they didn't look like a convoy to anyone who saw the trucks pass. At the first junction, she would go straight on, Jackson would turn left. The others, in the SUV, would turn right. From that point on, all anyone would see was a solitary and perfectly ordinary truck passing them.

The Marine was almost at the bottom of the rung ladder, his feet just above the top of the pipe. He lowered his upper body until he was in a crouched position. Holding on with his left hand, he slipped his right hand into his pocket and again withdrew the inspection camera. He could hear nothing, but his orders were for maximum caution: the hostiles were to be taken alive.

He bent the gooseneck on which the head was mounted into a right-angle. He then eased the head of the camera beneath the roof of the pipe and looked east. Blackness. He turned it to face west. Blackness again. He switched to infra-red. Nothing. He turned it 180 degrees. Still nothing. He switched back to visible light and flicked on the light. Nothing and no-one in either direction.

He descended the remaining distance until he was standing in the bottom of the empty pipe. He reached for his radio and hit the transmit button to report all clear.

Sullivan's satnav unit, like those in the other rig and the SUV, was following a route Chung had plotted in Garmin's Basecamp software. Unlike just entering a destination into the unit directly, this allowed the precise route to be chosen. Up ahead, she would turn left, then right onto the freeway. Neither she nor Evans had said anything beyond Evans' confirmations that the road was clear on his side as they turned at junctions.

"Ok," said Timpkins, as the third 'all clear' report came in. "Clear them to advance."

The order cleared the second Marine of each party to descend. The pair to the east would then proceed westbound, the pair to the west eastbound and the pair in the middle would stay put. Within a few minutes, they would have swept the section of pipe they'd identified as that most likely to contain beached boats.

Each Marine was using active night-vision goggles. Passive night-vision goggles were just light amplifiers, turning even starlight into something bright enough to see by. But in the unlit pipes, there was no light at all. They were thus using the goggles in active mode: infra-red vision with a small but powerful IR lamp. Each Marine also had a flashing infra-red beacon attached to his helmet: nothing would be visible to anyone else, but with the night-goggles they could spot each other as they converged.

The innocuous-looking Fedex truck proceeded along the 287 freeway leading south-east out of Fort Worth.

"You think we can relax yet?" asked Evans, finally.

"I must admit I feel a lot more comfortable now we're clear of Fort Worth," replied Sullivan. She glanced at the distance-to-destination figure on the sat-nav display: 298 miles.

"I'll check on the others."

Evans switched on his iPhone and opened the Find My Friends app. The phones had been bought for cash as unlocked devices, and they'd used the Apple Store wifi to register fake Apple IDs attached to throwaway Gmail accounts that, too, had been registered on public wifi hotspots. If the phones ever fell into the wrong hands, there would be nothing to tie the phones to any of them.

It was a small risk, linking the IDs in the Find My Friends app, as it meant that if one of them were caught, the authorities might be able to track the others if they thought to examine the phones during the time the trucks were en-route. But it was one Sullivan felt it was the lesser risk: it allowed any of them to track the progress of the two other vehicles. Since they all intended to drive non-stop to Galveston, a truck stopped for longer than a traffic signal would indicate trouble. It also eliminated the need for phone calls.

Evans scrolled out on the moving map until both dots were visible. The SUV was ahead of them, the other rig was making its way past Fort Worth now. In around six hours, they'd be at the port. It would be a very long day.

In the pipe, one of the two Marines waiting by the central access point tapped his colleague on the arm and pointed to the dimly flashing light visible in the green glow of the night goggles. The other man nodded and used an infra-red flashlight to give the 'friend' signal: short flash, short flash, long flash, short flash. The morse code for F, indicating friend.

The code was acknowledged with short flash, long flash, short flash: R for Roger.

Both men now turned their attention to the opposite direction. They didn't have long to wait: within ten or so seconds, a pair of flashing infra-red helmet lights were spotted, and the exchange of codes was repeated.

Now all six Marines knew they were alone in the section, they wasted no time in gathering together. Mindful of how far voices can carry underground, they kept their voices low.

"I'll report in," said one, heading up the ladder back to ground level.

"Guess they got further than the boffins calculated," said another.

"Looks that way."

Major Timpkins didn't look happy when he received the report.

"Understood. Proceed towards the outflow. Do not engage unless forced to, report in when location of hostiles identified, acknowledge."

"Proceed outflow, scout and report only unless engaged."

"CAG."

Timpkins turned to the tower manager.

"Get hold of the E-3 and ask them if there is any sign of activity at the outflow."

"On it, Sir."

Timpkins looked around the table at the others. They didn't need to hear the update from him, it was obvious.

Pritchard studied the plans again.

"There!" he said, pointing to a section marked with the letters CLV, an 8-digit number and a dotted line. "What's that?"

"I'll find out," said Daniels. He picked up his phone and called the water plant control centre again. He got straight through to Watts.

"Agent Daniels here, we have a marking CLV with a reference number and a dotted line – what's that?"

"Oh, that will be a culvert."

"Culvert? You mean there's another outflow?"

"Oh no," said Watts, "this is a drainage inflow."

"So what is it, a pipe?"

"Let me check ..." There was silence on the line for a few seconds. "Ok, it looks like a drainage ramp."

"A ramp?" echoed Daniels? The others looked at him sharply. "What sort of a ramp? What size are we talking about.?"

"They're usually quite wide, but shallow."

"Ms Watts, how wide?"

"Ten feet? Maybe fifteen."

"Are you telling me this is something wide enough to get a vehicle onto?"

"Um, I guess."

"Why the hell didn't you mention this before?"

"You asked where the water exited," said Watts, sound hurt. "I gave you the information you asked for. This is an inflow, not an outflow."

Daniels took a deep breath.

"I'm sorry," he said, "it's not your fault. I appreciate your help. I'll be in touch."

"Fuck!" he said, as he hung up the phone. "We need to get troops here, now."

"Mason!" called Timpkins. Lieutenant Mason was over by one of the consoles. "Grab this grid reference, and task the E-3 to get eyes on it." Without pausing for breath, he turned the other way. "Morris, get ground forces there."

"Sir!"

"Major."

Pritchard needed no prompting: he was already on the phone coordinating the police response.

"This is a fucking mess," said Timpkins, to no-one in particular.

Daniels just nodded, unable to believe they could be this close, have all these resources and still be duped.

"That's it," said Evans to Sullivan, "the other truck is clear of Fort Worth."

"Scott is maintaining proper spacing?" asked Sullivan. Although each of the trailers carried a different branding, they didn't want even the small chance of anyone remembering they'd seem two rigs travelling in line. They would keep at least a mile away from each other.

"Yep," said Evans, "he's five miles behind us."

"Perfect," said Sullivan, checking the distance-to-go on the satnav display: 274 miles.

"Major, I have the first of the ground teams for you. They're at the culvert."

Timpkins strode over, took the headset and held one side to his ear.

"Report."

"There's no-one here, Major, but we have a lot of tyre marks. There have been a number of vehicles here, at least two semis, we think."

Timpkins didn't often swear in front of his men. He thought it unbecoming of an officer of his rank. He did on this occasion, loudly and with feeling.

"Secure the scene," he said, more calmly. "We'll get civilian forensics there, until then, no-one in or out, and don't let anyone trample over everything any more than they have done. CAG."

Timpkins turned to the tower manager. "Get the E-3 tasked to check all roads out of there, looking for semis. Probably two. Then get hold of the choppers. Same deal."

"Sir."

Timpkins turned to the others at the table.

"Tyre tracks from two semis, both gone."

"Fuck," said Daniels.

"How the hell did we let this happen?" asked Pritchard.

"I'm sure that's a question that's going to be put to us quite a few times when we report in," said Daniels.

"We always seem to be one step behind these guys. I fucking hate being one step behind. We're supposed to be out-thinking them, not the other fucking way around." He took a deep breath. "Ok," continued Pritchard, "enough of the feeling sorry for ourselves. Let's get police forensics in there, and let's get road-blocks set up."

"How wide a radius?"

Pritchard looked at his watch.

"Hell, they could be miles away by now."

They both knew the numbers: as the radius increased, the resources you needed to cover the perimeter increased dramatically. A five-mile radius meant a circumference of more than 30 miles; a 25-mile radius, almost a 160-mile circumference - and up from there. Count the number of roads out of a 160-mile circumference, when you had to cover everything from major freeways to dirt tracks, and you started using up police departments pretty quickly.

Pritchard sat down.

"Let's leave this to air surveillance for now," he said. He picked up his phone and gave the instructions that would have every police helicopter in the state looking for a truck convoy.

He hung up.

"We need to approach this intelligently," he said.

"We thought we had been."

Pritchard shot him a look.

"Sorry," said Daniels.

"Ok, you've just filled two semis with a billion dollars in cash. We're pretty sure you're not headed to an airport, because you'd have flown it out directly. So where are you going?"

"No further than I have to," said Daniels. "The longer I'm on the road, the greater the chance that I'm going to get caught. I want to hole up just far enough to be away from the focus of attention, but close enough that I can get the trucks under cover before anyone gets the chance to spot me."

"Right," said Pritchard, "and with a billion dollars in brand new, sequentially-numbered bills, I'm not going to want to rush out to spend any of it."

"Agreed," said Daniels. "So they'll sit tight. Wait for things to calm down, then slowly start laundering the money, bit by bit."

"Ok," said Pritchard, "we'll get the cops to pull any apparent convoys, but we focus resources on checking out likely hiding places. Anywhere big enough to get a couple of rigs under cover. Warehouses, truck depots, barns, you name it."

"Got it," said Daniels, grabbing his phone and making a call.

"In the meantime, I'll get the serial numbers circulated so we're ready whenever the first report comes in."

* * *

It had been a very long drive after a very long day, and Sullivan was shattered. She'd expected to feel elated at this point, but instead she just felt exhausted. Right now she wanted nothing more than to walk through a hot shower en-route to a soft bed. But there were 36 pallets to transfer before anyone was going to do any sleeping, and the only bed any of them were going to see tonight were the ones in the tractor cabs.

The two semis were parked up inside a warehouse ten miles from the Port of Galveston. The warehouse was virtually empty aside from five container trailers, each with two half-sized containers: ten in all. Three of them were hooked up to tractor units, the other two would be hooked up to the tractor units they'd driven from Hicks. Each container and tractor unit wore a different livery: none of them would appear to be related. Beyond the trucks were a set of lockers along one wall, and a desk containing nothing other than an expensive-looking paper shredder.

The team gathered round. They all looked the same. No whooping. No congratulatory cries. Just tired smiles and nods.

"Ok," said Sullivan, "we're almost there. We're all dog-tired, I know, but we need to get the pallets moved into the containers ready for the morning. Let's get to work."

The transfers took them just under an hour. They now had ten loaded shipping containers, six of them with four pallets each, four of them with three pallets. As soon as each container was closed, Pugh added the final touch, then stood back to admire his work. All was set.

Sullivan looked at her watch. "The first of the containers needs to be in the loading area in just over seven hours. I want to allow an hour to get there, just in case of hold-ups, so that gives us six hours. If two each take 90 minute guard duties, that gives us four and half hours sleep each.

"It's ok," said Perez, "Scott and I have it covered. You guys sleep, we'll catch up on sleep tomorrow."

"Why?" asked Sullivan.

"Guard duty is boring. Couple that to being tired to start with, the chances of falling asleep are high. But we're ex-military. We have experience, we won't fall asleep. Honestly, leave it to us."

"You're sure?" asked Sullivan.

"Not a problem," confirmed Jackson.

"Well, ok," said Sullivan. She didn't like last-minute changes of plan, but the argument made sense, and she was bushed. She wouldn't argue at an extra 90 minutes' sleep – assuming she managed to get to sleep. She still felt very keyed-up; she wouldn't really relax until the shipping containers were on their way – if then.

Jackson and Perez looked at each other and nodded slightly. In truth, it was something they'd planned all along. Sullivan was adamant about no weapons, but they took a slightly different view. They had no intentions of any kind of armed stand-off with the authorities: if the Feds caught on, there was no realistic prospect of escape so they wouldn't resist. On the other hand, there were random robberies from warehouses and semis all the time. With a billion dollars at stake, they didn't want to risk being robbed by some two-bit punks: they each had a handgun in the SUV, and they intended to be prepared for any unwelcome visitors.

Sullivan woke with a start to find Evans grinning at her. Sexism had its benefits: she and Lewis had been given the bed in each semi while the rest had dozed in the seats of the trucks and SUV as best they could.

"Room service. I believe you ordered breakfast in bed?"

"What time is it?"

"5.30am. Half an hour before we need to set off. Here."

Sullivan took the carton of orange juice and the breakfast roll he was holding out for her: a packed breakfast they'd stashed in a coolbox in the tractor unit of the semi.

"I can't believe I actually slept straight through," she said. "I wasn't sure I would sleep at all."

"You needed it. It's been a busy time."

"For all of us."

"Yep," said Evans, "but more so for you: you always feel like it's all your responsibility."

"Well, it was my idea, and my job was to make sure all the angles were covered."

She shook her head; she was thinking of it in the past tense. The job wasn't over yet, and the next bit was a critical one: smuggling a billion dollars of stolen, sequentially-numbered bills through an international port shortly after the theft. Normally, even the idea would have been madness, but until the detailed forensic analysis of the trucks was complete, the authorities ought to believe the cash had been destroyed.

She had no way of knowing that she was dead wrong, and that right now every cop, Federal agent and customs officer had been briefed to conduct searches for the cash.

Sullivan popped the lid on the OJ and took a large swig.

Twenty minutes later, she had eaten, pushed a brush through her hair and put on a fresh Fedex uniform. She climbed down from the cab.

"Morning," said Pugh. "Your ID pack." He handed her a wallet. Inside it were the documents he'd prepared for her: a fake driving licence, Fedex identity card, two credit cards – and the digital tachograph card that Chung had created. Every semi driver has to insert a personal smartcard into a slot in the dash of the tractor unit. The cards record driving hours, distances and speeds. Police are entitled to check the details at any time. A printer in the dash would print out details of the last 28 days of data. Except, in this case, all the data on the card was faked. What would be printed out was a record showing that for the past fortnight, she'd spent most of her time driving back-and-forth between the Port of Galveston and a particular warehouse close to League City, some 26 miles away.

"And your shipment paperwork." He handed her a ring-binder containing the shipping documents she would need to produce on arrival at the port.

"Thanks," she said, looking around at the others. It was an amusing sight: between the eight of them, they were wearing the uniforms of five different transport companies.

"Sleep well?" asked Jackson.

"Better than I would ever have imagined. But you must be exhausted."

"I'll live – and I'll have plenty of time to sleep over the next few weeks."

"That's true." They all would. There wouldn't be much else they could do, in fact.

"Everyone set?" she asked.

"Ready to roll."

"Ok," she said, "let's do it. Trucks exit at five-minute intervals, and nobody gets too close to any of the others en-route to the port. We don't want this looking like anything other than five completely-unrelated trucks."

Customs Officers Michael Lawson and Chloe Cook were not amused. Yesterday they'd finished their six days of duty and today should have been the first of their four days off. Instead, they and the rest of their off-duty colleagues had received an early morning call telling them all leave and rest days were cancelled, and they should report for duty immediately. To cap it all, the coffee machine was on the blink and they were waiting for the kettle to boil to make some instant with a jar of cheap granules that looked like it had been there for several years.

"You heard anything about what this is all about?" asked Lawson.

"Not a thing," said Cook, "just got woken by a call telling me to get my ass down here pronto."

"Must be something big," said Lawson, gesturing to the massed swathe of uniforms gathering in the customs hall outside the portacabin that served as a kitchen and refreshment area. The kettle switch popped off and he poured the boiling water over the granules in the two styrofoam cups.

"Sure looks that– Oh for fuck's sake!" She slammed the fridge door shut.

"No milk left?"

"If there's one thing worse than instant coffee, it's instant coffee without milk," said Cook.

"Well, guess we'd better go find out what this is all about."

The two of them picked up their styrofoam cups and walked out into the crowded customs hall, joining the massed ranks of their colleagues. On a typical shift, there would be 36 officers on duty; today there were three times that number.

"Maybe we didn't get the worst deal after all," observed Lawson. "At least we got some sleep – the night shift must be pulling a double."

"Right," said Cook. "You ever known that happen before? Three shifts called in at once?"

"Nope."

"Nor me."

The customs hall was built like a small aircraft hanger, with four lanes of traffic running through it, a dozen inspection bays off to each side and a dedicated x-ray lane with a huge metal framework that looked like a giant Meccano set. This was a Rapidscan GaRDS, a backscatter x-ray machine capable of rapidly scanning the interior of any size vehicle from a compact car to a semi. Any vehicle they wanted to x-ray was positioned at one end of the lane, then when the operator in a nearby booth pressed the start button, scanners tracked down each side of the framework, relaying the x-ray image to the screens in the booth.

The scanner was capable of scanning the contents of a 40-foot semi in just two minutes. The computer system it was linked to interpreted the strength of reflected radar signals to generate an annotated, colour image giving the operator a detailed view of the contents, enabling them to distinguish different materials. One of the main jobs of the software was to automatically highlight a wide range of suspicious items, from firearms to powder that might be cocaine. One of the items it could identify and highlight from the special inks used was bank notes.

"Ok," yelled the Customs chief, "quieten down."

He waited for the chatter to subside.

"First up, sorry to those who got the pleasure of a double-shift, and to those of you called in from rest days or leave. You know it's not something we do lightly or often."

Some of the faces looking back at him appeared slightly mollified by the apology, others remained looking distinctly grumpy.

"Second, as much as I'd love to tell you the reason for it, I can't – because I haven't been told myself. I'm going to tell you everything the powers that be have told me, which isn't much."

He could see he had their attention now. While there were regular routine security alerts, and they often didn't know the reason for them, this was anything but routine. They'd expected to be told exactly what it was all about.

"So," he continued, "what I have been told is that we're looking for bank notes. A lot of bank notes. US fifty dollar bills. The new design, unmarked, sequentially numbered. They are probably in containers, but may have been broken down into pallets placed in the back of small trucks or panel vans. It's even possible they've been split up into batches that can fit in car trunks. So condition Red Alpha is in operation."

There were some groans at this. Standard procedure was for a very select number of vehicles to be inspected. Some based on intelligence, some from hunches – anything that didn't look right – and some randomly-selected. There were then different levels of alert requiring a greater proportion of vehicles to be checked. Red Alpha was the highest alert level, meaning almost every vehicle passing through the port needed to be inspected, either by x-ray machine or by hand. The x-ray machine would help, but couldn't cope with Red Alpha: they were going to spend the entire shift being run ragged.

The chief held up his hands.

"I know. It's not going to be easy. But we wouldn't be doing it unless someone thought there was a good chance of catching some bad guys. So let's focus on that thought, eh?"

Customs work was mostly routine, often tedious, but all of them were, he knew, motivated by the satisfaction of catching the bad guys in the act.

"Ok, gate guys, you make it look like business as usual. We don't want anyone being spooked before they enter the port and high-tailing it out of here. So bored, friendly, casual. All the activity will be in here. Questions?"

There were none; they all knew their jobs.

"Ok, let's get to work."

Sullivan's semi approached the port entrance first. She indicated, slowed and carefully turned the rig into the port approach road and eased it to a halt just short of the barriers. She lowered the driver-side window and reached for the wallet and ring-binder Pugh had prepared.

A bored-looking port security official approached the cab, clipboard in hand, and stepped up on the platform. A few feet away was an equally bored-looking US Customs officer with some kind of handheld scanner.

"ID, please."

Sullivan handed her fake Fedex ID card and driving license. The official glanced at each and handed them back almost immediately.

"Shipping documents."

Sullivan snapped open the ring-binder and extracted the first of the sheaf of documents required to ship a container out of the USA. She handed over the Ocean Bill of Lading. This claimed the contents of the container were security papers, destined for Nigeria, intended to be used for printing share certificates.

The description was intended to be a reasonable thing to export to an African country – a known import for the country – and to pass the most casual of visual inspections. Anything glancing into the containers would be expecting to see pallets of paper, and that's what they would see. It would, though, pass only the most cursory of examinations.

Again, the security officer barely glanced at it before ticking a box on the form on his clipboard and handing it back.

Within a minute or so, Sullivan had handed over and received back four of the six other documents required, including the one showing on which ship the container would be loaded. Next up was the Importer Security Filing Form, required for Customs. Only a government, she thought, could require a document labelled 'Importer' in order to export something.

The security officer glanced at that, ticked another box on his form and then handed the form to the Customs officer. The officer scanned it, nodded, and handed it back to the security officer, who passed it back to Sullivan.

Last up was the Class B Security Transfer Certificate. This too received a glance and a tick from the security officer, and more careful study by the Customs officer, before being returned to Sullivan.

"Won't keep you a second," said the Customs officer, speaking to Sullivan for the first time.

The officer walked to the rear of the truck. Sullivan's stomach felt tight, and she glanced at the digital clock on the dash. Watching the Customs official in her side mirror, he disappeared out of sight behind the rear of the container, where the steel doors were located. Sullivan had to remind herself to breathe.

Ten seconds went by. Twenty. Could Pugh and Chung have screwed-up, she wondered? Thirty seconds. Christ. Forty. This was too long. Far too long. Fifty. Fuck! She wanted to be anywhere else right now. One minute. The Customs officer reappeared in her mirror, walking slowly back towards the cab. He was raising a radio to his face. Sullivan's heart felt like it was about the explode.

The officer replaced the radio mic in his lapel clip and nodded to the security officer.

"Ok," said the security officer, "once you're through Customs, follow signs to Lane 26."

Sullivan nodded, not trusting herself to speak for fear her voice would break.

The barrier was lifted, and she eased the rig past the gates and toward the hanger-like building that stood between her and the docks beyond. What the hell had that radio message been about? This should have been a totally routine check that the paperwork was all present. She hadn't even reached the Customs checkpoint yet. That was ahead of her. She would arrive there in less than one minute.

In the Customs hall, Chloe Hall clipped the radio mic back to her lapel.

"That was the gate. The Fedex truck on the way is a Class B," she said to Lawson.

"Gotcha."

On the approach to the hanger, Sullivan passed three sets of signs. The first, 20mph speed limit signs. Next, 10mph. Finally, 'Dead slow.' She carefully complied with each.

As she approached the entrance, a large sign announced:

US CUSTOMS CHECKPOINT

STOP WHEN INSTRUCTED

ALL VEHICLES SUBJECT TO SEARCH

Research she'd done had suggested that random inspections were carried out on roughly one vehicle in twenty. But right now, she was expecting heightened security. Very heightened. She knew every port in the country, sea and air, would be looking out for the small matter of a missing billion dollars in cash. One hundred and twenty-eight million of which was sitting inside the metal shipping container behind her.

She'd done her homework carefully, and she trusted both Chung and Pugh implicitly. All the same, she thought, if either one of them had missed something, even the smallest detail ...

Chloe Hall spotted the Fedex truck as it entered the hall, and signalled it to stop.

Usually with a Class B shipment, the truck would simply be waved on through after it had been checked at the gate. Not today. Everything would be double-checked.

Sullivan was terrified. All her research had told her that she shouldn't be stopped.

Customs carried out their searches of shipping containers in one of two places. The port was the obvious place, but it wasn't the ideal one. There was a constant stream of trucks arriving, and ships waited for no-one. While Customs officers were perfectly entitled to take all the time they needed to check out a shipment, causing a container to miss the sailing of a ship had significant cost implications for the companies concerned, and inevitably led to complaints.

Customs officers much preferred to conduct their searches before the containers reached the ports. This was made possible by a network of bonded warehouses. To ensure a smooth flow of exports, many companies would stockpile shipments at warehouses close to the ports. Customs officers were based in those warehouses, and would carry out their checks and searches at the warehouse.

This arrangement suited everyone. Customs could take their time over searches, with no time pressure, and companies had the reassurance of knowing that once a container had been cleared at the bonded warehouse, it should be able to pass through the port with the absolute minimum of delay.

Once a container had been cleared at the bonded warehouse, the container doors were sealed shut with a special Customs seal. It was nothing particularly hi-tech, but the seal was impossible to remove without breaking it. Each seal carried a unique barcode serial number that was logged on a computer system accessible to Customs staff at both the warehouse and the nearby port. The officers at the port checked that the seal was intact, and used handheld scanners to read the barcode number. The scanner was similar to a mobile credit card reader: it contained an LTE data SIM that connected to an online database, passed on the serial number and got back an OK or ERR code. Finally, a paper document was given to the driver to certify that the check had been complete.

Pugh had been able to forge the seals and certificates with ease, but doing so was pointless if the serial numbers weren't logged in the Customs database. Forged seals and certificates coupled to access to the Customs database, however ...

Chung had hacked the database and created fake entries for the ten containers, serial numbers matching those on the seals and certificates Pugh had forged. According to the database, these containers had been sitting in the warehouse for the past ten days and had been searched. The seal and database checks should have been carried out at the gate, so why was she being stopped now?

The female Customs officer who had signalled her to stop was approaching the cab door. Sullivan lowered the window.

"Morning, Ma'am."

"Morning," said Sullivan, trying to sound casual.

"I just need to double-check your Class B Security Transfer Certificate, please."

Fuck, thought Sullivan: that was the document supposedly issued by the bonded warehouse. Had Pugh screwed-up? The gate officer spotted something that didn't look quite right, and radioed through to the checkpoint to examine it more closely?

She forced herself to smile.

"Sure," she said, "one sec."

She flipped through the ring-binder and extracted the certificate, handing it over.

The Customs officer studied it carefully. Sullivan counted, silently. One, two, three, four, five ... how long could anyone take to study a single piece of paper? Not longer than five seconds, surely, if it looked ok? Six, sev–

"Thank you," said the Customs officer, handing it back to her.

"No problem," said Sullivan.

She glanced in the mirror as another Customs officer came back into view from behind the container. She saw him give a thumbs-up to the officer standing next to her. Their instructions were that no vehicle passed through the port without being searched, and the checks they had just completed confirmed that these vehicles had already been searched and that the seals were still intact.

"You're good to go, Ma'am."

"Thanks," said Sullivan.

She eased the rig forward. Christ, she'd be glad when this was over.

The drive was a short one, to the secure loading area, were the container would be offloaded, then to the long-term parking area where they'd arranged two month's parking for the tractor units. On their return, the tractor units would be retrieved and sold.

"This is a fucking mess," said Pritchard.

"You're telling me," agreed Daniels.

"They must have missed something."

"The Police Department swears they have searched every single warehouse, barn and aircraft hanger within a 20-mile radius," said Daniels. "Every rig they found, they opened up and checked the contents. Nothing. Same with the airport and port authorities: every trailer has been searched, nothing found."

"How the hell do we explain that someone stole a billion dollars from right under our noses, then simply vanished into thin air?" asked Pritchard in exasperation.

Daniels said nothing. There wasn't anything to say.

"Ok," said Pritchard, "let's walk through this from the beginning, figure out what the hell we've missed."

"Ok," said Daniels.

"If they intended to take the money out of the country, they could have flown it out direct from the base. They had the Galaxies as hostages, and could have been in international airspace before they allowed them to land."

"Right."

"They could have forced the Galaxies to land anywhere they wanted, within reason. Even out in the desert somewhere: C-5s can land just about anywhere."

"Check," said Daniels.

"So, they chose this location for a reason. One reason is now painfully obvious: the pipeline. But they also wouldn't want to be on the road for any longer than they needed to be, so they had to be headed somewhere local."

"Maybe."

"Maybe?" asked Pritchard.

"The Galaxies took off from here to fly in different directions. The further out they got, the longer it would take to get them landed in one place, and the longer the whole operation would take. It would make sense to get the aircraft landed as close as possible to the take-off point."

Pritchard looked at Daniels for a couple of seconds.

"Ok," he said. "So they could be headed anywhere."

"I'd say so," said Daniels. "Given the search results, I think we have to assume so."

"So why not fly out out from the base? This was obviously a very well-resourced, well-planned heist. Getting hold of a suitable aircraft and pilot couldn't have been beyond them."

"A plane is easy to track. Granted they might assume we could do nothing about it once it left U.S. airspace, but we'd still know where they'd landed. You have to admit, their disappearing act – however it was achieved – was a better approach."

"Leaving us clueless as to their whereabouts," said Pritchard.

Daniels nodded.

"Alright," said Pritchard, "so they've left the immediate area. We have every airport and sea port on maximum alert, absolutely no truck of any size enters an airport or port without being searched, and they haven't yet turned up anything, so right now they are holed up somewhere outside our search radius but they are still somewhere in the country."

"Doesn't narrow it down much, does it?"

"This is a fucking mess," repeated Pritchard.

* * *

The secure loading area of the Port of Galveston wasn't the most hospitable of places to hang out, thought Sullivan, as she waited for the others to arrive. A fenced-in parking area reserved for high-value cargo, its amenities comprised one single-storey building with a draughty waiting area, one unisex toilet and three vending machines dispensing hot drinks, sodas and candy. The hot drinks machine was broken.

The 'secure' part of the description also left a little to be desired, she felt. A small gatehouse with a lone security guard who looked like he was about 100 years old. If anyone really wanted to make off with any of the rigs parked up there, she suspected the guard wasn't going to put up too much resistance. But none of them would be leaving their rigs unattended until the containers were safely loaded aboard their respective ships. Two of the team would then be travelling aboard each of the four cargo ships, accompanying them on their journey.

Not many people knew that you could book passage on a cargo ship. It wasn't the most glamorous way to travel, with meals generally limited to eating what the crew ate and with few passenger amenities. You couldn't even rely on many of the crew speaking much English, despite it being the official language of the sea. But that suited them: the fewer questions they were asked, the better. Even the captains would know nothing more than the company shipping the security paper insisted on its own representatives travelling with the cargo.

Sullivan and Young were booked on the first ship to depart. Their ship would be carrying three of the containers, calling first at Port Lagos in Nigeria, where the first two exchanges would take place. One with Nigeria, the other with Chad. She didn't know what deal, if any, the President of Chad had done with Nigeria to enable safe passage of its container. She suspected none: it wasn't difficult to arrange for a rig to pass through both Port Lagos and the border between Nigeria and Chad without its contents being inspected if you had a few brown envelopes to hand out.

After that, it was on to Equatorial Guinea for the third exchange. The total voyage would take 27 days; plenty of time to catch up on sleep.

Scott and Raul would be sailing to the port of Bandar Abbas in Iran. They got to do all three of their exchanges in one port: with Iran itself, Uzbekistan and Turkmenistan. They did, however, have the longest time at sea: 40 days.

Mike and Katrina got Syria before a cruise through the Suez Canal to Sudan. Ryan and Aaron had a single exchange to conduct, in Venezuela.

Six ports, ten exchanges of shipping containers for diamonds.

It was, literally, a world tour of the world's most corrupt regimes. The only thing keeping them safe would be their cover as agents of the US Government. None of the men they were dealing with would hesitate to kill a common criminal, but none would want the wrath of the United States descending on them. Ryan and Mike had between them created cover identities that would stand up to the closest of examinations, with everything from diplomatic passports to online identities that would give each of them a suitably shadowy existence in unspecified government roles.

Young was the second of the team to arrive. There were CCTV cameras all around them, and they didn't want to be a recognisable team, but drivers passing the time with each other would be nothing out of the ordinary here. There was nothing else for drivers to do while waiting for their cargo to be loaded. Young and Sullivan nodded at each other and ensured their body language suggested nothing other than a casual conversation. They doubted the cameras had microphones, but they wouldn't be taking any chances. Conversation would be limited and neutral.

"Smooth passage?" asked Sullivan.

"Yeah," replied Young, "no bureaucracy."

"Good to know."

Twenty-eight minutes later, all eight of them were in the dismal building, having casually introduced themselves to one another for the benefit of the cameras. Now all they had to do was wait for their containers to be loaded aboard their respective ships before the final step of the U.S. stage of the operation.

* * *

Pritchard had argued hard that he and Daniels should be allowed to remain in Fort Worth to coordinate the operation locally, but the appeal had fallen on deaf ears. His boss, Jason Carter, hadn't minced words. "Given the fucking results of your fucking coordination efforts so fucking far, I'd say you aren't exactly going to be fucking missed there – get your fucking asses back to fucking DC today" had been his exact response.

The two of them had spent the flight back to DC trying to work out what they could say in their defence. They hadn't managed to come up with anything. The walk down to the corridor to Carter's office felt like a very long one.

The door to Carter's office was open and he looked up as they walked in.

"Close it," he said.

Pritchard closed the door behind them.

"Sit."

The two of them sat in the two guest chairs opposite Carter's desk. There were two small sofas and a coffee table off to one side. Carter had a reputation for informality, and all the previous meetings they'd had in his office had been sat around the coffee table. Not today.

Carter looked at them. None of them said anything. Pritchard and Daniels didn't know what they could say. They'd been in the office now for about 20 seconds, and only three words had been spoken. Carter finally broke the silence.

"How the fuck could you let this happen?"

It was a perfectly reasonable question, thought Pritchard: that was the hell of it. In Carter's position, he'd be asking exactly the same question, probably word for word. There was no point making excuses.

"We screwed-up," he said, simply.

"That much I know, Pritchard. What I want to know is how you screwed up and what the fuck you're going to fucking do about it. The fucking President of the United fucking States was pulled into this one, and in ..." he looked at his watch, "seven minutes, I have to leave for the fucking White House to explain to the NSA what the fuck happened. Then when I've done that, I have to tell her what the fuck we're doing about it, so that she can tell the President. So you tell me what the fuck I'm going to tell her."

Carter usually liked his direct reports to address him by his first name. Pritchard decided that when your boss is about to be hauled before the National Security Advisor to explain how two of his most experienced agents had screwed-up, usual didn't apply.

"Sir, what happened is we were outwitted. As simple as that. We failed to contain them, and that means we have to fall back to tracking them via the bills. As you know, Sir, these are brand new, sequentially-numbered bills. The number range is now top of the watch list at every bank in the country. We've also circulated the numbers to Interpol. Bottom line, the minute one single bill turns up anywhere, we'll be alerted. Then we close in that way."

"They could sit on these bills for years. That's what you want me to tell the NSA? That we're going to wait and fucking see?"

Daniels felt he had to support his colleague.

"Sir, this was a sophisticated operation. Financing it would not have been cheap. They likely had to borrow the money, and the sorts of people who would finance an operation like this are not noted for their easy payment terms. We're betting they need to start laundering the cash sooner rather than later."

. "That still sounds to me like you want me to tell Ms Lloyd that our plan is to sit on our hands until the bad guys screw up as badly as we did. As you did."

Pritchard stepped back in.

"Sir, you can walk in with my resignation in your hand if you think it will make it any easier."

"And mine, Sir," added Daniels.

Carter looked from one man to the other.

"I'll let you know," he said.

* * *

Chung and Lewis watched the crane lower the second of their containers into the hold of the ship.

"I don't like this bit," said Chung.

"Leaving it unattended?" asked Lewis.

"Yeah."

"Me neither. But truck drivers don't travel with their cargo, they drop it and leave, so that's what we have to do."

"I know," said Chung, "but let's wait until we see another container get dropped on top of ours. We have time."

"Ok."

They didn't have long to wait: the crane operator manoeuvred the giant machine with practiced ease. Within two or three minutes, another container was sitting atop theirs.

"Let's go," said Lewis.

The drive back to the warehouse was uneventful. When they climbed down from the cab, the rest of the team was waiting for them. Pugh stepped forward.

"I'll take your old identity documents."

Both handed over all their driver identification documents. Pugh handed each of them a manilla envelope.

"Your new identities, as passengers. You are now State Department employees with rather vague job titles. Thanks to Mike's work," Pugh smiled at Chung, "these identities will also pass any background checks that might be carried out, either at the port or by our ... customers. Those roles are sufficiently senior that any questions you are asked at emigration control at the port can be answered with a tight smile and a simple 'State Department business' or words to that general effect."

"Perfect," said Evans.

"You'll find locker keys in your packs. Inside the lockers are a change of clothes together with packed bags for each of you containing everything you might need for the voyage."

"Thanks," said Lewis.

"We have a minibus arriving in five minutes," said Sullivan, as Pugh stepped over to the desk and began shredding their driver identity documents. The shredder was a top-of-the-range one, reducing both paper and plastic to 1mm squares. Once complete, the shredded paper would be used as packing material in a box containing an expensive-looking glass ornament. Both ornament and shredded paper would be dropped into the ocean once Pugh's ship was well into its voyage.

"We'll be ready," said Chung. The two of them headed for the lockers.

Pritchard and Daniels were at their desks when Jason Carter got back from the White House.

"My office," he said, without pausing in his stride.

The two men looked at each other as they stood up and went to follow Carter out into the corridor. When they entered his office, Daniels didn't need to be told to close the door behind them.

"The President is not a happy bunny, which means the NSA is not a happy bunny which means I am not a happy bunny. Guess what that makes the two of you."

"Unhappy bunnies, Sir."

Pritchard noted the lack of expletives; that at least suggested progress of a sort. Perhaps they still had jobs.

"So," said Carter. "The position is this. So far, the media hasn't caught onto this. The no-fly zone we imposed and the military hardware dashing around the place been put down to an unspecified terrorist threat later found to be a false alarm. That statement can, just about, be considered true: none of our C-5s got blown out of the sky, at least. The heightened security at ports and airports likewise attributed to non-specific concerns about terrorism; also technically true. The bills have been cancelled, as you know, so in principle at least, there is no financial loss."

Pritchard and Daniels merely nodded. It didn't seem a sensible time to be saying anything.

"Provided there is no fall-out from this, and provided we can capture the bad guys and recover the cash, we all still have jobs. I've been asked to give daily progress updates, which means you'll do the same with me. Note: that's daily progress updates, not status updates. Which means I expect daily progress. Clear?"

"Sir," said Pritchard.

"Ok," said Carter, "get to it."

The Port of Galveston was used by a number of cruise liners as well as cargo ships. The port gate the minibus had entered was the passenger entrance. That had different staff to the freight gate, so they would not meet any of the same port staff – and with their new identities, there was nothing to suggest any connection between the freight drivers who had arrived and left earlier and the State Department staff arriving now. Their passage through security and passport controls had been uneventful.

None of them had wanted to hang around in the passenger terminal building any longer than necessary, however: they had said their goodbyes and then gone to the information desk to arrange shuttle transfers to their respective ships.

Sullivan and Young had been met at the gangway by one of the ship's officers, who showed them to their cabins. Sullivan had been given the Owner's Suite, and Young the Captain's Cabin. Once Young had dropped his bag in his cabin, he wandered next door to the Owner's Suite. It was large and beautifully appointed, with real oak panelling, a huge bed and a generously-sized en-suite with what looked like real marble.

"Impressive," said Young as he looked around.

"I reckon I'll be ok slumming it here for the duration," replied Sullivan. "What's your cabin like?"

"Not quite so grand, but still surprisingly spacious and well-equipped. I'm just wondering where the captain will be sleeping, given I appear to have been given his cabin." asked Young.

"Probably he got bumped to the First Officer's cabin and everyone on down from there got similarly bumped down the hierarchy. There's some cabin boy somewhere who got turfed out of his hammock and is sleeping in one of the lifeboats," said Sullivan with a grin.

"It's a bit schizophrenic, isn't it? All this old-world luxury aboard the modern equivalent of an over-sized tramp steamer."

"I guess for the price we're paying, we ought to get some luxury for our money."

Once the cheapest way to travel, booking passage on a cargo ship was now considerably more expensive than a first-class flight due to limited cabin availability and the length of the voyages. Passengers tended to be wealthy eccentrics doing it for the romance, or through a fear of flying – or security personnel accompanying valuable cargo because the cost of the passage was a small expense compared to the cargo they were safeguarding. It was not unknown for a valuable container to be ... accidentally offloaded at the wrong port, never to be seen again. Neither ships crews nor port staff were well paid.

"Personally I reckon I'd sleep for a week if all they gave me was a straw bed in the hold," said Young.

"You and me both. But if there's one thing we're going to have time for on this trip, it's sleep."

"True, the passenger amenities seem to be somewhat sparse."

"If by sparse you mean non-existent, yes," said Sullivan.

"Hey, there's Internet," said Young with a smile.

Chung had warned them that on-board Internet would be both slow and expensive. All Internet data had to be sent 22,300 miles into space to a satellite, where it was relayed, sometimes via other satellites, to an Earth station somewhere on land. Satellites offered limited bandwidth, meaning that trying to do anything more than send or receive a few emails was frustratingly slow. Web-browsing was impossible.

Unlike cruise liners, which at least offered wifi, the ship had one Ethernet connection at a desk in the crew room. Only one person at a time could use it, and they'd be paying a dollar a minute for the privilege.

Their travel bags contained iPads which Chung had loaded up with a wide selection of both movies and ebooks. That would be their only real form of entertainment for the voyage.

* * *

Three weeks later, Port Lagos

Sullivan and Young were leaning on the rail as the ship finally pulled into the harbour of the busy trading port. The captain had visited them earlier to ask them to accompany him into the hold and confirm the containers that would be offloaded in Lagos. They had done so, and at a signal from the captain a crew-member used a can of spray-paint to mark a large orange circle on each. The captain had politely thanked them, and accompanied them back out of the hold.

A pilot boat led the way as the ship followed.

"Nervous?" asked Sullivan.

"You betcha," said Young.

Their assumed identities ought to protect them: the man they were dealing with might be ruthless, but he would not want to take on the US Government. Their identities had been created in depth, and ought to stand up to rigorous scrutiny. But there was no way to know for sure what resources the regime had at its disposal, what backdoor contacts it might have within the administration, what they might be able to learn.

One thing was certain: if their cover didn't hold, they had a few more minutes to live. The men they were dealing with wouldn't part with the diamonds if they could instead safely kill the men accompanying the cash.

Nothing more was said as the ship came alongside its mooring, and they watched as the ship's crew and dock workers made the process of securing the ship to the quayside look deceptively easy. First, small-diameter ropes known as heaving lines were thrown down from the ship to the dock workers. The ship's end of these lines were attached to the far thicker mooring lines that would be attached to steel-and-concrete bollards on the quay. The dock workers reeled in the heaving lines, took hold of the mooring lines and positioned the large loops over the bollards. While all this took place, the bridge crew had to use the ship's engines and bow-thrusters to hold the huge vessel motionless in the water.

Once the mooring lines were in place, winches aboard the ship were used to tension them. It required a total of six mooring lines to hold the ship fast. The entire process took just a few minutes. A gangway was positioned just as quickly and secured to the ship by the crew. Usually, the huge crane on the quayside would swing into action to begin offloading the containers within seconds of the ship being secured, but today it sat motionless: they had been given their instructions. The dockside crew withdrew, leaving the quay empty but for a forklift truck and a motorised dolly: a trolley used to extract pallets from confined spaces.

A small convoy drove slowly along the dockside and came to a halt next to the gangway: two black SUVs, a large limousine with tinted windows and Nigerian flags on each wing, and an army truck. Nobody got out.

"Looks like our cue," said Young.

"Right."

The two walked to the gangway, then descended. They could feel the eyes of the crew on them: clearly word had been given that they were to secure the ship to the quay and then await instructions.

As they descended the gangway, all four doors of the lead SUV opened and five soldiers emerged. One, an officer with an impressive amount of gold braid, had a side-arm in a holster. The four others had MP-5s slung around them. They formed a line leading from the gangway to the limo. The weapons were pointed at the ground, but their fingers were in the trigger-guards.

Trying his best to maintain an unconcerned air, Young stepped off the bottom of the gangway and came to a halt. Sullivan did the same. Nobody moved.

There was no visible communication from anyone, but the crane suddenly swung into action. It was apparently rearranging containers in the ship's hold, uncovering the marked container. There was still no movement from the limo, and the five soldiers stood impassively, staring straight ahead.

Young noted the crane's arm start to move, and looked back to see the container moving in an arc from above the ship's hold to above the quayside. It was expertly lowered no more than five or six feet in front of the lead SUV and a similar distance from the forklift truck. Once it was on the ground, the rear doors of the second SUV opened. Two soldiers got out, approached the container, broke the seal and swung the doors wide open. The pallets, still wrapped in the black saran wrap, were visible. The soldiers returned to the SUV, got back in and closed the doors.

The front passenger door of the SUV opened and a man in a black suit and black sunglasses got out. In his right hand was a large knife. Sullivan and Young glanced nervously at each other. The man walked over to the container, walked inside and used the knife to slice a hole in the saran wrap, at the bottom left of the first pallet. He used the knife to lever out one strap: a block of 100 bills.

He placed this on the floor of the container and did the same about halfway up the pallet, a little off-centre. He placed this strap next to the first. He then repeated the procedure with the three other pallets, choosing different locations in the pallets each time. He then placed the knife on the floor of the container, picked up the eight straps and walked back to the SUV. He climbed inside and closed the door behind him.

Nobody moved. It was around 40 degrees, and Sullivan and Young had no protection from the harsh sun. Sullivan could feel the sweat running down her back.

Several minutes passed before the passenger door of the SUV opened again. The man walked to the rear, left-hand door of the limo. The tinted window was lowered a fraction, and a conversation took place; Young couldn't hear any of it. It was obvious they had tested the bills. That was no problem: the bills were the genuine article and would pass any test. The problem was that they would conduct that test whether or not their cover had held.

He remembered his meeting with the President: all charm and perfect English. If everything was ok, surely he would have stepped out from the limo and exchanged pleasantries? Or at least beckoned them over to the window? Instead, they were being ignored. Young felt a growing tightness in his stomach. If their cover was blown, the only way they would leave this dock would be inside a wooden box.

Or perhaps they wouldn't even merit a coffin. Perhaps it would be a rough sack, or a crate. Perhaps their bodies would simply be pushed off the side of the dock into the waiting water.

To have come all this way, to put in so much work, to have pulled off the world's biggest heist – and it could all end here in a heartbeat. A single word from the man inside the limo, a nod from the man in the black suit, a raised rifle, the crack of two shots breaking the oppressive silence, two bodies on the dockside that those aboard the ship would carefully fail to see. He watched intently.

The limo window was raised again, and the man in the black suit walked back to the SUV. He said something to the soldiers. This was it. If the order had been given, it had now been passed on. How long did it take to raise a rifle, aim, pull the trigger? Two seconds? Three? Was that how long he and Sullivan had to live? Three seconds?

Two of the soldiers walked over to the container, while the other two walked over to the truck. Young watched the two heading for the container. One took the handle of the motorised dolly and manoeuvred it into the container, a second got into the forklift truck and drove it forward until it was directly along side the container.

The loading was apparently about to begin. Did this mean anything? Did the fact that they were still alive mean that their cover had held? That the exchange was now taking place? If so, where were the diamonds?

The diamonds wouldn't take much space: their portability was the reason the team had opted for diamonds. But $128 million in diamonds was still roughly 150 pounds in weight. That was a crate of some kind. Young looked around. There was no sign of any crate anywhere.

The soldier backed the motorised dolly out of the container with the first of the four pallets on board. He lowered it to the ground and reversed the dolly out. The forklift driver picked up the pallet. The soldier was clearly skilled at operating the machine: he did a smart 180-degree turn and drove the pallet to the rear of the truck. The forks lifted as he was still approaching the truck and by the time he was at the rear of it the forks were at the right height and the pallet went straight inside. Young couldn't see inside the truck, but guessed there was another dolly in there. The forklift truck driver did another neat 180-degree spin and went back to the container, where the next pallet was already sitting outside the container.

Young realised he was surprised at the slickness of the operation. He supposed he'd always had the banana republic image of African countries run by dictators, but the soldiers appeared extremely professional. He imagined that if they were called on to dispose of the two foreigners once the loading was complete, that too would be efficiently taken care of.

The second pallet was lifted onto the truck, and the procedure repeated for the third pallet. Finally, the driver returned for the fourth and final pallet. Young had no real sense of time. There was a dreamlike quality to the scene. How long would it be until the fourth pallet was loaded into the truck? Thirty seconds? Forty?

The pallet was lifted, the forklift swung around and driven the short distance to the truck, again the forks expertly raised to the correct height during the brief journey. The pallet disappeared inside the truck. About ten seconds later, the two soldiers inside jumped down. The four soldiers met back at the SUV.

The front passenger door of the SUV opened. The man in the black suit got out again. Young looked around again for a crate or bag or anything that could be large enough to contain 150 pounds of diamonds. There was nothing.

The soldiers were all looking at the man in the black suit. He nodded. Young always thought that when people talked about swallowing when scared it was just a figure of speech. It seemed not.

The soldiers walked around to the rear of the SUV. One of them opened the two-piece hatch: one half lifted, the other dropped down to form a kind of shelf. The four soldiers reached in and pulled out a battered-looking metal case. Black in colour, it looked like an old ammo case or over-sized toolkit. There were two simple clasps on one side, each with a thick padlock through it. The diamonds. It had to be! Young felt almost drunk with relief. He hadn't realised until that moment just how rigidly he had been holding his body, and his legs felt like they were about to buckle as he relaxed for the first time since they had walked down the gangway.

It took two of the soldiers to carry the case, and even then they looked to be struggling. The soldiers approached, lowered the case to the ground. Three of the soldiers turned away without saying a word. The fourth reached into a breast pocket and held out a keyring with a worn leather fob and two keys. Young took the keys. The soldier nodded, turned and followed the other three back to the truck.

Young watched them as they climbed into the back of it. He looked back at the SUV to see that it was already swinging round in a U-turn. The limo followed, then the truck.

Less than a minute later, the three vehicles had turned a corner and were out of sight. Young and Sullivan looked at each other. Neither yet dared to smile. They looked around the quayside at the now-empty container and the abandoned forklift truck and dolly.

"Christ," said Sullivan, finally.

"Yeah," replied Young.

"I thought we were dead."

"Me too."

Sullivan nodded toward the case in front of them.

"It could still be full of lead bricks," she said.

"Could be. But we're alive."

"There is that."

Young placed the keys in his right pocket, and the two of them bent to grab a handle each of the case.

"On three," said York. "One, two, three."

"Umph!"

"Can you manage it?" asked Young.

"It's bloody heavy, but yeah, a short distance at a time."

No crew members had come down the gangway to help. He wasn't sure he trusted anyone to even touch the case anyway.

It took ten minutes before they were finally in Sullivan's cabin with the case in front of them. Young pulled the keys out of his pocket.

"I guess this is where we find out whether we have 128 million dollar's worth of diamonds, or a few hundred bucks' worth of lead," he said.

"Go ahead," said Sullivan.

Young looked at the two keys. They appeared identical. He crouched down and inserted one of the keys in the first padlock. He turned the key and the padlock clicked open. He pulled it free from the hasp and placed it on the floor of the cabin next to the case. He inserted the same key into the other padlock and turned it. The second padlock also clicked open. He removed that one and set it next to the first. He flipped open the two hasps.

"Would you like to do the honours?" he asked Sullivan.

Sullivan shook her head.

"You do it."

Young lifted the lid. It lifted just past 90 degrees, where two thick canvas straps held it in place. The two of them stared at the contents.

Say 'diamonds' to most people and they think of brilliantly sparkling clear crystals, beautifully cut. Rough diamonds look far less impressive. Randomly shaped, they have a rather muddy appearance, with a range of colours, some yellowish, some blueish, some looking almost grey. Only a minority of them looked transparent.

Young and Sullivan were not most people. They knew what rough diamonds looked like.

Neither said anything. For several seconds, they simply stared. Then Young reached in and picked one out. It was grey-looking, about the size of two peas joined together. One end was bulbous, the other end was pointed.

Young walked over to one of the paintings on the wall of the cabin. He placed the pointed end against the bottom-left corner of the glass covering the painting. He applied pressure and dragged it along the bottom of the glass, about an inch. He lifted it and repositioned it on the left-hand edge, an inch above the corner. He again applied pressure and dragged it down to the corner. Finally, he positioned it back where he had started the previous cut and dragged it diagonally across the corner. He used the palm of his hand to tap the outside of the frame, hard. A triangular-shaped piece of glass fell out. This was a diamond.

Still not a word was spoken. Young walked over to the sofa and sat down. Sullivan came and sat next to him. He handed the diamond to her. Sullivan took it, examined it and the two of them then turned their gaze back to the contents of the case.

"One hundred and twenty-eight million dollars," Young said, finally.

Nothing more was said for thirty or forty seconds.

"Round two," said Sullivan.

Young nodded. The second handover was to Chad, a landlocked country whose capital, N'Djamena, was just beyond the border with Nigeria. They had arranged to do the handover here in Lagos. Young wondered whether the Nigerian president had been informed and was taking a further cut, or whether bribes were being handed over at lower levels to ensure safe passage through the country; he hadn't wanted to enquire.

They climbed back up to the deck. Young pulled out a phone and hit a speed-dial number simply labelled Chad.

"Yes?" asked a voice which answered the call.

"We're ready," said Young.

The line went dead.

They walked down the gangway ready for the next exchange.

* * *

Pritchard and Daniels had taken all the steps they could to ensure that any of the bills surfacing anywhere would be reported to them. Every bank branch in the USA had a record of the bill numbers, with strict instructions to call the Secret Service immediately any of them appeared. Bank

Compliance Officers had received memos requiring them to ensure that any Suspicious Activity Report, or SAR, they filed with the Treasury Department was also copied to the Secret Service.

Banks were required by law to complete a SAR anytime a cash deposit of more than $10,000 was received without obvious good cause. The SAR detailed the account owner's details, the total amount of the deposit, the breakdown of the bills deposited and the range of bill numbers if they were sequential or three sample bill numbers if not. The arrangements Pritchard had put in place meant that copies of SARs received by the Secret Service were immediately forwarded to him personally: he wasn't going to leave it to anyone else to check the numbers.

It was a tedious business. Pretty much the only large cash deposits accepted without question were recognised businesses dealing in large volumes of cash week in, week out. A single large cash transaction to someone personally known to bank staff and for which there was a known and reasonable explanation was acceptable – but for everyone else an SAR was likely to be raised. There were hundreds of these a day, almost all of them innocent: an individual selling a car to someone who ran a cash business, for example.

Pritchard and Daniels faithfully checked each one, looking for bill numbers in the range of the stolen batch. They had done little else. Pritchard was about three-quarters of the way through his pile of SARs when something caught his attention. He looked up. Across the desk, Daniels had sat up abruptly. He was holding a SAR in his hands, staring at it.

"You got something?" asked Pritchard.

"Check me," said Daniels, tonelessly.

Pritchard reached for pen and paper.

"Go ahead."

Daniels read the serial numbers slowly, each digit distinct.

"P40268372T to P42828372T."

Pritchard wrote them down, then frowned and reached for a calculator. He tapped some keys.

"That can't be right," he said.

"It can be," said Daniels.

Pritchard reached for his desk calculator.

"But these are fifty dollar bills. That range adds up to 128 million dollars."

"Check them," said Daniels, without comment.

Pritchard checked the range against the range of the stolen bills. He took a breath, and kept his voice even.

"Let me confirm those numbers back to you." He took the same care Daniels had to read out each digit distinctly. "P40268372T to P42828372T."

"Correct," said Pritchard.

"We've got a match," said Daniels, matter-of-factly before he could keep it up no more. The pitch and pace of his voice both increased rapidly: "We've got a fucking match! We've got a fucking match for one hundred and twenty-eight million fucking dollars!"

"Where?"

"Bank of America, New York City."

"And the account owner?" asked Pritchard.

"It's registered to a small hedge fund. One principal only. A Mr Abasi Mbadiwe."

Daniels was grinning broadly. Pritchard was puzzled for a second, trying to place the name, before he realised that wasn't the reason Daniels was so happy. It was not the name, but the amount.

"$128 million – that can't be a cash transaction ..."

"Right," said Daniels, still grinning.

"So we have a source account."

"Right again."

"Where?"

"Nigeria."

"So the SAR was triggered by a bill-check," said Pritchard.

"Yep."

Most electronic transfers between banks involved nothing more than electrons in a computer. If John Doe transfers a hundred bucks to his mum's account, all that happens is one bank makes a note that it has $100 less and the other bank notes that it has $100 more. There's no physical transfer of cash, and no reference to bill numbers.

But when an American bank receives a large transfer from a Nigerian bank, it wants to be certain that the money actually exists. It requests a bill-check. The originating bank has to demonstrate that it is in physical possession of the cash by supplying either the range of serial numbers or a sampling of them. A range of checks are then made to verify that the bills exist and are not logged as showing up elsewhere.

"Call the bank," said Pritchard. "Tell them that under no circumstances are they to reverse the transaction without express authority from me personally."

"On it," said Daniels.

Whenever a transaction failed the bill-check, the receiving bank simply reversed the transaction: rejecting the transfer and debiting the receiving account. This ended the fraud attempt, but the bank that sent the funds would immediately be advised that the transaction had failed. It would then reverse the transaction at its end, put a hold on the funds and advise the account holder. At that point, whoever sent the funds would know that the authorities were aware. Pritchard didn't want them to know a thing at this stage.

The bank would be asked instead to place a 'silent hold' on the amount. To the account holder, the amount would appear to be in their account, it simply wouldn't be allowed to be withdrawn. Unless the account holder planned to forward the money elsewhere, they would be completely unaware that anything was wrong.

One of the privileges of being a senior Secret Service agent was access to a telephone directory full of unlisted numbers. Everything from the cellphone numbers of senators to the private offices of bank presidents. Three minutes later, Daniels had the assurance they needed.

"Ok," said Pritchard, "let's get to work on finding out who really owns both the originating and receiving accounts."

* * *

Two months later, New York City

"Everyone enjoy their round-the-world voyages?" asked Sullivan with a smile.

"Just don't ever suggest a cruise ship holiday," said Young.

"Only after I stopped being seasick," said Chung with feeling. "Three days. Felt like three years."

"And me," said Lewis. "The thing they say about seasickness is completely and utterly true: at first, you're afraid you're about to die, then you're afraid you're not."

"I am never setting foot on a ship again," said Jackson. "If God had meant us to travel by sea, he wouldn't have created the Wright brothers."

"It was kind of ironic," said Perez. "There we were on a ship, each with $125M worth of diamonds, and I'd have gladly have handed over every last one of them to have had a helicopter fly in and get me the hell off that ship."

"I didn't get sea-sick," said Pugh.

"You know we hate you right now?" asked Evans of Pugh.

The group exchanged war stories about the storms and the scary handovers, with much laughter. Scary stories are always the funniest after the event, thought Sullivan.

She noticed Young's smile seemed a bit forced.

"Hey, you ok, Sam?"

"Sure. I mean, we're all multi-millionaires, we'd be up there somewhere in the Rich List if anyone knew."

No-one would know. Converting the money to diamonds had made the money easier to spend. Unlike cut stones, uncut stones weren't traceable, and Chung and Pugh between them had created a dozen new identities for each of them – each with a paper and electronic trail that showed each of them to be in legitimate possession of a modest number of uncut stones.

Each of those identities could use the same provenance repeatedly to sell stones to different dealers, thanks to the anonymous nature of uncut stones. Each of those borrowed identities could bring in $100k or so a year without attracting any attention, so each of them could pull in a little over a million each a year in total. The problem was that they couldn't consolidate that income: they couldn't buy a penthouse apartment overlooking Central Park because that would require a single identity having a very visible sum of money.

But each of them could, with care, live an extremely comfortable lifestyle for the rest of their lives. You wouldn't have guessed it from Young's voice.

"Your tone seems less than celebratory," said Sullivan.

"I guess this is the moment I dreamt of all my life. The big one. The last job. The one that sets you up for life and means you'll never need to work ever again."

"But ... ?"

"Well, this is it, isn't it? For us, I mean, as a team. We've done it. We won't ever need to do another one. We're done. The team is done."

"Not as friends," said Sullivan. "We'll always be friends."

"Yeah, I know, but ... it won't be the same, will it? Not without a project to work on. Who we are as a team, that's done. I'm not sure it'll ever be quite the same, just getting together for dinner. It kind of feels like what makes us ... us ... will be gone."

Several seconds passed. Then several more.

"It doesn't have to be," said Lewis, finally. She looked around. "I mean, sorry, I don't mean to speak for anyone else, but for me, I mean, it doesn't have to be the end of us as a team."

"You mean do another job?" asked Jackson.

"Yeah."

There was more silence.

"We don't need the money," said Perez. "Well, I don't, anyway. Tell you the truth, I'm going to end up quietly giving away much of it to a bunch of charities."

"Me too," said Jackson.

"Now you guys tell me!" said Sullivan, with a laugh.

"We're not complaining," said Pugh. "Being able to donate money to good causes, especially small ones who really struggle for funding, is the biggest buzz in the world. I wouldn't swap it for an executive jet."

"Yeah," agreed Evans, "I wouldn't have missed the for the world, and being in a position to not even to need to think when someone needs a helping hand – that's a fantastic feeling."

"Yeah," said Chung, "I'm not sure how I'd ever spend it on myself, even if we didn't have to be careful. Funnelling most it to good causes was my plan too."

"So no-one was planning on moving to a Caribbean island?" asked Sullivan.

"Not really my style," said Perez.

"There's only so many Mai-Tais you can drink," said Lewis.

"Those 'What will you do with your share?' conversations never went very far, did they?" asked

Evans. "It's like we didn't want to think about what happened when it was all over."

"We didn't want to jinx ourselves," said Perez.

"Sure," said Young, "it was partly that, or not quite able to believe we would actually pull this one off, but I think it was also ... this. Not wanting it to end."

"It would be a hell of a risk," said Pugh. "Another job, just for kicks. Can you imagine what it would feel like to get caught, knowing it was all basically pointless?"

"What if it wasn't pointless?" asked Sullivan.

"When we're each sitting on $125 million?" queried Pugh.

"Well, it seems we each want to give away most of it. But there's a problem: each of our borrowed identities can only give away maybe $10-20k a year without attracting undue attention. After all, they each only bring in $100k or so. So we can, in any given year, give away something in the $100-200k range, right?"

"Right," said Pugh. "But that can do a lot of good, in the right hands."

"It can," said Sullivan, "but what if you could give away millions at a time, even tens of millions if you wished, without attracting any attention?"

"That would be nice," said Pugh.

"I thought so," said Sullivan.

"You've clearly been giving this some thought," said Lewis.

"Well," said Sullivan, "sitting in a cabin at sea bored out of my mind did give me a lot of time to think ..."

"And you have a plan another job that would allow us to give away millions at a time, without attracting the attention of the authorities?"

Sullivan nodded. "Well, not yet a plan. But an idea. An idea with a little research behind it. Want to hear it?"

"Can't hurt to hear it," said Pugh.

"Don't you believe it!" said Perez. "Look at what she talked us into last time!"

"True," said Pugh. "But what the hell, let's hear it."

"So," said Sullivan carefully, "the question I kept asking myself during the voyage was how the hell do we top stealing a billion dollars?"

"Steal two billion?" asked Jackson, deadpan.

"Exactly," said Sullivan.

"I was joking," said Jackson.

"I'm not," said Sullivan. "And if we do it right, they won't even know it's gone."

The team was seemingly getting more used to her bombshells: the silence this time lasted only a couple of seconds.

"What the fuck?" asked Katrina Lewis, their electronics wizard. "I couldn't think last time where the hell we'd find a billion dollars in one place, but you found somewhere. But two billion? Who the hell has two billion?"

Sullivan flipped open her laptop and turned it to face the group.

"It's right here."

The group moved closer, to peer at the photo of the building on the laptop screen.

"Two billion?" asked Lewis. "In that one building?"

"Yep," said Sullivan.

"In cash?" asked Pugh.

"Not cash," said Sullivan, "but in a form which can be readily converted to pretty much any form we want – including large-scale donations to charity."

"And we steal it without the owners knowing it's gone," repeated Perez.

"That's the plan," said Sullivan.

"You'd better start at the beginning," said Young.

To be notified when The Two Billion Dollar
Heist is available, please visit
www.airbookpublishing.com/tbdh/

Afterword

A novel is, of course, a work of fiction. However, it is written somewhere in the small-print of the contracts where technothriller novelists sell their souls to the devil that we shouldn't take too many liberties with the technologies on which the story relies.

Most of the technology described in this novel is real, and could work roughly as described. Most scarily of all, the hack of the South Houston Water Plant which gave rise to the idea for the escape plan really occurred, and the lamentable lack of security in web-accessible SCADA systems is fact rather than fiction.

There are any number of utilities whose control systems are accessible via the Internet and which rely on default logins or use access systems which can be easily compromised. Unless we address this, there will inevitably be those who take advantage of this fact, and the chances are high that they have something more sinister in mind than stealing money.

It's something we really ought to fix.